THE Perfect GAME

By

W. William Winokur

Kissena Park Press
An Imprint of Starlight Runner Entertainment

Kissena Park Press
An Imprint of Starlight Runner Entertainment

Published by
Kissena Park Press
5 Union Square West, 4th floor
New York, NY 10003

Jacket design: Chrysoula Artemis & Maurce Kessler
Cover: Jake T. Austin from THE PERFECT GAME film
Book design and layout: Helane Freeman
Printer: Berryville Graphics
Printed in the United States of America

Library of Congress Cataloging-in-Publication "Data"
Winokur, W. William, 1960
The Perfect Game

ISBN 978-0-97685-081-6
0-97685-081-8

To Cesar Faz, Harold "Lucky" Haskins and the Monterrey Industrial Little League team, without whom there would have been no miracle.

And in special memory of Norberto Villarreal, Baltazar Charles, Fidel Ruiz, Alfonso Cortez and Francisco Aguilar, who are no doubt having a catch somewhere—waiting patiently for the rest of their team.

Also by W. William Winokur

MARATHON

"Sometimes a week might go by when I don't think about *that game*, but I don't remember when it happened last."
—*Don Larsen, New York Yankees Pitcher on his 1956 World Series Perfect Game*

As always, there are far more people to thank than are or can be enumerated here, but I would like to give special acknowledgment to the following: to Adolfo Franco and Vidal Cantu of Kenio Films for their moral support; to La Mesa players Lewis Riley, Joe McKirahan, Richard Gowins, Francis Vogel, David Musgrave and their teammates; to Lance Van Aucken and the Little League organization in Williamsport, Pennsylvania; to Eloy Cantu Jr.; to the government and people of the State of Nuevo Leon; to Carlos Slim, Carlos Bremer and Cristobal Pera for helping bring this story to the Mexican people; to Jeff Gomez, Mark Pennsavalle, David Zeichner and Chrysoula Artemis of Kissena Park Press without whom this book would not be in your hands; to Stephanie Castillo Samoy for her keen editing eye; to Helane Freeman for her limitless patience in laying out this book; and, as always, a special acknowledgment to my wife, Maggie, and our children, Leo, Emma and Ian, without whose encouragement this writer can't write.

By

W. William Winokur

Prologue

An Old Radio

Padre Esteban carefully placed the charcoal and herbs into the brass *incensio*. He didn't have any frankincense, so sage, which grew in abundance in the surrounding mountains, would have to do. The sun still burned brightly outside, but the inside of Iglesia de San Juan Bautista was enveloped in shadows. The sparse light that streamed through the small windows was filled with dust which danced in seemingly random movements.

The church was in Monterrey, Mexico's Colonia Cantu, which like the surrounding barrios was a shantytown for families whose fathers and sons labored day and night in this industrial city's factories. It was 1956 and the end of summer drew near.

The padre began to dress for Mass. Taking hold of the white amice's two strings, he tied it about his neck and then fastened his alb with a rope around his waist. It would be hot inside the church for anyone, but for a priest, it bordered on unbearable. He had always seen this as his minor penance, infinitesimally small when compared to the trials of Moses or Job.

There was no one else in the church except Arturo Rodriguez Diego. Padre Esteban began to light dozens of candles. The church, being near the center of town, was one of the few structures that had electricity, but the lights were never used during services. Built during the Spanish Colonial period, the Church of San Juan Bautista was simple, yet dignified. Barren stuccoed walls were broken only by framed paintings of Christ's final journey on *Via Doloroso*. Heavy hand-hewn beams held up the roof, and below lay stones that were quarried hundreds of years earlier.

The second of three sets of bells rang out, and soon parishioners would file in and take their seats in the rows of pews. The priest had delivered Mass so many times that his biggest challenge was breathing life into the words that rolled from his deeper memory. But it wasn't Sunday and this wouldn't be a typical Mass. Today, the spirit of Arturo Rodriguez Diego would be given up to the Lord.

Funeral Masses were the part of the padre's duties that he least relished. He had presided over the burial of many men and women, but this day was worse. Arturo was a child. When parents and grandparents died, Padre Esteban could eulogize that they lived good lives and made beautiful families to carry on the Lord's work. He could not look at the Diego and Rodriguez families and utter those euphemisms. Arturo was eleven years old and his death had been senseless. There was only one word that captured the truth: *tragedy.* The kind of gut-wrenching event that tested the faith of even the most pious.

Arturo and his friends had been playing at Fundidora, the steel foundry. On a dare, Arturo had climbed atop a tall iron ladder, lost his balance and fell twenty feet to the ground below.

Arturo's death made Padre Esteban at once sad and angry. He knew there were only two social classes: business owners and workers, the latter being little different from the ancient *macehualles*. Instead of playgrounds and parks, the children of Monterrey ran freely among the factories, exposing themselves to all types of hazards and disposed wastes. There was little incentive for academic education; the young had but one future to which to aspire. Boys would replace their fathers in the foundries or fabrication mills, and girls would marry these boys. Hundreds of thousands of idle and unexploited minds was the most hazardous and wasteful by-product that every factory made.

Many years earlier, the priest had presided over the death of another child, Pedro Macias—the firstborn of Umberto and Oralia Macias. He remembered it all too well because Pedro had been the first person to whom he had delivered both first and last rites.

⋘⦿⋙

With everyone present, Padre Esteban blessed the simple pine coffin with holy water as one of the older altar boys began to sway the *incensio* back and forth—first over the coffin and then down the center aisle. Cries of lamentation rose from those gathered. Arturo's mother and aunt passed out and had to be held up by relatives. Others gnashed their teeth and pounded on their chests. It was best this way. To get past death, one had to immerse oneself in the most intensely emotional way.

Through it all, the priest remained calm. *"In manus tuas, Domine, commendo spiritum suum,"* he solemnly spoke.

Since no photos existed of Arturo—his family was far too poor to own something as luxurious as a camera—pictures drawn by some friends were placed on a table off to the side of the altar. The table also had bunches of wild plants and some flowers, which neighbors had gathered earlier that morning. Death of the old was often an occasion of celebration, but today the mood was somber and severe. It was simply unnatural for parents to bury their child.

". . . For men are not cast off by the Lord forever. Though He brings grief, He will show compassion, so great is His unfailing love," Padre Esteban finished his recitation from the book of Lamentations 3:31-32. While he spoke to his congregation of Juan Diego and the Miracle of Guadalupe, he found himself silently asking God, *Why a child? Aren't their lives already difficult enough?* And then he quickly stopped his train of thought, angered at his weakness in questioning the Lord's will.

Finishing his sermon, he led the procession along El Campo Santo. Padre Esteban walked with a slight limp; it was the only remnant of his brush with the Spanish Flu almost four decades earlier.

"Why did the Dark Virgin send her message through Juan Diego?" the priest overheard one child ask his mother as they continued down the street. "He was a nobody."

"God works his miracles through the meek, not the mighty," Padre Esteban interjected.

"That was a million years ago," the boy said.

"Only four hundred," corrected the priest as if the distinction would make the story more acceptable.

The boy's eyes grew cold, and as he looked away he whispered, "There are no more miracles."

The funeral was heartbreaking enough, but the boy's comments echoed an even deeper despair.

Padre Esteban bit his lower lip and kept walking. He would cry later, long after the family and neighbors had dispersed. It wasn't that he felt it unseemly for a priest to cry; it was just that he knew the family looked for his guidance through their grief. No, he would wait until he was alone and then he would weep for young Arturo and the life that would never be.

❦

Padre Esteban closed the church's heavy wooden doors but did not lock them. It wasn't necessary; kids were usually trying to find ways to get *out* of church. He entered a smaller building attached to the rear of the church, which served as the rectory. Before he retired for the evening, he brought in two large buckets of water from which he filled a small wash basin on his dresser. Other than the bed and end table, it was the only piece of furniture in the room. Above it was a mirror, and Padre Esteban looked at himself for the first time that day.

His face was layered with soot, both from the factories and the incense inside the church. Tears made rivulet-like traces down his cheeks. He cupped his hands in the water. It was already warm, but it still felt soothing as he brought his hands to his brow and let the water cascade down his aging countenance. He was barely sixty years old, but a hard life had weathered his face and his soul. Through a small window, he saw that the skies had filled with dark, gray cumulus clouds. They portended rain and that would be a welcome relief from weeks of parching heat—the kind that suffocates and crawls all over one's body.

Padre Esteban lay down on his bed. He had a sheet, but he rarely used it. Monterrey was a city devoid of material comforts, so it was good that he had chosen a vocation that rewarded austerity. He did, however, have one luxury: a Colonial Radio Company Silvertone, model no. 4569, built specially for Sears & Roebuck in 1937.

At nearly twenty years old, the radio had been dropped often, but despite its age and being scuffed, it was still in perfect working condition. Rectangular in shape, it had a huge gold-colored dial with a "tuning-eye," and Padre Esteban admired the craftsmanship in its multigrained wood veneer. It had been a gift from Señor Don Fernando Alvarado, one of the wealthiest and most powerful men in Monterrey. Padre Esteban had been summoned to give Señor Alvarado's mother her last rites while the family's priest was out of town. She recovered and Señor Alvarado had associated this fortunate turn of events with Padre Esteban's appearance. When she finally did pass away, he gave Padre Esteban the radio she used to listen to.

As Padre Esteban turned off his bedside light, he turned on the radio. Using shortwave receivers and then rebroadcasting through local transmitters, Mexican stations could deliver live broadcasts from NBC in New York City or the BBC in London—delayed only a few minutes for the Spanish translation. There were lots of news and dramas, but there were so many American corporate advertisements that old-timers called Mexican radio "spiritual tequila."

The priest's favorite shows were Saturday night's *Hit Parade* and *Hacia un Mundo Mejor*, which was on from seven thirty to eight o'clock on Sundays. Both played the music of Pedro Infante, the poor carpenter who crafted his own guitar. His *boleros* and *rancheras* touched a chord in the poor and the oppressed. Even the rich begrudgingly admired him, though it was a sin for them to feel *simpatico* with the pain of his songs.

Padre Esteban could barely distinguish between the static crackling from the radio and the rain hitting the corrugated metal roof of the rectory. Soon, however, the static overpowered the music, a result of the storm that howled outside. He slowly turned the tuning knob until something caught his attention. It was different than anything he had heard before. It wasn't music, yet it had a lyrical quality to it. Suddenly, he opened his eyes and stared at the crucifix on the wall opposite his bed.

A wide smile overcame him as an idea took shape in his mind. He knew it lay somewhere between insanity and heresy, and he prayed the Lord would understand his plan.

Padre Esteban's eyes squinted in the darkness, the only light emanating from the golden face of the radio. "Eight, three, zero. . . eight, three, zero. . ." He juggled the station's frequency over in his mind to ensure he'd be able to find it again.

The Spanish announcer's voice grew increasingly excited.

"Duke Snider hits one deep into right center, Musial's back, back, back. . . it's gone!" crackled the broadcast as the roar of a cheering crowd echoed through the rafters of Ebbets Field in a faraway place called Brooklyn, New York.

Part One
The Dirt Field

1

The Palm Frond

An emaciated dog tugged at a pile of garbage, strewing it across the manure-covered street. The houses of Colonia Cantu looked more like afterthoughts of what to do with cinder blocks and scrap metal than a planned housing community. San Francisco Oriente, like most streets in this colonia, wasn't paved, and the tracks from horse-drawn carts, which had been made during heavy rains, had dried into petrified ruts.

Almost a year had passed since Arturo Rodriguez Diego's funeral and other than a small PELIGRO sign posted near the place where he had met his death, little had changed either at Fundidora or in Monterrey as a whole. Workers toiled day and night in behemoth drones that swallowed their souls and their children; not necessarily like Arturo, but in the way they absorbed each generation without offering any hope from their monotonous cycle of birth, grueling labor and then death.

For the boys of the parish of Iglesia de San Juan Bautista, traces of a different world filtered through Padre Esteban's radio each week as they gathered to hear men they'd never seen play a game they knew little about. Last season, the boys' adopted team, the Brooklyn Dodgers, lost the final game to the New York Yankees. The announcer described the Yankees in terms more befitting devils than baseball players.

This morning on San Francisco Oriente, besides the clucking of several chickens and the growls of the hungry dog as he eyed the scavenging birds, there was only one other discernable sound. It was the hymn *Cristo, Eres Justo Rey*.

The voice's angelic quality seemed completely out of sync with its surroundings. It came from one nondescript shack, near the center of the block, owned by Umberto Macias. Next to it was a plank-fenced pen that was home to several pigs. Animals that didn't yield milk or lay eggs had little to look forward to on special religious days.

"Quiet down, I'm trying to sleep!" boomed Umberto's voice.

Following its source, Oralia Macias entered the bedroom of the house. She was a tiny, dark-haired woman who looked even shorter because of the long cotton dress that flowed down to her ankles. Petite yellow flowers adorned the lightweight fabric, and over her shoulders was draped a wool shawl made by her sister. It covered her neck and shoulders so that they wouldn't be seen by any man besides her husband.

Between her feet and the compacted dirt floor were her *chanclas,* sandals made of pigskin which clung to her soles in the most primitive way. They were the only things she owned that protected her feet from the broken rocks, which lay half-buried in the unforgiving soil.

Oralia looked across the small room to her husband, who still lay in bed. His long cotton pajama pants and trimmed T-shirt were once pure white, but nothing in Monterrey stayed that color for long.

"If you didn't drink all night, maybe you wouldn't sleep so late," she said.

"Just make him stop," said Umberto as he sat upright on the edge of the bed and began to rub the sleep from his bloodshot eyes. The strains of the hymn could still be heard from the next room.

"He has to practice for choir."

"Choir? You're turning him into a woman," he grunted.

"And *you're* showing him what a *man* is?" she replied.

"Shut him up or I'll do it myself." These words were spoken so loudly, and with such vehemence that the singing suddenly stopped. Satisfied, Umberto flopped down and pulled the sheet back over his head.

Returning into the shack's main room, Oralia stood before her son, a twelve-year-old boy named Angel. She gazed at him with a look asking, *Why did you stop?*

"It's okay, Mama. I was finished anyway."

"He didn't mean it," she tried to comfort him, but after dozens of such episodes, the sincerity in her words had diminished.

"Is he ever going to get better?" asked the boy.

"I don't know," his mother answered.

"Padre Esteban says that anything is possible with the help of God."

"God has more important things to worry about than us," she said, eyeing a small shrine above the mantle containing some mementos of Pedro, her firstborn child who had died many years earlier. In the center of several candles was a picture of Our Lady of Guadalupe, over which was draped a medallion of the Dark Virgin that had been Pedro's. It wasn't much, but to a grieving mother, it was everything.

"You should wear something nicer to the church on this day," she added.

"I have nothing nicer," answered Angel.

"Hold on," she said and left the room for a few moments. When she returned, she was carrying a folded shirt and a pair of pants.

"Pedro never had a chance to wear these. They should fit you now," she said.

"Mama—"

"No time to argue. Now go change or you'll be late," she said with a sigh.

∾⊙☙

It was not yet ten o'clock and already Calzada Francisco I. Madero was filled with people. Thousands waved palm fronds in the air as they awaited the procession of Jesus Christ and his entrance into the Holy Land. This year, the one chosen to re-enact this ritual was Señor Claudio Villarreal.

April 15, 1957 was *el Domingo de Ramos*—Palm Sunday.

"As our Savior rested on the Mount of Olives, he sent two disciples ahead to get a donkey and her colt," Señor Villarreal explained to his son, Norberto, who helped him ready his mount with a blanket over its back. Norberto was born in the small agricultural town of Sabinas Hidalgo. When a terrible drought forced many of its residents to leave, the Villarreals moved to Monterrey. Their four children, all boys, sold newspapers to contribute to the family. The Villarreal brothers shared a fierce competitiveness and that was where Norberto got his nickname *el Verdugo,* the Executioner. Though he never backed down from a scrap with his siblings, Norberto was a gentle soul.

"How did he know there'd be a donkey there?" he asked his father.

"He's the son of God, of course he knew," replied Señor Villarreal, confident that his answer would suffice for any question his son might ask.

In a few minutes, Señor Villarreal would head down the Avenida Zaragoza and make his triumphal entry into Barrio Antigua, the oldest part of Monterrey.

Near the Plaza del San Juan Bautista, Angel Macias and two of his friends, Enrique Suarez and Mario Ontiveros, were fighting to the death—at least for that day. They had discovered that if one held a palm frond by its leaves, the hardened end narrowed into a point and made the perfect sword.

"Stand back or *Casanova* will end your life!" Mario threatened Enrique. Enrique was taller than Mario and had a very dark complexion, which was why they called him *el Cubano.* A look at his father, one of the more handsome men in Monterrey according to the ladies, explained his swarthy features. Mario was small, but his looks fell more into the realm of cuteness, which was a big plus in the eyes of similarly aged girls.

"Take that," answered Enrique with a thrust of his own palm frond.

Pretending to be run through the heart, Mario fell backwards, and feigning a lengthy dying scene, he staggered over to a group of *chicas* who had been eyeing them.

"It's going dark, I'm fading fast," said Mario with his eyes closed. As he neared the girls, the darkness apparently explained his need to grope forward with outstretched hands.

"One kiss for a dying hero," he said to one girl who also

pretended to veil her face. Mario puckered his lips and moved in her direction, but as he stepped forward with his eyes closed, he accidentally walked into Padre Esteban. Mario's mother saw the collision and yelled out to her son.

"Mario! This is a holy day. It's not a time for games."

"Okay, boys, hand over your weapons," said Padre Esteban with a sternness that pleased Señora Ontiveros as she grabbed Mario by the ear and led him away.

"We're sorry, Padre, we didn't—" began Angel.

"If God hadn't intended for us to play games, he wouldn't have made them so fun," interrupted the priest with a smile as he brandished one of the confiscated fronds.

The boys of his parish had no toys, except those they fashioned from raw materials they found in refuse or scrap heaps. Recreation was secondary to survival, though Padre Esteban perceived that the two were not mutually exclusive.

"*¡En guarde!*" the priest said as he suddenly chased Angel and Enrique around the square, their younger legs easily outpacing his.

Padre Esteban's hollowed cheekbones and square jaw made him appear more like a *gringo* than a typical Mexican of Indian or Spanish descent. The nature of his vocation, with its long hours indoors and his being fully garbed, contributed to his being relatively fair-skinned for a Mexican. In fact, Padre Esteban *was* part *gringo*. Though he and his parents were born and raised in Mexico, his mother's parents had been missionaries from the Ohio Valley who had come to Mexico to spread the Gospel in the late 1860s. They had died when Padre Esteban's mother was a child, so very little was known or spoken about them. Besides the physical inheritance, they left him the legacy of service to Christ—a mantle he'd worn ever since he entered the seminary at the age of fifteen.

❦

Later, Angel and Enrique took their places in the church's choir. As Angel looked at the faces of those gathered for Palm Sunday Mass, he could see his mother and bleary-eyed father seated in opposite pews. It was a tradition for women to sit on the right and men on the left, except for young boys who often sat with their mothers.

After Mass, Oralia approached her son.

"You have the voice of an angel," she said.

"Mom," Angel whispered forcefully while looking around to see if anyone heard.

Changing tack, she asked, "So, big game today?"

"Opening Day against Philadelphia," he nodded.

"*Ooh*," she sighed, trying to sound genuinely interested.

"Well, be home by supper," she added and then kissed him. Angel squirmed. He loved being kissed by her, but at twelve, squirming away was protocol. He ran to the back of the church and grabbed a broom handle.

꧁∞꧂

Next to the church was a dirt alley; its only patches of green were clumps of weeds. A half-dozen boys from the Iglesia de San Juan Bautista choir waited anxiously as Hector Martinez repaired the ball. It was nothing more than a sock stuffed with dirt and straw and then tied several times around with thinly torn cloth. The broomhandle, devoid of its bristles, served as their bat, and certain clumps of weeds were designated as bases.

Though a few positions were recognizable, the odd shape of their field and their lack of experience meant there was a pitcher, a catcher and everyone else.

There was baseball in Monterrey. Americans—businessmen, entrepreneurs, and hopefuls with maps of gold and silver mines—had brought the game with them into Mexico, but there were no organized leagues for the young.

Hector threw a pitch and the batter hit the ball sharply toward third base where Enrique stood ready for it. He fielded the ball and threw it to Ricardo Treviño who was positioned at first.

Ricardo attended the Diego de Montemayor Elementary School, the same school as Enrique, but Ricardo was younger and two grades behind. His father, Eusebio Treviño, left his family when Ricardo was very young and moved to the United States. Ricardo saw him for a few weeks each year before he would take off again, leaving his family to fend for themselves.

"It's my turn!" called out Angel from behind the plate.

"You're the catcher," chided Hector.

"Sandy Koufax doesn't catch," said Angel, referring to one of the Dodgers' newest pitchers, and the player Angel imagined himself to be.

"First of all, you aren't him. Second, you're both too thin to make it as pitchers."

"What makes you the expert?"

"I made the ball," sneered Hector.

Angel crouched behind the plate again and mumbled to himself, "We're not too thin."

Hector fired a pitch to the next hitter, Norberto, who swung and missed the ball.

"You're out!" yelled Hector.

"I tipped it," claimed Norberto.

"No you didn't."

"Did so!"

"Boys, it's time!" came Padre Esteban's voice, interrupting their intractable argument.

As the boys ran into the deserted church, Norberto made sure that everyone knew he *had* tipped the ball and wasn't really out.

⤜◎◎⤏

Sitting on the ground before the altar, the boys formed a semicircle around Padre Esteban's radio, its tuning needle pointed to 830.

"Gil Hodges steps to the plate. One more out and the Phillies will take the opener," filtered through the church as the Spanish announcer continued his broadcast of the last inning of the Dodgers' opening game.

"Do you think our Dodgers have a chance?" asked Angel.

Enrique shook his head solemnly. "With two outs and down by three in the bottom of the ninth?"

"I meant this season," corrected Angel.

"Yankees beat'em last year in the series. They look too tough," Hector said. "They got lucky," chimed in Norberto.

"Lucky? You call Don Larsen's perfect game lucky?" asked Ricardo.

"A perfect game! And in a World Series," sighed Enrique. They were referring to game five of last year's series. Don Larsen, the Yankees pitcher, hadn't allowed a single Dodger batter to reach base.

The term first appeared in 1908 in the *Chicago Tribune*. In describing a game won by Cleveland Broncho pitcher, Addie Joss, the Tribune's sportswriter called Joss's performance on the mound, "An absolutely perfect game, without run, without hit, and without letting an opponent reach first base by hook or by crook, on hit, walk, or error, in nine innings."

"Have you ever seen a perfect game, Padre?" asked Norberto.

"To me, baseball is always perfect," answered the priest.

"And do you boys know the beautiful thing about Opening Day?" he asked.

After a pause and no-takers, he said, "No matter what happened last year, today every team is in first place."

"And that's ball four. Hodges walks, moving Duke Snider to second. . ." continued the announcer.

Angel looked up at the priest shyly, his brown almond-shaped eyes squinted in the dim light of the church. "Why can't we just start over like that?"

"Until the last out, there's always hope," said Padre Esteban. Before Angel or his friends could respond, the broadcaster's voice became noticeably more excited.

". . . Sandy Amoros hits a deep drive, Repulski back to the wall . . . It's gone, a home run! The Dodgers have tied the game. Unbelievable!" he exclaimed.

"See. Our Dodgers have spirit," the priest responded to the announcers' call.

"I'd still rather have Don Larsen," quipped Enrique.

Even Padre Esteban had to laugh.

⌖

Umberto and Oralia Macias had almost finished their dinner. The meal, like their house, was very simple. Frijoles, tortillas and some squash, which Oralia had made into a soup. On special occasions, she would add some cow intestines or some other cheap cut of meat. And, of course, in every Mexican kitchen there were always chilies being soaked, peeled, chopped, ground, stuffed or dried. *"Sin chile, no creen que estan comiendo* [without chilies, the natives don't believe they're eating]."

Umberto looked up as his son, Angel, entered. "You're late," he grumbled.

"The game went into extra innings, Papa. We won seven to six." Angel went to take his place at the table, but Umberto stiffly held out his arm and stopped him.

"No! If you can't be home on time, you don't eat. Do your chores. When you're finished, you can clean out the hog pen. It's needed doing for weeks."

"Umberto, he's just a child," interjected Oralia.

"When I was his age, I had to help put food on the table," barked Umberto, whose word would not be crossed, even by Angel's mother.

Turning to his son, he scowled, "Go!"

⁕

His father had been curt, but it could have been much worse. Out back, Angel shoveled manure into a mound on one side of the pig pen. He held the back end of the shovel with his right hand, putting all of the pressure on one shoulder. No stranger to an empty stomach, he was not in a hurry to finish his task. Here in the pen, his solitude gave him a temporary feeling of safety.

"Your mother thinks I'm too hard on you," a voice came from behind as Angel glanced sideways to see his father watching him. "Well, the world is harder."

Angel stood still, hesitant to turn fully toward the sound and yet sensible enough not to turn away. Finally, he lifted the shovel again, and then dropped it as a strong pain cut deeply into his right shoulder. He instinctively rubbed it.

"What's wrong?" his father asked.

"Nothing," replied Angel, releasing his shoulder and looking straight at his father's dark eyes. He knew better than to admit weakness in front of him.

"Why don't you change sides? Try it with your other arm, switch it around," offered Umberto with unexpected concern.

Angel pulled the shovel from the filthy ground and clutched the end with his left hand, his right arm now only guiding its motion. The ache in his right shoulder decreased as the one in his stomach became more demanding.

"Good," said Umberto as he placed a plate of food on an upside-down pail, then turned and left.

Angel ignored the pungent odor of the sty as he sat and ate.

"You think the pigpen is hard? Well, the slaughterhouse is harder," he mockingly told the oblivious hogs.

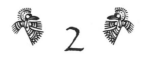

A Siesta, Ruined

The dawn of the twentieth century brought the Industrial Age to Monterrey as plans for the Compañía Fundidora de Fierro y Acero de Monterrey were formally announced on May 5, 1900. In three years, the first High Alloy Steel Foundry in Latin America opened.

During the construction, men were being trained in the terminology of their future jobs. Iron and steel would become more than a source of employment; they would set the life rhythms of generations of *Regiomontanos*—the local word for an inhabitant of Monterrey. When the whistle blew on the factory's first day of operation in 1903, fifteen hundred workers entered through its wooden doors. That year saw almost one hundred thousand tons of steel forged. By 1957, the foundry was producing three-quarters of a million tons of steel annually. In many ways, Monterrey and Fundidora had become one in the same—as if the bones of its people were made of the steel it produced.

Enrique Suarez's great-grandfather, nicknamed Papá Fito, had been the first butler hired by the Departamento de Aceración. They were called butlers because they served the needs of the furnaces at all times of the day or night. Required to be close by, they were given small apartments in Colonia Acero. Even though the midnight whistle signaled the darkening of the factory's lights and the closing of the main entrance, the butlers were frequently woken up in the middle of the night by the giant monster who demanded their attention.

The steel they forged was everywhere: in the plow and the tractor of the farmer; in the hammer and the chisel of the bricklayer; behind every wall; under every street and in every car.

"Even in my hallway I hang the Virgin de Guadalupe with a steel spike," Papá Fito would proudly tell Enrique's father when he was a boy.

⋯⊙⊙⋯

Angel, Enrique and Norberto made their way along the north side of the Santa Catarina River toward Fundidora, which lay on Monterrey's more isolated east side.

They were met by Hector. "Where are you guys going?" he asked them.

"My dad forgot his dinner," said Angel, holding up a paper bag.

One could enter Fundidora's grounds from almost any side by simply walking along the dirt trails formed by large trucks that entered and exited all day long or on the rail tracks that brought raw materials from Durango, Coahuila, and Oaxaca. The clamor of the machinery, the movement of throngs of men, the smell of *chapopote* and the orange glow that radiated twenty-four hours a day from Fundidora's thermal core made *Regiomontanos* believe that it was really alive.

As the boys neared the entrance, something made Enrique freeze in his tracks.

"What?" asked Norberto.

"It's her. . . my girlfriend," Enrique answered, motioning toward a young, well-dressed girl who walked out of a building that housed some of the foundry's offices.

"Girlfriend? You've never even met her," said Angel.

Gloria Jimenez stood for a moment and turned her head to face the four boys. She smiled ever so slightly, though it wasn't clear at whom the smile was directed, if at any of them. But the fact that she had smiled in Enrique's general vicinity was all the proof he needed.

"See, told you she likes me," he boasted.

"She could've been looking at a bird behind you, stupid," came Hector's disparaging remark.

"What birds?" Enrique asked, gazing behind him toward a couple of scraggly, soot-covered trees. Neither looked as if it offered sanctuary to any birds, but the argument was rendered unimportant as Gloria was suddenly joined by Señor Jimenez, who spirited his daughter into a waiting automobile.

"Girls like her don't go out with boys like you," Hector added as the automobile sped off.

"What do you mean, *like me*?"

"Well, for one thing, try poor," said Angel.

"I ain't gonna be poor forever."

"Oh no?" chimed in Hector. "How are you gonna get rich melting iron?"

"Maybe I won't work at Fundidora," said Enrique, but his statement was so absurd that it didn't immediately register with his friends. Even if he decided to forgo the foundry in order to melt silicon at Vitro Glassworks or grind and burn calcium carbonate at Cementos de Mexicana—the prospects were equally barren and unforgiving. But Enrique had something else entirely in mind. "Someday I'm gonna be an engineer," he added.

"You've got about as much chance of becoming an engineer as you do of dating Gloria Jimenez," said Hector.

"What makes you so sure?" Enrique defended himself.

"You gotta go to school to be an engineer. And that takes money, which is something you ain't got, *amigo*," said Hector.

Enrique went to answer, but he realized that as harsh as his friends' words were, they probably were right. The odds of someone born in his station in life going to university was about as likely as him winning a Nobel Prize or meeting his country's president.

∾⊙⊙৹

The first shift at Fundidora began at six in the morning when roosters still crowed on the farms that ringed its eastern perimeter. Workers wore blue overalls and silver helmets, one of the only pieces of safety equipment issued by the company. Veterans of the factory knew that these didn't prevent or mitigate the accidents, nor did they protect workers from heat exhaustion or respiratory diseases.

They simply reminded them that Fundidora owned their heads and everything below it.

"*Regiomontanos* should be born, grow, study, learn a craft, and finally work at Fundidora," stated one of its first presidents. That workers were free to quit gave the illusion that it wasn't slavery, but anyone who was born at the company's Maternidad Maria Josefa, sheltered in Colonia Acero, schooled at Escuela Acero, and lived within blocks of the hypnotizing sounds and fumes of this ferrous giant would always have steel in his blood—as a stigma and as a way of life.

Inside Horno Alto #1, huge furnaces blazed as Umberto Macias, Fecundino Suarez, Claudio Villarreal, and other sweating and overstressed workers toiled. From raw iron, they would forge steel and bend it into the shapes demanded by a rapidly industrializing world.

It took at least eight men to perform the Acid Bessemer process, which gave the steel the purity required on the international markets. It was also one of the most exhausting and dangerous parts of the job.

Claudio Villarreal and his team refined the molten pig iron by blowing air through it in the converter, an egg-shaped container that could hold up to twenty-five tons of terribly hot liquid minerals. Fecundino Suarez monitored the mix of alloys at his end of the line; the oxidation of the liquid's impurities raised the charge and caused an intense flame at the mouth of the converter. Umberto Macias and his team were responsible for maintaining the steel's temperature above its transformation range.

The air inside the plant was always dense with metal particles, which found their way into men's lungs, and nearly invisible specks of burning steel embers constantly pricked the skin and eyes.

Each cycle lasted only twenty-five minutes, but in this short period of time there could be no mistakes or men would die, or possibly worse: suffer the living death of extreme burns for which there was no treatment. Fundidora, was quick to remind complacent or forgetful employees of the fragile demarcation between life and death.

Just a few months earlier a malfunction occurred on the mechanical arm holding a twenty-foot diameter crucible of molten metal in the Department of Steel Casting #2. As the massive pot keeled over, steel magma at a temperature of more than 2,700 degrees poured out uncontrollably.

A dozen workers never returned home that day.

⋘⊙⊙⋙

"You got twenty minutes!" yelled the foreman who vanished just as quickly as he had appeared. Fecundino and Claudio found a place to sit and pulled out their dinners. Monterrey's factories were terrifying in the enormity of scale, which made a man feel small and vulnerable like Lilliputians in a world of Gullivers. The proportions of everything seemed unimaginably large: rivets larger than a man's head, chain links the size of an automobile, and of course the *sopladores*—smokestacks that towered two hundred feet skyward in a country whose tallest building was three stories. It was as if men didn't really belong here and their intrusion, while necessary, was an afterthought of Fundidora's creation.

"Where's that kid?" asked Umberto, anxiously looking around. Though Umberto and his colleagues had found a place of relative quiet, he was still shouting. That was normal in the factory, even to be heard by the man next to you.

"Hey, what happened to Ruben?" asked Fecundino.

"Got burned pretty bad yesterday over at Horno Alto #3," answered Claudio.

"They couldn't care less about our safety," Fecundino replied as he tried to wipe some grease from his forehead, but the harder he tried, the more it smeared.

"Complaining only gets you a worse shift," noted Claudio.

"We should organize," suggested his co-worker.

"Organize? You mean like a union? I don't know. I got eight kids to feed. I can't afford to lose my job. What do you think, Umberto?" asked Claudio.

"I think you two should mind your own business. Ruben was just unlucky, that's all," said Umberto as he pulled out a small tin flask and brought it to his lips.

None of the men heard or saw Angel as he quietly stepped closer.

Fecundino watched Umberto take several hearty swigs from the bottle. "You're not gonna find answers in there."

"Where then?" snapped Umberto.

"In God," said Claudio.

"One Palm Sunday playing Jesus Christ and you're suddenly a prophet," Umberto said. The veins on his forehead began to appear through the sweat laced hair that matted to his brow.

"At least I'm smart enough not to mock God."

"God . . . ? God took my son," said Umberto. His gaze burned with the intensity of the inferno that both punished and provided his existence.

"And *He* sacrificed *His* only Son," said Fecundino with a tone of sympathy. "At least you have the blessing of Angel."

"He'll never be the son Pedro was."

Despite the background noise, the men heard a side door slam shut. They walked over to inspect but saw no one.

"Who was that?" Claudio asked.

Umberto didn't say anything. He knew who it was. He felt a tinge of remorse as he reached down and picked up the paper bag that contained his dinner.

⁓◈◑◈⁓

Angel ran and ran and ran some more. He felt his heart pumping so fast he was sure it would burst, yet he wished he could run all the way out of his own skin and wake up as someone else.

He finally collapsed when his limbs could no longer find the strength to propel him forward. He lay in a weedy, rock-strewn lot. His feet felt warm, but he knew it was from the blood that oozed from cuts and tears.

Suddenly, he saw something that appeared out of place. It was only a few feet from his face; its silhouette was being gently washed by the light of a full moon. Crawling to it, he picked it up and held it high above his head. For a moment it eclipsed the moon and a halo formed around its circumference.

It was worn and beaten, but nonetheless it was a real baseball. At that moment, it was the most beautiful thing Angel had ever seen.

⸎⸎⸎

Early the next morning, Oralia Macias retrieved a small cloth from a cabinet beneath her washbasin. She brought it, along with a water-filled bowl, into the room where Angel slept soundly on a pile of straw. She bit down on her lip at the sight of where his blood had matted down the straw. Kneeling, she began to wash the dried blood off his feet.

Angel writhed but did not wake. Oralia studied him closely as she finished her task. Returning to the kitchen, she hung up the cloth, emptied the bowl and picked up the two buckets that needed to be filled. The walk to San Juan Bautista Square wasn't so bad when the buckets were empty, but the way home was getting harder with each passing year.

She got to the well and pumped the iron lever until water trickled out and cascaded into her bucket. Before she had finished filling the second one, the flow of water decreased to a trickle, and then to nothing.

"It's run dry again," said an old woman behind her. "It'll be a few hours before it'll flow again."

"Here. Take one of mine," said Oralia.

"Are you sure, dear?"

"I have more than I need for now," she lied, but she would come back later after the pump had been primed again. Oralia carried the water to the old woman's home; it was only a few blocks out of her way. After completing this task, she headed home when Norberto recognized her from his vantage point in the alley next to the church.

"Señora Macias, where's Angel? We need him for our game," he called to her.

"Not today, boys. He's hurt his feet," she replied.

"We don't need his feet—just his arms," laughed Enrique.

⸎⸎⸎

It would be two weeks before Angel returned to the dirt field where he found the baseball. It was a large expanse next to what appeared to be an abandoned factory, though it had no smokestacks or conveyers.

He walked over to the building. Its windows were either broken or missing, and gaps in the plaster showed the cinder blocks behind its veneer. After a further search, Angel found a rusting metal bucket. He propped it on a small ledge on a side wall of the building. Pacing back about fifteen long strides, he turned and looked at it. It sure appeared a lot smaller from forty feet away.

Angel took a few minutes to make a little pile of dirt and an indentation from which he could push off with his back foot. Proud of himself, he stood defiantly on the mound and focused on his makeshift strike zone. Winding up, he let fly with his best pitch. Missing the target by at least three feet, the ball struck the wall with a deadening thud.

"Who did that?" came an unpleasant voice that startled Angel. An unkempt and disheveled looking man appeared at a doorway in the building. His demeanor suggested anything but cordiality.

"Me," Angel said.

"And who are you?" the man growled.

"Sandy Koufax," Angel answered with a mix of arrogance and apprehension as he picked up the ball.

"Well, Koufax, you ruined my siesta."

Angel wound up and let fly another pitch. This too missed the strike zone and impacted the building with another loud thud.

"By the way, Koufax is a lefty," the man grunted.

Angel retrieved the ball in silence, went back to the mound, casually switched hands and fired another pitch using his left arm. Another miss. A loud whistle blew from somewhere nearby. The older man looked in the direction of the sound and then added, "And he's Jewish."

"I'm . . . *Joodish*."

"Jew-ish" repeated the man.

"That's what I said, *Joorish*." Angel reared back and threw a fourth pitch that missed by more than his three previous misfires.

"Well it sure hasn't helped your aim," said the older man,

shaking his head.

"What do you know?" said Angel with all the condescension he dared.

The man stared for a moment at Angel before walking over to him. Angel stood his ground, fully expecting the back side of the man's hand, but instead the man took the baseball from him and backed up slowly until he was about sixty feet from the wall. Without a word, he wound up and fired a bull's-eye into the bucket's center.

Angel's mouth dropped open as the man turned and said, "Now go away."

⋞◉◉◉⋟

The man left the dirt field and returned to Vitro Glassworks where he was greeted by his boss.

"Valve won't close in furnace three," said the foreman. It needed to be fixed, and as little as the foreman liked the man who never took siesta with his colleagues, he knew there was no better machinist on the floor.

"That valve's holding back a thousand pounds of pressure," the man said. "It's not safe to work on yet."

"It needs to be done now."

"You don't pay me enough to risk my ass."

"Don't push me, *pocho*," snarled the foreman.

The man grabbed a tool belt and headed for the troubled area.

"What's with that guy?" one of the other workers asked the foreman.

"He lived in America. He thinks he's better than us," he answered.

"Why don't he go back there?"

"I heard he can't," stated the foreman.

"Maybe he killed someone," speculated another.

"Why keep him?" the first worker asked the foreman.

"*You* wanna go up and open the valve?"

The workers all looked down; no one volunteered.

"Besides, he can assemble a turbine engine with his eyes closed," added the foreman.

"Still, someone ought to teach him some manners," said the first worker.

"Yeah? Maybe you'll be the one," his colleague goaded him as the men laughed and got back to work.

⁂

Thud. . . thud. . . thud.

"You again?" asked the annoyed man as Angel rained one pitch after another on the side of the building. It had been two days since Angel had been here, but as the other day, he awakened the same man from his afternoon siesta.

"What's that for?" the man asked, looking at a second glove the boy had brought.

"A pitcher needs a catcher. I thought we could play catch," answered Angel.

"Sorry, I'm busy."

Angel threw another pitch at the bucket on the wall.

"Why don't you find your own field?"

"This *is* mine," replied Angel.

The unshaven man merely grunted and went back inside the dilapidated structure.

⁂

Later that evening, Umberto sat at his table drinking a beer while Oralia prepared supper. Angel slipped through the front door, and holding the baseball behind his back, he tried not to garner his father's attention.

"What are you hiding?" snapped the older man.

"Nothing."

"Come here!" said Umberto as his eyes narrowed.

Spinning Angel around, the ball came into view. Umberto hastily grabbed Angel's wrist and pulled it toward him, ignoring the wince of his son.

"Who did you steal this from?"

"I found it, Papa," said the frightened boy. Umberto stared for a moment at Angel and then took the ball from him.

"I don't believe you."

"Umberto!" pleaded Oralia desperately.

Umberto stood up with the ball and walked toward the door.

"I'm not going to have a thief for a son! I'm going to the *cantina* to see if someone lost this," said Umberto as he exited through the improvised metallic door that helped the place look less of a mess. Umberto was not really looking for the owner of the ball; he saw this as an opportunity to change it for a few drinks and laughs.

Angel, timidly following his father onto the street, said, "I found it near the factory that time when you forgot your dinner. I swear!"

Umberto stopped and remembered the incident. He turned around and looked painfully at his only living son. For an instant, he imagined he saw another boy, from another time, but it was not a memory of Angel's brother Pedro. Umberto felt an echo of himself standing on a rain-drenched street, pleading for his father to come home.

"Next time don't be late with my supper!" replied Umberto as he rolled the ball through the mud back to Angel.

❦

For the third time that week, the man was awakened by the sound of cork-filled leather striking the wall behind his head. His eyes opened slowly, but he was too tired to move except to roll over and cover his ears with one of his arms.

"Not again!" he grumbled as he got up and went to the door. There was that nuisance of a kid with his two gloves. Angel made no attempt to approach or retreat.

"Are you sure you don't want to play catch?" Angel asked the man, unfazed by his rejection the day before.

"As sure as I've ever been," the man sternly replied.

"Okay, I'll just have to practice by myself. . . every day." Angel began to wind up.

"Every. . . single. . . day," he said as he threw his next pitch.

"Okay, give me the glove," the man snarled.

"Really?" Angel's eyes lit up.

"Anything to stop that noise. Tomorrow, you find someplace else to pitch, got it?"

"Sure!"

The man hobbled out onto the field as Angel retrieved the ball.

"You limp, like our priest," said Angel.

"I slept funny," he replied. "Just give me the glove, Koufax."

Angel handed one of the gloves to the man. It was pretty shoddy and looked more like a glove made in the 1920s.

"It goes on your left hand," Angel said.

"I know how to wear a glove, but what's this thing?"

"It used to be my friend Norberto's. His mom made it."

"Figures."

Standing about twenty feet apart, the two began to have a catch. Neither one spoke for a few minutes, and as the ball flew back and forth, the only sounds were the flutter of the wind and the snap of leather on leather.

Angel excitedly fired one with particular speed, but it flew wildly by.

"You're throwing too much with your arm," the man said.

"How else can you throw?"

"A great throw comes from here," he answered, tapping his index finger on his temple.

"Our priest says that baseball is a game of God," said Angel.

"How'd he figure that?" the man asked as the two continued to throw and catch.

"When you look out from home plate, the field has no end. And until the final out, you can play forever."

"So?"

"Only God can make something infinite and eternal," Angel said very solemnly.

A factory whistle blared in the distance.

"I gotta go," the man said as he tossed the glove back to Angel, but he held on to the ball as he walked away.

"That's mine," Angel said.

"The field may be yours, but the ball's not," the man told him.

"I found it, it's mine."

"Then why does it say *Property of the St. Louis Browns* on it?"

When the man was about thirty paces distant, Angel called out to him, "I can't read!"

"You can't pitch either," the man said without glancing back.

⏤⏦⏤

On Monday afternoon, the man prepared for his usual siesta. He'd already eaten lunch and washed it down with a couple of beers from the Cuauhtemoc Moctezuma Brewing Company. They weren't as cold as he liked them, but they went down fine just the same.

He took his usual place in the old building and was about to lie down when he checked outside for the pesky kid.

No one.

He smiled and lay down, ready to enjoy a much-deserved nap. The building was once used as a barracks for migratory workers before the shantytown was haphazardly built around the factories.

Suddenly, it was too quiet, and as he opened his eyes he saw the kid, sitting next to his two gloves, arms folded, just staring at him.

"You sleep a lot," said Angel.

The man rubbed his eyes, hoping it was just a weird dream, but the kid was still there.

"I thought we had a deal."

"I'm not pitching."

"Good!" the man replied, unsure of what to say. He closed his eyes again and tried hard to fall back asleep.

"You took care of that," added Angel.

"Not one more word about the ball," he growled.

A half-minute later, Angel asked him, "You got kids?"

"No!"

"Why not?"

"No wife."

"How come?"

"Cause they usually want kids."

Angel stood up and looked out the door at the dirt field beyond. "I won't bother you again," he said as he stooped to pick up his gloves.

The man watched him for a moment; the boy was barefoot and

his pants were tattered around his shins. He also noticed the small bruise on the boy's wrist where Umberto had unintentionally grabbed his arm a bit too hard the evening before.

"What happened to your wrist?" he asked Angel.

"My father thought I had stolen the ball. Guess he was right," said Angel as he walked out of the building.

The man turned back over and closed his eyes, but he had no chance of falling asleep. *"Argh!"* He bolted upright, grabbed the baseball and ran out toward Angel.

"Hey, wait a minute!" he called out, making Angel stop and turn.

"I'll trade you the ball for your extra glove."

"What for?" the young boy asked.

"A pitcher needs a catcher. . . and a ball," the man said, realizing that from this day forward his siestas were all but ruined.

Batboy

ach day after school that week, Angel made his way to the dirt field where he and the man would don their gloves and play catch.

"Do you have another name, besides Koufax, I mean?" asked the man.

"My friends call me Angel."

"That's a good name. Why call yourself Sandy Koufax?"

"He's my hero."

"*Hmmp*. Well, don't spend too much time worshipping heroes. You'll only be disappointed," said the man.

"Who are you?" asked Angel.

"Willie Mays."

"Really?"

The man smiled and stared at Angel, unsure of who was pulling whose leg.

"Haven't you ever seen Willie Mays?"

Angel shook his head, sensing that he should be embarrassed.

"Willie Mays is. . . colored."

"Like Jackie Robinson?"

"Yeah, that's it, like Jackie Robinson."

"What color are they?" Angel asked. He'd heard the term, but he'd never seen a televsion broadcast.

The man realized he had dug himself a little hole, but the whistle had just blown and time was money. Hurriedly, he continued. "Well, brownish—"

"Like me. So I'm colored too."

"No, well, sort of. Of course you and I have a color, but in America there are. . ." Angel looked more confused the more the man tried to explain.

"Never mind! Just call me Cesar Faz."

"You're not from here, are you?" asked Angel.

"Why do you ask?"

"You talk funny," Angel answered.

"Maybe 'cause I'm not from here." Cesar's answer was intended to stifle, not provoke Angel's inquisitiveness, but it served only to encourage more questions. *Where are you from? Why did you come here? Who are your parents?* And so on and so on.

There is an old Mexican saying, "to know a man today, you must know who he was yesterday," and there on the dirt field, between the intermittent snapping of leather gloves, Cesar began to share who he was.

⌘

The War of 1845 was the defining event in a centuries-old clash between the two dominant North American cultures. In the treaty of Hidalgo-Guadalupe, Mexico forfeited more than a third of its territory. *Tejanos*, as people of Mexican descent were called in Texas, were beaten and often murdered as squatters quickly occupied their lands. Systematically stripped of political power and cultural identity, *Tejanos* found themselves treated as aliens in a land that their ancestors had occupied for tens of thousands of years.

A revolution swept across Mexico in 1910, precipitating a decade of civil war and anarchy. During that period, large farms, railroads and mining companies in the United States demanded workers who were willing to perform grueling work in unsafe conditions for low wages. The result was a mass migration northward across the Rio Grande. Among these emigrants were José and Felicitas Faz.

In 1918, while the United States fought in the trenches of Europe, raiders like Pancho Villa crossed the border to loot and plunder. In a secret message from the German foreign minister to his envoy in Mexico, Germany proposed an alliance with the understanding that Mexico would reconquer its lost territories. The *San Antonio Light* reported that if a German-Mexican army invaded Texas, just like the Alamo, Texans would fight to the death.

It was in this year and into this racially divided America that Cesar Leonardo Faz was born in San Antonio, Texas.

By the time Cesar was ten years old, San Antonio was Texas' largest city with a population of more than two hundred thousand people, one in four of who was a *Tejano*.

José Faz would bring his son on errands to the Mart down on Euclid and Flores streets. There, men would gather around a radio and talk about politics and money.

⚬⚬⚬⚬

"Every reason which calls for the exclusion of the most wretched, ignorant, dirty, diseased and degraded people of Europe or Asia demands that the illiterate, unclean, peonized masses moving this way from Mexico be stopped at the border. . ." crackled a speech by a Texas congressman.

"We take the worst jobs for the worst pay, and if we complain or try to organize, we're taken across the border and dropped off, even if we are citizens," groused one listener who was a friend of José Faz.

"Call the police," answered José.

"What good does that do?" grumbled another in response. Even when arrests were made, white juries never convicted their peers, and it would be decades before Mexican-Americans would have the legal right to serve on a Texas jury.

"Look at what happened to that Espinoza girl. Choked to death right in front of her friends," said the first man. "They weren't allowed to get water for her from a Whites-Only fountain just a few feet away."

Behind their dialogue, the congressman's address continued. "The Mexican peon is a mixture of Mediterranean-blooded Spanish peasant with low-grade Indians who did not fight to extinction, but submitted and multiplied as serfs. Into that was fused much Negro slave blood—"

José turned off the radio.

"You're not going to get anywhere by whining. You have to work hard and show them we're just as good," he said.

"That's easier for you to say," said one of the men. "You're in a union."

"Perhaps he's becoming white," joked another, but the humor masked an underlying question of why José Faz had moved his family from Salinas Avenue on the west side, where most Hispanics lived, to a tract home in a predominantly white neighborhood.

⊷⊙⊶

Like his brothers before him, Cesar attended elementary school at San Fernando Cathedral. It was only a few blocks from his home, so Cesar walked. Even if it had been farther, he still would have walked.

One day, Cesar's brother, Jorge, came home wearing a baseball uniform.

"I'm the bat holder for the Mission," Jorge announced. Major League Baseball's westernmost franchise was in St. Louis, which hosted two teams: the National League Cardinals and the American League Browns. Texas didn't have a major league team, but the San Antonio Missions were a double A squad and a farm team of the Dodgers, known then as the Brooklyn Robins.

"What does it pay?" asked José Faz, that being his usual first concern.

"Nothing," admitted Jorge.

"Then what kind of job is that?"

"The best in the world," added Jorge.

In October 1929, Cesar's father lost his savings when the Fifth National Bank failed. Fortunately, he managed to keep steady employment at Pabst Engraving.

Though employed, times were extremely hard. But Cesar never dwelled on how little his family had. Doing without had become part of the national psyche. But one thing they did have was a Westinghouse Junior cooler. Made especially for Coca-Cola, it had the company's logo on both sides, as well as the inviting words ICE COLD just below them. San Antonio summers are scorching and its winters freezing, so the cooler doubled in the off-season as a wardrobe for Cesar's clothes.

Three times a week, Cesar borrowed a neighbor's wagon and brought home blocks of ice to fill the cooler. Delivery trucks used to service the neighborhood, but since the 1929 stock market crash, they only ventured into the most affluent parts of town. Cesar took advantage of this and began delivering ice to the neighbors for a penny a trip. He'd then head across town to the Fair Maid Bakery to buy day-old bread at a quarter of the price of a fresh loaf.

His escape was baseball. There were no organized teams for youth, but in fields, in sandlots or in the middle of streets, give young boys a ball and a stick and they'd create the game.

Cesar and Jorge were in the Knot Hole Gang, kids whom the Missions let in for free in return for their hooting and hollering for the home team.

Soon Jorge passed the cut-off age for batboys. When he gave his younger brother the uniform he'd outgrown, Cesar felt like a prince accepting a crown without a monarchy. He slept in it every night until he finally grew into it and then it was time for him to stake his claim.

Before tryouts had even begun, a confrontation occurred between a few boys and the only colored kid who showed up to apply for the position. Cesar's friends made no move to get involved, but Cesar interceded.

"Hey look, spic, you're no better than—" began one of the bullies, his words cut short by Cesar's fist.

In the midst of the fight, which lasted only about four or five punches, no one noticed that the colored boy had already run away.

"What goes on here?" bellowed the voice of Segundo "Mercy" Montes. Now the Mission's rubdown man, he had once been a professional boxer from Cuba. He was in charge of hiring batboys.

"He started it," said the bully, pointing at Cesar.

"Did you?" asked Mercy.

"Yes, sir."

"There's no room for that kind of behavior on this team," he said, dismissing Cesar.

At home, his mother brushed aside a few strands of Cesar's hair, which had become tangled with the sweat and blood from his brow. Dipping a washcloth into a tin basin of warm water, she wrung it out and dabbed it gently across a cut on his forehead.

"Ouch," came his muffled cry as she cleaned the remaining traces of dried blood. The bruise would disappear in a few days but not his humiliation.

Felicitas looked up when she heard a knock at the door. It was Mercy Montes.

"Sorry to bother you, ma'am. Do you mind if I talk to your son for a few minutes?"

After Felicitas had left Cesar with Mercy, the older man turned and said, "One of the kids told me what really happened. You did the right thing."

"I shouldn't have bothered."

"Why do you say that?"

"The kid I was sticking up for ran away. He didn't stay to help me."

"You can't be responsible for the honor of others, what's important is that you kept yours."

"That's easy for you to say, you're a boxer."

"I wasn't born one. I learned to fight because I was small, much smaller than you. And from what the Lambkin boys told me, when I was your age I didn't have half the jab you do. Good thing, too, 'cause there are sure gonna be some jealous kids when they learn you're going to be our batboy."

⚬⊙⊙⚬

"I was in heaven," Cesar told Angel. "I picked up bats, chatted with the umpires and kept track of the players' hours. Instead of pay, they let me keep broken bats, which I fixed and sold. But the best moment was when I met Babe Ruth."

The Vitro whistle blew.

"You met the *Bambino*?"

"Sure did. The St. Louis Browns took spring training at Mission Stadium. One day they played an exhibition game against the New York Yankees. I made sure to fill the water cooler in the Yankees' dugout all afternoon."

"Did you ever meet the Brooklyn Dodgers too?"

"Yep."

"Who?"

"Another story for another day," Cesar said as he rose to his feet and headed back to the factory.

4

One Real Game

Angel and his friends were joined by Fidel Ruiz. He worked as a delivery boy for his mother after school and on weekends. The six of them stood with their mouths agape in the lobby of the Gran Hotel Ancira. It was Monterrey's oldest hotel, built before the Mexican Revolution; its opulence was reminiscent of the colonial period of great excesses.

"She comes here every Saturday to swim," said Enrique.

"They have a pool?" asked Ricardo.

"Yep," replied Enrique.

"A pool. . . inside a building?" asked Norberto in awe.

"How do you know she swims? You see her in her bathing suit?" teased Fidel.

"He wishes!" laughed Adolfo.

The lobby's ceiling was three stories tall with lights placed above a layer of smoked glass, and its walls were a combination of wood paneling and stone columns. Parrots and toucans preened themselves in huge gilded cages suspended by cables from the ceiling. The marble flooring felt cold to their feet, and they shifted nervously from side to side taking in the splendor.

The boys' tattered appearance was tolerated by the guards; they even made no move to stop the boys when they swiped some food from one of the tables in the open restaurant. Most of the guards came from the same neighborhoods and understood that these children were about to have their fun stripped away by early employment and responsibility. However, they couldn't ignore it when they saw the boys tossing bits of tortilla into the birdcages, and moments later escorted them out to the Plaza Hidalgo.

"Now we're going to look stupid," said Enrique.

The boys separated to unique vantage points from which they could see Gloria Jimenez approach. Enrique stood behind the statue of Don Miguel Hidalgo y Costilla.

Fifteen minutes elapsed and there was still no sign of her. Enrique began to get discouraged and thought that perhaps she wasn't coming, when a large bus pulled into the square and partially blocked his view of the hotel's entrance. Moving from his perch, he walked around the back of the bus.

At that moment, Enrique looked down the street and spotted her.

"*Callate*, there she is!" he exclaimed to his friends who lost all pretense of hiding and gathered so close to him that they nearly shoved him off the curb.

"Go on. Talk to her," urged Ricardo, also unable to take his eyes from the beautiful girl, who approached like an angel drifting down the sidewalk.

Enrique froze, but a hard shove from Ricardo placed him right in Gloria's path.

"*Hola*, Gloria. What a surprise."

Gloria stared for a moment as if unsure of who had addressed her.

"My father works for yours," Enrique added.

"Oh yes."

"Are you. . . swimming?" he asked.

"I come here every Saturday," she said, raising the towel that she carried under her delicate arm.

"Really? I was thinking of swimming also," he said, eliciting a laugh from Gloria.

"In those?" she asked as her gaze lingered on his dirt-stained street clothes.

Enrique turned to Norberto and snapped, "*Idiota*, I told you to bring my bathing suit."

"What suit? You don't have—"

Enrique elbowed Norberto and quickly finished his sentence, ". . . have time to get it now."

"Oh well, nice seeing you," Gloria said as she turned.

"Wait!"

Gloria angled her head back toward Enrique.

"Maybe I can walk you home after your swim?"

At that moment, Juan Zaragosa, a tall, fair-haired boy came out of the hotel dressed in a crisply pressed, white and green baseball uniform. Obviously a *madre patria*, descended of purebred Spaniards, he carried himself with a cocky, worldly-wise confidence. Even Enrique and his friends stared in awe at this gleaming figure as he moved without any notice of his surroundings. He stepped in between Enrique and Gloria and addressed her without even acknowledging the *mestizo's* presence.

In gracefully enunciated Castillan Spanish, he said, "They told me Monterrey had the most beautiful girls in Mexico. Too bad I must leave."

Though she tried to appear offended, Gloria's giggle gave her away.

"Yeah, too bad," Enrique said, trying to find his way back into the conversation that now seemed to have escaped him. "Gloria, about that walk, I—"

"Sorry, my father picks me up," she said to Enrique, her gaze still lingering on Juan as she walked into the hotel.

Juan turned his attention Enrique and sneered, "*Ooh*, picked off base! Nice try."

Before Enrique could assimilate how badly his encounter with Gloria had gone and before he could formulate a response to Juan's snipe, Ricardo stepped in front of the tall stranger and said, "I'll show you, *puerco*. You, you. . . *guero*."

Juan was then joined by a half-dozen of his teammates, most of whom were Caucasian and as sons of diplomats, industrialists and bankers, were obviously from the United States. They were dressed in the same baseball attire, and all were bigger than Ricardo and his friends. A fight seemed imminent, when the door of the bus swung open and its driver stepped out and opened the luggage compartment.

"Come on, we've got a long drive to Texas," he called out.

Juan looked down at Ricardo and scoffed, "You guys aren't worth getting dirty over." He and his teammates boarded the bus as the driver loaded their duffel bags and baseball equipment.

"Who are they?" Enrique asked the driver.

"Mexico City All-Stars," the older man answered after a pause, as if to imply that the answer was too obvious to merit the question.

"What are they doing in Monterrey?" asked Adolfo.

"They're on their way to play some exhibition games in Texas," he said and returned to his task.

The boys coughed as the diesel fumes from the bus filled their lungs. They sat dejectedly on the curb.

"America," said Angel with a dreamy sigh.

"I should've punched him. I had him right where I wanted him," argued Ricardo.

"It wasn't your fight, it was Enrique's," insisted Adolfo.

"He insulted all of us," Angel said as he looked up at the large clock in the square.

"We could've taken those all-stars," added Norberto.

"You mean all-jerks," corrected Ricardo.

"I'll never get Gloria," moaned Enrique.

Ricardo put his arm around Enrique's shoulder as if to comfort him. "Yeah, you see the way she drooled over that pretty boy?"

Norberto stood up and pretended to dance with himself and said in a girl's voice, "*Oh guero, mi amor.*"

Enrique just hung his head lower.

"You have no more chance than Tizoc," added Fidel. Tizoc was a peasant in a movie, who fell in love with a society woman who could never be with someone of his class. The film ended with Tizoc killing himself. "Face it, we're always gonna be on the bottom."

Enrique noticed the clock. "We better get outta here before Gloria comes back out—"

✺

That night, Angel was awakened by a voice at his window.

"Angel, wake up," said Enrique.

"Enrique?"

"I got it!"

"What, a *chapulin* in your underpants?"

"No, *estupido*. I've got an idea. . ."

"Go to sleep."

"I can't."

"Why not?" asked Angel.

" 'Cause I got an idea."

ᥰᐲᏮᥰ

Shadows played across Padre Esteban's room as the night ceded the sky to the approaching dawn. He had always been an early riser, but the pounding on the church's outer doors woke him before his customary time to rise.

Opening the door, he was greeted by Angel, Enrique and Norberto.

"Padre Esteban, Padre Esteban, we need to talk to you!" came several anxious voices.

"What time is it?" asked the priest.

"Morning," said Norberto.

"What's wrong?"

"Enrique had an idea," said Angel.

"Come in, come in. . ." said the priest, stepping away from the doorway.

Sitting on the floor of Padre Esteban's tiny room, the boys outlined their simple plan. It all revolved around an organization in the United States called Las Ligas Pequeñas.

"There was a team from Mexico City staying at the Gran Ancira hotel," said Enrique.

"We want to make a team too," said Norberto.

"*Hmm*," muttered the priest. "I'm sure with prayer and hard work, you can make it happen."

"But we need it now," said Enrique, respectfully yet firmly.

"What's the hurry? Good things come to those who wait."

"We're twelve," interjected Enrique.

"I know. I baptized all of you. What a wonderful age—so much time ahead of you," Padre Esteban said smiling.

"By next season, we'll be too old for Little League," added Norberto.

"I see. You boys have natural baseball talent, that's for sure. But a real team takes training and learning strategy."

"You can teach us," said the boys in unison.

"Look at me," said the priest, taking a few steps across the floor, his right leg taking its steps noticeably slower than his left. "I'm afraid age now offers me the ability to desire without the desired ability."

"We won't make you run. . . promise," said Enrique.

"No, you need help from someone who's really played the game, and I don't mean in sandlots. You need someone who knows how to coach and I don't know anyone like that in Monterrey."

"I do," said Angel.

⸎⊙⸎

The sun burned brightly on this cloudless day. In the distance, the Sierra Madres appeared awash in the deep green and yellow hues of sprouting wildflowers. There was a slight breeze in the air, which felt good to Angel as he raised his arm and leaned forward.

"Not bad," Cesar said as the ball sailed into his glove. "So why won't this kid, Adolfo, let you pitch?"

"He's always been our pitcher. Besides, he's bigger than I am and can throw harder."

"Try holding the ball with your fingers on the stitches like this," Cesar demonstrated. "It'll give the ball more control. The velocity doesn't come from your arm, it comes from your back leg. Use it. Push off. Think about lunging forward so far that you can shove the ball right into your catcher's glove."

Angel knew that he had found the right man for the job, all he needed to do was convince the man.

"There! That's it!" Cesar yelped, feigning pain in his gloved hand as Angel's fastball struck the webbing. "You didn't think too much. It was perfect."

The next ball flew so high that Cesar had to jump to catch it at his fingertips. Angel slapped his hip with his bare hand.

"It's okay. You felt her rhythm once, she's still there waiting to be summoned again," Cesar said. "You have the potential to pitch well, but you aim too much and it hurts your control."

"It's worse when a batter's at the plate," answered Angel.

"Unfortunately, that's the only time pitching counts."

Angel shrugged.

"Were you a pitcher?" he asked.

"No, but I hung out with a lot of guys who did. The one thing they all had in common was that when they were on the mound, they could blank out the whole universe except one thing—their catcher's glove."

Pulling out his lunch box, Cesar began to roll some corn tortillas stuffed with frijoles and handed one to Angel, who downed it in two quick bites.

"Slow down, there's plenty. Don't they feed you at home?" He caught Angel's eyes before the young man turned his gaze sheepishly away.

"How did you end up coaching baseball?" Angel asked.

"Eventually I outgrew the job of batboy, but I still hung around the field, taking practice with the team whenever I could. The St. Louis Browns took spring training in San Antonio, and shared the field with the Missions. Little did I realize that I had been noticed. One day my Spanish teacher yelled at me across the schoolyard and said, 'Faz! Principal wants you in his office now!' I assumed it was because I was failing his class."

"You were failing Spanish? That's pretty stupid."

"When I got to the office, my mouth went dry. Next to the principal stood Rogers Hornsby, the Browns' manager. I could not have been more impressed had President Roosevelt been waiting there."

"What did he say to you?"

"He said, 'Hey, kid, I been watching you at the field. How'd you like a chance to play for the Browns?' 'Uh, uh, uh. . .' was all I could muster. 'I'll take that as a *yes*. When school's out I want you to come to St. Louis and report to Coach Sewell,' Hornsby told me right there in the principal's office."

Angel sat transfixed. Cesar's story was an experience so far beyond his reality that Cesar may as well have been describing a safari in Africa or a flight to outer space.

⊷⊙⊚⊙⊶

Within a month, Cesar had moved to St. Louis. His mother, Felicitas Faz, warned him that the women there were faster and wilder than the mujer católica joven, the good churchgoing girls from San Antonio. He took his mother's admonition in stride and prayed she was right. He found a roommate, and the two shared a studio apartment on the south side of town off Manchester Avenue. Each day, he'd take the electric streetcar to Spring and Sullivan streets, which dropped him off behind the right field wall of Sportsman's Park where the Browns and Cardinals played.

Cesar suddenly found himself surrounded by some of the greatest baseball players who ever took the field, heroes whom the children from his old neighborhood only read about in newspapers or listened to on radios.

"There are only five things to learn in all of baseball. You learn them, you can play in the big leagues," barked the assistant coaches he worked with. "Running, fielding, throwing, hitting and hitting with power. That's it," they reminded Cesar every day.

⊷⊙⊚⊙⊶

"Under Hornsby, I learned everything about baseball, from sewing a button on a uniform to the proper way to put on the high socks and to scuffing a ball so that it would dance the Charleston on the way to the plate. But I did notice one strange thing about him," Cesar said.

"What?" asked Angel.

"*Rajah*—that's what we called him—never read the newspaper or watched movies. 'Spoils the battin' eye, kid,' he told me."

"You could have played for the team," Angel said eagerly.

"Yeah, maybe I could've, but Rajah was grooming me for something more important," said Cesar while he prepared another bean taco. "He always told me a team had many good players, but only one manager."

"Your father must have been very proud," sighed Angel.

"When I went home to visit my folks in '39, they told me they were moving back to Monterrey and wanted me to come."

"But you were with the St. Louis Browns!" exclaimed Angel.

"To my father, a baseball job, whether it paid or not, was play, and he always told me that when he had a choice between work and play, he chose work. Following in my father's footsteps, my oldest brother, Joseph, became an engraver. Jorge was in school and Manuel had a job as a mechanic, which meant I was the black sheep of the family. I told them I would never live a single day in Mexico." Cesar stood up to resume their play.

A few minutes later, Angel asked, "What's America like, Señor Faz?"

"I don't know. Big cars, green lawns, tall buildings. . ."

"I'm going there," stated Angel abruptly, as if the quicker he said it, the more true it would become.

"Really?"

"Yeah, I'm going to play baseball. My friends and I are making a Little League team."

"Why?"

"We wanna play against a real team, with our own uniforms."

"So make some uniforms."

"The Mexico City All-Stars went to Texas."

"Did they win?"

"No."

"Figures. Angel, American kids have the best equipment, the best training, the best of everything, and you guys. . . well, you don't have. . . anything."

"We have. . . spirit," Angel said, recalling Padre Esteban's optimism.

"Spirit, huh? How does that help you hit a fastball?"

"Padre Esteban could tell you."

"I'm not exactly on God's starting lineup," Cesar said. A slight breeze blew the dirt beneath their feet into a small swirl. As Cesar tried to wipe a speck that had lodged itself in his eye, he grumbled as the dirt on the back of his hand only exacerbated the problem.

"He teaches us a lot," continued Angel.

"Like how to pray?"

"Why do you make fun of him?"

"I don't even know him," said Cesar.

"You could. Why not come to Mass tomorrow?"

"Sorry, I'm busy."

"You have no family, no one expecting you—"

"Thanks for the reminder, but still *no*."

That was when Cesar noticed a particularly beautiful woman passing by. It wasn't the first time he'd seen her, but today he couldn't take his eyes off of her. There was a confidence and ease in her stride that made it appear to him as if she were drifting by in slow motion.

"*¡Ay, tantas curvas, y yo sin frenos* [Wow, so many curves, and I with no brakes]*!*" Cesar whistled under his breath.

"You like her?" asked Angel.

"Who?" responded Cesar.

"I think you are in love," Angel snickered.

"There are plenty of fish in the sea," he tried to appear nonchalant.

"But not like that mermaid."

"Do you know her?" Cesar asked.

"No. But I know where she'll be tomorrow. . ."

❧⊚⊚☙

Although Cesar Faz was baptized Catholic, he felt strangely out of place in the pews of San Juan Bautista the next day. He wasn't sure when to stand, when to sit or when to speak out loud. In one such miscue, the other parishioners sat, leaving him conspicuously as the only one standing. He sat abruptly, which made the entire bench move a half an inch and caused the most awful sound. At least it afforded him an unobstructed glimpse of Maria del Refugio Gonzales. He assumed she saw him, too, even imagined that he had detected the slightest smile. Then his excitement morphed into anxiety: What if it wasn't a smile? What if she were laughing at him?

"The Holy Scriptures teach us that there are three kinds of miracles," Padre Esteban continued his sermon. "*Semeion* is the one you *see*. *Teras* is the one you *feel*. . ." Cesar shifted uncomfortably in his seat. It was warm inside the church, even though it was only May. He tried to peer between the heads of several people to get another look at Maria, but he couldn't get a clear line of sight.

". . . and *dunamis* is the one you *create*. The third miracle is the most divine of all."

⸎⊙⊙⸎

After the services, Padre Esteban stood on the steps of San Juan Bautista, wishing the parishioners well as they slowly filed out. The boys had run out first, taking their usual positions in the alley. Cesar approached the priest.

"Padre Esteban, I'm Cesar Faz," he said, extending a hand. Cesar was impressed; the priest had a firm grip, the kind that signified a man who was strong in his core, yet gentle in his demeanor.

"Ah, Angel's coach."

"Coach? No. We just toss a ball around sometimes. It's nothing."

"To him, it is everything."

"Yes, of course," Cesar replied with a half-vacant acknowledgment. Clearing his throat, he suddenly saw Maria over Padre Esteban's shoulder. She tried to look away but couldn't avoid glancing at Cesar for a moment as their eyes locked.

"I hope you'll join us again," said the priest, but Cesar's attention was elsewhere as his gaze followed Maria down the steps.

"Yes, it's been a long time," he responded in a way that obviously had nothing to do with Padre Esteban's last comment.

"Angel tells me you coached the St. Louis Browns."

"Yeah," he said as his mind snapped back to the conversation at hand.

The two men walked next door to the alley where the game was just about to start.

"That's him," Angel said to his peers.

"He doesn't look like a baseball player," sneered Adolfo.

"He's a great ballplayer," replied Angel emphatically.

"Are you going to help us make a team, Señor Faz?" asked Enrique as Cesar drew closer.

"Yes, we want to play in the United States," said Norberto, leading the boys to a chorus of reasons why it would be the coolest thing in the world to form a team. Eyes full of hope, heads full of dreams, and the excitement of having nothing to lose or to look up to struck Cesar full force.

"Please, show some respect for Señor Faz. You've just met him. Don't ask him for anything," admonished the priest, but Cesar already had a suspicion Padre Esteban was in cahoots with the boys.

"You're just setting yourselves up for disappointment," Cesar said.

"We don't care if we lose," said Angel. "We just want to play a real game."

"That's why we need a coach," Ricardo chimed in.

"Even if I wanted to, I couldn't get off work to take them," Cesar said to Padre Esteban.

"I can take them, but I can't teach them," the priest replied.

Cesar turned his attention back to Angel and his friends. "Do you have any idea what this means? You just don't call yourselves a team and magically become one. It's a lot of work and dedication, and to travel that far just for one game?"

"Ah, but what a game it would be," said Padre Esteban, confirming Cesar's suspicion that he supported this half-baked idea.

Looking at the priest, Cesar said, "Sometimes it does a man good to know when he can't win."

"We are talking about the boys, aren't we, Señor Faz?"

After a pause, Cesar said to the priest, "It's just not realistic."

"I've always believed that an army of men is no match for one child with faith," countered Padre Esteban.

"Well, the Texas tournament starts in a month and this army doesn't even have a field. Sorry, boys," were Cesar's parting words as Angel's heart sank into a pit deep in his stomach.

5

Dames and Fly Balls

"Faz, we're running low on salt cake. Take a few guys over to Vidriera and ask for Señor Galeana. He'll know what to give you," barked Cesar's manager at Vitro. Vidriera was a glass bottling factory, and salt cake, a by-product of aluminum, was a small but necessary ingredient in glass.

"Juarez, Vallarta, Peña, come with me. *El Gerente's* orders," Cesar chose three of his coworkers.

They would have to lug back hundreds of pounds of the material for Vitro's furnaces.

At Vidriera, while Cesar waited for Señor Galeana to process the paperwork for the loan of the salt cake, a large hook made its way across the floor. Were it not for the intervention of a man who bodily tackled him, Cesar would surely have taken the hundred pound hook in the back of his head.

With the wind knocked out of him, it took a moment for Cesar to open his eyes. Above him stood a tall, white-haired, barrel-chested man offering his hand. It was the second time they'd met. The first time was in 1944 and back then, the older man was dressed in khakis with Lieutenant Commander Insignia on his epaulets.

❧

At a meeting in Monterrey between U. S. President Franklin Delano Roosevelt and Mexican President Avila Camacho, Mexico committed El Escuadron Aereo de Pelea 201, *the Aztec Eagles, to the allied war effort.*

Cesar's older brother, Manuel, joined and became a maintenance engineer in the first Mexican armed force to fight overseas.

Felicitas took the news in stride; at least Manuel would not be at the front line. She already had enough to worry about: A year earlier Jorge had joined the U.S. Army and Cesar had enlisted in the U.S. Marine Corps. Felicitas, who had lived and fought many smaller wars and revolutions herself, asked the Virgin de Guadalupe to safely back bring her sons. A friend from her old neighborhood in Texas sent her three blue stars, which she placed in the window of their home. It wasn't a custom in Mexico, but everyone seemed to understand what it meant, and no one dared to ask.

While Angel Macias and his friends were being baptized in Monterrey's Holy Water, Cesar's outfit was being baptized by fire in the Marshall Islands. Rewarded with a week of R & R in the Philippines, Cesar entered a waterfront bar, anxious to enjoy his shore leave.

"Care to dance?" asked a pretty woman who introduced herself as Eleanor.

"I got a girl back home," Cesar said, soliciting a laugh from the woman. It was nice to hear the sound of laughter. For months all he had heard were artillery barrages and the screams of men killing and being killed.

"I ain't asking you on a date, soldier, just a dance," she said with a soothing voice, and immediately he felt embarrassed by his comment. "'Sides, honey, I'm married."

"Where's your husband?"

"Navy—in Halsey's Battle Group. Don't rightly know where he is now." Eleanor was a volunteer in the USO. No sooner had Cesar led her out to the dance floor when a sailor tapped him on the shoulder.

"Mind if I cut in?" he asked.

"Sorry, we've just started," Cesar answered, though the sailor's question had been more of a command.

"Why don't you find one of your own girls," said the persistent intruder. There was no mistaking his meaning.

"Sailor boy, why don't you cool off at the bar? You'll get your turn," said Eleanor, trying to diffuse the situation. But it clearly wasn't about dancing anymore.

"This is between me and Private Pepe, ma'am," said the sailor with increasing hostility.

"Leave him alone," said another man who had overheard the exchange.

He was tall; at least a half a head taller than Cesar, and his hair was prematurely turning silver.

"Who the the blazes are you?" snapped the rude sailor as he turned to face the man who had interceded.

"You mean, 'Who the blazes are you, Lieutenant Commander?'" the tall stranger corrected his fellow seaman.

"What's this grunt to you. . . sir?"

"Just a grunt."

Backing down, the sailor went on his way. Cesar finished his dance with Eleanor and then joined the officer at the bar. The two men drank and talked about women and home and the lousy war, though they mostly drank.

The lieutenant commander knew that men were in the service for many reasons—some volunteered, others were drafted—but he was surprised to hear Cesar give his reason.

"I just needed to get away for a while."

"You wanted by the law?"

"Hah! Jail would be a step up in the world from this place," Cesar slurred.

"At least it's for a good cause."

"To the cause!" Cesar raised his glass. "To liberty and justice for all. . . as long as you ain't Black or Chicano."

The lieutenant commander was happy to make the toast. He didn't really catch what Cesar had said, but they were in a bar and Cesar was buying and that was all he needed to know.

Four hours later, in the wee hours of the morning, Cesar and his newfound friend zigzagged their way back to the docks where an MP shined a flashlight in their faces.

"You're drunk, sir!" the policeman said to Cesar's companion.

"I sure hope so. If not, the ship's sinking," he said as two of his shipmates helped him reboard his vessel.

Cesar stumbled back alone toward his hotel. It started to rain, first softly, then in a downpour. He had never experienced precipitation like in the South Pacific. Lonely and drenched to the bone, Cesar realized that the closest friend he could think of in the whole world was an inebriated lieutenant commander whose name he didn't even know.

⌒⊙⌒

"You?" Cesar managed to utter as the wind gradually came back into his diaphragm.

"Seems I'm making a habit of bailing you out, *amigo*," said the tall man who stood above Cesar.

"What on earth are you doing here?" asked a bewildered Cesar. He knew he recognized the man, but it was so out of context it took Cesar a moment to pull together where and when they'd met.

"I live here."

"What's it been. . . twelve, thirteen years? How did you recognize me?" asked Cesar.

"I didn't. If I knew it was your thick skull in the way, I wouldn't have bothered," he said, causing the two men to break into laughter. Given the nearly fatal accident, this only convinced the onlookers that the two were completely mad.

"Harold Haskins. . . my friends call me Lucky," the tall man said, extending his hand to help Cesar up. His nickname was born when a kamikaze struck the forward gun turret he manned on his first ship, the *USS Henley*. Though dozens around him were killed, he walked away with barely a scratch.

That evening, the *viejos amigos* made up for lost time at Cantina el Indio Azteca in the heart of Monterrey's oldest barrio. Though a dozen years and a world away from the waterfront Filipino bar, after a round or two, the scene begged little difference to the last time they'd met.

"I just got tired of Wisconsin winters," Lucky continued his story as he and Cesar talked down a bottle of tequila.

A few years after the war, Lucky had moved to Monterrey where he helped American employers recruit legal temporary workers from the State of Nuevo León. In the mid-1950s immigration policy shifted; the U.S. government began mass round-ups and deportation of anyone suspected of being Mexican, in a program called Operation Wetback. With his recruiting business dried up, Lucky put his life savings into a small bottling company.

"I remember you had a kid."

"Got four now."

"They home with the missus?"

"Not anymore. One day, she sent me a telegram from Laredo: 'YOUR KIDS ARE AT THE HOLIDAY INN STOP I'M LEAVING STOP SUGGEST YOU COME GET THEM STOP.' They've been with me ever since, though sometimes I think I was more cut out to be an officer than a father."

Lucky tilted his head back and poured the clear liquid down his throat. He coughed for a moment and rasped, "I've siphoned diesel weaker than this stuff."

Cesar laughed. "All she lacks to be meat is the bone."

"What brought you here from St. Louis?" asked Lucky.

"Had to take care of my mom after my father died. She's gone now."

"Sorry. You just decided to stay, I guess?"

"Got no good reason to go back and plenty not to," Cesar replied.

"What about that woman. . . the one you told me about. . . what was her name?" Lucky asked.

"Tammy."

"Didn't go so well when you got stateside?"

"About as well as Pearl Harbor."

"Didn't the Japs toughen you on Iwo?"

"Yeah, except they just tried to kill me, not steal my gal," slurred Cesar, pouring another round.

"Another guy?"

"Her dad. Apparently he never approved of her dating someone from my side of the tracks. Figured he didn't need to say anything before I shipped out 'cause he assumed I wasn't coming back."

"Was he worried or just hopeful?"

"First her letters became kinda formal and then less frequent, until there were none. Finally, even the ones I'd written started coming back undelivered."

"Dames are nothing but trouble," Lucky said to Cesar.

"You can say that again. If life was a fly ball, a woman would be the sun in your eyes," Cesar philosophized as he raised his tequila and their two glasses came together with a loud clink.

eↄ☉ⓖ☉ↄ

An hour later, Lucky excused himself.

"You got a curfew or something?" asked Cesar.

"I'm exhausted. Hey, don't you have a job to go to tomorrow morning?"

"I'll be fine, old man," boasted Cesar.

"Suit yourself," Lucky smiled as he left Cesar at the bar.

Even though it was Tuesday night and almost eleven o'clock, the cantina was packed with workers from one of the numerous factories that ringed it. Men from Cemex, Vitro, Vidriera, Fundidora and American Smelting were all in various stages of inebriation.

A rousing chorus of *El Rey* could be heard. It was the *machismo* anthem, and rarely could one visit a *pulqueria* without hearing at least several of its verses:

Con dinero y sin dinero,	With my pockets full or empty,
hago siempre lo que quiero,	I just do whatever's tempting,
y mi palabra es la ley.	And the law is what I say.
No tengo trono ni reina,	I have no throne and no queen,
ni nadie que me comprenda,	And no one knows what I mean,
pero sigo siendo el rey.	But the king I always stay.

At the far end of the bar, Cesar watched a man down his third mezcal and haphazardly make another attempt to flirt with a waitress, who couldn't seem to avoid him no matter which route she took across the dank, smoke-filled room. The man, like the rest of the establishment, smelled of alcohol and sweat, and even if his wife hadn't walked in, he would have held no special appeal to the female server he was vainly trying to charm.

From behind him in another corner of the bar, Claudio Villarreal and Fecundino Suarez tried unsuccessfully to hold back Umberto Macias from approaching Cesar.

"You're that baseball man my son goes on about," said Umberto as Cesar swiveled around.

"You're Angel's father?" surmised Cesar as he reached out his hand, which Umberto allowed to dangle in midair.

"You've been filling his head with crazy ideas." Umberto replied sharply. "Stay away from him."

Taken aback, Cesar responded, "I'm just teaching him baseball.

What's the harm anyway? He's having fun and he's pretty good at it."

"Yeah, well, he needs to learn his place."

"Where's that? A slow death sentence in the steel foundry?"

"My father died in the middle of his shift. I had to work for food," Umberto said. "There was no time for games. But I made it. I survived. And someday Angel will take my place on the line."

"Maybe Angel has his own dream."

"Dreams don't build cities. Men and iron do."

Across the bar, the argument between the man and his wife was escalating. Umberto noticed it first and thought for a moment about interceding, but then decided it was not his business. Cesar, on the other hand, could not let it pass.

"Come home, the children need you," the wife pleaded.

"That's why they have a mother," the inebriated and apathetic husband answered. "Leave me alone."

"Javier, it's been days," she tugged at his sleeve.

"I thought I told you to go home. Can't you see that I'm busy?" The man didn't see Cesar coming up behind him.

"Where I'm from, we don't treat women as property," Cesar told the man. Cesar was an imposing figure, not tall but stocky, and his face was blistered from the sun and dozens of fights and accidents.

"I know all about you *pocho*. This ain't the United States."

Putting up with racial slurs from whites was one thing, but Cesar didn't have the patience to take it from a Mexican.

Standing up and turning his back on Cesar, he said to his wife, "I said beat it, whore!"

"Bastard!" she yelled back at him so loud the room fell quiet.

"I'll see you dead before you speak that way to me—"

Javier raised his hand to strike her. His arm began its swinging motion, but it stopped in midflight as if it had hit an invisible wall. He stared back in disbelief as a hand wrapped around his wrist. When Javier turned to face Cesar, his gaze was met by a look that probably hadn't been seen by anyone since Iwo Jima.

With instinctive aggression, the man redirected his hostility toward Cesar and swung as wildly and violently as he could. That was another of Javier's errors in judgment. When he awoke later, far from the bar, he barely recalled what hit him.

Cesar was detained by several policemen as one of them searched for a witness who wasn't too inebriated or tight-lipped to help. The waitress, who had been the object of the victim's flirtation, looked over at Cesar and said to the policeman, "Fight? There was no fight. That guy just hit the son of a bitch once."

Cesar and Umberto never did get to finish their conversation. And though Umberto told his friends that Cesar got what he deserved, what bothered him most was, Cesar was the man whom Umberto had once been.

Bar fights happened, and unless someone was killed, there were usually no arrests. However, though the guy Cesar decked may have been a son of a bitch, he was also the nephew of a judge.

"He's in jail, you know," said Angel as he and his friends walked down the railroad tracks that paralleled Calle San Nicholas.

"For a few days," said Norberto. "You hear what happened to the guy he hit?"

"One punch I heard," Angel answered.

"My dad said it took six guys to pull him off," Norberto said.

"Great idea asking him to coach," said Adolfo with obvious bitterness.

"He's the best," said Angel.

"Yeah, I hear he thinks he's too good for his own people. Growing up in a big house in America and all," Adolfo added.

"He's not like that," argued Angel. "He was once really poor."

"Like us?" Enrique asked.

"No way," said Adolfo.

"One winter he nearly froze to death. He and his friend used to go down to the tracks and get coal from moving locomotives," Angel said.

"How?" Adolfo asked suspiciously.

"Whenever one passed, they'd hurl rocks at it. The train engineers fought back by pelting them with chunks of coal."

"Really, he stole coal?" asked Norberto, impressed.

"He didn't steal it. They threw it at him, *estupido*." Enrique put Norberto in his place.

"I gotta get going," Angel said. "If the sty isn't clean when my father gets home, I'll be grounded. Tomorrow, after school. Don't forget! Tell the rest!" Angel yelled as he diverted down a narrow street on a shortcut back to *2a. San Francisco Oriente*.

⌘

"I'm worried about you spending time with that man," Oralia said as her son handed her the clothes that he had worn for days.

"He was defending a woman's honor," said Angel. The house smelled of the corn tortillas and tamales that his mother had made earlier. If there were two overwhelming odors in Monterrey's barrios, they were *maize* and manure.

As Oralia blew out the candle, the last vision she had was of her only remaining child staring hopefully at her in the enveloping night.

⌘

The group of boys came to a stop. Angel was the only one smiling.

Finally, Norberto said, "So, this is it?"

"Yep," answered Angel.

"You couldn't find a place with more rocks, huh?" asked Adolfo.

"Nope."

"This is stupid," Adolfo griped. "This place'll never be a field." He sat down on the sideline.

"This will get us to the United States," Angel told his friends.

The rest of the team took some time to assimilate Angel's dream. Then it was all hard work driven by passion.

Each day after school the boys returned to the dirt field, and one rock or piece of glass or metal at a time, they placed refuse in a pile. Others made rakes out of scraps of metal and leveled the dirt and filled in the many pits and holes.

"You got 'em!" exclaimed Angel as he saw Enrique and Ricardo dragging a bag of cement they had "found" at the nearby Cemex plant.

"There and there," said Angel, pointing to what would be the first and third base lines.

⸙⸙⸙⸙

"You Chicanos and your *machismo*," Lucky said to Cesar as he sat in a chair opposite Cesar's holding pen. "It ain't pretty, even when you guys are sober."

Cesar knew the charges against him would be dropped in a few days. His detention was more about separating the combatants and letting one of them, in this case Cesar, cool down.

"You should see the other guy," Cesar quipped.

"At least he's still employed."

"Who needs Vitro?"

"You do, you hothead. When you get out of here, you're gonna go down there and beg to keep your job."

"That bastard got what was coming to him."

"Maybe, but what's gonna come to you if you lose your pay-check?"

It burned him to plead for his job, but groveling to *el Gerente* was still preferable to work in the bean fields.

After Lucky had left, Cesar lay on his cot and thought about another night, the first time he came to Monterrey.

⸙⸙⸙⸙

It was the fall of 1949.

"Monterrey, una hora," Cesar recalled the driver announcing over the speaker that dangled from a single wire. Two hours earlier, they had crossed the Rio Grande at Laredo, Texas. Though the river, known to Mexicans as Rio Bravo del Norte, appeared as a thin blue line on a map—it was a border between time and cultures.

José Faz had passed away two years earlier and Cesar's brother, Joseph, had told him that their mother, Felicitas was having a relapse of pneumonia. He and his brothers would take turns in Monterrey, caring for her until she got better. Since Cesar was available, he would go first.

It was still dark outside though one could see the faint outline of the Sierra Madres. Its long ridge appeared like the cartilaginous plates along the spine of a stegosaurus. On the eastern spur lay the Royal Mountains for which Monterrey was named. Its granite towers opaquely masked the stars on the horizon, but even in silhouette Cesar could distinguish the saddle formation of El Cerro de la Silla. The valley below was as dark as a black sea.

"Ultima pa-r-r-r-ada, Monte-r-r-r-ey," said the driver, his r's rolling off his tongue as the bus pulled up to its last stop. Monterrey was first and foremost a factory town. The entire city seemed constructed only to service these man-made monoliths that rose from the valley floor. They held nothing of beauty or majesty. Steel, glass, textile, cement, metal fabrication, breweries, smelting—there were dozens of major production facilities. Rail lines fanned across the valley and branched out at the terminus of each factory like dozens of smaller arteries feeding the city's organs. At night they were even more terrifying, appearing as spiderlike monsters out of War of the Worlds, *which at any moment might rise up on their mechanical legs and consume everything in their paths.*

Cesar grabbed his duffel bag and stepped out into the warm morning air. Pausing now and again for directions, he soon found himself standing before a house that looked like its roof didn't cover the entire structure. It was on Matamoros Oriente where that street dead-ended at the Rio Santa Catarina.

"What kind of place is this?" he said aloud to no one while wiping the sweat from his forehead and checking the address again. He was about to retrace his steps when something caught his eye. There in the window, held fast by some yellowed adhesive, were the remains of three faded blue stars.

Having finished high school gave Cesar more of an education than most of the local working class. It didn't translate to value on the factory line, but his military service did. He could fix just about anything made of metal, he understood bureaucracy, and after clearing jungles full of enemy soldiers, nothing in a factory scared him. Besides, he told himself, this was only temporary. Soon, Jorge or Manuel would come, and he could move on.

Built during the first half of the century, at a time of great growth and anarchy and before environmentalists existed, Vitro Glassworks was a living, smoking monster. Its six hundred-foot tall silos held the powders of aluminum-silicate, soda ash, limestone and silica sand, which were mixed in precise ratios called batches. Mixed with cullet, waste glass from previous melts, the batch travels to the furnaces in hoppers and conveyer belts. It's heated to 1,500 degrees for about twenty-four hours. Once a furnace fire is lit, it is kept burning, even on Sundays, since the stresses of heating and cooling would diminish its lifespan. It is only extinguished at the end of a campaign when the plant's refractory brick walls need to be replaced.

Cesar worked at the hot end of the factory. It was not for the meek. Like most jobs in Monterrey, there were about a thousand ways to get hurt. But one benefit of spending all day near molten metals is that the outside temperature always seemed a pleasant relief, no matter how warm or humid. And while rain was a blessing, the poorly built pluvial system made the town look like Venice until the hot sun could evaporate the pools and cake the mud.

Little had prepared Cesar for the depths of poverty he encountered here. Not in San Antonio during the Great Depression nor in St. Louis' worst neighborhoods did he find such squalid living conditions. From the surrounding arid lands to the dust that swept the city to the settling of factory soot on sweat-coated bodies, one just accepted that cleanliness was a relative concept.

Cesar's brothers never came, and after eight years of "temporary" work, he was still grinding it out each day at Vitro. Just as a man who limps adapts to his handicap and soon can't remember what it was like to walk straight, Cesar no longer remembered why he came or why he couldn't leave. Rather he relegated himself to the reality that this was his life.

⚜

Cesar was released without charges in a few days. When he returned to Vitro, his manager poked his head out of his glassed-partitioned office.

"Faz! They want to see you upstairs, right away!"

Cesar shrugged. He was in no mood to deal with this right now. Defending his job had become a ritual.

He entered Señor Calderon's office. "I'm sorry about the incident at Indio's the other night. It won't happen again," Cesar said.

"How long have you been with Vitro?" his manager asked, though Cesar knew that he already knew the answer.

"Almost nine years."

"And you're still working on the line. You ever wonder why?"

"Figured someone else had already done the wondering for me."

"You're pretty smart, too smart for your own good."

"I just want to do my job and stay out of everyone's way."

"You're on a short leash, Faz. I know you're good, but no one's that good."

"Yes, sir," said Cesar. That was that. He left his manager's office.

Pleading cut against every fiber of pride in his body. After work, he wanted to be alone, but he didn't want to go home yet.

He entered the abandoned barracks the same way he always did. The walls were dilapidated structures made of cinder blocks, whose grouting had seeped through myriad cracks only to freeze in midflow like some sort of concrete moss. The ceiling rafters, or what was left of them, were made of layers of rusting corrugated steel. The slab of the floor was cool, even during the heat of the summer. Though the cavernous space was dark and shadowed, sunlight streamed through several gaping holes in the rotting metal roof. In the distance, through the crisscrossing grid of steel I-beams, which remained open to the elements, he could see the imposing blower stacks of Fundidora's blast furnaces numbers one and two.

His thoughts were interrupted by the distinct yet familiar sound of a thud.

"Angel?" he called out as he moved toward the opening. The dirt field was all but unrecognizable. So immense was its transformation that he did a double take to see whether he had, in some confused state, walked out the wrong door.

He hadn't.

Cesar gazed out at a baseball diamond etched into the hard earth. It was chalked on each baseline with a long line of cement powder, the empty bags of which made the three bases. Nothing demarcated the infield from the outfield, and the lines were clearly not straight or perpendicular where they should have been, but it was a baseball field—of that there was no doubt.

They even had created a small grotto to Our Lady of Guadalupe alongside the pile of cinder blocks that served as the backstop.

Cesar walked out to the circular pile of dirt in the center of the diamond that was obviously the pitcher's mound. As he did, the boys drew closer to him.

"Well, we have a field," said Angel.

As their semicircle collapsed upon him, Cesar stretched his arms wide to envelope the boys in one embrace.

Part Two
The River

6

A Tall Order

I t was 10:20 AM Pacific Standard Time in La Mesa, California. Francis Vogel's mom pulled the string taught around the roast she was preparing. Her butcher always gave her the best cut of meat. Mr. Vogel had recently gotten her the wall-oven she'd wanted. With it preheated to 375 degrees, she slid the roasting tray in. There were mashed potatoes, string beans, fresh baked bread and a large pot of cream of mushroom soup, her in-laws' favorite. Mrs. Vogel could have made the soup from scratch, but why, when Campbell's made it so convenient?

"I need you to clean this room before your grandparents get here," she said to Francis and his two siblings who were sitting on the carpeted floor, watching television in the den.

"Kids, I'm talking to you," she repeated. It was always hard to get their attention during the middle of *Gunsmoke*. The boys had been building a model B-29 Bomber, and pieces were strewn all around in various stages of completion. Francis' sister had set up her Suzy-Homemaker oven and was "baking" chocolate cakes and serving her brothers. A checkerboard and Spirograph set completed the mess of toys on the floor.

In a few minutes, Mr. Vogel came in from the garage; he'd been building some shelves to store his tools. The Vogels' home was fairly typical: a stuccoed ranch house with a red-tiled roof and a swimming pool in the backyard. It had a two-car garage, but the family had only one car, so Mr. Vogel used the extra space as a workshop. On weekends, he enjoyed working with his hands, a break from his white-collar job as a regional inspector for the Metropolitan Water District of Southern California.

Perched on rolling hills east of San Diego, La Mesa was the quintessential American suburb with paved roads, a municipal sewer system, good schools, and plenty of parks and recreational areas.

"Honey, can I steal Francis? I promised him we'd stop at the sporting goods store this weekend," said Mr. Vogel.

"He's in the middle of cleaning up."

"Please hon, my dad's dying to see him in his full uniform. This is going to be his big season," Mr. Vogel pleaded.

Sportland was located in the quaint shopping district along La Mesa Boulevard. Francis tried on cleats and special catcher's gloves and swung various bats until he found one he liked. The team supplied him with his uniform shirt and pants, but Sportland outfitted him with the thin white socks and special T-strap oversocks in the appropriate colors. He and his dad picked out some baseballs, a practice "T" for hitting, and a netting device that would catapult the ball back to Francis when he was throwing by himself.

"Why don't we get two pairs of cleats," his dad said to the clerk as they checked out. "In case one gets wet," he added even though it didn't rain very often in Southern California during the summer.

❧◈❧

Little League didn't exist when Cesar was twelve. When it was founded in 1939 by Carl Stotz, there were just three teams: Lycoming Dairy, Lundy Lumber and Jumbo Pretzel, all from Stotz's hometown of Williamsport, Pennsylvania. Carl's Lycoming Dairy beat George Bebble's Lundy Lumber by a score of 7-2 in the inaugural game.

In 1947, the league organized the tournament that would end each season with four final games played in Williamsport. There were no teams outside the United States, but it was to be called The World Series.

America embraced baseball as its favorite national pastime, but organized baseball did not embrace all Americans. Until 1947, Major League Baseball enforced a strict whites-only policy. Returning African American soldiers who had helped breach Germany's Siegfried Line were told they weren't good enough to cross the color line of professional baseball. They were relegated to competing in their own leagues, and their names were as colorful as their teams: "Smokey" Joe Williams, Dick "Cannonball" Redding, John "Pop" Lloyd and Ted "Double Duty" Radcliffe. Hispanics, many from Cuba, were already in the Major League, but they often changed their names to sound more like the acceptable Italian lineage.

By 1957, though many rosters had Black and Hispanic players, these athletes often couldn't eat in the same restaurants or sleep in the same hotels as their white teammates. On and off the field, they lived under the specter of being booed, spat upon and having their lives threatened. This hostility even came from teammates and fellow ballplayers.

Little League rules had never specifically mentioned integration, but to its credit, the organization never wavered from its inclusive policies. That position was severely put to the test in 1955. South Carolina's Cannon Street YMCA became the first team in that state to field children of color. In actuality, the whole team was comprised of African American boys. When other teams balked at playing them, Williamsport issued an ultimatum: Play or forfeit. When they still refused, all sixty-one white leagues in South Carolina were disqualified.

✑◉◍◈

The banging on the door did not go away as Lucky had hoped it would. He bumped into his end table as he made the way to his front door and grumbled, "Who is it?" His mouth felt like it was stuffed with wads of cotton.

"Lucky, it's me."

"Faz?" Lucky replied, opening the door.

"Hope I didn't wake you," Cesar said with rhetorical politeness, even though the man who stood before him was dressed in his underwear. Lucky looked outside to see where the sun was, but it hadn't made its way over the horizon yet.

"The last time someone got me up this early, Jap Zeros were aiming for my ship."

"No such luck today. You gotta moment?"

"I'm pretty busy right now," responded Lucky with his normal sarcasm, which Cesar often failed to interpret.

"Sorry, I can come back later," Cesar said, turning to go.

Lucky reached out and grabbed his sleeve. "Just kidding, *amigo*. Come in."

"Your kids?"

"They spend Saturday nights at a friend's place; they call her Aunt Carmelita. Just give me a second," Lucky said, ushering his friend into his living room. Cesar peered in carefully, in case Lucky had an overnight guest.

"I'm alone," said Lucky, reading Cesar's thoughts.

"Does it ever bother you?"

"I do all right for myself with the ladies."

"You know what I mean."

After a long pause, Lucky said, "Sure, it gets lonely. But don't think having a wife is the end to your problems. Never forget that women are the givers of pleasure. . . and pain."

"I must be hurting, asking advice from a guy wearing boxer shorts."

"I forgot what time I printed on your invitation," Lucky laughed and excused himself. Entering the bedroom, he walked over to his nightstand on which were a basin of water and a half-empty bottle of beer. He scooped up a handful of water and splashed his face and hair. Refreshed, he pulled on a white undershirt and a pair of crumpled slacks and returned to the living room, but not before picking up the beer and downing the other half of its warm, flat liquid.

"I know you didn't take the streetcar all the way across town to ask about my love life," Lucky said as he picked a few items of clothing off the only place the two of them could sit.

"I need you to pull some strings to get a Little League franchise for some local kids."

"Little League? I thought you didn't like children. You going soft on me?"

"They're going to embarrass themselves enough. The least I can do is teach 'em some rules. . . so they won't give baseball a bad name."

"That's a tall order—it's already June."

"I saw the damage you could do on a one-day shore leave," Cesar said, playing the ego card.

"Oh, I didn't realize you were giving me a whole day."

They talked awhile, then Cesar abruptly stood up.

"I gotta go," he announced.

"Where are you in such a hurry to get to on Sunday morning?"

"Church."

"Is there no end to your surprises?"

"There's a *señorita* who goes there—"

"A dame! What about the 'if life was a fly ball, a woman would be the sun in your eyes' speech?"

"Well, you still need to catch fly balls to win games," said Cesar, as he bounded out the door and ran down the street.

"Don't come crying to me when the fly ball hits you on the forehead!" yelled Lucky.

The Trinity

nfortunately for Cesar, an electrical outage had temporarily
stopped the streetcars. He ran all the way to Padre
Esteban's church, but missed both Mass and the one
parishioner he hoped to see.

Later that day, Angel and Enrique dragged Cesar to Colonia
Cantu's outdoor market. It was a good place to find potential
ballplayers and their parents. Not only did they need to find boys
who wanted to play, they also needed to find ones whose parents
would let them travel hundreds of miles to the other side of the Rio
Grande.

"You really should get Padre Esteban to do this," Cesar said to the
boys.

"Señor Faz, he's busy with church matters," said Angel with some
astonishment.

Their first stop was to a vegetable stand owned by Francisco
Aguilar's father. Francisco was the oldest of ten children raised by
Clemente Aguilar and Reynalda Dávila in Guadalupe, Nuevo León.
It was a humble and crowded home, so Francisco had started
working at a very early age. He began each day delivering
newspapers for *El Norte* and gave the money to his parents. He had
a hard childhood, and Señor Aguilar believed that being invited to
play on the first Monterrey Little League team was an experience
he could never have afforded to give his son. Señor Aguilar was
receptive to allowing his son time off from his chores to practice on
the team with one condition. "You work him hard, Señor Faz. I don't

want him to grow soft playing baseball," he admonished.

"Oh, don't you worry," responded Cesar, turning to leave. "He'll be very focused," and with that, Cesar backed into a pile of avocados that had been stacked in a tall pyramid. Apologizing profusely, he fell to his knees to pick up several that rolled under other stands.

Standing up with the last errant avocado in his hand, Cesar found himself face-to-face with Maria. The incandescence of her soft brown eyes drew him in like land lures a long adrift sailor. But just as suddenly, she walked slowly past him.

"Wait a minute," he said as he took several hurried steps to get in front of her. "I saw you at church a few weeks ago."

"You don't go often."

"Why do you say that?"

"It was obvious," she smiled.

"Well, I'm a little rusty."

"I'm Maria," she said after a pause in which she waited for Cesar to make the introduction. He smiled but didn't take the hint.

"Do they use names in the country you come from?" she finally asked.

"Yes, yes! I'm Cesar Faz."

"Cesar Faz?" she asked with surprise.

"Do you know my name?"

"People talk."

"You come here to buy food?" he asked.

Maria looked at him curiously and answered, "Yes, Señor Faz. Does that surprise you? It is, after all, a food market."

"Of course it is. Please, you must call me Cesar."

"Okay. Did you come to steal an avocado, Cesar?" she asked, gazing down at the one still in his hand.

"Of course not," he stated. "I was just holding it."

"You shouldn't squeeze it so hard, it'll bruise the fruit inside," she said, smiling. "I have much shopping to do, but it was nice meeting you," she added and walked away.

After Cesar returned the avocado, he hurried to catch up to her again.

"So, where was I?" he asked as he stood in front of her.

"Blocking my view," she said with some aloofness.

"Which view?" he asked, looking behind him and then moving slightly to one side.

"The one you're standing in front of."

"At least let me help you with those bags," he said as he took one from her.

Cesar accompanied Maria as she filled a second large bag with fruits and vegetables. The subject of his recent incarceration came up, and he realized that everyone had heard only the part about his powerful temper, not about the waitress to whose aid he had come.

"Well, that's all I came for," she finally announced.

"Maybe I could go out sometime," he blurted, afraid to lose the moment, yet causing Maria to laugh. Cesar was falling in love in a way that only a few can survive. "I mean, *we*. . . Maybe we could go. . . Maybe you and I can eat—"

"Are you asking me on a date?"

"Yes."

"I'm afraid that's impossible."

"Why?"

"I doubt my father will approve of me going out with a strange man, especially one who's been in jail."

"But you know the truth."

"But he doesn't."

"Can I meet him?"

Maria paused and looked at her two bags of groceries. "I suppose you could join my family for dinner tonight."

"Tonight?"

"I thought you wanted to meet him?"

"Of course I do. I'll be there."

"Seven o'clock," she said as she left the square.

"Señor Faz has got a date!" came a young boy's voice. Cesar spun around to see Enrique and his friends spying on him from behind some produce stands.

"What are you guys gawking at?"

"Do you love her?" asked Francisco.

"It's just dinner," Cesar replied.

"Don't forget flowers," said Angel. "Mario says that women love them."

"The day I need advice on women from a twelve-year-old, I'll be too senile to use it!"

Later, when he was sure the boys couldn't see him, Cesar doubled back to a stand where he remembered an old woman was selling fresh gardenias.

As he was about to leave the market with the bouquet of flowers under his arm, he encountered Padre Esteban.

"I've been looking all over for you, Cesar. Come, I've arranged a meeting with Señor Alvarado. He might be able to help us get those bats and baseballs," said the priest.

"But. . . I have supper plans."

"You'll still have plenty of time to keep them."

"But—"

"Cesar, this is for the kids!"

❧

Señor Don Fernando Alvarado lived in San Pedro, Monterrey's most exclusive neighborhood. Most of the haciendas couldn't be seen from the street, but as Cesar and Padre Esteban were led through the wrought iron gates, the patron's enormous home came into view. The house was built in the Spanish Colonial style, yellowing stucco beneath a multi colored clay-tiled roof. Bougainvilla-covered fountains trickled water as the men walked down a stone path to the main doors' nine feet of hand-carved, dark, knotty alder with rubbed-bronze *clavos* adorning them.

Another servant answered the door and informed them that Señor Alvarado was just finishing supper and that they should wait on a side veranda. Sitting on the limestone tiled terrace, Cesar looked up through the heavy wood-beamed pergola at the sky. He had never been in such a home, even in the United States. The wait was far longer than Cesar had expected and he nervously looked at a clock visible through the glass doors. Señor Alvarado was not the type of man who could be rushed. He was in the ruling class, which meant that other people's lives and needs revolved around his.

It would be more than an hour before they were received.

". . . so that's why we were hoping you could help," Padre Esteban explained to the wealthy patrician, who listened quietly with respect to the priest who had once come to comfort his ailing mother.

"And what is the advantage to me?" His response held compassion laced with skepticism.

"The children are good, Señor. It'll make the whole town look good. Isn't that right, Cesar?" Cesar's attention was glumly fixed on the hacienda's clock. It was now 8:15 PM.

∾⊚⊚⊷

Maria sat quietly at her family's dining table. No one spoke, not even her father. Moments earlier, when her brother had tried to take some food from a tray that Maria had carefully prepared, she had stabbed his hand with a fork.

So they sat and waited.

Señor del Refugio was angry, but it paled in the face of his daughter's wrath.

∾⊚⊚⊷

"Right, Cesar?" the priest prompted him again.

"Yes, yes, they're very good. It'll definitely help the town's image," he finally responded.

Señor Alvarado cut the end off a cigar and took his time lighting it. He took a few puffs and its end burned brightly in the cool darkness of the veranda. Standing up, he walked over the stone balustrade that overlooked the city beyond and its gritty landscape of working factories.

"Image?" he asked. "Do you think people care?" Señor Alvarado brought the cigar once again to his lips.

∾⊚⊚⊷

Maria rose from her seat and served dinner to the brother she had stabbed. Wiping a tear from her eye, she finished serving everyone else, except her own plate, which she picked up and put back in the cupboard. Not a soul looked at Maria or dared to point out that she had been stood up.

❦

As Señor Alvarado's front door closed behind Cesar and Padre Esteban, the priest said, "There are others we can go to."

"They'll all say the same thing. Nobody cares about these kids," said Cesar.

As they made their way back down the garden pathway, Cesar glanced upward to the veranda where he could still see Señor Alvarado standing. A cloud of cigar smoke curled upward from his lips and dispersed in the night sky.

The flowers had held up pretty well all day, better than Cesar's plans had. Bouquet still in hand, he found Maria's home but saw no lights on. He had blown it and he knew it. Turning away, he made his way, alone, down the dusty street.

❦

It was the boys' first official day of practice, and they were eager. They tossed the ball around, ran up and down the base paths, and hooted and hollered for the benefit of some parents, friends and other strangers who sat on the dirt or on upside-down empty fruit crates, watching this mysterious game.

Though it was nearly ninety degrees, Padre Esteban arrived in full priestly regalia to bless the team and sanctify their field. The boys gathered around him at the pitcher's mound as he sprinkled Holy Water onto the parched dirt.

In a few minutes, Cesar joined them and asked, "Can any of you tell me the Holy Trinity of baseball?"

"The Father, the Son and the Holy Spirit?" offered Angel.

"Close. *Home runs, batting average* and *RBIs*." Cesar held up the baseball and continued, "And they all revolve around this. For the next few weeks you will have to eat, sleep, and breathe this and only this."

"How can we eat that?" Norberto quietly asked Ricardo.

"Who wins the World Series every year?" Cesar continued.

"Obviously the best team," answered Adolfo. Though he had not helped create the field, he was all too eager to reinstate himself as the team's *de facto* leader.

"No. It's the team that plays best," Cesar answered. "You have a lot to learn in both mind and body, but today we'll start with the body. Everyone line up for exercises."

"Exercises?" came the communal groan.

"Yes, let's start with twenty jumping jacks."

"We want to hit and throw. We shouldn't have to do twenty jumping jacks," said Norberto.

"Norberto's right. Let's make it forty."

8

The Unexpected Play

A blindfolded Baltazar Charles swung his stick wildly at the target that floated in the air above his head. Children shrieked out directions to help their disoriented friend: *Más arriba, Abajo* or *enfrente*, the equivalent of "You're getting warmer or colder."

The object of Baltazar's aim was a clay pot adorned with protruding points which gave it the appearance of a seven-pointed star. An icon at a child's birthday party, the *piñata* was originally used by Spanish missionaries to teach the natives the *catequismo catolico*. Each point represented one of the seven deadly sins, though all Baltazar and his friends thought about at this moment were the nuts, candies and dried fruits that lay within, ready to be freed with one good swing of his stick.

All the while, children and adults alike sang the traditional *piñata* song:

Dale, dale, dale, no pierdas el tino.
Porque si lo pierdes, pierdes el camino.
Esta piñata es de muchas mañas, sólo contiene naranjas y cañas.
La piñata tiene caca Tiene caca: Cacahuates de a montón.

Hit it, hit it, hit it, don't lose your aim.
'Cause if you lose it, you lose the way.
This *piñata* has a lot of tricks and only has oranges
and sugar canes.
The *piñata* has pee—peanuts in a pile.

Finally, with one tremendous *whoosh*, he crushed the clay pot, and its contents spilled out into the groping hands of excited boys and girls.

Norberto had told Angel about Baltazar, a boy who kept mostly to himself, but Norberto knew he would be at the birthday party of Francisco Aguilar. As Angel and Norberto watched from the other side of a broken fence, they knew it was no accident that Baltazar was known as the *"piñata buster."*

Baltazar Charles and his family, like the Villarreals, lived in a small house on an unpaved street with no lights and no running water or sewage, the latter functions being relegated to a hole in the ground behind the house. Drinking, bathing and cooking water had to be brought in each day from a public well, and his mother washed the family's clothes in an *arroyo*, a gully cut by draining rainfall.

Balta, as he was called by his friends, was the son of Baltazar Charles Martinez, a worker for Companie de Trokeles y Esmaltes, and Maria del Rosario Montes de Oca Cruz, an artisan who made intricately decorated bowls, plates and jugs for the few who could pay for such luxuries in Monterrey. Her palms were brittle and cracked from applying chemically harsh lacquers with her bare hands, instead of using brushes, which she could never afford.

Balta walked to Escuela Revolución, a school in one of the most destitute barrios in all of Monterrey. His family's poverty didn't allow Balta to dream about a bright future. For him, life was limited to school, chores and caring for his younger sister, Patricia, who had been very sick ever since she was a little girl. She had a form of juvenile arthritis, brought on by diabetes, that made her weak and kept her in pain most of her life. Normal activities were difficult for her, and she always needed someone nearby for assistance. Since both parents worked, much of that responsibility rested with Balta, the oldest boy still living at home.

⚬⚬⚬

The darkened cavern of the blast furnace suddenly exploded with light as a liquid cylinder of molten steel was released from Ladle No. 2. Its intense illumination was bested only by the sun. The pour could take no longer than two and a half minutes to maintain the integrity of the magma's temperature. Recaptured in its mold, it would rest for several days, cooling into the form prescribed by the men who tamed it.

Señor Rafael Estrello overheard several of his coworkers talking about a baseball team for twelve year olds. After work, Señor Estrello stopped by Iglesia San Juan Bautista to speak with Padre Esteban.

"It would be great for Rafael to try out," said the priest.

"He's very shy. Maybe some of the kids from the team could speak with him."

In a few minutes, Señor Estrello led Angel and Norberto toward his neighborhood of Villa de Guadalupe. It was a good stone's throw from Fundidora on the southeastern bank of the Rio Santa Catarina. Its residents lived in conditions that made Colonias Fundidora and Acero seem luxurious by comparison. The Estrellos embodied the well-known refrain *Mientras hay lucha hay vida, y mientras hay vida hay lucha* [While there is struggle there is life, and while there is life there is struggle]."

Rafael was not home.

"He's probably at my brother Ramon's furniture store. He works there after school," Señor Estrello told the boys who accompanied him.

"There's no time for him to play ball. I need him here in the store," Ramon told his brother.

"Their fathers let them join the team. Right, boys?" he asked Angel and Norberto.

"My papa is very excited about my playing baseball," said Norberto.

"And yours, too, I bet," Rafael Sr. said to Angel.

"Yes, sir," answered Angel, saddened that he could not give the same answer as Norberto without shading the truth.

"You see," Rafael Sr. said to Ramon. "Besides, it'll be good for him to play with other boys his own age."

"I bet he won't even be interested," said Ramon.

"Let me ask him. Where is he?"

"I sent him to fetch some materials from Fabricacion de Maquinas. He should be here any minute," Ramon answered. "Why don't you two wait outside for him," he said to Angel and Norberto.

Soon, Rafael arrived, and Angel asked him if he'd like to play baseball.

"Sure!" said Rafael enthusiastically as he donned an extra glove.

The boys' play was abruptly curtailed as the noise of screaming children approached. Ramon and Rafael Sr. rushed to the door to see the cause of the commotion. Dozens of children were running wildly down the dusty street in every direction. Hot on their heels were men in white coats, sent into the barrios by the State Health Department during annual vaccination campaigns. Some children ducked inside doorways; some dove under carts; others climbed trees; but most made their way toward the Rio de la Silla whose craggy banks offered a myriad of hiding places where they would wait until dark when it was safe to come home. Drowning in the river or falling from a tree seemed preferable to the doctor's needle.

Later that evening, when the boys returned from their hiding places, Rafael pleaded with his mother to let him join the team.

"Why do you have to go all the way to Texas?" she asked. Rafael was her only child and she was very protective. He also wore glasses, which Señora Estrello felt made him a target for jokes.

"That's where teams from south of the border have to play," he answered.

"That's very far away."

She then addressed her husband. "When would Rafael come home?"

"It's only for a couple of days," responded her husband.

"I don't know what to say. Rafael has never left home and, well, I don't know what to say."

"Please, Mama, let me go with the team. Please," begged her son.

"He's a good boy, and this trip will be a growing experience for him," added Rafael Sr.

"You are my baby, Rafael. Promise me you'll be careful," she cried as she hugged her son.

"Don't worry, Mama, I'm not afraid. The Empress of the Americas will guide us."

❧ ◎ ❧

There is something about a hard wooden bat striking a leather-covered baseball that made a sound unlike any other Cesar Faz had ever heard. There was a baseball field in San Antonio three blocks away from his home, but even through trees, neighbors' houses and street traffic, he could distinguish the faintest *thwack* of a batted ball, which told him that it was time to get his glove and hurry there before sides were chosen.

Such was the phenomenon at the dirt field in Monterrey's poorest barrio as boys were drawn in; many with handmade gloves, most of them barefoot, but all eager to play *biesbol*.

Enrique and Angel had brought three new kids to tryout.

"What about him?" Cesar asked about the one already standing in the batter's box.

"That's Baltazar Charles," said Enrique. "Throw him a pitch."

Cesar pitched one toward home plate where Baltazar stood with his stick ready. With a purposeful swing, as if at a *piñata*, he sent the ball soaring high over their heads.

"Not bad," Cesar said, shaking his head. Having to pick up and carry his sister regularly had made Balta very strong for his age. The muscles in his arms and shoulders were far more developed than those of his peers, a result that would serve him well when throwing or hitting a baseball.

"And him?" Cesar referred to the second boy waiting in line.

"That's Fidel Ruiz," said Angel. "Race him to first."

"Race him to first? I'm on the mound. I've got a five-step head start. Besides, he's a little kid."

"He is old," Fidel said of Cesar. "Would the señor like me to run slower?" he said to the coach.

"Okay, wise guy, go!" Cesar yelled as he took off for first. Fidel beat him by a full two strides.

"Speedy little kid," said Cesar as he caught his breath. "He's in."

Fidel had been born in the zone of the city reserved for its military camp. He was the son of a well-respected and strict sergeant, Emilio Ruiz. His mother, Adelaida España, had agreed to move with the whole family into *Ciudad Militar*, the military base where Fidel and his sister, Guadalupe, would be schooled. Living among soldiers and uniformed men made Fidel's childhood a very disciplined one.

Fidel began working when he was a child which allowed him to leave the Military Camp and run all the way to the center of Monterrey to sell the food that his mother had made. It was a hard job for a child, but it gave him a reason to wander and the ability to see a world beyond the high cinder block walls of the base. After his deliveries, he would gather with street children and walk through Monterrey unsupervised and free from the rigors of the strict world of his sergeant father. Once he and his friends stole some cookies from a grocery store, and when they were detained and brought back to the military camp, he was put in a small prison cell to learn a lesson—one he'd never forget.

"What's that kid good at?" Cesar asked, pointing at the one who was noticeably smaller than the others.

"That's Mario Ontiveros. Try throwing him a strike," challenged Angel.

"I can't take a kid just 'cause he's got a small strike zone."

"Just try," Angel cajoled.

A dozen pitches later Cesar hadn't thrown anything resembling a strike.

After the thirteenth pitch bounced skyward off the lip of the plate, Cesar grunted. "Okay, it's hard to pitch him, but I need a better reason to pick him."

Enrique drew closer to Cesar and whispered, "Please, Señor Faz, he knows all the girls!"

Cesar looked at Mario and said, "You got a glove?"

Mario was born to Victor and Sara Ontiveros in Colonia Industrial. The second of six children, he was the firstborn male, which meant a lot of responsibility for him. At first, his parents didn't want him to try out for the team. In order to participate, he'd have to walk two miles each way. Mario had to convince his parents that he would continue to study hard and to help around the house.

⋞⊙⊙⋟

"Why haven't you come back to church?" Enrique asked Cesar at the end of practice.

"I'm not much of a churchgoer," Cesar replied.

"She misses you," said Mario, the team's honorary expert on women.

A chorus of "Who misses him?" followed.

"Maria del Refugio," Norberto answered.

"She's beautiful," said Ricardo.

"I'm sure she doesn't," said Cesar.

"I saw how she looked at you at the market last week," Angel said.

"That was before I stood her up and embarrassed her before her family."

"You must go to her," Mario advised.

"It's not that simple."

"Why not?"

"You're too young to understand," Cesar said. "Okay, boys, tomorrow at the same time."

After Cesar left, Mario called his teammates together.

"What's up?" asked Angel.

"Señor Faz needs help with this Maria."

❧❦

Angel and Enrique solicited Maria's address from Padre Esteban, and before practice the next day, they made their way to her house. When they were within a few blocks, the boys made sure they had their story straight, then ran as fast as they could to her door. Besides being in a hurry, it was important that they looked out of breath.

A panting Enrique spoke as Maria opened the door.

"Señora, Padre Esteban told us you're a nurse."

"I am, but. . . Is someone sick?"

"Please come, our friend's been hurt," said Angel, also breathing rapidly.

When Maria arrived at the field, she saw the rest of the team gathered around home plate, standing over Mario who lay on the ground, moaning. Pushing her way into the center of the group, she knelt down to tend to the injured child.

"What happened?" she asked.

"There was a play at the plate and he slid badly into Beto's leg," said Enrique.

"Yeah, it really hurt," said Norberto, eliciting an elbow in his ribs from Angel, who could barely hold his laughter.

"Can you move your leg?" she asked Mario.

"I'll try. . . owww!" came his agonized whine as he moved it slightly. Mario, besides being a *suavecito* with the ladies, was also one of the greatest actors of his time, or at least he thought he was.

"Perhaps we should get him to the hospital," she said.

Mario's eyes widened as the boys looked at one another in fear.

"Don't be frightened. They make people better at the hospital," Maria added.

"Wait," pleaded Mario. "Maybe just a few more minutes—"

Just then, Cesar arrived for the start of practice and ran over to the group.

"What's going on? What are you doing here?" a startled Cesar asked Maria.

"I'm a nurse. His friends summoned me," she said.

"Maybe if I try to walk on it," suggested Mario as his act began to fade.

"I better get a doctor," Cesar said.

"No!" shouted Enrique. "I mean, I think he's moving it okay. Right, Mario?"

"Yes, it's feeling better," said Mario, who stood up and began to walk around, his leg taking a miraculous turn for the better.

"Wait a minute," said Maria. "If you slid, why aren't your pants dirty?"

The kids all looked at one another, realizing the small detail left out of their plan.

"Boys?" said Cesar sternly, smelling the con.

"We'd better get the field ready for our scrimmage," they said as they quickly scattered to distant parts of the field. Maria turned toward Cesar.

"If you wanted to speak with me, you—"

"I swear, I had nothing to do with this," Cesar interrupted.

Maria studied his eyes for a moment. Satisfied that he, too, had been caught unaware, she said, "Well, at least nobody's hurt." She turned to go.

"About the other night—" Cesar began to say.

Maria turned sharply.

"There's nothing to say about it, Señor Faz. Really, nothing."

"I couldn't help it," he continued. "I had to meet a man and—"

"You should've told him you had a previous commitment."

"You don't tell that to an important man like Señor Alvarado."

"So my father is not an important man to you?" she snapped.

"It wasn't for me, it was for the kids. If we can't raise the money to go to the Little League tournament, all their efforts will be for nothing."

"It was for them?" she asked.

"Yes."

"I'm sorry, I didn't know. I suppose I can forgive you this once. But if you stand me up again, my father will surely kill you."

"Señor Faz, it's time to practice," called the boys.

"Meet me tonight," Cesar asked Maria.

"That is not possible."

"Why not?"

"My father would not approve of me being out at night alone."

"But you wouldn't be alone, you'd be with me," said Cesar.

"To him, that would be worse."

⚜

"Hurry, Enrique needs us," the fleet-footed Fidel told Baltazar when he found him the next morning at the open air market. Enrique had been cornered by the Mexico City players who were returning from their exhibition tour. Heated words were exchanged, and Enrique challenged Juan Zaragosa and his friends to show up at their dirt field. Their differences would be settled on the baseball diamond.

As visitors, the Mexico City All-Stars batted first. There were no spectators, no uniforms, no umpires; the results would be written only in the minds of the participants.

Adolfo wound up and let his arm come quickly forward, but his nervousness didn't allow his hand to release the ball until it had passed its apogee. The ball drove into the ground a bat's length in front of home plate and careened off Norberto's shoulder all the way to the backstop, causing the batter to laugh.

Adolfo looked around in embarrassment and motioned for Angel and the rest of the infielders to come over to him.

"My arm's hurt from sliding yesterday. You come in," he said and handed the ball to Angel.

"I was with you all morning and your arm was fine," Ricardo accused Adolfo.

"You calling me a liar?" fired back Adolfo.

Angel thought for a moment and then said to Ricardo, "If Adolfo says he's hurt, then he's hurt."

As auspicious a start as this was, it would be the high point for Monterrey.

When Mexico City batters weren't being walked, they were pounding the ball all over the field for extra base hits. So many of them crossed the plate that they mercifully lost count after each had batted twice in the inning.

It wasn't completely Angel's fault. Once chaos crept in, any semblance of organized baseball fled the Monterrey team. Adolfo sat on the sideline watching. He was glad not to be a part of the beating.

Padre Esteban had told them that baseball could be eternal, but right now the boys prayed for its mortality. With no clock, no mercy rule and darkness hours away, it seemed as if nothing would rescue them from this purgatory.

They were saved by boredom. The Mexico City team finally lost interest and left.

⎇⎇⎇

Later that day, when Cesar showed up for practice, he found Angel sitting by himself.

"They all went home," said Angel.

"Who canceled practice?"

Angel told Cesar the details of the earlier event with the Mexico City players.

"Your padre said an army was no match for a child with faith. It sure didn't take much to make this one desert. I want everyone here tomorrow at five, and I mean everyone!" he barked.

"What for?" asked Angel.

"Tell them to be here, or I will find every one of them and drag them here myself," he said as he turned and left. Angel knew that Cesar was not joking.

⋘◉⋙

The next day at four o'clock, the door of the cantina across the street from Peñoles flew open, its hinges making a loud creaking noise. Peñoles was Monterrey's mining company and it employed a lot of Americans.

"I need some guys who've played baseball," Cesar announced.

⋘◉⋙

The bells of the Metropolitan Cathedral rang loudly and struck five times, signifying the hour. Not one boy dared to be late for this appointment. Cesar Faz stared at them; none moved or so much as whispered to the boy next to him.

"If you wanna quit, fine. But not on my watch. You're going to finish the inning you started. I don't care if it's the last one you ever play."

"Who are we going to play?" asked Enrique.

"Them." Cesar pointed to the group of men he'd recruited that afternoon.

The boys stared with apprehension at the older men; Cesar had found seven. They appeared like an over-the-hill gang, but when they took the field and tossed a ball around, the ease with which they practiced clearly intimidated the Little Leaguers.

"They're so much bigger!" Norberto said.

"Are you going to carry them?" asked Cesar.

"We couldn't even get the kids our own age out," Fidel said.

"I have all night!" barked Cesar.

"But, Señor Faz, they're real American baseball players," added Baltazar.

"Wrong!" said Cesar. "They're the Yankees and you are the mighty Brooklyn Dodgers. You're going to avenge last year's World Series!"

Cesar then turned to Ricardo Treviño and said, "Let's go, Gil Hodges. First base."

He went down the squad, and for each boy at each position, he called them by his Dodger equivalent. "Pee Wee Reese, third base, Duke Snider, center field. . ." They all began to smile and get excited as he called out the roster. "Sandy Koufax, take the mound," he said to Angel.

"My arm feels better today," stated Adolfo.

"That's good news, but let's see how Angel does," Cesar answered.

"We all saw how he could do yesterday," said Adolfo

"It's all right, Señor Faz, I stunk yesterday," said Angel.

"All the more reason why you're going to get back in there and try again," Cesar replied firmly.

"Adolfo, take a turn at second base," the coach offered.

"I only pitch," replied the young man.

"Play second or don't play," Cesar commanded this time. Adolfo begrudgingly took his position.

The men from Peñoles were neither great ballplayers nor bad ones, but they knew enough of the game and their muscles retained just enough memory to play it with a semblance of precision.

Angel threw four pitches and walked the first batter. Cesar walked to the mound and said, "Angel, look around. What do you see?"

"American baseball players, my friends, some of my friends' families, some people I don't even know and—"

"Funny. I only see Norberto's glove," said Cesar. "Don't even see Norberto, I just see his glove." He walked back to the sideline.

Angel closed his eyes and opened them, focusing on the small basket of leather that Señora Villarreal had sewn for her son's hand. He saw its coarse stitches and when he strained even harder, he could see the grains of the leather. His next pitch fell squarely in its padded webbing. He soon found his rhythm and with it, his confidence. After a few more strikes, Angel could even detect the slightest brown mark where the animal had once been branded.

The game continued, and though a few errors were made, the boys managed to finish the first inning after giving up only one run.

In the bottom of the first inning, Fidel and Enrique got on base.

Adolfo was the next batter, but when Cesar called out the boy's name, Norberto told him, "He said he'd be back when you needed him to pitch."

"When you see him again, tell him I'll miss him."

The boys held the old-timers scoreless for two more innings, but more importantly, they were having fun in the context of competing. They loaded the bases with one out and had just scored their first run on a clutch hit by Baltazar. They proved they could score, and every boy knew the significance of the moment. Suddenly, taking the lead seemed a real possibility.

"Okay, that's it!" yelled Cesar. "It's getting dark."

"But, Señor Faz, we're about to score again!" exclaimed Rafael.

"Yeah, and it's not that dark, We can still see," Francisco added.

"We want to keep playing. We don't want to go home now!" came the resounding comments from the boys.

"Remember, you all quit yesterday. Now you can go home with clean consciences," Cesar said as he and the men from Peñoles walked off the field.

❧❧❧

Lucky joined Cesar at the same cantina where he had recruited the men. The old-timers were enjoying the round of drinks Cesar had promised.

Cesar and Lucky listened to them as they regaled one another with tales of great players and plays and never-ending *what if* scenarios and *what-might-have-beens*. These men may have forgotten most of their lives, but they vividly recalled game-winning hits and diving catches that they made in the long ago sandlots of their youths.

"So I hear you got a pitcher who fancies himself to be Sandy Koufax," said Lucky.

"Yeah. That's his hero."

"Why him? He only won four games in his first two seasons? Why not Newcomb or Drysdale?"

"Do you know what Al Campanis said of Koufax when he had the kid throw him some pitches in a tryout?" Cesar asked. Al Campanis was the Brooklyn Dodger's scout. "He said there were only two times in his life when the hair on the back of his neck stood up. The first was when he saw the ceiling of the Sistine Chapel, and the second was when Sandy Koufax threw him a fastball."

"Well, at least one Mexican kid believes in him. Hey, I think you owe me a beer," said Lucky. Cesar ordered one for his friend, and then turned to the old men who were still talking about their baseball outing.

"Thanks for making it look close," Cesar said to them as he raised his bottle of Cuervo.

"I don't know about you guys, but I was trying to win," said one of the men.

"Here, here," chimed in his friend, who then downed his enrtire beer without surfacing for air.

❦

The sun barely clawed its way over Mitras Hill when the knocking began at Cesar's door. He leaned against it and smiled, but he remained still. The knocking persisted. He had allowed the boys to rediscover their desire and he wanted to savor the moment.

"We're not leaving until you come to the field," Angel said through the thin glass window.

"You're lucky I have nowhere to go this morning," Cesar said as he came out of his house a few minutes later.

Cesar looked up and down the row of boys who stood on his doorstep.

"Anyone even thinking of quitting again is gone for good. Understand?"

"*Sí*, Señor Faz," they responded.

❦

That afternoon, the boys tried various positions while Cesar barked out scenarios in what he called "situation ball." Lucky came to the field to check up on the newest incarnation of the Brooklyn Dodgers.

"Runners on first and—" he began when he was suddenly

interrupted by Angel.

"What runners, Señor Faz? There's no one on base."

"Pretend."

"How?"

"Okay," Cesar said, taking a deep breath. "Mario, get on first. Fidel, you run from home plate the moment I hit the ball. Satisfied?"

The boys nodded.

"Now, runners on first and second with nobody out. What're you going to do if the ball comes to you? On the ground, in the air, on one bounce? Think," he said and hit a hard grounder between shortstop and second base.

Mario and Fidel took off as the two infielders let the ball pass, each thinking the other would field it. Enrique made a throw from center field toward first base, but the runners had already passed there, which forced a throw to second base, which overshot the base back into the out field. Only a pinpoint throw from Gerardo Gonzales managed to catch Mario at the plate.

Cesar shook his head from side to side.

"¡Cosas inesperadas en momentos inesperados [The unexpected play at the unexpected time]!" he said loudly.

"But we got Mario out," proclaimed Norberto.

"You turned a routine play into one that required heroics. That's not good baseball. What distinguishes great ballplayers is being prepared for what you can't imagine. The base runner who stumbles, a wild throw, a ball that ricochets off a base. . ."

Cesar hit a grounder to third base and again, the ball made its rounds.

"It's a lot to take in. Except for a few innings with the Mexico City All-Stars and your gray-haired brigade, these kids haven't really seen the game played," said Lucky.

"There are only five things to learn," Cesar lamented. "Running, catching, throwing, hitting and hitting harder."

"They look like they can already do those things," Lucky observed as the throw came into third base to catch a sliding Fidel. "You just need to teach them when."

"Okay, let's try again," Cesar called out. "Nobody on base, two outs, play to first." Cesar hit the ball to the outfield where Enrique, thinking Cesar was going to hit another grounder, stood unprepared. Racing back to get the ball, Enrique missed his cutoff, but his throw reached home on one clean hop to get Francisco Aguilar out.

"See what I mean?" Lucky commented. "Nice throw."

"They use great athleticism to compensate for strategic errors," Cesar replied.

"Enrique," Cesar yelled out, "the unexpected play at the unexpected time."

"Sí, Señor Faz," replied his winded outfielder.

Lucky joked, "Well, Yogi Berra said ninety percent of the game is half mental."

"Yeah, and I must be a hundred percent mental to think I can teach them baseball in four weeks. How'd you like to create order in this chaos?"

"Holler when you're hurt," Lucky laughed.

⌘

The boys had natural athleticism and showed signs of individual brilliance, but they moved together like a broken clock whose gears were out of sync. The problem exacerbated one afternoon when a "gear" from the other side of town showed up.

The boys were taking a break when an expensive car drove up and parked at the edge of the field. Out of the black sedan stepped a boy and his father, who was dressed in a suit.

Who's that?" Cesar asked Padre Esteban, who had come to watch the team's progress.

"That's Señor Maiz. He's the head of a much respected family," answered the priest.

As Cesar and Señor Maiz conversed, his son walked over to the group sporting a brand-new glove and baseball cap.

"Who are you?" asked Angel.

"I'm Pepe. I play left field."

"Gerardo plays left," said Enrique.

"We'll see," said the new boy.

After Señor Maiz drove off, Cesar returned and said, "Boys, meet your new left fielder, Pepe Maiz."

"Told you," Pepe snickered to Enrique.

"You think your dad can buy your way on the team? Money isn't everything."

"Only when you don't have any," replied Pepe, "and you never will."

"At least I'll always be able to kick your ass," said Enrique. He and Pepe stood toe-to-toe, neither willing to back down.

"Play's to second!" Cesar yelled and hit a line drive to center field. Enrique saw it too late. He took off after it, but instead of an easily fielded ball, it rolled all the way to the street.

"Enrique, pay attention!" Cesar yelled.

"Nice play! You'll be collecting splinters on the bench soon," quipped Pepe.

"Okay, that's it!" Enrique threw down his glove and went for Pepe. In seconds, the two were throwing punches and rolling in the dirt.

"He threw the first punch," Pepe said as Cesar pulled them apart.

"He started it," countered Enrique.

"Silence, both of you. There are only two kinds of baseball players: Those who can play as a team and those who won't be on this team. Don't either of you move."

Cesar grabbed an empty cement sack and took out his pocketknife. Cutting two long strips from the material, he tied them together at one end and brought it to the boys.

"Put your legs together," he ordered and tied Pepe's left ankle to Enrique's right one. Helping them up, he led them to the shortstop position. Going to home plate, he turned and called out to them, "Okay, time for teamwork lesson number one. Play's to first."

Cesar hit spanking grounders directly at the hapless two. One after another, balls careened off different body parts because they couldn't get out of each other's way. Even when one managed to get the ball in his glove, the other one's jerking motion caused the throw to fly wild.

Finally, after pushing, shoving and blaming each other, Pepe dropped his glove. Enrique snagged the next grounder and flipped it to Pepe who then fired it to first base.

Cesar cut the rope and the two fell to the ground, rubbing their sore ankles.

"From now on, leave your grudges at home."

Cesar left Angel in charge to pitch some batting practice. Pepe called first up. As Angel served one right down the middle of the plate, the new kid hit the ball dead on its sweet spot and watched it sail over the outfielders' heads. It went so far that it bounced on the street and hopped into the back of a horse-drawn hay cart.

At once, they all realized the consequence of what happened.

"Our ball!" the boys yelled and took off running down the street after the cart.

❧

Without enough bats and balls to go around, Cesar became more inventor than coach. He began devising different games, each of which was designed to improve the boys' reflexes, stamina and camaraderie.

The ankle-tying experiment with Pepe and Enrique had proved so successful that several times a week, he tied the whole team together and had the boys run errands around the city. It was a comical sight to see the dozen or so bound-at-the-ankle boys falling down or trying to fit through doorways, but Cesar wanted them to understand their teammates' intentions from the slightest movements.

Cesar also kept them busy by working together on their field. They foraged the local factories for pieces of wood, metal, cinder blocks and other materials that might improve it. To disguise the calisthenics they hated, he had them move wood beams and cinder blocks from one end of the field to the other while he decided where to construct bleachers.

With his help, they also began to fashion a makeshift scoreboard, and a scavenged section of chain-link fence became Norberto's catcher's mask.

After practices, when their arms were too sore to pick up a baseball and their legs felt like railroad ties, he taught them the rules, strategies and silent hand signals that communicate stealing, hit-and-runs, and bunts.

Cesar sat on the sidelines during one practice and worked on the roster for Padre Esteban.

"Cesar?" asked the priest.

"Yes, Padre?"

"With Adolfo Martinez gone, don't you think it's time to choose a second pitcher?"

"For one game?"

"What if Angel gets hurt or. . . or can't get out of an inning."

"Good idea," said Cesar. He called the boys to the mound.

"Okay, Angel, I want you to catch. Everybody else, make a single line at the mound." The boys did as they were told. "I want every one to throw five pitches."

Francisco was first, followed by Roberto Mendiola and Alfonso Cortez, two of the team's newest recruits. None of their pitches flew close.

"It's Angel's fault," whined Fidel, the next one to throw. "He makes a bad target."

"You want a target?" yelled Cesar. He stood on home plate with his back to the mound. Bending all the way over, he presented his backside and dared Fidel to hit him. One by one, the boys failed until Enrique took the baseball.

The sting of the ball striking Cesar's rear end could be felt a block away and Cesar's yelp was drowned out by the sound of the boys congratulating Enrique for his timely bull's-eye.

"I have four more pitches, Señor Faz," said Enrique, smiling.

Anticipating the consequences, Cesar dutifully bent over again. When a second fastball impacted his bottom, Angel winced. "That's going to leave a mark."

⚬⊙⊙⚬

"Here you go, señora," said the owner of a tannery as he rolled up a sheet of leather. Señora Ontiveros reached for her small purse.

"What do you need so much for?"

"Gloves for my son's team," she answered.

"Why didn't you say so before? Hold on a minute," he said as he climbed a small ladder and retrieved a different, darker hide. "This one is much better."

"I don't think I can afford it. I—"

At that moment, the boys ran down the street. They were all blindfolded, except for Norberto who guided them.

"Please, señora. Just wish them luck," said the shopkeeper as he made her put away her money.

Later that afternoon, Cesar stood on a street corner with Norberto.

"Go!" Cesar yelled. That was Norberto's cue to throw the ball down the street toward Enrique as Mario started singing one of the team's favorite hymns. Enrique caught the ball, pivoted and threw it down an intersecting street to another teammate. In this way, the ball traveled a circuit around the neighborhood, easily followed by the barking dogs and frightened chickens taking flight, until the last boy in the chain fired it back to Norberto. When it hit his glove, Mario stopped singing.

"How was that?" Cesar asked Mario, the team's musical "stopwatch."

"Four bars better."

"Good. Okay, Norberto, get ready. This time, throw it the other way."

"But, Señor Faz, you didn't tell them—"

"Exactly. *Cosas inesperadas. . .*"

⌇⌇

"You see the top of this hill?" Cesar pointed to the steep incline that looked more like a small mountain than a hill. The boys nodded. "Well, on top is buried a treasure. And no one knows it's there but me. But we have to get it right away or it will be gone forever."

With that, the boys began to run up the side of the craggy mound. Rocks gave way and several boys' footing nearly sent one or two of them on a nasty slide down its jagged surface. By the time they had reached the top and searched for the treasure, all they found was a new baseball. Back at the bottom, Norberto said, "There was nothing there but this."

"Touch it, everyone. Feel it carefully," Cesar said as the boys passed it around. Several rubbed it across their cheeks.

"This isn't a real treasure," said Enrique angrily.

"If I had told you that the only thing up to here was a baseball, would you have run so hard to make it to the top?"

"No," came the response.

"When you are ready to run up a mountain, swim through a stream or cross a desert for a baseball, you will be ready to play against American baseball players."

"Do they practice this hard?" Angel asked.

"Every single day of their lives," answered Cesar.

Except for Angel, the boys dispersed to go about their day's activities. Angel stared up at the precipice from which they had just descended.

"What are you thinking about, Angel?" Cesar asked.

"If I run up this mountain every day, can I be a professional baseball player?"

Cesar didn't know how to respond. His only goal was to teach them enough baseball to make a respectable showing in McAllen, Texas. He held no illusions of what their efforts would bring, but this was something new and Cesar wanted no responsibility for dreams that had no chance to rise.

Brown Paper Bags

It was the third week in July. Backstage at Broadway's Winter Garden Theater, final auditions were being held for a new musical called *West Side Story*. It portrayed a group of white neighborhood kids defending their turf against a gang of Hispanic immigrants. In Alabama, Martin Luther King Jr. returned from Washington, DC, where he'd been received by Vice President Richard Nixon in the nation's Capitol, even though in his own state capitol he couldn't drink from the same water fountain as a white janitor.

The Brooklyn Dodgers had won four games in a row and were currently in second place. Today, they would play a doubleheader against the Chicago Cubs at Ebbets Field.

In La Mesa, California, Dennis Hanggi and his family packed towels, chairs and an ice chest in the family station wagon for a day trip to South Mission Beach, north of San Diego's naval station. They would play a game unique to Mission Beach, a three-on-three version of baseball called Over-the-Line.

In Monterrey, Padre Esteban finished Communion and now sat at the altar listening to the boys in the choir. A young boy approached him and whispered something in his ear, eliciting a slow nod from the priest.

After the hymn, he took his position behind the pulpit and, as was the custom, prepared to make his weekly announcements.

"Thanks to your prayers, Señor Montez's boils have finally healed. Señora Santana has given birth to twins. . . And lastly," he paused and looked over at the choir, "Monterrey has just been officially invited into the American Little League."

The *whoops* from the usually solemn choir began before he had finished his sentence.

Baseball skills alone wouldn't get them uniforms or transportation to Texas—money would. After visiting Señor Alvarado, Cesar and Padre Esteban called upon other industrial barons and patriarchs of Monterrey. Most were polite, like the mayor, who said that he didn't have enough in his budget to pay for schools or roads let alone a traveling baseball team, but all of them were dismissive. One even warned the priest that he was leading lambs to a slaughter.

There was one man, Señor Bremer, whom Cesar and Padre Esteban were obliged to leave a message upon learning that he was in Mexico City. Upon Señor Bremer's return to Monterrey, he instructed his chauffeur to drive through *Colonia Cantu*. He heard rumors of boys running blindfolded through the streets and up the sides of hills until they couldn't walk.

Through the side window of his Packard Clipper Deluxe, he watched Angel and his teammates carrying water. The poles and buckets seemed oversized on their bony bare shoulders. They'd be paid a few pesos for each bucket delivered—they were determined to pay for their trip if no one else would. Señor Bremer had been born into wealth, his childhood held little from which he could relate to the experiences of these boys. But he admired those who worked hard, and for this alone, he felt compelled to reward them.

❧◉☙

"Are you kidding?" asked a dumbfounded Cesar Faz as he sat in a small metal-framed chair on the opposite side of his manager's desk at Fundidora.

"No," came Señor Calderon's reply.

"I've done everything you asked me to do. The dangerous jobs, the garbage ones. . . No thank you," replied Cesar.

"It wasn't a request. Señor Bremer has asked Vitro to become one of the team's sponsors and he wants you to go as their coach."

"If it were anywhere else but in the States—"

"Not my problem."

Cesar slumped down in his chair and stared out a small window in his manager's office. He would have to cross the river whose waters separated the sides of his life that had never coexisted in peace.

తించిన

Cesar arrived at the field carrying several boxes. Padre Esteban was already there with the final fourteen boys who had been selected for the traveling team. They were Angel Macias, Enrique Suarez, Baltazar Charles, Fidel Ruiz, Norberto Villarreal, Francisco Aguilar, Rafael Estrello, Jesus Contreras, Pepe Maiz, Gerardo Gonzales, Roberto Mendiola, Alfonso Cortez, Mario Ontiveros and Ricardo Treviño.

"They're very excited that you're coming with us," said the preist. "I knew God would guide you."

"Oh, *He* guided me alright."

During this dialogue, the boys remained seated by the grotto and Cesar noticed that they neither moved nor took their gaze from the statue of the Dark Virgin.

"Are they praying again?" Cesar asked the priest.

"No," he answered.

"Then what are they doing?"

"They're watching the little bird."

"What bird?"

"There, the little one. . . in the flowers."

Cesar strained his eyes and finally saw the object of the boys' attention. Seemingly suspended in midflight was a green and yellow hummingbird.

Padre Esteban pulled Cesar closer to him and whispered, "I told them that when they could see the wings of the little bird they could hit any pitch."

"You don't really believe that, do you?"

Padre Esteban shrugged. "They do. . ."

"That's some consolation for the forsaken."

"Perhaps, but it seems the Lord has provided," the priest said, looking at the boxes Cesar had placed on the ground.

In a few minutes, Padre Esteban asked the boys to gather closer to Cesar.

"Señor Bremer paid for these, but you boys earned it with your sweat," Cesar said and pulled open the flaps of the boxes.

There eventually would be several sponsors, Vidriera Monterrey, Cia Metalurgica de Peñoles, Anderson Clayton and Tubacero, and they would name the team: "Los Ligas Pequeñas Industrial de Monterrey, Association Civil."

José Gonzales Torres from Peñoles would accompany them on their trip to Texas as an assistant to Cesar. Ten years earlier, he worked for the American Metals Company whose headquarters were in New York. He had helped organize one of Monterrey's first baseball teams in an adult Catholic league.

The boys excitedly rifled through the cartons to find uniforms and cleats. They were so elated that they stripped down to their underwear and began to change on the spot. The families and friends who watched from the bleachers stood up and cheered as the boys paraded around in their uniforms for the very first time. Across each boy's chest was emblazoned the name Monterrey written in script.

"Padre, my coming along wasn't totally my choice," Cesar confessed.

"Even Moses resisted God's call to lead His people."

⋐◉◉◉⋑

Padre Esteban gathered the whole team at the church after practice. While they performed various chores, Cesar sat with Maria in the pews. Her attention was momentarily diverted when she observed several of the boys limping.

"What happened to them?"

"Nothing, I'm just making them wear their cleats all week."

"But their feet will blister," she said with some concern.

"Better now than at the game," he answered.

"I'm glad you're not my coach."

"Me too—I'd rather be your boyfriend. So how 'bout that date I've been asking you on for weeks?"

"Cesar, it's time for you to meet my father. It is only proper."

"I doubt he'll approve of me."

"I told him you were a manager in the American Major Leagues. That's very impressive."

"*Mmm*. . . I don't know."

"You can't play with my heart like it is a baseball."

"We leave for Texas tomorrow, but we'll be back by Wednesday. Tell your father I will come by that night."

"You sure you'll be there this time?"

"I promise."

"I've heard that before."

"I thought you forgave me," Cesar sighed.

"Yes. But that doesn't mean I believe you."

"Wednesday. I promise."

∾৩৩৶

The sun was about to roll down the far side of the Sierra Madres. Only a flickering of candles provided the scantest hint of illumination in the church. Sitting in a semicircle before the altar, the boys watched as the priest prepared a special jar of blessed ointment. Enrique, who sat on the far left of the circle, handed Padre Esteban his glove. He watched curiously as the priest slowly poured a few drops of sacred oil into its webbing.

"Ointment and perfume rejoice the heart: so doth the sweetness of a man's friend by hearty counsel," Padre Esteban said quoting Proverbs 27:9 (KJV), as he methodically rubbed the oil into the glove and worked the leather as if he were kneading a ball of dough.

"What does that mean, Padre?" asked Enrique.

"It means, tie this up with something round inside it and sleep with it under your pillow."

One by one, the boys handed Padre Esteban their gloves and each one received this special benediction.

∾৩৩৶

It was a particularly busy night for Padre Esteban. He paid a special visit to Baltazar Charles' family in their small house in Colonia Industrial. Baltazar's parents had asked the priest to come and speak to their son. Baltazar had cared so long for his sister, Patricia, that he was suddenly afraid to leave her. The priest talked to Baltazar for a while as he and Patricia prepared to say their bedtime prayers. In the end, they were his sister's reassuring words, not those of Padre Esteban, that eased Baltazar's mind.

"Balta, you must go. If you don't because of me, I'll never forgive you," she said.

"But who'll help you if—"

"It's only for a few nights. You can't stay with me my whole life," Patricia insisted.

Before Padre Esteban left, Baltazar implored him to make a special blessing for Patricia. The priest did and stayed until both children were asleep. Patricia slept in the only bed in the room, with Baltazar by her side on a makeshift mattress on the floor.

"Blessed are the pure in heart: for they shall see God," the priest whispered a phrase from Matthew 5:8 (KJV), as he left them for the night.

✍◎෮✍

"Don't you have to get up early?" Lucky asked Cesar as the two of them washed down their thirst at a local bar.

"Speaking of that, what are you doing for the next couple of days?" Cesar asked his unsuspecting friend.

"What I always do. Work—but, not that hard I hope." Lucky laughed and took another long swig of his beer.

"I was thinking you'd come with us to McAllen." These words precipitated Lucky's expelling a spray of beer onto Cesar's shirt.

"You always get in trouble when you do that," he said.

"What?" asked Cesar.

"Think."

"Sure, get the team its franchise and then bail out on them."

"Me bail? Until this afternoon you weren't even going. I've filled my quota of saving your ass."

"Come on, I could use your help. It's only for a couple days."

"What am I gonna do, tag along as their batboy?"

"I'll pick up your bar tab for a week."

"Two weeks."

"Deal. Let's drink to Monterrey Industrial and our luck," said Cesar as he raised his beer.

Lucky followed suit and said, "If I'm so lucky, why do I feel like a giant gift horse has been left on my doorstep?"

∾⊙⊙∾

That evening, as it always did, the Mitras Hill dismissed the day from the west side of Monterrey. Its religious profile is an eternal monument of the faith the working town has in God. At night, with no electricity to light homes or even streetlamps, Monterrey's poor *colonias* were shrouded in the kind of ink-black darkness that usually can be found only in the desert.

Few in Monterrey had watches or clocks, so time was demarcated by sunrises, sunsets and factory whistles. Even fewer people had calendars, as days blended into weeks, which in turn became years. Monterrey was a place of generations changed by not changing at all.

The boys, though were very aware of the date: July 28, 1957. In a few hours, they'd leave their families, their town and their country to play an official baseball game in McAllen, Texas. They'd played games amongst themselves, keeping score and calling balls and strikes, but this would be different.

Tonight they shared the restless thrill of an unknown journey that awaited them across the night's horizon.

∾⊙⊙∾

It was past midnight when Oralia entered Angel's room and sat down on the floor next to his bed. Angel held his string-tied glove tightly in his arms. His countenance bespoke a calmness that she rarely saw as her son forged through the daily storm that was his childhood.

"You fought me when you were born, as if you didn't want to come into the world, and now you're leaving me tomorrow," she spoke softly to his sleeping form. "Pedro would have been eighteen now." The doctor said I would never be able to have another, but six years later I carried you. It was a miracle, but then Pedro fell ill. I felt that God had punished me for something terrible, and Umberto. . .

he just closed his heart and crawled so deep in a bottle that he's never found his way out."

⌒◦⌒◦⌒

The next morning, as most of the team assembled in *Plaza de José Marti*, Angel was still at his house. He was in uniform, and Oralia was making sure he looked just right.

"Where does he think he's going?" asked a hungover Umberto, who had come out of the bedroom. It was a rare sight to see him awake this early.

"To Texas, with the team. Remember?" Angel said.

"I don't remember sayin' you could go," he gruffly told Angel.

"Umberto, you swore—" pleaded Oralia.

"Even if I swore to God, he's still not going. When I was his age, I could pour molten steel."

"Papa, I'm going," Angel stated as if there could really be no other possible decision.

The two stared at each other, and Oralia could feel Umberto's temper rising as he moved toward Angel. Breathing heavily through his nose, Umberto let out a nasty, cheap tequila odor that flew inside Angel's lungs, but the boy did not back away. He stood firmly, matching Umberto's gaze with no emotion in his eyes. Neither fear nor anger pervaded his expression. He was going, not to disrespect or spite his father, he just was.

Umberto exhaled sharply and turned his eyes away from his son.

"Why not? One less mouth to feed around here for a couple of days," he grunted.

⌒◦⌒◦⌒

Pepe Maiz arrived at the square before Angel could make his way to Colonia Cantu. His father's sedan was parked on the far side of the square from where the rest of the boys waited. Señor Maiz opened the trunk and handed Pepe a leather valise.

Pepe looked at his teammates and noticed that all of them carried brown grocery store bags.

"Wait, Papa," Pepe said to his father. He opened the valise and grabbed a single pair of underwear.

"What about all the nice things your mother carefully packed for you?" his father asked.

"It's okay, Papa, I'll be fine."

Pepe went across the street and sat down on the curb. Enrique walked over to him.

"Here," said Enrique, holding open his paper bag. Pepe put his extra pair of underwear in with Enrique's.

⌇⌇⌇⌇

It was only a few minutes after seven o'clock, but already Angel Macias' face was smudged with soot. He looked sheepishly down at his feet when Cesar called to him to get on the bus. Everyone was already seated, and the excitement was immense.

"Come on, Angel!" his friends called from the bus' open windows.

Angel appeared like a waif against the looming background of Monterrey's skyline of great, long stacks, which spewed columns of black smoke into the orange-and-gray-tinged sky.

With one big stride and bolt, he jumped onto the steps as the door of the bus closed behind him.

The boys of Monterrey Industrial were ready to go. They were ready to play ball.

10

The Long Walk

The doors of the old bus closed, and it headed out of Monterrey, bearing right at the fork that became Route 40. On board with Cesar Faz were the fourteen boys of the Monterrey Industrial Little League team, Harold "Lucky" Haskins, José Gonzales Torres and their priest, Padre Esteban.

As the bus wound its way out of town, Padre Esteban thought about how Monterrey, while poor, had no shortage of natural beauty. Each morning, the first rays of light bounce off the peaks of the majestic Cerro de la Silla, sun symbol of this northern sultana. As a guardian of the South-east, there is the imposing Madre Sierra that conserves in each extreme two beautiful canyons: the Huajuco, which can be seen from the Gulf of Mexico, and the Huasteca, which is lost in the search for the center of the republic. Completing the circle, to the north of the city extends the Picachos Mountains; through its folds men forged a route toward the U.S. border.

Jesus "Chuy" Contreras was so excited that he stuck his thin arm out one of the windows and waved to anyone whose attention he could get.

"Chuy!" Cesar yelled, nervously eyeing his dangling limb. A tragedy wasn't likely, but for these kids unlikely tragedies were part of their lives.

"Don't you know how to behave on a bus?"

"He's never been in one," said Roberto Mendiola.

"It's the same as a car, just bigger," said Cesar.

"I've never been on one of those either, Señor Faz," said Chuy.

"That's impossible!" exclaimed his coach. "How do you get to school?"

"I walk, Señor Faz."

Of course he did, Cesar sighed to himself as he gazed at the unwashed faces of the boys who comprised the Monterrey Industrial Little League team. They were heading for a competition in the home of the best baseball in the world, yet they seemed eager and unafraid, displaying only the exuberance of youth and its unfettered optimism.

Black emissions spewed from Monterrey's ever-exhaling smokestacks and could be seen for miles. Cut off from the Central Plateau by the Sierra Madre Oriental range, the pollutants formed a haze that continued until they were far from Monterrey's valley.

Few of the working class had the opportunity to leave Monterrey. One of the fortunate few was Baltazar Charles' Uncle Ramiro, who worked for many years as a chauffeur for a very important businessman in Mexico City. Whenever his employment took him back to Monterrey, Ramiro would stop by Baltazar's house where he would regale those at the dinner table with stories about his exotic travels.

"One time, my Uncle Ramiro went to Veracruz," Baltazar told Angel. "He said that he went into the ocean and had to fight a shark with his bare hands. He was so exhausted that he fell asleep in the middle of the sea and woke up in Cuba where a whole tribe of dark people took him and tied him up."

"What for?" asked Angel.

"They have magical powers and they eat people!" said Baltazar with a look of a child referring to a monster under his bed.

"No way," said Pepe as he and the other boys listened.

"It's true, I tell you," repeated Baltazar.

"I think he's right," Ricardo chimed in. "My grandpapa worked the sugar fields in Haiti. He told me about *Santeria*. . ."

"Voodoo!" came the muted whispers of some other boys.

"What happened to your uncle?" asked Norberto.

"He always carried a knife and candies in his pocket, so when the tribe left to gather vegetables for his cooking, he saw a monkey walking down the tree were he was tied up. He whistled and caught the monkey's attention. The monkey went in his pocket to get the candy and when he did, he knocked the knife out. When the monkey left, my uncle grabbed the knife with his foot, cut his ropes and escaped as the cannibals chased him with poison-tipped spears."

That was the end of it. Nobody questioned the veracity of the story, at least not publicly. They all dispersed slowly when Cesar yelled, "Boys, don't sit in the aisle! Go to your own seats."

The heat was stifling, and the men's T-shirts had already absorbed all the sweat their bodies had to yield. The boys seemed immune to the heat, perhaps lifted by the feeling of freedom that only moving through the world can provide.

"I've never gone this far," said Angel as he watched from the window.

"I'm a little scared," Norberto said. "Do you think we really have any chance to win?"

"Why not? No one knows us in Texas, they don't know what our fathers do, they might as well believe we're rich."

"Or winners?" Norberto added.

"Yeah, winners," Angel agreed.

⋘◎◎⋙

The desert spread in every direction like a vast sea of sagebrush broken by an occasional *saguaro*. Their multipronged arms stood in defiance of the parched earth below. Even fire, which had cut a black swath in the terrain, had failed to kill one such stubborn cactus. From its charred limb, Cesar could detect something green protruding from its burned shell.

"God can breathe life anywhere He chooses," said Padre Esteban, noticing the object of Cesar's attention.

"A fitting home for snakes and scorpions, not men," reflected Cesar.

"All places have their purpose."

"Here, a man can lose his mind."

"Or find his soul."

Cesar watched the desert undulating into the horizon, and between earth and sky appeared a thick clear liquid that appeared in constant flux without going anywhere.

"Would you care to join me and the team in prayer for a safe journey?" Padre Esteban asked, fingering the crucifix that hung from his neck.

Cesar shrugged his shoulders. "I used to pray for things, but they never came true."

"It doesn't work like that," said the priest.

"I guess not. These kids pray all the time and look at their lives."

"God brought you to them."

"Perhaps He was punishing them," Cesar teased.

Eventually, the bus pulled into its final destination at Reynosa's northernmost bus terminal. It had taken five hours. There was no bus service from here to McAllen, and they could not afford a private taxi service. They would have to walk the rest of the way.

Ahead of them lay the Rio Bravo del Norte and ten miles beyond that their destination: Baldwin Park in McAllen, Texas.

The boys waited while Lucky and Cesar went over the paperwork with the *Oficial de Migracion*. The Mexican official was friendly, bordering on indifferent. His job was easy. There was no alien traffic heading south, and it was no skin off his back if some of his fellow countrymen wanted to relocate north. He checked their papers with the scantest of scrutiny.

"*Buena Suerte. Lo miro en tres dias* [Good luck. See you in three days]," said the official, waving them through.

His U.S. counterpart at the International Passage, however, was very different.

"Purpose of your visit?" asked Sgt. Clayton Harbush, U.S. Army retired. He studied the boys' visas, and though Cesar had a U.S. passport, the sergeant looked at his with extra suspicion.

"Baseball," Cesar responded, hoping to elicit a smile from the taciturn official.

"*Mmm*. You fixin' to come back, right?"

"Of course."

"See that you don't accidentally leave any behind," snapped Harbush. He wasn't an evil man, but after twelve years of chasing thousands of illegals and the drowning of an entire family in the river the week before, he had exhausted his on-the-job humor.

Angel focused his gaze upon a photograph of Dwight D. Eisenhower.

"*¿Quien es ese hombre viejo?*" he asked, tugging on Cesar's shirt.

"What's he sayin'?" asked the gruff sergeant.

"He just asked who that old man was," Cesar answered.

"You tell that *mojadito* that this old man is the president of the United States, and we don't take kindly to folks who don't show respect, especially when they's guests." He then pointed out how he'd once seen "Ike" from a distance in Portsmouth, England, when he served in "W-W-Two" and how it would behoove all of Cesar's boys to remember their proper place.

With the team finally cleared for entry, they paused for a moment before continuing, with trepidation of what lay on the other side. It wasn't very far to Texas soil, not in terms of distance, but the slowly ebbing waters below had drowned the blood and tears of so many who had risked everything to cross it.

As they made their way across the bridge, they saw a sign at the halfway point that said, "Welcome to the United States." Below it was a bumper sticker that declared, "In God We Trust." Over the word "God" someone had handwritten "Texas."

"Is this America?" asked Ricardo, once they all stood firmly on U.S. soil. Ahead lay a flat and endless valley of dry sagebrush and chaparral; the no-man's-land between the river and the outskirts of the border city of McAllen.

With the mercury floating mercilessly around ninety-eight degrees, they began their long hike. Ten miles without water or shade, all just to play a baseball game that most likely would reward them with defeat.

Cesar turned to Lucky and said, "Imagine, a group of Mexicans just crossed the Rio Grande without getting their feet wet!" He had intended it to be funny, but Lucky detected the anger in his voice.

"Were you paranoid *before* everyone was out to get you?" asked Lucky.

"Why'd that guard question my passport while you breezed right through?"

"'Cause I left the chip on my shoulder at home."

Chip or not, Cesar's shoulder supported a bag of bats that he shifted from one side to the other. Cesar always knew he would return to the States, but he never envisioned it would be on foot, following in the shadow of a band of hapless Mexican children.

They walked double-file along Twenty-Third Street, which led toward the center of McAllen. Heat and dust combined to parch throats, and the street became so hot that the rubber tips of their cleats began to stick on the tar and asphalt.

"What's wrong, Beto?" Cesar asked his first-string catcher.

"Nothing, Señor Faz," replied Norberto. He had been lagging behind, and Cesar thought he detected a slight limp as the young player hurried to catch up.

Locals peered out of storefront windows to watch this strange caravan of uniformed boys carrying grocery bags, who walked proudly under the challenging sun. They were an unusual sight, but nothing compared to how strange America appeared to the boys. Everything was different: storefronts, telephone poles, cars, even the neat curb-lined streets and bright red fire hydrants.

They finally reached the Grand Courts Hotel, an inexpensive motel about a half-mile from Baldwin Park. It had nothing to recommend itself other than a small pool in the rear that was surrounded by a chain-link fence. As dismal as it was, it still appeared as an oasis for these thirsty, weary kids.

"A pool!" yelled Ricardo.

"Can we take a swim, Señor Faz?" asked Enrique, already unbuttoning his shirt.

"Yeah, a swim!" added several other excited voices.

"No swimming," Cesar sternly told them. It was not easy to avert their attention, having come so close to a cool body of water. "Look, boys, you can choose between five things: the movies, candy, sodas, swimming or being champions."

"Did you hear what you just said?" asked Lucky.

"Yeah, I said they didn't come all this way to fool around."

"Not that. . . you said *champions*."

"No, I didn't."

"Yes, you did," replied Lucky.

"You're hearing things, old man."

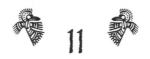

Opening Day

La Mesa's first game of the California State Tournament was against Rolando, and Joe McKirahan would be the starting pitcher. The McKirahans wouldn't need to travel very far for their opening games; they'd be played at Rolando Park. It was located at the corner of Vigo and Alamo Way in the heart of La Mesa. Two of Joe's friends played for Rolando, but that wouldn't stop him from trying to strike them out just the same.

Mrs. McKirahan had made Joe flapjacks with warm butter and maple syrup. Joe was already in his baseball pants by the time he came down for breakfast. There was no game today, but all the coaches and players were invited to the field for team photos. They'd all get to ride down Main Street in the town's fire engines, and the mayor would kick off the local tournament with a speech and a special raffle for a brand-new Stingray bicycle. Afterward, Joe and his friends would spend their allowances at the traveling amusement park that had been set up at the field.

Joe couldn't wait to get to the fair's rides and games. He always won the biggest prizes when the contests involved throwing balls at targets.

Mrs. McKirahan watched her son down the pile of pancakes and she smiled as Joe begged for seconds. As a waitress in a local restaurant, she was no stranger to making sure customers' appetites were satiated. Similarly, her husband, Ralph was no stranger to athletic competition. He directed the local YMCA, which made him a natural to be La Mesa's coach. But more importantly, he had already been to the Little League World Series. Two years earlier, Joe's older brother, Ronald, had played on the San Diego, team which had gone all the way to Williamsport, Pennsylvania. They didn't win the championship, but the McKirahan family had come close enough to taste it. Now it would be Joe's turn to strive for the ultimate prize.

⁊ᴏᏇᴏᴖ

Twenty-three-year-old Frances Maria Stevens worked for the *McAllen Gazette*. She was born two days after the St. Louis Cardinals beat the Detroit Tigers in the seventh game of the 1934 World Series. Her father had intended to name his son Frank—after Frankie Fritsche, his favorite player on the Cards—but after hearing the words, "It's a girl," his wife drew the line at the name Frances. Defiantly, he still called her Frankie and the nickname stuck.

Frankie studied journalism at the University of Texas in Austin and worked her way up the staff at *The Daily Texan*, the student-run newspaper. It was an era when only a minority of women matriculated at college and fewer pursued careers. Frankie applied for a job at *Life* and *Time*, but such positions were rarely available to young women. So she took the job at the *Gazette* and wrote stories about politics, international events and sometimes stories so mundane that not even the people mentioned in the articles found them newsworthy. Everyone assumed that her dad had helped her get the job, but in reality she was a very good journalist and the most competent member of Charlie "Mac" Thompkin's staff.

Frankie tore yesterday's page from her desk calendar and sat back in her chair staring at the date, July 29, 1957. It was barely ten o'clock in the morning and the thermometer broke ninety-five degrees for the sixth straight day. It's said that in the summer the devil prefers hell 'cause it's cooler than Texas.

Bobby Dawkins, the newest staff member at the paper, was adjusting the fan, and Frankie's other colleague, Hank Valerie, was tracking down an annoying fly with a rolled-up copy of yesterday's paper. As Frankie typed, she found her fingers synchronized with the rat-tat-tat of the fan.

Charlie, the editor-in-chief, came into the reporters' pool. No one looked up. They all knew he had an assignment, and only a fool or a masochist would want to go outside today. It wasn't much better in the office, but at least they had that fan and a water cooler.

Charlie was a burly man with a belly that hung over his beltless pants, which were held up by suspenders. Dangling from his lips was a severely chewed cigar.

"I need you to cover the Little League tournament," Charlie said to Bobby. Frankie and Hank tried to look busy without acknowledging Bobby's run of bad luck. That's what rookies were for.

But Bobby said something about his wife being pregnant and how her water was about to break, and frankly, he embarrassed Charlie enough that he turned to look at the others.

Hank's words came faster, "Chief, I got the Governor Daniels' story on deadline and I'm working up something on this record heat wave. Besides, Frankie here knows a lot more about baseball than I do." Hank sold her out faster than a dying man in a desert would for a canteen of water.

"Oh, come on, Charlie," Frankie pleaded, "a Little League game. . . ?"

"Krolick's Tire Company is a sponsor and they buy plenty of advertising space, so stop complaining and just cover the dang event," Charlie replied. "Besides, Hank's right. You know more about baseball than any guy on our staff."

"Yeah, and I hate the game."

"You hate baseball? What're you, a communist?" asked Bobby.

"When I was a little girl, my dad bought me a glove for my fifth birthday and a bat for my seventh."

"Didn't you play with dolls?" Bobby asked.

"Sure, as long as they had crew cuts and wore Cardinals uniforms. Besides, my camera is busted," she said.

"Here, take mine," offered Hank with a huge smile on his face.

"Thanks, buddy," she scowled.

"I hear there are two teams coming from south of the border," said Charlie.

"Is that allowed?" asked Hank.

"Guess so," answered Charlie.

"Well if that don't beat all. What's next, Russian apple pie?"

Bobby said, then mumbled something about it being unholy for foreigners to pose as baseball players. He spit a wad of chaw into a spittoon he kept next to his desk. He could hit that tin pot from five feet and not even touch its rim.

"I heard the team from Mexico City is pretty decent," said Charlie. "Half of 'em is white, you know, sons of rich Americans."

"Five'll get you twenty they don't score a single run against our boys," proclaimed Hank. "Whaddya think, Frankie?"

"I don't know," she said.

"You don't know? It'd be a miracle if they did," Bobby said, laughing.

She thought about his comment. He didn't have to convince her; she'd long ago stopped believing in miracles.

"Well, it's not a bad story line. Play up the invasion angle and how our kids are defending what our granddaddies fought for," added the editor-in-chief.

"And when our boys whup 'em, you can photograph those Mexicans heading home with their tails between their legs," came Bobby's added wisdom.

"Who's the other Mexican team?" Frankie asked.

"Ain't worth your breath," mumbled Charlie.

Charlie might have been a hard ass at times, but he was a good newsman. He had a nose for it. Nonetheless, his scouting report and tip on a story angle did little to pique Frankie's enthusiasm. This wasn't the sort of Pulitzer Prize journalism she had envisioned when she went to college or took the job at the *Gazette*.

Making sure Charlie knew her dissatisfaction, she grumbled as she grabbed her notepad and headed out into the early morning humidity. She had plenty of time, so she decided to grab some breakfast on the way to the field.

ଏ◈ତ

Baltazar pounded steadily on Cesar's door until the coach finally opened it. "What is it Balta?"

"It's Beto," said the out-of-breath boy as he led Cesar back to his and Norberto's room. Entering, Cesar found his catcher lying in bed, crying, his head covered by a sheet he had pulled over his entire body.

"You're burning up," Cesar said, feeling the young boy's forehead.

"What's up, Cesar?" asked Lucky, who had heard the commotion and joined them.

"Fever."

"Señor Faz, my foot, it hurts so much," sobbed Norberto. Cesar pulled off Beto's sock, causing the boy to let out a loud moan. The sole of his right foot had a cut that had become infected.

"How did this happen?"

"A few days ago, on our field—I stepped on a piece of glass."

Turning to Lucky, Cesar said, "I'm going to have to get him to a doctor. You take the team to the field and I'll meet you there."

"He's gonna die, you know," came Baltazar's sobering remark.

"He's just going to the hospital to have his foot fixed," Enrique assured his friends. In particular, Francisco, Rafael and Roberto were very worried about what might happen to Norberto.

"No, I'm serious. My uncle went into a hospital because he had a small pain in his arm and the next thing he is being buried."

"What if Balta's right?" asked Francisco. The boys continued their discussion about Norberto's odds of recovery when they were joined by Padre Esteban.

"Boys, we've got a game to play. Why are you still sitting around?"

"Will Norberto die?" Rafael asked.

"Eventually," the priest answered.

"See!" exclaimed Baltazar.

"Eventually," repeated the priest, and then he finished his original comment, "but not for a long, long time. He's young and has much life ahead of him."

"Arturo was young," said Ricardo, referring to the boy who had plunged to his death a year ago while playing at Fundidora.

"And Pedro. . . ?" shyly added Angel.

"Yes, sometimes death takes the young and innocent," grimaced the priest. "That's why you must always live the life you have without fear."

"Even in baseball?" asked Roberto.

"In everything," answered the priest.

A half-hour later at Texas Children's Hospital, Norberto was given a tetanus shot after a doctor had cleaned and stitched his foot.

"He won't play for a week," said the doctor. "And I'll want him to stay overnight for observation."

Norberto looked down and cried when Cesar translated this diagnosis. He would have to spend the night in a place where no one spoke his language, away from home and his teammates. But far worse than this isolation and the pain of his foot was the thought of missing the game.

Before Cesar left, he asked Norberto, "Why didn't you tell me when this happened?"

"I was afraid you wouldn't let me come with the team."

❧❧❧

The motor coach carrying the team from Harlingen pulled up to the field. As its passengers filed out, their coach, Trent Watkins, stared in disbelief. The *Regiomontanos* were rolling on the ground, flaying their arms and legs as if making snow angels in freshly fallen powder.

"Is my eyes deceivin' me? What're they doin'?" Coach Watkins asked Lucky.

"That's Monterrey Industrial," Lucky answered.

"Ain't they never seen a grass field?"

"'Fraid they haven't," Lucky confessed.

"Well, if that don't beat all," said Coach Watkins with a laugh as the Monterrey kids continued to press themselves into the green velvet-covered field.

"Coach," interrupted one of his players, "are we gonna play 'em or use 'em as fertilizer?"

"I dunno, but I bet they don't smell much better."

The Harlingen players got a good laugh at Monterrey's expense as Lucky waited for Cesar.

"Finally," Lucky said to Cesar when the latter arrived.

"Bad news," Cesar told him. "Norberto's out. I'm gonna replace him with Chuy."

"There's more bad news," Lucky added.

"Great, I haven't filled my quota yet."

"We drew Mexico City." Though the Little League draw was supposedly made by random selection, Cesar couldn't help but wonder if being paired against the only other Mexican team for the opening game was a coincidence.

"Neiderhouser?" asked Cesar.

"Yep."

A few weeks earlier, Lucky had traveled to Mexico City on business. Out of curiosity, Lucky dropped in on one of the Mexico City All-Stars' practices. When he returned, he told Cesar about an ace pitcher named Bobby Neiderhouser who threw a wicked fastball.

Drawing Lucky and Padre Esteban aside, Cesar whispered, "I have an idea."

With the two men briefed, he shared the plan with the players. "Boys, listen up. In a few minutes, it'll be our turn to take batting practice. I'm going to throw pretty fast—too fast for you to hit."

"If we can't hit, it won't make a good practice," said Enrique.

"Every third pitch, I'll ease back and throw one you can clobber. But don't say anything."

"Why, Señor Faz?" asked Baltazar.

"Don't ask me why, just get a bat and remember only to swing at the third pitch."

On the sideline, Lucky invited the Mexico City coaches to watch Monterrey's batting practice. Cesar fired a wild fastball, which ricocheted off the dugout, nearly hitting them. After another blazing fastball, he made a big wind-up and threw a normal pitch to Baltazar who sent it out of the field.

One by one, the rest of the team followed. Each time were two un-touchable fastballs and then a Monterrey hit.

"Your coach throws pretty hard to them!" commented one.

"Yes, our boys just love fastballs," said Lucky. "I hope you have a really fast pitcher for us."

Cesar's ruse worked. Before the last Monterrey batter had taken his practice, the Mexico City coach decided not to use his fastball pitcher, Bobby Neiderhouser. That decision was also based on the fact that the Mexico City coach believed his team would have an easier time against Monterrey than the winner of the

McAllen/Harlingen contest. It made perfect sense to hold Bobby in reserve to face a better team tomorrow. Bobby didn't see it that way at all and angrily slumped onto the bench in the corner of the dugout upon hearing he wouldn't be the starting pitcher.

⊷⊙⊶

It was almost 1:00 PM when Frankie Stevens arrived at Baldwin Park. McAllen's team was already there. Their coach, Chad Terrence, and his assistants were setting up their practice equipment. McAllen's game would be one of the first played. Frankie stood on the sideline and loaded film into Hank's Valerie model 150 Polaroid Land Camera.

Noticing the Mexico City team stretching and playing Pepper on the sideline, she walked over to take a few photos before their game. She was curious to see how these Mexican boys played baseball, even though Mac had instructed her to cover McAllen's game on the primary field.

"Excuse me, do you mind?" she said to Cesar who had moved into her line of sight while she was trying to photograph Bobby Neiderhouser.

"Sorry, señora?" came Cesar's reply.

"Do you mind?" she asked again, waving her camera, so he'd get her meaning.

Misunderstanding her gesture, he struck a pose. She rolled her eyes and took the photo, deciding it was faster to waste a photo than try to explain herself further.

"I'm Cesar Faz."

She said nothing.

"Coach of the Monterrey Industrial Little League team," he continued. Cesar noticed that she wore Levi's and light-colored snakeskin cowboy boots. Her hair was pinned up and nestled underneath a beige cowboy hat.

"Coach Faz, I noticed your team sat for about ten minutes over there at staring a birdbath. What were they doing?" she asked him.

"They were looking at the wings of a hummingbird, I suspect," Cesar told her.

Frankie stared at him and didn't speak. Cesar realized how silly what he just had said must have sounded, so he tried to explain. "Their priest told them that seeing its wings will help their batting eyes," Cesar added.

"Coach Faz, no offense, but a hummingbird flaps its wings more than sixty times a second. You don't really believe it's possible, do you?"

Cesar looked at her with his dark, penetrating eyes. "I never believe in anything I can't see."

⌀⌀⌀

Cesar called over Angel and Enrique.

"You've both worked hard, and you'll both get to pitch today, but only one of you can start. I'll leave it for you to decide," he said to them as he went to work on the rest of the lineup.

"You found our baseball," Enrique said rationally. "You start."

Just then, several of the Mexico City players recognized the Monterrey boys. "Hey look, it's the *puercos*," one said. "I can't believe they have a team."

"Do we have to play six innings? I want to eat dinner before tomorrow," sniped another.

Juan, their catcher, eyed Enrique. "Your girlfriend was so nice. When you get home tomorrow, don't forget to tell her who whupped you."

"No. You start, Enrique," Angel said, handing him the game ball. "It's your chance."

"For glory?"

"For Gloria," Angel said. The two smiled.

On their knees in the dugout, the Monterrey Industrial Little League team formed a tight circle around Padre Esteban.

"Holy cow, now they're holding hands," said one Mexico City player who observed the strange ritual from across the field.

"They're saying a prayer, stupid," answered Juan.

"They need one," teased their coach.

Who travels with a priest? Frankie wondered as she went back to the other field to cover McAllen. She presumed it was no stranger than letting the players believe they could see the wings of a hummingbird. Frankie shook her head, feeling at once pity and envy at their naiveté.

12

A Friendly Wager

"P-l-a-a-a-a-a-y b-a-a-a-l-l-l!"

If any words could define the spirit of baseball, it would be these two that Umpire Earl Mabry yelled at the top of his lungs. Earl worked as one of the mechanics over at Krolick's. All week, he was a grease monkey who had to lie underneath cars and snap to attention and say, "Yes, sir" and "No ma'am," while everyone complained about their cars. But the moment he yelled, "Play ball!" he was the master of everyone and everything on the field before him.

Enrique took his position on the mound. With his right foot perpendicular to the rubber, he rocked forward then back, tapping the rubber once with his cleat as his hands rose above his head, coming together at their highest point. His left leg coiled across his torso, momentarily suspended in the air, then sprang forward as his right arm sliced toward home plate like the blade of a windmill.

"Low, ball one," Earl said in a subdued tone.

The Texas Little League Tournament was under way.

Enrique understood the umpire's call. For weeks before their trip, the boys went to sleep at night, memorizing words that Cesar highlighted in his copy of the baseball rulebook. In school or at play, they practiced these words with each other, as if sharing a secret language that they alone understood: *bunt, steal, tag, home run, Take your base* and *Batter-up!* As long as they could count to four in English, *balls, strikes* and *outs* could be easily accounted for.

In the top of the first inning, Mexico City struck quickly. A walk and a couple of base hits had already brought a runner across home plate. The Mexico City kids were razzing the Monterrey team real good from their bench. Enrique was beginning to feel the heat.

"That's ball four," Earl sent another Mexico City batter on his way to first, loading the bases.

"Time!" Cesar called out.

"Time-out is called," confirmed Earl as Cesar crossed the third-base line on the way to the mound for a conference with his pitcher.

"Settle down, Enrique."

"Señor Faz, they won't shut up."

"Don't let them get to you," he said to Enrique while glancing over at the opposing team's bench.

"I wasn't talking about them, I'm talking about *them*," he said, gesturing to his own defense.

Cesar ran to the outfield.

"You're driving Enrique crazy. What's going on here?" he asked.

"I called Carl Furillo first," said Rafael Estrello.

"He was Furillo last week, it's my turn," complained Pepe Maiz.

"No, he's Duke Snider."

"You can be Carl Furillo," Cesar said, to Rafael, "but I hear that Duke Snider gets all the girls."

Pepe smiled, satisfied in conceding that Rafael could be Furillo. As Cesar walked away, Rafael turned to Pepe and told him, "Next time, I call Duke Snider!"

A refreshing breeze crossed the field, and with a little peace and quiet, Enrique got the next batter to pop up to Baltazar in the infield, preventing any runners from advancing. The boys congratulated one another; the last time they faced this team they hadn't gotten a single Mexico City All-Star out.

"Coach, you might want to remind your players it still takes three outs to end an inning," the umpire told Cesar.

Resuming their positions, Enrique struck out the next batter, and the final hitter bounced a grounder to Angel at shortstop to end the inning.

"Okay, boys, we only gave up one run. We're still in this game," Cesar rallied his team.

Several innings later, with Monterrey still down one to nothing, Mario Ontiveros drew a walk and jogged to first base. Next up was

Enrique who dug his cleats into the batter's box. He had struck out his first time up.

When the pitch came, Enrique and his bat remained frozen.

Strike one.

Rubbing his eyes, he stepped back in the box and stared at the pitcher who wound up and hurled another fastball. The same thing happened again; he didn't swing.

Strike two.

Juan, the catcher, made a sniffing sound. "Smells like pig around here," he continued taunting Enrique in a language the umpire couldn't understand. Enrique waited patiently.

The third pitch was delivered and Enrique clobbered it. It sailed over the chain-link fence in center field. As Enrique rounded the bases, his whole team came out of the dugout to cheer and meet him at home plate.

Cesar pulled off his cap. A home run! It was amazing. In one swing, Enrique had given Monterrey the lead for the first time.

Before returning to the dugout on the shoulders of his teammates, Enrique turned and gave Juan a long smile. "Not bad for a *puerco*, eh?"

To calm his own team, Mexico City's coach called out, "A lucky shot! Don't worry, boys!"

In the dugout, Ricardo Treviño congratulated Enrique again.

"It slowed down, Ricardo."

"What did?"

"The baseball. I swear I could see its stitches."

❧❦❧

Few local residents were interested in the outcome of the all-Mexican game, except for some migratory Hispanic workers who sat on a berm along the third-base line. Frankie watched the McAllen game and found her mind wandering from boredom. The most entertaining thing about it was the commentary of the fans. Frankie was amazed at how caught up in the game the parents got—especially the fathers who tried to relive moments of sporting glory or compensate for athletic careers that never blossomed. If a child bobbled a ball or threw it to the wrong base, his dad would spit some chaw and look as dejected as if his son had been diagnosed with some shameful disease.

"Friend of mine went to Mexico once, staking out a silver claim," a spectator remarked to Frankie, referring to the contest taking place on the other field. "Said it wasn't much better than a cesspool. Folks living on dirt floors, eating food that spoiled almost as fast as they could get it."

"Well, you'll be playing one of those teams tomorrow."

"Good, we could use an easy one," he said, laughing.

"You've got to win today first."

The man grunted and then said, "I'm gonna get me a *dawg*."

She'd once read that Humphrey Bogart said that a hot dog at the ballpark is better than a steak at the Ritz. She doubted it would taste that good and she wasn't really that hungry, but she figured getting it would be something to do.

"Sounds like a good idea," Frankie stood up and stretched her legs.

There was an old man called "Pop" who had a little food concession at the field. Folks could get anything they wanted, so long as it was a hot dog. Smoke rose from his little shack; it had to be 130 degrees inside.

Frankie took hers with mustard and bought an orange soda to wash it down.

"Anyone tell you the score of the other game?" she asked Pop.

"Two to one."

"Really? I didn't think the Monterrey team could keep it so close," she said, shaking her head.

"They's the ones with the two," said Pop.

⁂

By the bottom of the fifth inning, the Mexico City All-Stars' bench was quiet. Monterrey still held on to its fragile lead. Desperate and realizing his mistake too late, Mexico City's coach asked Bobby Neiderhouser to go in the game and relieve their starting pitcher. Still offended, Bobby refused.

Bobby's father headed the Ford Foundation in Mexico City and he had grown up in the halls of influence and power. There was little the coach could do.

Conversely, though Cesar had originally planned to pitch both Enrique and Angel, he held off, realizing that should his team win, he'd need Angel tomorrow.

A combination of cockiness and some inspired play by Mexico City allowed them to rally with two outs and score the tying run. Only a great play by Pepe prevented the go-ahead runs from crossing the plate.

The Mexico City bench came alive. In the Monterrey dugout, the mood swung from eager anticipation to morbid despair.

"Keep your faith," said the priest.

"God rarely rewards arrogance," Cesar said to Padre Esteban.

"He's testing their mettle," answered the priest.

"He's testing my sanity," said the coach.

Cesar gathered the boys. "You all look like there's a funeral. They just tied the game, that's all. It's part of baseball, so get used to it. Sometimes we score, sometimes they do—that's how it works. Remember, victory is like the beautiful woman who waits on the dance floor for the last man standing, the one who didn't quit."

If his boys didn't keep their cool, the momentum of the game would surely change. Cesar watched nervously as Jesus "Chuy" Contreras grabbed a bat.

"Don't be scared, Chuy," Cesar consoled him.

"I'm not, Señor Faz. If I die, I want my mama to know that I didn't run away at the last moment."

"Who's talking about dying?"

Chuy didn't get a hit, but he did foul off four straight pitches until the Mexico City pitcher lost his concentration and walked him.

A rally had begun.

Baltazar and Pepe followed with hits to load the bases. Once again the Mexico City coach asked Bobby Neiderhouser to go in and once again he refused.

The *Regiomontanos* sent the tide that a half-inning earlier had flowed against them back over the Mexico City team like a crashing wave, stunning them by scoring seven runs. When the final Mexico

City pop-up fell squarely into Ricardo's glove, the team mobbed Enrique at the mound.

"El Cubano" savored this moment. It was one of three things a pitcher never forgets: his mother, his first kiss and his first win.

No one was more surprised than Cesar. He had doubted them, even as they practiced long and hard hours under the Monterrey sun. They proved that they could win a baseball game, but more importantly they showed Cesar that beneath the emblazoned MONTERREY of their uniforms were great hearts that were willing to sacrifice a lot.

ᏋᏬᎾᏌ

McAllen won the game that Frankie covered, though it ended without the drama that marked Monterrey's debut. McAllen's coach, Chadwick Roy Terrence III, invited Cesar and the boys to his home for a real Texas barbeque.

"It is very kind of you to invite us, Mr. Terrence," Cesar told his host. The Terrences lived in a split-level house on Cypress Street, about three blocks from the downtown district. It was a typical house on one of McAllen's typical streets, except tonight its backyard was overrun with American and Mexican Little Leaguers.

"Please, call me Chad. Mr. Terrence is my dad," he answered with a good-natured smile. "Your boys played a helluva game today. No offense, but I never expected you'd win, let alone beat Mexico City nine to two."

"Neither did I. . . neither did I."

Both teams were seated at one of three long picnic tables that had been set up in the Terrences' backyard. "Your kids looked like they could've used a good meal," their host said.

"I think you're just trying to weigh them down for the game tomorrow," said Cesar, laughing.

"They'd have to eat more food than I got to get weighed down. You sure they's twelve?"

"They're tiny, but don't let that fool you. They're pretty gutsy."

"Believe me; I don't intend to underestimate them after today. Hey, how come some of them ain't touched my barbecue? It's larrupin' good!"

"This is more food than they see in a month. Some probably never eat meat at all."

"No wonder my wife's PB and Js are going like hotcakes at a county fair," Chad said and then turned to address his son. "Hey, Jarrett, bring me some more of them ribs."

Down the long table, Mario was struggling to get his mouth unstuck. He'd never experienced the effects of peanut butter before. Lured by its sweet flavor, he was quickly trapped by its pasty consistency.

"What is this stuff?" he barely managed to ask Enrique.

"I don't know, but I can barely breathe," his equally incapacitated friend answered.

Meanwhile, Jarrett brought a huge tray over to his dad. On one half were large beef ribs, slow-cooked in Coach Terrence's smoker. The other side of the tray had warm cornbread and ears of grilled corn, each cob with a long skewer through one end, dripping with butter and mixed with the juices from the meat. Cesar's stomach jumped with excitement.

"Son, say hello to Mr. Faz."

"How do you do, sir?" came the polite response from the crew cut, lightly freckled boy.

"Just fine. Are my boys behaving themselves?"

"I guess so," he shyly answered.

"They aren't?"

"Well, sir, I don't rightly know. Me and my friends can't understand a word they's sayin'."

Cesar grinned. "I watched your team practicing earlier. You got a knack for the game."

"Thank you, sir."

"Careful, son," said Chad, winking at Cesar, "he was just spyin' on us to find our weaknesses."

Cesar laughed and then whispered to Padre Esteban, "*El sabe lo que tu estas haciendo* [He's on to me]."

As the sun set and night critters began to fly around the Terrences' backyard, the kids moved into the family's living room. Coach Terrence had set up a movie projector on which he ran a reel of the 1956 Little League World Series. The Mexican boys were transfixed; few had ever seen a movie.

"So how's about a friendly wager on your team's chances?" asked Chad.

"You mean to see if we go to the World Series?"

"Don't be ridiculous. I mean whether your team makes it to Wednesday."

"I don't know, Chad, I really can't afford to make a bet." Cesar wasn't exaggerating. He barely had enough to last for two more days.

"I don't want to take your money, coach," Chad said, looking at the smaller Mexican kids. "That wouldn't be sportin'."

"Then what do you have in mind?"

"We win, and you have to spend the rest of the day wearin' a ten-gallon hat. Whaddaya say?"

"Fine, but what happens if we win?" Cesar asked him, soliciting a chuckle from Chad.

"Oh, of course. If you win . . ."

❧❦❧

Inside the Terrences' home, Ricardo leaned out of the bathroom's doorway and caught Enrique's attention, signaling for him to come over. Entering the small room, Enrique watched as Ricardo turned on the water in the sink. The two boys stared at the stream of water pouring from the spout.

"This one makes the water hot!" Ricardo said of the other spigot.

"¡Orale!" screeched Enrique.

Ricardo laughed. "Watch this," he said. First he went to the shower and turned it on and then he flushed the toilet. Enrique had to try this one for himself.

"So much water inside a house! Where do they keep it all?"

The boys continued to play with the water, turning on the hot, then the cold, and then taking turns flushing the toilet.

Meanwhile, in the kitchen with Jarrett, Angel was having his own moment of discovery. Jarrett poured two glasses of milk from a bottle he took from the refrigerator.

"Milk," said Jarrett, and then he repeated slowly, "M – I – L – K."

"M – E – E – L – K," mimicked Angel.

"Good!"

"*Bueno*, meelk—*leche*," Angel said.

"Lay chay," said Jarrett, causing Angel to giggle.

"*Si, leche*. . ."

"You want an oatmeal raisin cookie? My mom makes the best," said the McAllen boy, but he could see that Angel didn't understand. Retrieving four of them from a jar on the counter, he gave two to Angel.

"Watch," he said as he proceeded to show Angel how to properly dunk his cookie in the milk. "Like this. *Mmm*, good!"

Angel timidly tried to do the same, but he accidentally dropped his cookie in the glass. Embarrassed, he began to fish the cookie out, but the more soaked it became, the more it crumbled.

"*¡Ay Dios mio, lo siento—se cayo la galleta* [Oh my God, I'm sorry— I dropped my cookie]*!*"

"It's okay, don't panic. It happens to the best of us. Here," Jarrett handing Angel his own glass of milk and last cookie. He watched and laughed as Angel ate them. But his laughter concealed a touch of sadness because Angel consumed his cookie as if he were dining on filet mignon, picking up each crumb from the table and savoring them.

∽◦◐◐◦∾

The boys' jubilation continued at the hospital, where the team went to visit Norberto. Satisfied that their friend was not going to die, the boys jumped on the adjacent empty bed and banged on bedpans, trying to raise Beto's spirits. More than a few times nurses had to ask them to be quiet. The good news was that he'd be released the next day, but the doctor was quite insistent that he not play in their game against McAllen.

∽◦◐◐◦∾

The Grand Courts Motel appeared to be a dive to most Americans. Even truckers who passed through McAllen stayed only as long as they had to before climbing back in their tractor-trailers and hitting the road. But from the boys' perspective, it was luxurious.

They stayed four in a room and though it was well past lights-out, Cesar knew his team would stay up talking well into the night about their escapades that day. Just yesterday they were waiting for a bus in Monterrey; tonight they were the unofficial champions of Mexico. No matter what tomorrow would bring, this evening they were going to cherish their victory like it was the last one they'd ever have.

Cesar also stayed up past his self-dictated curfew, but he wasn't thinking about the victory that afternoon. He thought about Norberto and his lonely night at the hospital, and a torrent of memories came to him about his own mother.

༄

Felicitas Faz worked at the Santa Rosa Hospital on the west side of San Antonio. It was the poorest part of town, and disease and epidemics were commonplace and the hospital was always teeming with people in need of the most basic medical attention.

Cesar couldn't have been more than nine or ten years old at the time. His throat had been hurting for weeks, so each morning he and his mother walked several miles along the brook of San Pedro to reach the hospital's free clinic. After many visits, the triage nurse determined Cesar needed emergency surgery. His tonsils were removed by the on-duty doctor. When he was discharged, his mother was there to meet him for the long walk home.

The hospital was located on La Plaza de Zacate. Here, contractors came to hire day laborers to work the cotton and beet fields. Foremen would cherry-pick the workers who looked like they would give the hardest day's work without complaining. It was a large gathering place where one could walk from one end to the other and hear people reading aloud everything from Mexican newspapers to La Biblia.

Cesar watched a group of workers getting in the back of a pickup, which seemed stuck for a moment before it lurched forward so suddenly that one man fell out the back. He ran to catch the truck, but when he grabbed on to the back gate, another worker ground his heel on the poor man's hand making him fall again into the dust of the street. Perhaps it was an old grudge, or just about getting a little more elbow room for the drive to the fields.

"I hate these people," Cesar told his mother in a whisper since his throat hadn't fully healed.

"Don't ever say that again, Cesar. They're your people, they're just less fortunate," Felicitas replied.

Cesar swore that he'd never become like them, that he'd never work the beet fields or sit around muttering passages of the Bible while praying for Providence.

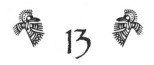

13

A Close Shave

rancisco Aguilar rose the next morning somewhat disoriented. Perhaps it was the unfamiliar look of the smooth white ceiling that stared down at him, or maybe it was the sound of automobile traffic coming in through the slightly ajar window. Whatever the cause, for a few moments, he completely forgot where he was until he began to piece together his memory of the long bus ride and the arrival at the McAllen motel. Searching for something familiar, his anxiety was immediately fueled by the fact that he didn't see Chuy in the bed next to his. Jumping up, he found his friend curled in a fetal position on the floor between their two beds. Chuy was tangled in a single sheet that had been pulled onto the ground.

Jesus "Chuy" Contreras was born in Ramos Arizpe, Coahuila but was brought to Monterrey as a newborn when desperate conditions forced his father to seek work in Mexico's industrial center. The family settled in a small shack in Colonia Lagalde. They shared it with another family. There weren't enough beds to go around, so Chuy and several of his siblings slept on the floor. It was pretty cramped and devoid of comforts, but it had the benefit of being near his father's job at the oldest factory in Monterrey, Cervecería Cuauhtémoc Moctezuma Brewing Company. Its popular Indio beer was actually named something else, but since few people could read, Mexicans asked for it by the picture of a young Indio girl on its clay bottle.

Next to the brewery was Parque Deportivo Cuauhtemoc y

Famosa, a recreation area for management. The park was more than an escape from the barrio's gritty architecture; it provided an opportunity for Chuy to help support his family. He worked for a man who had an old mill on which he hand-pressed *aguamiel,* a kind of Mexican soda made from sugar cane. There was also a tennis court for the highest executives who paid an entrepreneurial Chuy a few pesos an hour to be their ball boy. A month before the McAllen trip, the assistant coach, José Gonzales Torres, had seen him sprinting to catch errant tennis balls and throwing them to the server. José didn't know if Chuy could hit a baseball, but he saw that the young boy had coordination and tremendous stamina.

"Are you hurt?" Francisco asked Chuy after he had shaken his roommate awake. The commotion also awakened Pepe and Roberto.

"Why?"

"I better get Señor Faz," Roberto said. "You fell on the floor."

"No," Chuy grabbed Roberto's arm and pulled him closer. "Please, guys, I don't want to get in trouble. I didn't fall. I just don't know how to sleep in a bed."

Cesar, meanwhile, had already risen and left the motel. It was still too early to get Norberto discharged, so he decided to take a walk through the main part of town. He struck up a conversation with an old African American fellow named Moses who was sweeping the sidewalk in front of his store, a combination barbershop and shoe shine stand.

"Don't recognize you. You with one of them teams here to play baseball?" asked Moses.

"I coach Monterrey Industrial."

"You done come all the way from Mexico?"

"Yep."

"Didn't know kids played baseball there," said Moses.

"It's our first team."

"Ain't that somethin'. Looks like you need a trim and a shave," Moses said to Cesar.

"I've got to get to the hospital," Cesar responded.

"Is everything okay?"

"One of my players cut his foot. He'll be fine if he lays off it. I have to pick him up soon."

Moses smiled and said, "A man always gots time for a shave."

Cesar stood frozen at the threshold weighing which was worse: admitting his poor financial state or hurting the old man's feelings. Moses looked Cesar up and down for a few moments and comprehended Cesar's predicament.

"Come on in and sit down. Your first visit is on the house."

"You sure?"

"Sure I's sure. 'Sides, a busy-looking barber draws more customers."

After a quick trim, Cesar settled back in Moses' chair. The old man tucked a towel into Cesar's collar and layered steaming hot towels over his face, leaving a small hole for Cesar to breathe through. Cesar heard Moses sharpening his straightedge on the long leather strap that hung from the chair. It was an odd fact that when Moses' razor glided over a white patron's neck, the same men who wouldn't tolerate him riding in the front of a bus suddenly trusted him with their lives.

Out on the same street as the barbershop, Ricardo, Angel and Baltazar were looking for Cesar.

"Balta, go on that side," ordered Angel. "Ricardo and I will stay on this one."

As Baltazar slowly passed a small liquor store, a thrift shop and several diners, something caught his attention. Staring at the rotating red, white and blue stripes of the barbershop's "Marvy" pole, its motion momentarily hypnotized him.

"I think one of your players is here," Moses said as he continued sharpening his blade.

Cesar mumbled through the face towels for Moses to invite the boy in.

One glimpse of Moses holding a razor over a man's towel-covered face, however, and Baltazar was flooded by the memories of Uncle Ramiro's stories. Suddenly Baltazar's biggest fears materialized in the welcoming smile of good, old Moses who waved him to come inside. Baltazar ran as fast as he could, leaving no chance for anyone to question his motives.

"Guess he had somewhere to be in a mighty hurry," Moses casually commented. He peeled back the hot towels and began to apply a thick layer of warm lather. "Your team's playing the hometown favorite today," he added and began to glide the blade along the rough surface of Cesar's stubbled face.

"*Mmm hmm*," Cesar said without opening his mouth or moving so much as a hair's width.

"Would be something if you won," Moses smiled. "Yep, it sure would be something."

⌘

The doctor at the hospital had told Cesar that Norberto's foot would need a week to fully heal, but the young catcher was having trouble accepting this prognosis. All the way back to the Grand Courts Motel and then at the field, Norberto pleaded with Cesar to let him play.

Cesar continually denied him; he even resorted to having Padre Esteban talk to Norberto and explain to him what could happen if his foot became infected again or if the stitches tore. But Norberto was relentless, showing Cesar that he could walk just fine.

"Look, Beto, I see that you can walk now, but you can't run," said an annoyed Cesar. "How can I play you if—"

Cesar hadn't finished his sentence when Norberto took off and ran the base path as fast as he could.

"All right, all right. Get a glove and warm Angel up."

"You're starting him?" asked José as Cesar finished the lineup card.

"How can I say no to that kind of courage," replied Cesar.

⌘

When it was McAllen's turn to take the field for its warm-ups, Coach Terrence ran an extension cord and plugged in a mechanical pitching arm. In a moment, its lever wound around slowly, picked up a baseball in its cuplike hand and hurled it at the first McAllen player to take batting practice.

"Jarrett, why don't you start loosening up," the coach said to his son, who took off his pitching jacket and reached for a bag of rosin.

After their allotted time, Coach Terrence called his team in and as the two teams passed, Mario dropped his glove and nearly tripped over it. A McAllen player, Jake Lambeau, picked it up and held it out, but when Mario went to retrieve it, Jake held it up higher. Mario, the second shortest player on the Mexican team, stretched upward and couldn't reach it even when he jumped.

"Hey, guys, y'see this thing? Looks like his mama made it," Jake teased and was quickly joined by several of his teammates in mocking Mario.

"Come on, Jake, give it back," Jarrett interceded.

Jake lowered his hand as Mario grabbed his glove.

"Ain't gonna help him none. This is gonna be like fightin' a one-legged man in a butt-kickin' contest."

Warm-ups were over, and the game was going to start in a few minutes. The groundskeeper was putting the finishing touches on chalking the lines and making the batters' boxes. Cesar loved this moment, the crisp lines were straight and gleamed white. Once the first batter stepped in, the lines would be scuffed by cleats and would never be as perfect as they were right now.

After the teams were announced, all the players stood on their respective baselines. A recording of the "Star Spangled Banner" was played and Cesar made sure his boys held their caps to their chests.

As Angel threw his last practice pitches, Cesar became a little worried as he watched Angel struggling to find his accuracy. Two warm-up pitches flew wild, illiciting some laughs from the McAllen bench. The McAllen team's boys boasted to each other how they couldn't wait to get up and cream a pitch, assuming Angel could throw a single strike.

The game began, and Angel hurried his pitches, not finding the strike zone in any of his first eight tries.

Cesar quickly called time and joined Angel at the mound. His young pitcher shifted nervously from side to side.

"I don't think I can pitch in America," Angel said.

"Do you know an amazing thing about baseball?"

Angel shrugged.

"God made the pitcher's mound the same distance from the plate everywhere in the world," Cesar assured him. "It's no different than our field at home. You just need to slow down a bit. You're rushing your delivery."

"But they're in the batter's box so quickly, and the umpire's already in position—"

"When you pitch, the birds in the sky, the waters of the river, even the sun will wait until you're ready. Understand?"

"Sì, Señor Faz," said Angel.

"We want a pitcher, not a glass of water. . ." came the chant from the McAllen bench as Cesar strolled back to the dugout and play resumed.

The McAllen team's razzing continued louder. "Come on, pitcher, we ain't got all day!" Even if Angel could have understood their words, it was unlikely they could have pierced his concentration as he drifted deeper inside his soul.

When Angel was ready, he began his windup. His eyes narrowed into a singular focus as his arms rose above his head, his head turned slowly to his right and his left leg kicked high. His right arm propelled forward and his hand released the ball at the perfect point in its arc.

"Steeeeriiiiike one!" yelled the umpire.

Okay, not bad, Coach Terrence thought. *Kid's got an arm.*

That arm would confound the batters for the first three innings. It was during this first half of the game that Cesar began to notice it. *It* wasn't that his young pitcher had recorded five strikeouts, three weak groundouts, an infield pop-up and had coolly pitched his way out of two jams. Similar statistics were sure to be happening this afternoon somewhere else in America on the hundreds of Little League fields hosting the tournament. No. . . *it* was the look in Angel's eyes as he bore down on batters to whom he had fallen behind in the count with runners threatening to score. Cesar had seen that look before in Mission Stadium and Sportsman's Park. *It* was the fire that separated the great players from everyone else.

Growing stronger each inning, Angel was unaware of any distractions around him. What made this even more amazing was the effect it was having on his teammates.

Angel was raising the level of play for each and every *Regiomontano*. Players hustled an extra step quicker; and "around-the-horn" throws were delivered with enthusiasm and pride, even following only one out in a long game.

On offense, Monterrey's hitters slowly built a lead of several runs. Victory was far from certain, but with each run scored, the boys' confidence grew as they began to believe that they were just as worthy as any other boy who wore a Little League uniform.

In the fourth inning, Jake's father, John "Boomer" Lambeau, made his way down from the bleachers until he was standing next to the McAllen dugout.

"You can't be serious, lettin' a bunch of wetbacks kick your asses out there."

"Now don't get all swolled up, Boomer," Coach Terrence said. "The boys are doin' the best they can."

"Well maybe that just ain't good enough," he replied. Turning to Jake he added, "*Dangnabbit,* son, you're losin' to a bunch o' midgets!"

Jake walked away from his father.

"Hey, boy, I'm talkin' to you! Come back here!"

Jake turned and looked his father square in the eye. "Dad, I'm on deck."

Before he could take any practice swings, the umpire's voice rose above the noise from the bleachers.

"Steeeeriiiiike three!" yelled the umpire as the side was retired.

The next inning, Monterrey capped off its scoring with their fifth, sixth and seventh runs. Coach Terrence tried to rally his team, and they managed to load the bases in their last at-bat, but it was too little, too late. McAllen went down seven to one.

"Cesar, what's this I heard about a bet you made on the game?" asked Padre Esteban as the boys went to congratulate their opponents.

Cesar laughed. He wasn't sure which punishment Coach Terrence was going to find worse: losing or having to walk around town all day wearing a *sombrero.*

In the parking lot, Boomer got in his car and slammed the door. He barely looked at Jake who slid in the passenger seat. Mario saw this and felt bad for Jake, even though he had taunted him before the game. Mario was surprised that a father could be so angry with his son for losing a baseball game.

Frankie grabbed her camera and walked over to Cesar.

"I'm Frankie Stevens, *McAllen Gazette.* I spoke to you yesterday," she said.

"Yeah, I remember."

"This is the first time Monterrey's been represented in Little League competition. Do you think this game was. . . What're you staring at?"

"I didn't know there were any female sports reporters. Bet it makes you pretty unwelcome in the locker room."

"I'm not a sports reporter, and I bet your beating the home team makes you 'bout as welcome in McAllen as a skunk at a lawn party," she retorted.

"Better to smell funny than lose," Cesar answered.

"Maybe tomorrow you can do both," she said.

He had to admit, she had a sense of humor and she wasn't bad looking either.

"Anyway, mind if I ask them a few questions?" she motioned toward the players.

"They don't speak English."

"How come that kid keeps saying *Geel* Hodges?" she asked, pointing to Ricardo. "And he," she motioned toward Mario, "told those girls he was Duke Snider."

"That's their secret weapon." Frankie looked at the Monterrey players.

"What is?" she asked as she turned back toward Cesar, but he had already walked away.

❦

News traveled fast. Moses overheard two of his white patrons discussing what the world was coming to. Soon, the caravan of Monterrey Industrial boys appeared outside the window as they walked by his shop.

"I bet they think they's hot stuff today," said the man seated in the barber chair next to his friend.

"Well, they better enjoy the win 'cause they'll get their comeuppance tomorrow," said the one waiting his turn.

Moses merely smiled as he applied some Vitalis to his customer's hair.

Back at the Grand Courts Motel, Cesar called the boys together near the pool for a team meeting.

"Now can we swim?" came the familiar question.

"No," followed Cesar's equally familiar answer.

"What are we going to do then?" asked several players.

"We're going to go over some plays and see what mistakes were made," Cesar said, sending José inside for his blackboard.

The boys groaned, and Padre Esteban gave Cesar a look that showed he questioned the coach's wisdom in reviewing a game that the boys had fought hard, played well and won.

Even Lucky threw in his two cents. "Cesar, it's a hundred degrees in the shade here. Let the boys rest."

"We won, but tomorrow we'll play a team that also won its game today, and they won't take us for granted when they realize we beat the home team."

The discussion could have continued were it not for the gesture of Monterrey's catcher who tried to quietly sneak away from the group.

"Beto, where are you going?" Cesar asked. The young catcher sheepishly returned, and Cesar noticed Beto's cleat was soaked with blood. He had suffered in silence during the entire game. Hidden from the eyes of the spectators and the press, few besides these *Regiomontanos* knew of the heroic act that had happened on a small baseball field in the huge state of Texas.

"Maybe a little rest is fine," Cesar said, dismissing the team. "But no swimming."

⋯⊙⊙⋯

"So no water breaking, huh, Bobby?" Frankie asked her colleague who had used that excuse to get out of this assignment the day before.

"False alarm, Frankie. Imagine that."

"Yeah, imagine," she said.

"You got that story for me?" Charlie Thompkin asked her as he came out of his office.

"Almost," responded Frankie.

"So how'd they do it? They got ringers? Maybe some fourteen-or fifteen-year-olds?"

"Are you kidding? They barely look ten," she said. "They just beat the pants off the home team. I did your story, now don't ask me to explain it."

14

Strike Two, You're Out!

Early the next morning, Cesar and José walked down the hallway whose carpet smelled of mold and stale beer. They alternately opened the doors of their players' rooms to make sure the boys were awake and getting ready. Monterrey's game was scheduled for ten o'clock in the morning.

Behind one door, José found Angel sitting fully dressed on his bed, looking apprehensive.

"What's wrong?" the assistant coach asked.

"It's Enrique. He's been in there since I got up," said Angel, gesturing toward the bathroom door.

"Seems all that peanut butter and Wonder Bread they ate has things backin' up," José told Cesar. "Enrique and Mario are ready to burst like overstuffed *piñatas*."

Cesar sent the team ahead to the ball field. Every border town has a *bodega*; he just needed to find one.

Lucky, José and Padre Esteban took the team to the field and prepared for the start of the game against Mission, Texas.

"I'll need your lineup card," Earl, the umpire, asked Lucky, presuming him to be the manager.

"Same positions as yesterday," Lucky told the boys in his awkward but passable Spanish. He actually spoke it reasonably well, but his Wisconsin accent was so thick that Mexicans were constantly asking him to repeat himself. Or worse, they would just said "Sì," even when they didn't have a clue about what he was saying.

"Angel's not allowed to pitch two days in a row," José pointed out.

"Who then?" asked Lucky.

"Enrique, can you try?" José asked the intended starter, but his question only elicited a moan from his crumpled-over pitcher.

"Who's going to pitch?" asked Pepe.

"You," said José.

"Me?"

"You got the next best arm on the team," the assistant coach replied.

Pepe looked at the faces of the other players. He didn't believe that they shared José's confidence.

Enrique, sensing Pepe's hesitation, said, "Listen, everyone! Pepe's pitching and he's going to give his best, so you give him yours." As the team headed out of the dugout, Pepe turned to look back at Enrique.

"Thanks," Pepe said.

"Don't forget, I can still kick your ass," said Enrique, causing Pepe to return the knowing smile.

ᴄⱭᴑⱭᴐ

The proprietor of the *bodega* laid out an assortment of peppers on the counter for Cesar to make his selection. Every Mexican knows that not all peppers are created equal. The bell pepper is the mildest. Next comes the poblano, jalapeño, chipotle, cayenne, Tabasco and at the top of the scale the dreaded "make-a-man-out-of-you" habañero.

For Cesar's purposes, two large, dark green jalapeños would do the trick. They were raw and had been aged in the hot Texas sun. He shoved them in his pocket and ran to the field, arriving in the bottom of the second inning.

Pepe Maiz was pitching well. Mission had their chances, but strong defense had quashed each attempted rally. Fortunately, no balls came to Enrique or Mario who looked like a couple of hunched-over old codgers.

At the inning change, Cesar handed these two their "medicine" and an inning later, both boys sprinted for the public facilities. Obviously relieved, they took their next turns at bat. Enrique homered to trigger a big inning for Monterrey. Shell-shocked and clearly thrown off their game plan, Mission found itself in one interminably long inning after another, watching the opposition score. It's not that they played poorly, it's that the *Regiomontanos* did everything right, taking advantage of every opportunity at bat and on the field.

The final score said it all: Monterrey 14, Mission 1.

ⅇⅇⅇ

At a diner closest to the motel, Ricardo ordered his second plate of "tortillas with syrup." They were American pancakes and Ricardo decided he'd eat them for breakfast, lunch and dinner. He would roll them up like gigantic tacos and open his mouth as wide as he could manage to eat them. Cesar was happy to see the boys eating heartily, but with every extra helping came the reality of dwindling reserves and the likelihood that they'd soon run out of money—an enemy they couldn't defeat on the baseball diamond.

"I haven't paid the motel yet for tonight," answered Lucky.

"Why not?"

"Did you want me to grow their food?"

The owners of the diner had generously offered the boys double portions at half-price, but it was still a drain on their meager resources.

"Okay, how much do you have?" Cesar asked pulling out a few bills and loose change from his pocket. Lucky did the same. The total amount barely exceeded sixty dollars.

"Here, Señor Faz," said Pepe, handing his coach an American fifty dollar bill. He had overheard their entire conversation from the next booth.

"Where did you get this, Pepe?" Cesar asked.

"From papa. He told me to spend it if I had an emergency, and this seems like one."

"What did you think you heard?"

"Everything."

"And them?" Cesar gestured toward the others.

"It's okay, Señor Faz. We're young, but we're not stupid. They had no money in Monterrey, why should it be different here?"

"Come with me," Cesar motioned for Pepe to follow him to the cash register. Lucky was surprised that Cesar was taking Pepe up on his offer.

"Cesar—?" Lucky began with disapproval, but Cesar had already turned to leave and didn't respond.

Cesar asked the cashier to break the fifty into singles. When she was finished counting them into his palm, Cesar turned to Pepe and said, "I won't take your money, and that's final. But if you want, you can divide it up among your friends. You say nothing of this conversation to anyone on the team."

"Yes, Señor Faz."

When Cesar returned to the booth, Lucky said, "That was the right thing to do, Cesar."

"Yeah, nobility is sure expensive. Still doesn't solve our problem."

"Here," said Lucky as he loosened his wristwatch and handed it to Cesar. "For the team."

Cesar noticed Padre Esteban sitting by himself, looking anxiously at an unfolded paper that he had withdrawn from his pocket. Cesar knew that something was wrong.

"Why aren't you celebrating, Padre?"

"Our visas expired today."

"Why didn't you remind me yesterday?" Cesar asked.

"I didn't believe we'd win three games," the priest said sheepishly.

"Oh my God, it's Wednesday!" sighed Cesar.

✧◈◈◈✧

In Monterrey, Maria and her family waited once again for a man who wasn't coming. She had prepared a local delicacy, *los cabritos* (goat). It is usually roasted whole over a mesquite fire, but for the special occasion, she had chosen to make a stew in which the marinated goat was mixed with avocado leaves, *guajillo chilies*, *ajo* (garlic), lime, cumin and other spices, and then slow-cooked it in her cast-iron pot until the meat fell effortlessly from its bones. It was a feast that took her all day to prepare and cost her father a day's wages.

Her brother looked at her hungrily, but dared not move. Maria looked down at her empty plate, said a prayer, and then served her family and quietly left the table.

⚭⚭

Later back at their motel, several of the boys tried to console Cesar.

"It's not your fault, Señor Faz," Angel said.

"I gave her my word that I'd come to meet her father tonight."

"She'll understand," Enrique added.

"No, this was the second time I let her down."

"Señor Faz," perked up Mario, "that's only two strikes! You get one more swing."

"Love isn't like baseball," he groaned.

"It's not?" asked Mario.

As the boys left his room, Cesar tried to rub the fatigue from his eyes. In his pocket, one of the jalapenos from earlier that day had split open, spilling some of its seeds. The acidity immediately made his eyes feel as if someone was touching them with a hot poker. Frozen in the hallway, the boys heard his cries coming through the motel room door.

"Poor Señor Faz. He's taking this pretty hard," said Mario.

⚭⚭

Maria and her family weren't the only ones in Monterrey who were stood up that evening. In the Plaza de José Marti, anxious parents waited for the bus coming from Reynosa. As the last one stopped without the passengers they were anticipating, some were concerned but most just went home, assuming that some inefficiency or mix-up had been the source of their children not returning.

The next morning, they learned the reason. *El Norte* had printed a headline on its third page: "Monterrey Bulldozes Mission, Wins Third in a Row."

15

The Good Neighbors

On the fourth day, Enrique Suarez, the dark one of Colonia Cantu, dominated the team from Weslaco, Texas.

Some locals, aware of the *Regiomontanos'* eroding financial condition from Frankie's newspaper articles, stopped by the Grand Courts Motel to bring fruits and other snacks. Others volunteered their cars to shuttle the team to a diner that one of their friends owned. *The Busy Corner* had offered to feed the kids for free.

As the carpool approached the diner, the hand-painted banner hanging from its silver ribbed roofline became visible: "The Busy Corner Welcomes Monterrey Industrial."

"Betty recommends the fried chicken," said a pink-aproned waitress, referring to Betty Little and her husband, Benny, the proprietors. Betty worked the register while Benny took care of business in the kitchen.

"Fried chicken, *mmm.* What do you think?" Cesar asked Padre Esteban.

Before the priest could answer, the waitress yelled, "Benny, gimme four baskets of fried chicken!"

"Great. How 'bout the fried chicken then," Cesar said, folding the menu.

"Fried chicken, I guess," added Lucky.

While they waited for their food, Lucky fed a couple of nickels into a juke box and Norberto made his buddies laugh when he danced to the rhythms of Buddy Holly and the Crickets' "That'll Be The Day."

"By any chance, do you have any chocolate syrup?" Cesar asked the waitress as they waited for their food.

"Sure do, honey," she said, returning a few minutes later and placing a pitcher of milk and tall bottle of Hershey's syrup on each table.

"Order's up!" yelled Benny.

"What is they doin' to my special fried chicken?" Betty shouted a minute later. The boys were dousing their chicken pieces with chocolate syrup.

"They think it's *mole*," said Lucky.

"What in God's name is mo-lay?"

"A Mexican chocolate sauce," he replied. "It's kinda like their version of ketchup." *Chocolatl* was a distinctly Aztec creation once reserved for nobility; King Moctezuma was said to have consumed fifty cups of this beverage a day.

Betty yanked the Hershey containers off the tables and grumbled, "Mo-lay or no-lay, I ain't lettin' them make sundaes outta my chicken."

After the meal, Cesar approached Betty at the register. "I'm sorry about the chicken," he said, while taking out some money.

"Keep it, Coach. I offered a free meal."

"But they got chocolate all over the place."

"Did they like my chicken?" she asked.

"They sure did," Cesar said. As she turned away, he could swear that he caught her smiling.

As the Monterrey Industrial team came out into the still warm McAllen night, the same people who had driven them to the Busy Corner waited patiently to take them back to the Grand Courts Motel. They called themselves the "Good Neighbors of the Texas Valley" and without their help the team would not have managed to scrape by and play another day.

⋘◎◎⋙

"You're pushing them pretty hard, Cesar," said Padre Esteban, who realized that the players were emotionally and physically drained. They were back at the motel and Cesar had sent Angel to bring everyone to his room for a strategy session.

"What's with you and Lucky?" Cesar snapped. "I learned baseball in the school yards of San Antonio, and believe me, it's going to require a lot of technical preparation and physical sacrifice if we're going to have a chance."

"Who's chance, your or theirs?" asked the priest. "They just came here to have fun and play one game. They've already achieved more than they could have hoped for. Why not reward them for what they've already accomplished?"

"You're right, Padre. I'll go easier on them," Cesar seemed to acquiesce.

A few minutes later, Cesar addressed the assembled team. "Some people," he began, casting a glance over toward Padre Esteban and Lucky, "have suggested that I'm driving you too hard. They think I'm not rewarding you enough. Okay, here's the deal: Tomorrow, if you win, you swim."

❦

The next day against Brownsville, the boys did just that. Just as remarkable as their continued winning streak was the fact that during the game Angel alternated pitching with both arms. There are many players at the higher levls of baseball who can hit with ease from either side of the plate, but far fewer who can throw with equal proficiency right or left handed. The occurence of a player who can pitch well with either arm is one of the rarest phenomenons in the game, at any level, anywhere.

By the fifth day since arriving in the United States, Monterrey Industrial had defeated every team they faced in McAllen and won the right to play again in another American city, though that afternoon their singular thought was of the small pool at the Grand Courts Motel.

The closest they had previously come to it was when Cesar had them wash their uniforms in its shallow end. Today, it became their oasis in the desert after having been denied it for six days.

Lucky could not resist making a somewhat irreverent reference to Genesis, "And God blessed the seventh day and made it holy, because on it Cesar let them swim."

"Good thing the padre can't hear that."

"Good thing you let them swim or you'd have a full-scale mutiny."

"That's why I brought you along, skipper," Cesar stated.

"Don't *skipper* me. . . if they revolt, I'm with them," Lucky said, laughing.

The Good Neighbors of the Texas Valley arranged a caravan to transport the team to Corpus Christi later that day. While the boys frolicked in the pool, Cesar contemplated the next game.

"The winds off the Gulf are pretty strong there," he told José as the two studied the weather reports.

"Yeah, the papers say it's going to affect visiting teams who don't know the climate."

"That doesn't give us much time to get to know it then," Cesar said.

⋘⊙⊙⋙

Yesterday, the Little Giants from Monterrey beat Weslaco 13-1. Today, the favored team from Brownsville fared little better, falling 6-1. Angel Macias, who during the game pitched with both hands, had cold water running through his veins. Never have I seen a kid—or a grown-up pitcher—so focused and so efficient. By the end of the game, a contingent of local fans were chanting, "Los Niños Maravilla" (the Amazing Kids). Now it's on to the next round in Corpus Christi for this surprising team from Mexico. This reporter wishes them the best of luck. . ."

The *chuck-chuck* of the Smith-Corona's keys chattered like the muted whisper of a locomotive's wheels. Frankie was typing the last sentences of her article when suddenly she felt her editor behind her.

"I'd never have thought they'd win five straight," said Charlie.

"Me either," Frankie said, continuing to type.

"Why the oxymoron?"

"Little Giants? You gotta see how small they look next to our boys," she said as she finished the draft and pulled out the single sheet of bond paper. "You wanna proof it first before I give it to Esther?"

"Nah, you're doing fine."

"Thanks." Frankie skimmed the copy for corrections and continuity, but noticed above the paper that Charlie neither moved nor took his eyes off of her.

"Why are you looking at me like that?" she asked him.

"Corpus, huh?"

After an uncomfortable silence, she got his drift. "No. No way, Charlie. I'm not covering them in Corpus."

"It's a great story. Got folks glued to the sports page."

"If it's so good, why don't you cover it?"

"'Cause I sign your paycheck. Unless, of course, you want to put an apron on and—"

"Say that again and I *will* punch you in the nose."

"That's the spirit! C'mon, Frankie. What're we talkin' about here? A game, maybe two. I'll pay your expenses and an extra five bucks a day."

"Make it ten and you still owe me, Mac."

"I'll remember you at Christmas."

"I'm renting a car *and* you're springing for a decent hotel."

಄ல௫ல

The team was housed in dormitories on the University of Corpus Christi campus. On Sunday morning, Padre Esteban and José took the boys to Mass at a nearby Catholic church. From there, they would join Cesar on the field at Bear Park, where he was speaking with Frankie.

"It sure is thirsty weather," she said.

"Yeah, it's so hot the trees are bribin' the dogs."

"Impressive analogy," she rolled her eyes.

Cesar tried to be polite to her, but they rubbed each other like steel wool on rust.

"Where's your team?" asked Frankie

"At Mass."

"I hear they pray a lot."

"Every day." Cesar noticed Frankie writing down what he just said. "Why are you taking that down?"

"Always looking for an angle to a story."

"There's no angle."

"You think it helps?"

"You mean, does praying improve their baseball skills?"

"I guess that's my question."

"Missy, anything a baseball player imagines is helping *is* helping."

"Thanks. By the way, call me *Missy* again and I'll give you a black eye."

Cesar blew the air hard out of his mouth and said, "*Gallo, caballo y mujer, por la raza has de escoger.*"

"That better mean 'I promise to be respectful to women,'" she stated.

"Absolutely," he said, though the literal translation had something to do with comparing a woman to a horse and a rooster.

"I know all about Mexican men and your *machismo.*"

"I'm from Texas," he corrected her.

"So are you a Texan?"

"Guess I ain't sure anymore," he sighed.

Cesar had become like the mythical *Axolotl*, a salamander known to the Aztecs as a water dog. It never morphs completely from an aquatic larva into a terrestrial form, always staying in between, unsure of whether it's a fish or a reptile.

In a similar way, American society was a veneer over two very different realities. In one, television portrayed happy families who represented the typical American values, though everyone was white and comfortably middle-class. People of color or obvious ethnic descent were never seen as neighbors or friends, and any hint of romance between different races was not only absent from television, it was illegal in many states.

"Don't you ever give them a day off?" Frankie asked as she watched the Monterrey team arriving and getting ready to practice.

"I want them to get used to the direction of the wind and sun."

"It's Sunday. Are you sure you're just a Little League coach?" she asked.

"What about you? Why are you here?"

"Just checking out the field, like you."

"No, in Corpus Christi, I mean."

"Seems my editor-in-chief thinks your story's interesting. Shows how little must be happening in McAllen."

During their conversation, Cesar noticed a group of men sitting in a vehicle parked at the curb. The motor was running, and there were already three or four cigarette butts on the ground below the driver's rolled-down window. Upon being spotted by Cesar, the car suddenly sped off.

Cesar would not have given the incident a second thought had it not been for the arrival of another man who approached him in a suit.

"I'm Jeb Lansing. I run the Corpus Christi Little League," he said.

"Nice to meet you, sir," answered Cesar.

"Did you know it's against town regulations to practice baseball in uniform on a Sunday?" he asked.

"No, I didn't know," said Cesar and then turned to call his boys in to home plate. "It seems kind of harmless, and believe me, these boys are very religious and meant no disrespect."

"I'm sure they didn't, but unfortunately a grievance has been filed. I have no choice but to suspend your team, subject to a hearing on whether you'll be disqualified."

"I can't believe anyone would have lodged a complaint about a few kids in uniform," Frankie interjected.

"This ain't about uniforms," Cesar said. "My boys just came from the wrong side of the river."

"What's that supposed to mean?" asked Frankie.

"What do you expect from a place where children are taught about the Alamo before the alphabet."

The next morning, Cesar had no choice but to tell the team what had happened and that he wasn't sure whether they'd be playing that afternoon. Their morale was low as he tried to use the time etching out plays on his chalkboard. Padre Esteban joined them, and he could see that the boys were not anxious to absorb Cesar's strategy lecture.

"Cesar," Padre Esteban pulled him aside, "maybe the boys could use a break from baseball for a few hours."

"A break?"

"Well, they've never seen an ocean," suggested the priest.

⌒◯◯⌒

Cesar stood at the water's edge, skipping stones into the surf that gently lapped at the shore. In the distance was a two-mile-long jetty that served as a breaker for the waves. The priest was right: The boys had never seen an ocean or a beach. He hadn't either until he was almost twenty-six years old, and then the shorelines had been littered with metal obstacles, incinerated tanks and the floating bodies of dead marines.

In the surf and dunes behind him, the boys played and for a little while forgot about the tournament and the suspension. He admired that they could shut out the world so easily and find joy and fascination in something as simple as a horseshoe crab or half-buried water-eroded beam.

Cesar wondered whether God favored these boys or had it out for them. It seemed like no matter how hard they tried, their reward was to awaken to a fresh day with new obstacles to overcome.

⌒◯◯⌒

"I don't get why you, of all people, is gettin' all lathered up about this," Mayor Jim Pratt said to Slim Pembroke, who sat in a high-backed leather chair across from the mayor's desk. Frankie sat on a couch on the far side of the office, having already spoken her piece and watching her words fall on deaf ears.

"'Cause it ain't right," answered Slim.

"You wanna win?"

"Yeah, but not that way."

"I heard they goes about town in those uniforms all the time as if they's showin' off or somethin'. I know they won in McAllen, but that don't give the no right to be rubbin' it in our faces. And now I hear they's running around in underwear. I tell you, a grown man and a bunch of kids in underwear, it just ain't natural," said the mayor.

1. Fundidora, the steel foundry. Built in 1905, it symbolizes the heart and soul of the industrial city of Monterrey.

2. Silhouetting Fundidora are the imposing *Cerro de la Silla* (saddle back) mountains.

3. The Vitro Glass factory where Cesar Faz worked.

4. Cementos Hidalgo de Mexicana factory.

5. Norberto and Enrique walk home.

6. The Bishop's Palace. Church, fortress and one time hideout for Pancho Villa.

7. & 8. Above and below, Monterrey boys play stickball in an abandoned dirt field. In the photo below, note the homemade ball in flight.

9. Angel practices pitching at home.

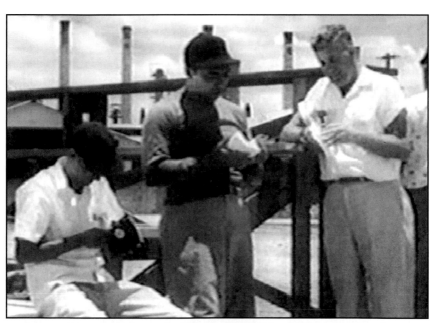

10. Cesar Faz, Jose Gonzalez Torres and Harold "Lucky" Haskins study the rule book in the shadows of Vitro Glass.

11. & 12. Cesar Faz
believed in discipline
and endurance training.
The team (above) gets
an education by running
up the Mitras Hill.
Never expecting of
others what he would
not demand of himself,
Cesar (at right) makes
the same grueling
ascent.

13. Sandy Koufax's rookie year (1955) baseball card.

14. A Sears & Roebuck Silverstone radio. Mexicans could hear Spanish translated broadcasts of their favorite shows from the U.S.

15. The heroes of Flatbush—the Brooklyn Dodgers.

16. Cesar Faz lectures on the fine art of baseball.

17. The Little League credo: "Character, Courage and Loyalty." Monterrey Industrial joins the league in 1957.

18. Monterrey boys practice on their converted dirt field.

19. Monterrey Industrial hopefuls on the eve of their first game.

Angel Macias

Enrique Suarez

José "Pepe" Maiz

Norberto Villarreal

Baltazar Charles

Ricardo Treviño

Rafael Estrello

Fidel Ruiz

Gerardo Gonzales

Jesus "Chuy" Contreras

Mario Ontiveros

Roberto Mendiola

Alfonso Cortez

Francisco Aguilar

20. & 21. The Monterrey Industrials on the road to McAllen. It would take four hours to reach Reynosa, Mexico on the southern banks of the Rio Grande.

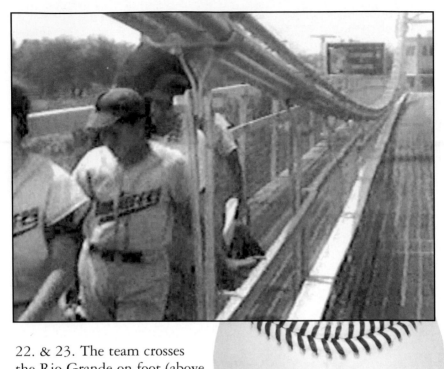

22. & 23. The team crosses
the Rio Grande on foot (above
and below). They would have
to walk the remaing twelve
miles to McAllen.

McAllen
TEXAS

24. Cesar Faz carries the bag of bats in McAllen, Texas.

25. Enrique Suarez (right foreground) leads his teammates on the walk to the McAllen Little League ballfields.

26. Posing after a hearty meal at the Busy Corner Diner.

27. Gerardo Gonzales admires one of Angel's pitching arms.

28. After five victories, Cesar finally lets the boys take a swim.

29. Cesar going over strategy before a game in Corpus Christi.

30. Fidel Ruiz about to make a tag play at third base.

31. Ricardo Trevino
is safe at home!

32. Later, Ricardo
takes a collision at
first and has the
wind knocked out of
him. He's one tough
kid, and refuses to
be taken out.

33. Cesar
pretends to
struggle with
English as
he waits for
his missing
pitchers to
find the field.

"It's all they got," said Slim.

Mayor Pratt paused and contemplated this last comment. He glanced over at a picture on the wall of his dad taken during the Great Depression. His father held the reins of a pony. The pony wasn't his; it belonged to a man who regularly came through the neighborhood with the animal and a camera.

Mayor Pratt reached down and pressed the button on his intercom. An older-sounding woman came over the speaker.

"Yes, Mayor."

"Madge, would you be a doll and get me Jeb Lansing."

⌒⊚⌒

Out of the corner of Cesar's eye, he watched a boy ride his bike to the sand's edge, leap off and run as fast as he could toward him.

After listening to the boy's message, Cesar yelled out, "Hurry, boys, we're playing Laredo!" The league had summarily dismissed the complaint. "We'll dress at the field," he said, picking up the bundle of uniforms in his arms.

The team would have to get back to Bear Park the same way they'd gotten to the beach—hitchhiking. Each car that stopped was asked to take a handful of players. When they separated like this, Cesar remained anxious until they were reunited at their destination.

At Bear Park, the boys began pulling baseball pants over their sand-covered feet and legs and Cesar found himself holding two empty uniforms.

"Our pitchers!" Cesar cried out to Lucky.

"What do we do?" Lucky asked.

"I'll stall the game while you look for them."

Lucky took off in the car of a stranger who volunteered to drive him around searching for the missing boys.

⌒⊚⌒

"Pepe, warm up," Cesar said as he was summoned to home plate to join the Laredo coach in a pregame conference with the umpire.

"No, no, *señor*. *Scusi*, is foul ball? *¡No comprende!*" Cesar said, feigning a lack of English proficiency.

"I said it's a *fair* ball if it *hits* the field umpire. But the play is dead," repeated the frustrated umpire.

"¿*Muerto?* Dead?"

"Yes, dead."

"Umpire *es* dead? ¡*Ay Dios mio!*"

Angel and Enrique had run down Main Street in their underwear, asking everyone they met, "¿*Beisbol estadio?*" They finally arrived at the field to a burst of laughter from both teams. Seeing that his delaying tactic worked, Cesar said, "Ready, *Señor* Umpire."

"What was that about?" Frankie asked Cesar when he came back to the Monterrey dugout. "What's with the '¿*No hablo de Ang-lay-zee?*'"

"I almost lost two players," he said, looking over at the end of the bench where Angel and Enrique were pulling their jerseys over their heads. "Fooled the ump and that coach though."

"By the way, that coach you *fooled* is the same one who got the complaint about the uniforms tossed."

"Him? Why did he help us? We're—"

"Visitors?" she interjected.

☙◦◷◦❧

"Look how small they is. Ain't none of 'em over twelve, that's for sure. Shoot, they don't look but nine or ten!" marveled one spectator as he watched the first Monterrey batter get his bat and stride toward the plate.

"Must have been some kinda fluke, them winnin' in McAllen," chimed in one of his cohorts.

"Yeah, too many Mexicans down there. Made 'em soft. Wait 'til they get a whiff of Jimmy Stokes' fastball," said the first man.

Jimmy Stokes, the Laredo pitcher, delivered a solid fastball to Baltazar who got a whiff of it, just long enough to send it over the left field wall.

CORPUS CHRISTI, TEXAS, AUGUST 5, 1957 – A crowd of more than three thousand were in attendance at Bear Park for the Little League

Tournament today. The Monterrey team started nervously against Laredo. No doubt they had never seen so many spectators, made worse when many came to see them lose. There were so many roaring for Laredo that it was nice to see a small contingent of fans near the visiting team dugout, cheering for the phenoms from Mexico. After settling down, the Monterrey pitcher, Enrique Suarez, dominated and didn't let Laredo make a move while Baltazar Charles destroyed their pitcher with two homeruns giving, the "Little Giants" another win, 5 - 0.

こめのの

Monterrey Industrial dined in the dormitory's cafeteria, along with the players and coaches of West Columbia, the team Monterrey was to play next. They had two Black players, who sat by themselves at a separate table.

"Why are they sitting alone?" Angel asked his friends.

"Maybe they did something bad," replied Baltazar.

Despite this speculation, the boys urged Cesar to ask the West Columbia coaches if the two players could join them at their table. When Cesar returned, he said, "They won't let them come over to your table."

"Why not, Señor Faz?"

"I don't know, but it's none of our business."

As the boys continued their meal, Baltazar felt a growing uneasiness. He grabbed his tray and walked over to the table where the two boys sat like marooned sailors.

"What does your boy think he's doing?" Hank Aubrey, the West Columbia assistant coach, asked Cesar.

"Balta?" Cesar said to his player, but before he could answer, Pepe stood up and brought his food over to join Baltazar and the two West Columbia outcasts. One at a time, the rest of the Monterrey Industrial team did the same thing without speaking a word to one another.

"I told you guys they couldn't sit with you," Cesar finally said.

Baltazar sighed and told Cesar, "No, Señor Faz. You only said they couldn't come to *our* table."

ॐ

Every night since arriving in McAllen, Cesar would fall asleep at around eleven o'clock, but by two in the morning, he was wide awake, feeling the burdens of the world on his shoulders.

Knowing he'd be awake for hours, Cesar went to check on his team, pausing in each room to take off sweaty socks, open windows, disentangle bodies tired from playing, fix pillows, and finally to make sure that all the kids slept as comfortably as possible.

The incident at dinner had provided the fodder for this night's insomnia. Cesar recalled another evening and another racial slight from which he did not back down. It was in St. Louis, and Cesar had taken Tammy Grolich and a friend of hers named Sara Joy to the Chain of Rocks Amusement Park.

ॐ

"Oxtail sandwich?" Sara Joy laughed after hearing Cesar's order. "I don't know anyone who eats that."

"It's my favorite," Cesar lied. The added wheel on the date didn't really bother him, except after the two girls had ordered, Cesar realized he barely had enough in his pocket to cover the meal. He couldn't tell Tammy how skint he was so he frantically searched the menu for the only item he could afford.

The order arrived, but before Cesar could take a bite, they were interrupted by a couple of roughnecks from Tammy's school.

"Well if it ain't Miss Grolich," said Tully, the larger of the two boys. "Why don't you cut loose and come with us? We're goin' for a swim in the river."

"One of these days you're gonna drown and it'll serve you right Tully Barnes," said Tammy.

"I don't have a bathing suit," said Sara Joy with something less than innocence.

"That's the idea," replied Tully's friend, Stitch, while elbowing Tully in the rib.

"Whaddya say, Tammy?" Tully asked. "Sounds like your friend wants to go."

"I'm busy," she said, casting a glance toward Cesar.

"I didn't know we had lettuce fields here," said Tully as his eyes squinted.

"He's with the Browns," Tammy said, lingering on the last word for an extra beat.

"Shucks, they're cellar-dwellers," said Stitch.

"Mr. Hornsby told Cesar he'd manage the team someday," said, Tammy laughing.

"A Mexican manager? I don't think so," laughed Stitch.

"I ain't Mexican," Cesar's replied. "I was born here, just like you."

Tully looked at Cesar with disdain and said, "If you's American, then the dog musta been keepin' your mama under the porch," which in local parlance questioned the legitimacy of Cesar's breeding. But before Tully could finish his sentence, Cesar's shoulder barreled into his chest, and soon fists and French fries were flying everywhere.

ecoGoo

The next morning, Alfonso Cortez and Roberto Mendiola found an old washing machine in one of the school buildings and did the team a great favor by washing all of their clothes. Roberto was used to hard work and household chores. His family had moved to Monterrey from his birthplace of Real de San Carlos de Vallecillo, a tiny village about a hundred miles away. When Roberto was old enough to learn his way around the Centro de Monterrey, his father gave him and his older brothers boxes of limes, which he had picked from the fields surrounding the city. Roberto and his brothers sold them door-to-door to help their family.

With clean uniforms, Monterrey teed off against West Columbia at one o'clock that afternoon. On the mound, Angel didn't allow a run, and at bat, both Baltazar and Enrique hit home runs. Enrique's shot was the longest anyone remembered seeing in Bear Park.

After the game, the boys climbed into the stands with their hats turned out for loose change. Their ability to get to Fort Worth and the Texas State Championship was in serious doubt, and though some in the stands were offended or apathetic, many were touched by the humility of the team's condition and reached into their pockets for coins.

Meanwhile, in California, local newspapers were abuzz with columns devoted to the commencement of the California State Championship, hosted by the city of Santa Monica. To advance to this round, La Mesa had beaten El Centro and four other teams, outscoring them forty runs to two. Remarkably, their opponents rarely got more than one hit a game! With a team batting average of .408 and a pitching battery of six aces, it was no surprise.

eᴼᴼᴼ

Señora Ontiveros walked slowly down the dirt street in Colonia Cantu. Under her right arm was tucked a copy of that morning's *El Norte*. Without the paper, none of the parents would have had any idea where their children were and whether they were coming home or forging deeper north into the United States.

As she walked down the road, she suddenly stopped on the corner of 2a San Francisco Oriente. Momentarily disoriented, she looked down the street at the façade that had drawn her attention.

A few houses off the corner, in front of the one owned by Umberto and Oralia Macias, was a planter of flowers, their vivid colors bursting forth in stark contrast to the muted hues of the drab street.

 **16**

Homesick

ocal guidebooks called Fort Worth, Texas, "the Gateway to the West." Situated on the Trinity River about thirty miles west of Dallas and six hundred miles northwest of Corpus Christi, it's been a little of everything since it was first settled: an army post, the last major stop on the Chisholm Trail, a meat-packing and cattle-shipping center, and eventually an oil town. Hell's Half Acre, in the center of town, was a well-known watering hole where a man looking for the devil could find saloons, gambling parlors and dance halls.

"Eighteen one-way tickets to Fort Worth," Lucky said to the clerk behind the ticket booth at the central bus station.

"Let me guess, you're the West Columbia team?"

Lucky shook his head.

"No? You with Kennedy?" the clerk guessed again. Both of those teams had prereserved their spaces before the tournament, each believing that they would win the divisional title in Corpus Christi.

"We're the team from Monterrey, Mexico," said Lucky.

"What about them other groups?"

Lucky smiled. "Trust me, they're not coming."

❧◌❧

The bus transporting Monterrey Industrial pulled into a roadside truck stop that was so small, the boys had to sit on the floor. There was only enough money to buy each person half a sandwich and share a container of milk.

"Cesar, we're really hungry," said Ricardo, several hours after that short lunch stop. Cesar tried to get them to sing, but it didn't take their minds off their hunger, so he offered the boys chewing gum.

"That only makes us hungrier," came the reply, but there was nothing Cesar could do to ease the ache in their bellies.

The bus entered Forth Worth around midnight. From this level of the tournament and higher, the league provided housing for visiting teams, but the *Regiomontanos* were arriving in their host city a few days before the league anticipated. With no formal destination, Padre Esteban led them to the Church of St. John the Divine's where he knew the priest. Several parishioners offered to accommodate the children, but it would require them splitting up into different homes. Padre Esteban thanked his fellow priest profusely for their kind gesture, but the boys had told him that they'd left Monterrey together and refused to be separated even for one night.

The boys huddled together for comfort on the church pews. As uncomfortable as sleeping on its wooden benches was, the next evening's accommodations were worse.

Lucky and Cesar found a cheap motel on the outskirts of town where big-rig drivers stopped to eat or sleep for a few hours before continuing on their long-haul routes. It was particularly grungy, and the truckers drank heavily. As the boys nervously prepared for bed, they could hear the sound of verbal altercations outside their thin doors.

"Don't just sit there, help me," Pepe whispered to his roommates.

Alfonso, Francisco and Roberto helped Pepe move a heavy dresser in front of the door. Next came the chair and the beds, with the boys leaning their backs into the upright mattresses.

"Get the lights," Francisco said to Roberto.

"You get them!" answered his frightened friend. Finally, Pepe crossed the room and hit the lights before rejoining his comrades who huddled quietly in the dark as some rowdy men—with two giggling companions—made their indiscreet way past the boys' room.

A loud knocking startled Roberto who almost began to cry. Pepe put his finger to his lips to hush his friends, but the knocking continued. The boy didn't breathe until it stopped.

"They must be asleep," Cesar said to Lucky as the two of them stood outside the room that had recently been barricaded by Pepe and his rommates.

❧◎◎❧

A world away, Lewis Riley and his younger brother screamed, "Dad, hurry!"

Mr. Riley had paused to rest on a bench that looked more like a rock. They had just finished cruising down the Congo River where they narrowly escaped hippopotamuses wallowing in the shallows and natives with blow-darts hiding behind palm trees. Trying to keep pace with his sons, Mr. Riley began to wonder whether a trip to Walt Disney's new theme park a day before the California State Championship had been such a good idea.

The strains of Don Defore's silver banjo filtered from around a bend in the road as Lewis and his brother pressed their father, "Come on, let's cross the Mississippi and go fishing!"

While Mrs. Riley took Lewis' sister to browse the shops on Main Street, Mr. Riley and the boys boarded the steam paddleboat to Smuggler's Cove.

"Let me just sit down for a minute, boys. I'm exhausted!" Mr. Riley said. Just then, Tom Sawyer, barefoot and dressed in tattered clothes, strolled by them, whistling a happy tune.

"Wouldn't it be great to live like him and not have to go to school?" Lewis' brother asked.

"Yeah, nothing but fishin', playing hooky, and goin' on adventures!" Lewis answered.

❧◎◎❧

On their third day in Fort Worth, the Little League organization sent word to Lucky that out-of-town teams would be berthed in the barracks of the Carswell Air Force Base. They were very clean, and each of the two floors had two long lines of metal cots divided by a center walkway that a commanding officer, or a coach, could walk down. Monterrey would share the top floor with the team from Waco.

Lucky and Cesar met for a couple of beers at the base's canteen.

"Whaddaya think?" Cesar asked Lucky.

"They look. . . big."

"What's new?"

"Waco's coach is ex-Air Force. Captain, I think he said."

"Fly boy, huh? Maybe we'll tell him what war looks like below twenty-thousand feet," Cesar said.

"Bet he runs a tight squad," surmised Lucky. The Waco kids were disciplined, but only at not getting caught. During rest periods, they had worked out a system of lookouts to watch for the coach. When he thought they were sleeping, they were actually having pillow fights. If he appeared, a quick signal caused his entire team to dive into their beds and feign sleep.

⚬⌘⚬

Cesar was now confronting a growing issue: homesickness. Unlike most victorious teams who could return home after each round and then travel to their next scheduled series, the *Regiomontanos* could only keep moving deeper into the United States.

One evening, Enrique startled Cesar by saying, "You know what, Señor Faz? The next time I pitch in a game I hope we lose, so we can go home."

Cesar immediately called the whole team together and asked them all to take a walk with him through town. Without any plan, they found themselves in front of a theater showing a double feature of *Francis Covers the Big Town* and *Francis Goes to West Point*. The owner allowed them all to come in for the price of one adult ticket.

The boys couldn't understand a word of it, but the movies' star, a talking mule, made them laugh and helped ease their longing for home.

Coincidentally, the next day happened to be Enrique's birthday, so to celebrate Cesar took the team to the Stockyard Championship at the Cowtown Coliseum. On Thursday's, the coliseum hosted bull riding, team roping, penning and barrel racing, and a re-creation of the original Pawnee Bill's Wild West Show. It was a welcome distraction from their heavy and unanticipated schedule of back-to-back baseball games.

The crowd suddenly let out a loud applause as a cowboy, who had moments earlier taken a nasty ride underneath the belly of his wildly bucking horse, managed to get up and walk back to the stalls. Unlike bullfighting where toreadors spent their time running away from bulls, in Texas, men jumped on their backs and rode 'em.

The boys loved every bit of the show, especially the choreographed stunts involving rows of riders who could touch the ground and spring up and over to the horse's other side while at a full gallop.

"Come on, the mayor wants to meet us," Lucky said, taking Cesar by the arm and leading him to the grandstands on the other side of the indoor arena.

As they got closer, Mayor Tom McCann was in the middle of a conversation with several of his invited guests, all political cronies. "You should've seen him, Earl. He was blacker than midnight under a skillet," said the mayor. "Coming down here from Washington all high and mighty like, telling me that we got racial problems here in Fort Worth."

Mayor McCann had been on the job only since April when a group of Black golfers, who were banned from both private and public courses, set up homemade flags on an abandoned marshy field and used coffee cups for holes. The press jumped on the story.

"What did you tell him, Tom?" Earl asked.

"I told him to come down to my club and he'd see we don't have any racial problems." Tom laughed and spit a huge wad of chaw on the dirt. "Well, he took off like the dogs was after him," he added.

The men surrounding the mayor laughed.

"Excuse me, Mayor, I have the gentlemen from the Monterrey team," interrupted Toby Allison, the mayor's assistant.

"'Scuse me, gents," Tom said to those gathered around him. "I want to greet the head of the posse who done beat up our boys in McAllen and Corpus Christi like they was rented mules."

The mayor turned to Cesar and Lucky and reached out first to the latter, clasping his hand. "I'm Harold Haskins, but my friends call me Lucky."

"Howdy, Mr. Lucky. I hope you bring some of that to our fair city," said the mayor, who wore a white embroidered shirt with metal tipped collars, down from which hung a bolo tie. That was held together by a detailed silver star slide with a blue onyx stone mounted in its center. "Helluva job coaching, Mr. Lucky, 'specially with what you had to work with."

"I'm not their coach," said Lucky as he motioned toward Cesar. "He is."

"I'm Cesar Faz," Cesar said, extending his hand.

"You'll forgive an ol' cuss. Of course the Mexican team's gonna have a Mexican coach," said the Mayor.

"Cesar's actually from San Antonio," said Lucky.

"Well if that don't beat all, a fellow Texan! What do you think about these here Yankees tellin' us what to do like they knows our city better than we do?"

"I never liked them Yankees," Cesar said sternly. "Personally, I'm a Dodger fan."

The mayor laughed. "Spoken like a true politician, sir. Who you playing tomorrow?"

"Houston," Cesar answered.

"Your little fellas done pretty good, but don't forget, you're in the heart of Texas now and we take baseball as serious as our rodeos."

◈

The next afternoon, Friday, August 9, Monterrey Industrial faced the Baytown League from Houston. Monterrey's pitching rotation had been established, so Enrique Suarez took the mound. After two innings, Monterrey was down four runs to nothing, and had it not been for outstanding defense interspersed with some luck the score easily could have been even more lopsided.

"Cesar, it's just a game," Padre Esteban said to the coach as he paced nervously back and forth. Houston had gotten their first two hitters on base and were threatening to score again.

"Yeah, it's all good playing for fun, but it's a long bus ride home when you lose," Cesar muttered.

Perhaps Monterrey Industrial realized that they had nothing left to lose or perhaps the truth is an overly confident Houston team let up a bit—this can be debated forever by baseball scholars—but whatever the cause, the effect was the *Regiomontanos* scratched and clawed their way back into the game.

"Didn't think it'd be this close," Frankie, who'd made the trip to Fort Worth to cover Monterrey, overheard a spectator say. The two teams entered the last inning with Baytown's lead now cut to one run, and Frankie tried hard not to bite her nails.

The hefty Baytown pitcher easily struck out Fidel and Angel. Next to bat was Norberto.

"Well, ain't no matter none. One more out and they can head back to where they done come from," noted the same spectator.

Stepping into the batter's box, Norberto knew he could be Monterrey's last hitter of the season.

After swinging wildly at two pitches, Cesar carefully admonished his young player, "Don't try to save the game with one swing, Beto. Just try for a single and get on base!"

Suddenly, Cesar noticed that Padre Esteban was pacing next to him in the dugout. "What are you worried about, Padre? Like you said, 'It's just a game."

"I'm worried he's never been in such a situation with so much pressure," said Padre Esteban.

"Every boy has been in this situation," said Cesar cooly.

He had been in this situation a hundred times before, not on a real field or in a real game, but in his mind. Norberto, like every boy who's ever played the game, had already imagined himself in every conceivable heroic scenario: the diving catch to save the game; pitching the final strikeout; crushing the last inning, two outs, two strikes homerun. All of this had been played out in daydreams or in sandlots with mythical announcers and the imaginary roar of crowds.

Norberto dug in as the Baytown pitcher served him a curve ball that didn't break.

Crack!

It is said that when a baseball is hit just right, the impact is no longer a violent collision, the batter feels as if he has swung through nothing but air.

In one swing, the boy who had stepped on broken glass and had

178 • The Perfect Game

limped with a bleeding foot across the Rio Grande had tied the game
and prolonged the season—at least for one more inning.

Norberto rounded the bases, crossed home plate and was met by
Cesar.

"You're forgiven," Cesar said.

"For not trying to get just a single?"

"No, for lying about your foot two weeks ago."

At the end of regulation, the score was four runs apiece.
Little League rules limited a pitcher to six innings per game and
prohibited him from pitching two consecutive days. Both Enrique
and his Houston counterpart had to abandon their positions.

"You gotta go with Angel," Lucky advised Cesar.

"Then who'll pitch tomorrow if we win?" Cesar asked.

"If we don't win, there'll be no need for a pitcher tomorrow,"
countered Lucky.

Should Cesar throw everything to the game at hand to increase
the odds of victory today or save Angel for a match-up that might
never happen? Monterrey's offense gave them a huge boost by
scoring twice in the top of the extra inning, so Cesar told Pepe Maiz
to start warming up.

Christened José Sebastian Maiz Garcia, "Pepe" was the oldest of
twelve children born to José Maiz Mier and Maria Antonia García. In
1938, his father began a construction contracting business that grew
into one of the more important companies in Monterrey, Pepe went
to elementary school at the Instituto Franco Mexicano where he was
a dedicated student and athlete, excelling in basketball and soccer.

Though his fortunate birth circumstance had made his acceptance
by Monterrey Industrial difficult at first, he had won their respect
by refusing to take advantage of luxuries that his father could have
provided to make his journey more comfortable.

"Look, Pepe," Cesar told him, "I don't want you to let anyone get
a run, because if you do I'm going to have to put in Angel."

Pepe got the first out, but the second Houston hitter walked.
Going out to talk to his nervous pitcher, Cesar tried to ease Pepe's
anxiety. "Let me give you a piece of pitching advice I once overheard
from the oldest rookie in the majors."

"What should I do, Señor Faz?"

"Just take the ball and throw strikes, and remember, home plate don't move."

Before Cesar could second-guess himself, Pepe struck out the last two batters to close out the game. Monterrey narrowly staved off elimination.

୬ର୍ଚ୍ଚ

The next day, they would play Waco for the Texas State Championship. The local headlines rekindled Cesar's childhood demons:

WACO LITTLE LEAGUE BRACES FOR
THE ALAMO!

In San Antonio, Cesar had been one of the few Hispanics in his class, so in the playground he was always forced to be the Mexican soldier when his classmates played a game called Remember the Alamo. That three-worded slogan so pervaded Cesar's world that no one living within a thousand miles of San Antonio was ever allowed to forget it. The real truth of the event was never told, but victors always write history and this was the way it was when you grew up in the shadow of the Alamo.

Cesar hated the story. It only reminded him of how different he was from the rest of his class, and today's headline shined a spotlight on how the Texans truley felt about playing a team from south of the border.

"Señor Faz, why can't they put up our flag?" Fidel Ruiz asked, tugging at Cesar's shirt when the team was introduced before the start of the game. Two flags flapped gently in the breeze atop poles in center field: the Stars and Stripes and the state flag of Texas. Being raised with strict military discipline, Fidel showed the most respect for his uniform of any of his teammates.

"When they play the anthem, tell each boy to look at the patch on the arm of the boy to his left," Cesar said. On each player's right shoulder was a crimson red emblem that had embroidered the word *Mexico* in white. This was the closest thing they had brought from home that symbolized their country.

Frankie was interviewing some of the local dignitaries on the sideline. One of them told her, "Heck, I admire these Mexican kids as much as the next guy, but for an American team to lose the Texas State Championship just wouldn't be right, if you know what I mean."

She knew exactly what he meant.

By the end of the first inning, Waco led two runs to nothing, but something was different than the previous times Monterrey found itself down. No one looked downcast or even anxious. The Houston game had let the *Regiomontanos* believe that they could come from behind in any circumstance.

Pepe was at bat. He missed after two huge swings, and as a good hitter the pressure on him to perform was great. Though he fouled off the last pitch, the contact had splintered his bat. He walked to the dugout to retrieve a new one, and was met by Cesar and Mario, the on-deck batter.

"The best way to kill a rally is to overswing. Remember, Pepe, the goal is to make it last as long as possible," said Cesar.

"It's like kissing a girl," said Mario, swinging his bat in the on-deck circle. "Just don't close your eyes."

Pepe proceeded to double one off the center field wall. Monterrey followed with a string of four more base hits. When the rally ended, Monterrey was up three to two.

In the bottom of the second inning, Angel struck out the first Waco batter and then faced Clyde Connors. During Waco's batting practice, Cesar had watched this lefty belting pitch after pitch into the outfield. Like most lefties, he was more effective when the pitcher threw right-handed.

"Time!" Cesar called and jogged out to the mound.

"I don't want Waco back in the game with one swing. Pitch him lefty," suggested Cesar.

A spectator turned to his buddy and said, "That there kid is one of them amphibians," when he saw Angel switch the glove to his right hand.

"You means *am-bye-doctor-us*, stupid," replied his more scholarly friend.

"Don't matter, Clyde hits just as good from both sides."

When Clyde noticed that Angel was preparing to throw left-handed, he reversed his grip on the bat and stepped into the opposite box. Angel glanced over at Cesar who signaled for Angel to switch back and throw right-handed.

Upon seeing Angel switch hands again, Clyde crossed the plate to bat lefty. Angel then switched his glove to his right hand and stepped on the rubber to throw lefty. Clyde quickly jumped across to the other side of the batter's box. The duel continued until the umpire finally yelled, "Batter, pick a side!"

Clyde frowned and dug in as a left-handed hitter. Angel made eye contact with Clyde, smiled broadly and switched his glove to his right hand one last time.

Monterrey Industrial's offense exploded for another seven runs in the bottom of the fifth and added another in the sixth.

Monterrey's opponents played their hearts out, but once Angel had settled down, he crowned the game by shutting out Waco the rest of the way.

In two hours it was all over. The prairie winds howled across the plains beyond and swept into the Fort Worth stadium. The field and the stands were empty except for an old Latino caretaker who was busy untying the Texas flag from its cleat on the pole in center field. Pulling on its rope hand-over-hand, it slowly lowered until he could gather it up in his arms. The caretaker carefully folded the flag and looked up at the scoreboard. The home team had lost eleven to two, and he could not have been happier.

As the Monterrey Industrial team set their sights on Louisville, Kentucky, the cities of New York, Chicago and San Francisco also prepared to receive Little Leaguers for their respective regional tournaments.

Even before their game against Waco, Cesar first heard talk of a team with giant kids from La Mesa, California, that was beating its competitors with an ease unlike any other.

On Bread Alone

Almost every home on the normally barren 2a San Francisco Oriente now had flowers. Several people stood outside their houses, watering new gardens or doing other odds and ends to beautify properties once assumed unworthy of such pride. One man was painting his façade, and several others had already done so.

A boy of eleven years of age named Hector Torres came down the block and stood in front of the Macias house.

"Señora Macias! Señora Macias!" he called out until Angel's mother came outside.

"What is it, Hector?" Oralia Macias asked.

"Have you seen the papers?"

"No," she answered.

"Angel won again! They're the Texas State champions," he blurted out before she had a chance to find the article that was the source of his exuberance.

What had begun as a story of local interest in McAllen, Texas, written by a woman who wasn't even a sports columnist, had now blossomed into bilingual coverage that spanned Fort Worth to Monterrey.

They were quickly joined by Señora Villarreal and Señor Yañez, the man who had been painting his house.

"It says they're going to Louisville. It's in Kentucky," said Oralia with some apprehension as she read the headline.

"That sounds far away," Señora Villarreal added.

"It's a good thing, Señora," said Señor Yañez. "It means they're winning! Imagine that—against those American teams." He took the newspaper from Hector and began to scan the article.

"I know, and I'm proud of him. I just miss him so much and hope he's okay," she said.

"Angel's won four games pitching," read Señor Yañez.

"Let me look," said Señora Villarreal and took the newspaper. A moment later, she exclaimed, "My son scored three goals in the game!"

"*Runs*, Señora Villarreal, not *goals*," Señor Yañez corrected her.

"Runs, goals, they still count," she stated with pride.

"Is the señor at home?" Hector asked Señora Villarreal.

"He went to gather materials for a project at the field," she said.

"Can you please give him this?" Hector said, handing her a small paper bag filled with pesos. "It's for the team."

"Hector, where did you get this?" she asked.

"My friends and I got the rich folks in San Pedro to pay us to deliver milk to them."

"Don't you and your friends want some of the money for yourselves?"

Hector merely shrugged. "It's okay, señora. We don't need anything right now."

⟨∞⟩

"*Mi trasero* is killing me," said Francisco Aguilar. They had been on buses for the better part of the last thirty hours.

"Stop whining, we all sit on the same place," countered Enrique.

"I wasn't even talking to you," Francisco replied. It was a good thing that they were arriving at their destination because the boys were starting to get on one another's nerves.

As usual, Monterrey Industrial arrived at their host city before the league-provided accomodations were available, so the team was obliged to spend their first two nights at a local YMCA that seemed to be sheltering the dregs of Louisville transient population. It was a rough couple of nights.

On the third day, they moved to the quarters arranged by the league, Nichols U.S. Army General Hospital. It was built on the south side of the city on Berry and Manslick roads as a temporary facility to treat wounded GIs. In 1946, it was turned over to the Veterans Administration until a new hospital could be constructed. Given its anticipated short lifespan, it was hastily fabricated. Now that all remaining patients had been moved and its medical staff transferred, its empty, decaying interiors had a ghostly aura.

"This place looks haunted," said Rafael Estrello.

"I'd rather sleep outside," said Ricardo Treviño.

Suddenly, Fidel Ruiz darted inside the building. Finding an open window on the first floor, he stuck his head out and called to his friends. "Come in, guys!" It was almost as much of a challenge as an invitation.

"Fidel, come out! It doesn't look safe!" Enrique yelled back.

"I've slept in worse places," Fidel said.

At once, they all realized how true his words were.

✐

"Mom, can I sit next to the window? Please, please?" begged David Musgrave.

"Of course, honey," answered his mother as she watched her son slide into the window seat. A green-suited flight attendant with a fetchingly tilted flight hat helped Mrs. Musgrave stow her carry-on bag in the overhead compartment. The airline's brochure likened the plane's cabin to a "living room on wings." "There is plenty of light and fresh air, and note that there is ample leg room for all passengers," it boasted.

David and his mother had boarded a Pacific Southwest Airlines DC-4 at San Diego's Lindbergh Field. Flight 125 was bound for San Francisco and would take a total of only two hours and thirty-five minutes, including a brief stop at the Hollywood-Burbank Airport. It was a good deal for $15.44 a ticket, and certainly took a lot less time than the train up the West Coast.

"George 'Machine Gun' Kelley and Al Capone were once inmates," Mrs. Musgrave read from a San Francisco guidebook about some of the famous "guests" of the penitentiary on Alcatraz Island. An eerie sight from almost any point in the surrounding San

Francisco Bay, it was still a fully operational prison.

David listened, but his attention was diverted by the high-pitched whine of the DC-4's engines. After a burst of black smoke, one of the two propellers he could see on the plane's starboard side began to whirl faster and faster. Moments later, its sister engine followed suit and then the two on the port side. With all four revved-up, the din inside the craft drowned out his mother's words, and the plane moved off its blocks and began to taxi out to the runway.

Behind the Musgraves sat the families of no fewer than four of David's teammates. Five hundred miles to the north lay the site of the Western Regional Tournament.

∾⊙⊙⌇

It was time for Monterrey Industrial to resume practicing, and this would take place at the old State Fairgrounds in the Parkland area of western Louisville. Founded in 1902 by the Kentucky Livestock Breeders Association, it was home to rodeos, horse shows and other activities that required animals to be kept under the stadium bleachers.

A huge downpour began moments after the boys arrived, and they were forced to practice underneath the bleachers with its long corridors of stalls, freshly soiled from a recent cattle exhibition.

Afterwards Cesar reviewed the myriad of secret hand signals, intricate gestures letting the team know when to swing away, bunt or let pitches pass; what to do when running the bases; where to position themselves on defense; and what pitches to throw. The boys practiced these all the time, even in quiet moments back in their rooms. In all the complexity of these silent communications, not once, in any game, would any player mix up a signal.

∾⊙⊙⌇

"We've been making Louisville Sluggers for the major leagues since 1884," said the guide at the Hillerich & Bradsby Company. As Enrique's birthday had prompted a visit to the rodeo, Pepe Maiz's special day was spent at the Louisville bat factory.

The guide continued as Cesar translated his comments into Spanish. "It all started in a small woodworking shop when Bud Hillerich hand-turned a bat for Arnie Latham in return for an oath that Latham would never tell anyone where he got the bat. The next day, Latham got three hits and promptly told everyone who'd made his good-luck bat. The rest is history."

The tour moved into a room where the walls were lined with bats in display cases. Cesar noticed that Angel looked bored and lagged behind the group.

"You don't find this interesting?" he asked his young pitcher.

"Bats only help hitters."

"So now you're a great pitcher, you don't need to learn anything about hitting anymore?"

Cesar gave the boys a few dollars in change and allowed them some free time in the gift shop. There was little they could afford, so they pooled their money and bought Pepe a package of Topps baseball cards. The boys watched eagerly as he opened it. Pepe looked through the cards and gave a slight and gracious smile. Though the set contained a rookie Frank Robinson and two other future Hall of Famers, its lack of a Brooklyn Dodger player eroded its sentimental value.

With what little he dared spare, Cesar bought a postcard.

❧☙

At the far end of the gift shop, two baseball players were signing their bats. Lucky asked the guide who they were.

"That's Red Hayes and Pete Grange. They're with the Baltimore Orioles." The Orioles were the successor team to the St. Louis Browns. Before Lucky could make the connection, the two players looked at Cesar with an air of recognition, but there was nothing in their gaze that suggested the warmth of reunion.

"Well if it isn't the Mexican," Pete said.

"Hey, Fazool, get me some towels," mocked Red, and the two began to laugh.

"Where are you going?" Lucky asked Cesar, who pushed by him to get to the door.

"Nowhere." He turned and stared sharply at Lucky. "Take the boys back to the dorms. I'll be back later."

Cesar had an appointment with an old lover whose name was "Mezcal," the daughter of the maguey plant. She is a cruel mistress; one night of her charms and she can make a sane man think he can dance with a moving train. "*¡Para el cruel destino, vino; para el fracaso, de tequila un vaso; para la tristeza, cerveza; para todo mal, mezcal* [For cruel fate, wine; for failure, a glass of tequila; for sadness, beer, for everything bad, Mezcal]*!*"

He decided he would have only one.

Cesar's head cocked back as the cool liquid seared the back of his throat. Slamming the glass down on the counter, he stared blankly at the mirror behind the bar. He didn't like what looked back at him, but he stubbornly refused to turn his gaze.

"Just one more," her spirit softly sang to him from the bottom of the empty glass.

⚬⚬⚬

The relative emptiness of the barracks added to the boys' already unsettled feelings, and they huddled in their cots like dwellers of a cave, unsure of what would spring upon them from out of the darkness.

"Where did Señor Faz go?" Gerardo Gonzales whispered.

"He left in such a hurry," Ricardo said.

"You guys don't have to whisper, we're all awake," came a voice from a few beds down.

"Yeah, none of us are sleeping," came another.

"I saw some men say something to him that made him really mad," said Enrique, who now had his teammates' attention.

"Maybe he went out and got into a fight," Ricardo said.

Lucky and José Torres had left Padre Esteban with the team in order to look for Cesar, but being unfamiliar with Louisville, they had no idea of where to begin. The priest joined the boys; he carried a candle, which made him appear ghostly.

Several asked Padre Esteban about Cesar.

"I'm sure he had some important things to take care of," the priest said. His comment garnered a few sounds of agreement, but neither he nor the boys believed what he just said. "Now it's important for you all to sleep."

"Tell us a story, Padre," said Alfonso Cortez.

"Yeah, a story," added Norberto.

"Which one would you like to hear?" Padre Esteban asked, knowing full well that they always wanted the same story, "The Miracle of Guadalupe." Though the facts never varied, he tried his best to make each retelling more dramatic than the last so that the story would never lose its luster. He realized that this was a vain concern, as if any man's oration could enhance or diminish that which was divine.

The boys drew closer around the priest's simple light.

"One day an Aztec peasant—"

"Juan Diego?" Norberto asked.

"Yes, but he wasn't called that yet. He was born Quauhtatoatzin."

"Talking Eagle," Ricardo said proudly.

The priest smiled. "Talking Eagle gazed up at the steps of the temple whose name meant "place abundant in hummingbirds." There, human sacrifices were made in bloody rituals. Forty thousand years before, his ancestors had arrived in this wild new continent. They were the chosen ones whose god had given them their name Mexica, and they, in turn, would honor him with human sacrifices."

Like a chilling ghost story around a campfire, Padre Esteban spoke of still-beating hearts cut from innocents' bodies and cannibalistic feasts. It amused him how much children, especially boys, were fascinated by this part of the tale.

"These brutal rituals sickened Talking Eagle, and he longed to awaken to a new world, but there was little he could do as a lowly *macehualles*. But his prayers would soon be answered. That day, news had reached Tenochtitlan that the fair-haired god *Quetzalcoatl* had landed and was approaching the city from Vera Cruz."

"Cortés," interjected Norberto.

"Yes, and within two years, Moctezuma's vast empire was razed to dust. Soon after, missionaries arrived. They were not like the conquistadors who preceded them. They obtained with compassion that which could not be conquered by force. In the Aztec peasant's fiftieth year, he was led into the warm waters of Lake Texcoco and baptized before God as Juan Diego."

The boys strained to hear every word as if feeling the power of "The Miracle of Guadalupe" for the first time.

The priest continued, "Juan Diego's wife died five years later, leaving him all alone. One day, in his darkest despair, he crossed Tepeyac Hill and the Virgin Mother appeared before him."

⊱◦◦◦⊰

There was no siren accompanying the flashing lights of the police cruiser as it rolled to a stop in front of the barracks. Lucky and José helped Cesar out of the back of the deputy's car.

Inside the building's lower level, Cesar stumbled down the hall, bleary-eyed and unabashedly soused. Lucky and the deputy stood conversing, as the coach leaned against a vending machine. He fed it several coins, but the machine ate them all and gave him nothing in return. He shoved the machine, eliciting a stern look from the deputy, and then stumbled farther down the long corridor.

Cesar managed to make his way up the stairs to the door that led to the main room, leaning into it for balance. Through it, he heard Padre Esteban's voice.

"The Dark Virgin told Juan Diego to go to Zumaragga and tell him all that he had seen and heard. But the Spanish bishop was more concerned with his own wealth and power than with obeying the word of God. Zumaragga shunned Juan Diego—"

Cesar barged in, and the boys stared at him with a mixture of fear, curiosity and pity.

"Why are you all still awake?" he growled.

"I was just telling them a story," said Padre Esteban.

"Oh yes, the one about how the poor peasant humbles the world. I've heard that fairy tale many times. Well, let me teach you something, boys—it's a lie."

"You're a lie" was all Angel could say, tears welling in his eyes.

"Angel, Señor Faz is your coach," said Padre Esteban.

Cesar scanned the boys who stared at him, his eyes narrowed and his brow tensed until small ridges appeared above his forehead. He then slurred, "Coach? I never asked to—"

"Cesar!" came the priest's stern voice. "That's enough now." He put his arm around the coach's shoulder. "Good night, boys," he said, leading Cesar away.

The boys were once again shrouded in pitch darkness.

❧❦

When Cesar opened his bloodshot eyes the next morning, he saw Padre Esteban sitting quietly on the other bed reading from his Bible.

"Did you get the license plate of the car that hit me?" quipped Cesar.

"You were in a car accident?" asked the priest.

"Never mind, it's an old joke."

"I see that the dawn has returned something the night had stolen—your sense of humor."

"Ugh," Cesar gurgled, "last night wasn't pretty."

"Really?" the priest said in a soft tone, but he knew that Cesar needed to be confronted. "You let down the whole team, especially Pepe."

"I'll try to make it up to him. . . and to all of them."

"You mocked the story of Juan Diego."

"Guess I don't believe the meek win just because they're pious."

"Neither did Juan Diego."

"How do you know the story wasn't invented by missionaries? Maybe it's a mirage, like those kids watching a stupid humming-bird."

"Is believing in the unlikely a sin?" asked the priest.

"What if you're making them believe in things that will never come true?"

"Cesar, the only true certainty of life is death. The only way to live is to detach oneself from the sadness of the past and to be unafraid of the variables of the future."

The priest suddenly noticed Fidel Ruiz standing at the partially opened door. "What do you want?" Cesar barked.

"I was just looking for Padre Esteban."

"He'll be out in a little bit," said Cesar as he closed the door.

"You hold so much anger, Cesar. What—"

"Who's angry? Nobody's angry!" Cesar replied, but hearing his own vitriolic intonation made him slump back on his bed and stare shamefully at the ground. "I'm just a little tense," he added in a softer manner.

"What happened when you coached the Browns?" Padre Esteban calmly finished his question.

After a pause, Cesar said ruefully, "Padre, I wasn't their coach. I was a clubhouse attendant."

"I see."

"No, you don't."

"Then help me to see," said the priest. He got up to sit next to Cesar, who didn't really want to talk about it, but he realized that Padre Esteban wasn't going to let up until he did.

"For years I bit my tongue while picking up their soiled towels and jockstraps," Cesar began. "I swallowed my pride when I had to sleep on the team bus in cities where I wasn't allowed in the same hotel as the players.I even took it in stride when they called me 'the Mexican.' The assistant manager's job that I had been promised finally came up, but I was passed over."

"Sorry," consoled Padre Esteban, "but that doesn't give you the right to behave like you did yesterday."

"I know...it's simply hard to forget. I remember sitting in Mr. Tanner's office, hearing him encourage me, 'You're doing great Cesar. Keep working hard and maybe next year. . .'"

"What did you do?"

"I looked for a job with another franchise, but the scouting report on me was hard-working but hard to work with. I found the source. It was Mr. Tanner, the new manager, the same man who to my face said, "Wait till next year" and then joked with everyone else about how he had the oldest towel boy in the league. I confronted him in the locker room and spoke a piece of my mind in a way that people like me just didn't do to white folks. I cleaned out my locker that evening."

"He fired you?" asked Padre Esteban.

"Does it matter?"

"One path means you ran away."

"Sorry to disappoint you, Padre," Cesar said and walked out closing the door behind him.

18

House Arrest

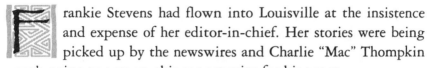

rankie Stevens had flown into Louisville at the insistence and expense of her editor-in-chief. Her stories were being picked up by the newswires and Charlie "Mac" Thompkin wasn't going to pass up this opportunity for his paper.

Frankie was having a late lunch at Ginny's Diner, which was a few miles down the road from St. Matthews, a suburb of Louisville. Ginny's was home to the "Sweet Daddy," a stack of three half-pound burgers topped with a mountain of cheese served with a side of "frickled pickles," battered and deep-fried dill pickles.

Frankie couldn't help but notice that a young man sitting alone at the next table hadn't taken his eyes off of her. She'd been extra careful not to make too much eye contact lest he misinterpret it as an invitation, but he sauntered over to her table and introduced himself anyway. She told him the purpose of her visit, and the whole incident would have remained insignificant had he not worked as a law clerk for the local judge.

"You're covering the Little League story?" he asked with amazement.

"What's wrong with that?" she stated.

"Nothing, but the Mexican team is under house arrest. Their case just came before my boss."

⚜

Sheriff Hayes, the officer in charge, knew the boys hadn't committed any crime that particularly concerned him, but he was paid $37.53

a week to uphold the laws of Jefferson County and that's all he was trying to do.

There was an Immigration and Naturalization Service office in Louisville, but the sole agent manning that branch had an appendectomy two days earlier and was on sick leave. An agent would have to be sent from Cincinnati. The sheriff's orders were to politely request that the Monterrey team await his arrival, but he was authorized to arrest them if they attempted to flee and hide.

He thought of the irony of the concern that these boys might escape and avoid detection. Fourteen kids, wearing baseball uniforms, who didn't speak English seemed as likely to blend in as a platypus at a beauty pageant.

"Sheriff," Cesar pleaded, "these kids are playing in the Southern Regional Chapionship tomorrow."

"I hope they're fixin' to play it in Mexico," said the sheriff, wishing this had happened in someone else's jurisdiction.

Cesar possessed a valid passport, so his movements were not restricted. He was feeling some withdrawal from the prior evening's binge of drinking on an empty stomach, so he decided to buy some spirits just for medicinal purposes.

Cesar found a check-cashing store that had what he sought. Inside, the clerk eyed him with a mix of disdain and pity. The proprietor was also Hispanic, though Cesar thought him likely to be from South America, perhaps Peru or Ecuador.

Cesar was counting out change on the counter when he noticed a small icon of Mary of Guadalupe atop the register. Just then, the bells of the Cathedral of the Assumption on Fifth Street rang out.

"Sorry" was all Cesar could say to the slightly annoyed proprietor as he picked up his change, put the bottle back on its shelf and walked out. He headed back to the Greyhound Bus depot where he had recalled seeing a Western Union office.

⎰⎱⎰⎱

"Where were you, Señor Faz?" a nervous Pepe asked him.

"I had to send a telegram."

"What's that?"

"It's a special message delivered on a piece of paper right to a person's door, no matter how far away they are," he explained.

The boys looked at one another, quite impressed with this "modern" marvel, which had been around for more than a century.

"Will they let us stay?" Angel asked.

"I'm not sure," answered his coach.

"Did we do something wrong?"

"No, Angel. Countries have rules about how long you can visit. We've just overstayed the time. But have faith, I'm doing everything I can."

Angel suddenly looked unhappy and a bit confused.

"What's wrong, Angel?"

"You tell us all the time to have faith, but you don't."

The rest of that day, the boys forgot about their past victories as a shadow descended upon them. Angel stood quietly in a dark corner and walked across the room, thinking, waiting and suffering.

Enrique had the opposite reaction to their temporary confinement. He was annoyingly energetic, impatient and hyperactive. Fourteen boys with fourteen different reactions to the same event, but one common symptom was the team losing the best thing it had: its spirit.

"Maybe it's best this way," Cesar said to Lucky while trying to find something to say to fill the awkward silence that pervaded the wait for news of their disposition.

"Being deported?" asked his friend, unsure if he heard Cesar right.

"No, leaving undefeated. At least they'll always remember being Texas state champions."

"What makes you certain they were going to lose?"

"All dreams end," said Cesar with the all the washed-out emotion of a man beaten into the dust.

∽◌⋐◌∾

Señor Bremer and his wife were enjoying tea on their veranda when their servant interrupted, handing him a telegram.

FWB65DB270 OB273

O.MTY193 PD=MONTERREY MEXICO 18 1110=

SEÑOR DON RODOLFO BREMER=

SAN SEBASTIAN ORIENTE 124=

HAVE BIG PROBLEM VISAS EXPIRED. BOYS REFUSE TO LOSE=

CESAR L. FAZ=

Señor Bremer had to smile, something he didn't do that often. He took a Hoyo de Monterrey from a small leather case, and his servant lit a thin strip of cedar and held the flame to the end of the Pyramides cigar until it glowed bright orange.

The patrician savored its dark blend of tobaccos from Cuba, Honduras and Sumatra. After several long draws, he turned to address his servant. "Bring me the telephone."

19

Biloxi Blues

Christian Archibald Herter graduated from Harvard University and had served as a US congressman and governor of the state of Massachusetts. Earlier in the year, he added to this pedigreed resumé his appointment as the undersecretary of state to John Foster Dulles.

1957 was a tumultuous year for the State Department. Hungary was overrun by the Soviets; Egypt nationalized the Suez Canal; the Chinese were supporting the Viet Minh against the French in Indochina; and the CIA had briefed Herter that the Soviets were working on a rocket that could carry a nuclear weapon thousands of miles right to the American heartland.

Herter dictated several communiqué's to his assistant, Mrs. Dorothy Berenson, and then asked her if there were any other pressing matters that required his immediate attention.

"The Philippine attaché dropped off the report on rubber exports," she said, handing him a manila folder. Herter perused it quickly and handed it back to her.

"Have Thompson at Agriculture handle it. Send it regular pouch. If that's all, I'll be at Delmonico's for lunch," he said as he reached for his Stetson. It would hit eighty-seven degrees today, but the undersecretary was a formal man who was rarely seen without a hat when he was in Washington, DC on public business.

"There is one more thing, sir. . . it's an appeal for a denied visa extension."

"Who's the VIP?" he asked, returning to the edge of his

mahogany desk.

"Some children who crossed the Texas border a few weeks ago."

"A bunch of Mexican kids?" asked Herter. With his back toward the door, he didn't see the impressively dressed gentleman who appeared at the threshold. The white fields on the man's French cuffs were accessorized with lapis cuff links and on the left cuff in a navy blue weave were the letters *RCH*. He was a Dartmouth man, and like Herter, he was of kind of blue-blooded lineage from which the State Department loved to recruit its diplomats.

"I'm the undersecretary of state!" exclaimed Herter with an air of indignation. "What piss ant got this bumped up to my office?"

"That would be me, Mr. Secretary," said the silver-haired man from the doorway, his lips curled into a slight smile.

"And you are?" asked Herter, turning toward the stranger.

"Robert Hill, US Ambassador to Mexico."

Ten minutes later, Ambassador Hill walked Herter across the street to his appointment at Delmonico's.

"I don't get it. What are these Mexican kids to you?" Herter asked.

"Just a bunch of Mexican kids," answered Hill.

"If I approved this, what kind of precedent would I be setting?"

"The kind you and I believed in when we first chose these jobs."

⋘⊙⊚⊙⋙

"They said the team can stay for 'thirty days or until they lose, whichsoever shall come first.' It's a blessing, Cesar." Padre Esteban repeated Cesar's words as the latter shared the news of the extraordinary visa extension. It had taken an act from the U.S. State Department to bypass and countermand the red tape that would have normally resulted in an immigrant's immediate expulsion.

Cesar watched as Padre Esteban continued his preparations to leave.

"You don't have to leave. They extended all the visas."

"I have a flock to attend to and Padre Velasquez must return to Saltillo."

"What am I going to do?" Cesar asked.

"You're their coach, coach them."

"And then?"

"Come home."

"Home? Where is that for me, Padre? I can't stay here in Louisville and I haven't got much to return to Monterrey for. I'm barely holding on to a bad job and I messed things up with. . . well, with just about everybody."

"To be forgiven, you must be able to forgive, and for that you will need to devote yourself, without reservation, to God."

Padre Esteban knew that when a man wandered into such an emotional desert, he alone had to seek salvation or perish in its burning sands.

"I've never found answers inside a church," Cesar said.

"You speak of our faith like it's a building. These boys who led us here, they're the real Catholic church. Not like a bureaucracy of religious know-it-alls." Cesar was surprised to hear a member of the clergy saying such things.

"What about the money? I spent a lot last evening on. . . beverages."

"All the more reason that I must return to Monterrey. It's one less adult to feed and I can do more for the team there than here. Now let me say my goodbye to the boys."

"You won't tell them about what happened in St. Louis?"

"I won't tell them, Cesar."

"Good."

"Because you will," Padre Esteban said.

Suddenly, a man who had faced enemy fire in war and had never backed down from a barroom scrape in peacetime now found himself terrified to confront fourteen children. Cesar didn't know why, but the real reason was that there were only two kinds of people who were incapable of veiling the truth: the very old and the very young. The former were usually too wise and the latter, thankfully, too naive.

On most nights when the boys prepared for bed, Padre Esteban would tell them stories. They were always about good triumphing over evil, with a moral lesson of how the faithful were rewarded and the wicked faced God's wrath.

But tonight was unlike any other. They hadn't traveled or played baseball, and the long hours of inactivity as well as the anxieties caused by Cesar's recent behavior and the potential deportation had taken their toll. The boys were upset, and a few cried themselves to sleep just wanting to go home and see their parents.

Cesar blamed himself, assuming that his behavior on the night that had culminated in his ride home in the deputy's car, had caused the problem. Yet as ugly an incident as it had been, it had absolutely nothing to do with the visit by Sheriff Hayes.

The real cause was a call by Sgt. Clayton Harbush, the border patrol who had screened the team when they first entered the United States. He had just read the *McAllen Gazette* and seen pictures of the kids who had crossed his post a little more than two weeks earlier with a three-day visa.

❧❦❧

The next day, Monterrey Industrial arrived at St. Matthews Park off Shelbyville Road. About seven miles from downtown Louisville, the community center was surrounded on three sides by potato farms and on the fourth side by encroaching suburbanization. After additional bleachers had been assembled, its two fields could accommodate more than five thousand fans. Behind the home plate fence was a large concession stand where the Louisville Ladies Auxiliary would sell baked goods to raise money for the local league. Over the next two days, they would bake and sell more than four thousand homemade cupcakes.

"Your team's causing quite a stir," said a reporter from the *Louisville Courier-Journal* who had cornered Cesar in the parking area of the field. "I'm referring to them begging folks for money after the games down in Texas. Don't you think it's embarrassing?"

"It sure is, but it was that or no food. I figure it was better to be embarrassed than go hungry."

"Do these children really have so little?" asked the reporter.

"Little?" Cesar said. "Try no gloves, no shoes. . . nothing but a sock-filled ball and a stick."

"They don't have shoes?"

"For some of them, cleats were the first thing they ever wore on their feet. Now they wear them everywhere, even to church." The reporter took notes about how fans had taken up collections at games to give to the Monterrey team. "Now all we have to worry about is money to buy food—and paying our way home," Cesar anxiously stated.

"Do you think you stand a chance against Biloxi, Mississippi?" the reporter asked, but the coach's attention was fixed on someone across the parking lot.

"Recognize someone?"

"It's some reporter who's followed us since McAllen. She swore the only direction we'd be leaving that town was due south."

"What's a dame doing covering a sports story anyway? She'd be better off sticking to a column about recipes or gardening," the reporter said laughingly.

The *Courier-Journal* reporter knew he had a good human interest story here. It always made for better reading, even among his ardent sports fans. Later that day, as he reviewed his notes and began to formulate his article, he thought of Cesar's worrying about how the team would get back home. He had never heard of any athletic team having such a dilemma. All they could do was forge ahead and pray for some miraculous solution to reveal itself.

He ended his article with, "Admission will be free, but a hat will be handy if you want to help the little Mexicans."

The boys of Monterrey Industrial sat in their dugout, watching their opponents take their final fielding practice.

The umpire stepped out in front of the plate.

"Play ball!" he yelled, but there was no movement from the Monterrey bench.

"Monterrey, where's your lead-off hitter?" the umpire called out to Cesar as Sam Hicks, the Biloxi coach and a man of very little patience, ran out from his dugout.

"Monterrey coach, come here now!" the ump summoned Cesar.

"I don't know how you start a game down there in Mexico," Sam said to Cesar as he joined the two men at the plate, "but here we gots two simple words: *play* and *ball*."

"Do you have a priest?" Cesar asked.

"A priest? Is someone dying?" asked the umpire.

"My boys won't play without a blessing. I'm sorry. Ours left a few days ago and they just assumed there'd be a priest here."

"We're starting a baseball game," said the umpire.

"I know, sir, but my boys said they're only here because of God's blessing and that honoring Him is more important than the game."

"Well, they better start now or else they's gonna forfeit," interjected Coach Hicks.

"Coach, I'm sure they can find one later. Why don't you try to reason with them," advised the umpire.

"Reason with those *bandidos*?" Cesar mumbled under his breath as the seconds ticked away with no motion from the Monterrey dugout. Unfazed by the impending forfeit, the boys discussed the dilemma at hand.

"Maybe it wasn't his fault," suggested Norberto.

"Who's could it have been?" asked Ricardo.

"Why are we even here in America? They don't want us anyway," said Gerardo.

"Not all of them. There are lots of good people here. How do you think we've been eating or getting around?" stated Pepe. "And it's not Cesar's fault if there's no priest at the field."

"But it is his fault that Padre Esteban left," said Fidel.

"We don't know that," said Pepe.

"He told Padre Esteban that Juan Diego was a mirage and that the hummingbird was stupid."

"Fidel!" snapped Francisco.

"Well, I shouldn't have heard it, but I did."

"If it weren't for Señor Faz, none of us would be here," exclaimed Pepe.

"You've always liked him 'cause he put you in left field. You're not really one of us. Right, Enrique?" Francisco began and was quickly silenced by Enrique.

"Pepe is as much my brother as any of you," he said with such command that left no doubt how much the bond between these two boys had grown. "Fidel and Pepe are both right, but we have to act as one," he added.

"Angel, you know Señor Faz longer than any of us. What do you think?" asked Ricardo.

"Coach Faz needs our help," answered Angel.

"So we play?" voiced several of his teammates.

"No, we can't without a blessing. It's for Señor Faz's own good."

"I don't get it," Norberto whispered to Pepe.

"He's saying we can honor God and help our coach at the same time—even if it means losing," Pepe told the catcher.

"Beto, whether we play or forfeit is in God's hands now," Angel finished.

"This is going to hurt," said Ricardo.

Cesar had just returned and spoke sternly to them. "No fooling, boys, you wanna lose and go home?"

"You lost our priest, you fix it," said Angel as he sat on his glove.

"Fine, Enrique's pitching anyway," said Cesar, but as he did, Enrique also took off his glove and sat on it.

"Pepe, start warming up," Cesar ordered, but Pepe took off his glove, too. One by one, each player followed suit until the gloves of the whole team were firmly nestled under immovable derrieres.

It was at that moment that Cesar realized that without a blessing, no power on earth was going to get his team off the bench. What made him angriest was they were just like him when he was a boy: audacious, reckless and romantic.

Cesar walked slowly back to the umpire and Coach Hicks at home plate with the news that Monterrey Industrial would be forfeiting.

Part Three

The Rose Garden

20

A Rose as Sweet

orry gentlemen, they're kinda stubborn," Cesar said apologetically.

"Well, ump," said Coach Sam Hicks, "there you have it! They won't put their team on the field."

The events of a Little League baseball game in Louisville, Kentucky should hardly have merited divine attention, but just as the umpire was about to call the game in Biloxi's favor, an angel's voice interceded.

"My neighbor's a minister," stated Rose Lee Simmons, an elderly African American woman who had walked onto the field from the first row of the bleachers. "Does that count?" she asked.

"What's it to you?" asked the Biloxi coach. Quickly scanning the field, he said, "You obviously ain't got a kid in the game."

"Rose lives nearby. She just comes to watch," said the umpire.

"I'm sorry for interrupting you fellas, but I could go get him," she offered.   "This is horse dung, ump. I demand that you disqualify these—"

"Coach, what's your last name?" came a second woman's voice, this one belonged to Frankie Stevens.

"Hicks!" he yelled out, trying to remain focused on his tirade. "Rule twelve, paragraph nine of the Little League handbook—"

While he was ranting, Frankie began simultaneously writing and reading aloud her words: "Louisville, Kentucky—Today Coach Hicks declared baseball *bigger* than God. . ."

"Hey, wait one dagnabbit minute! Y'all know I didn't say that!"

Frankie just stood there and batted her eyes.

"Here's my editor's number. Why don't you call him tomorrow. . . after you've read the morning edition," she said coolly.

Hicks looked back at the ump. "I demand you disqualify these Mexicans if they don't take the field right now!"

"You ain't in a position to be demanding nothing here," said a very annoyed umpire. "Bigger than God, huh?" he added, then turned his attention and a broad smile to Rose.

"Pay him no mind, Rose. You go get that neighbor of yours and let's have ourselves a ball game."

As the group dispersed, Cesar said to Frankie, "Never thought I'd be glad to see you. You really helped me out of a jam."

"Don't flatter yourself. I didn't travel all this way to cover a forfeit."

She could be hard as nails, Cesar thought.

"So, what happened to your priest?" she asked.

"I warned him not to drink the water here," was Cesar's reply.

ೋ⊙⊙ೋ

Rose returned, accompanied by an elderly African American man who at first appearance seemed to be in his sixties. His name was Clarence Bell, and he headed the congregation at Forest Missionary Baptist.

"Well, you'll get your blessing," Cesar stated.

But the boys still wouldn't budge.

"All right, now what?" a nervous and exasperated coach asked them.

"You've got to make one more promise, Señor Faz," demanded Ricardo.

"Anything, just take the blessing and take the field."

"When we return, you must make a visit to the Basilica of the Virgin of Guadalupe."

"Sure, okay."

"Swear?"

"Yeah, I swear." Cesar wasn't lying. He just knew it was an easy promise to make and because the Basilica was in Mexico City, it was just as easy to postpone indefinitely.

"Okay, we're ready," Cesar said to Clarence as he watched Coach Hicks slam down an ice chest in his dugout. "They'd like something from the book of Psalms."

"Any particular one?"

"The 108th is very special to them," Cesar answered.

"*Your loving kindness is great above the heavens*," began Clarence, in a language foreign to his flock, as the boys knelt before him, "*and your truth reaches to the skies. . .*"

∾⋅⊙⋅∾

The last few days in Monterrey, Mexico had seen a flurry of activity at the old dirt field. Local residents had been preparing for today's game. They raked out stones and glass, and watered it to reduce the lime dust that flew into the air with the lightest breeze or touch of a foot.

They had built a series of bleachers, four rows deep from which spectators could see the action. The work had spread to the inside of the adjacent abandoned barracks. Scaffolds had been erected, and men of different trades worked diligently, repairing roof rafters, shoring up timbers, chipping away the deteriorated masonry, and cleaning the twisted metal and concrete debris.

People began to take their seats and wait excitedly for the commencement of the "game." Several men sold tickets; all the proceeds would go to the Monterrey Industrial team. The only odd thing was there were no baseball players warming up on the sidelines, nor did the spectators expect any to show up. The "game" that everyone came to "watch" had actually taken place days earlier in Fort Worth, Texas. Señor Manuel Gonzalez Caballero from radio station XET's *La Voz de las Americas,* would re-create it through a microphone hooked up to some old speakers.

Señor Fecundino Suarez handed Señor Caballero several handwritten pages and asked, "Do you think you can make sense of it?"

"I'll do my best."

Working from box score diagrams, Señor Caballero would add color commentary to bring the action to life for those present, most of whom had never seen a baseball game played.

"It's another base hit through the hole. Peter Clark scores from second," he announced as the "game" progressed.

Or the next inning: "That's ball four. Fidel Ruiz walks, putting runners on first and second with one out."

And the next: "It's still Waco two, Monterrey nothing here in the bottom of the second but our boys are threatening. . . Baltazar Charles slaps one into center. That'll score Fidel Ruiz and Roberto Mendiola."

With the mention of any child's name, the crowd cheered and patted that boy's parents on the shoulders. And though the game's outcome was already known, nervous groans could be heard whenever a Waco player got on base.

Meanwhile, the work on the barracks continued. New cement was mixed from bags "borrowed" from Cemex as bricks and cinder blocks were laid. Windows, fashioned at Vitro, were fitted into their frames, and several men with specialized skills worked on the façade.

"Strike three! Angel Macias now has seven strike outs. . . A sharp grounder to shortstop, Gerardo Gonzales bobbles it. . . the throw. . . in time!" continued Señor Caballero.

As the crowd's excitement for victory grew with each passing inning, several workers stood back and admired their handiwork. A man driving by pulled his car over to the curb and looked in wonderment at the renaissance of a building that he had passed many times and known only as a crumbling ruin.

"Who hired you guys?" he asked.

"No one," answered Fecundino.

"Well, what's it going to be used for?" he asked Señor Claudio Villarreal.

"Don't know yet," Norberto's father answered, pulling off his gloves and wiping the sweat off his forehead.

"No one's paying you and you have no idea what it'll be? Why are you working on it?" asked the stranger.

"Needs doing," said Claudio.

⁂

On a field in Louisville, Kentucky, a live baseball game was about to take place.

Though Biloxi played aggressively, after an inning they had made little progress against Enrique Suarez's pitches. In the top of the second inning, Mississippi's pitcher gave up three straight walks to Fidel Ruiz, Gerardo Gonzales and Ricardo Treviño. Pepe Maiz stepped up to the plate with the bases loaded.

On the third pitch, he hit a thundering grand slam that ricocheted off the roof of an outbuilding past the center field fence. It was the first grand slam that the *Regiomontanos* had ever witnessed. It was a storybook homerun, and even the Biloxi players whistled softly with begrudging admiration.

In the bottom of the third inning with Biloxi at bat, one of their larger players collided full bore with Ricardo Treviño. His shins were already bruised from base runners sliding or running into him, and his left foot had taken the impact of dozens of cleats. Cesar, deciding to rest him as a precaution, shifted Angel from shortstop to first base. Angel, who'd been playing the infield right-handed, began to make practice throws with his left arm. The crowd stared in awe at this boy who threw with either hand as naturally as a man could walk with both feet.

Monterrey added nine more runs after Pepe's grand slam, many of them coming from an inordinate amount of walks surrendered by Biloxi pitchers. It turned into a rout, but Cesar celebrated with modest optimism. He knew he couldn't count on his players being walked to win tomorrow.

The Biloxi players collected their gear and reunited with parents who came down from the stands. One father tried to place blame for the loss. "Game would've been forfeited if it wasn't for that nosy colored gal."

"Dad, she wasn't the one who scored thirteen runs against us," said his son.

The *Regiomontanos* had played well, and in tallying thirteen runs, almost everyone on the team had gotten at least one hit, except Norberto who struck out all three times. He had been in a slump for a few days. Perhaps he was trying too hard, or perhaps his foot had been reinjured, or maybe sun or shadows played havoc upon his batting eye. Cesar couldn't figure out the cause.

Every player has days like that—it's a statistical eventuality. But today Norberto did have sun in his eyes, and it radiated from a beautiful girl in a white dress who cheered from the first row of the stands. Her name was Paulina Valenzuela, and her dad was a long-haul trucker who had read about these baseball invaders in a Spanish language newspaper called *Hoy en las Américas*.

Earlier, during warm-ups, Enrique had said to him, "Beto, there, see that pretty one?"

"Where do they sell tickets for that prize?" asked Norberto.

"She's looking at you."

"No, she isn't."

"Yes, she is," insisted Enrique.

"Go talk to her for me," Norberto pleaded.

Enrique finally agreed and made his way to the railing upon which Paulina had rested her thin and beautifully tanned arms.

"Good morning, señorita," he addressed the cute *chicana*.

"Who are you?" she asked.

"My name is of no consequence, but the message I bring is of such importance, it might change your life."

"Really?"

"Yes, señorita. You see that handsome *caballero* over there?" asked Enrique with a gesture of his head toward his catcher.

Paulina looked at Norberto, who pretended to be unaware.

"We call him *el Verdugo*," said Enrique.

❧◌❧

"Were your boys really going to forfeit if they didn't receive a blessing?" Clarence asked Cesar after the game.

"Yep," Cesar answered.

"Now that's a devoted flock!"

"Yeah, devoted—like the Spanish Inquisition."

Clarence laughed.

"If it wouldn't be too much trouble, would you come tomorrow and bless us again?" Cesar asked the minister.

"You sure your boys wouldn't prefer to find a Catholic priest, maybe one who speaks Spanish?"

"I already asked. They said that all men who feel God speak the same language."

Clarence smiled as he went to meet Rose in the stands.

Meanwhile, the victorious *Regiomontanos* awaited Cesar's instructions.

"Where are we gonna go now?" asked Baltazar.

"Nowhere," said Cesar.

"Why?" came the obvious question from his team.

"That was one of the sloppiest games I've ever seen," he began to scold them. "You're going to run some laps and then practice."

"We won thirteen to nothing!" answered Enrique.

"They made four errors and walked a dozen of you. Those are called gifts because you didn't earn them. How about that play in the fourth where Angel made a throw to second. That was your backup, Rafael."

"But, Señor Faz, there was no overthrow and the runner was out," said Rafael.

"*This* time," scowled Cesar. "And you, Norberto, you're Ricardo's last line of defense on an overthrow at first. Everyone give me three laps around. . . the long way."

"Señor Faz, we know why you won't be happy if we lose, but you don't seem happy when we win either," said Angel.

"I just don't want to see you come this far and lose over a stupid error."

"Is that what's really bothering you?"

"Angel, in America you have to be twice as good to be treated half as good."

"It's okay, Señor Faz. If we lose, no one will blame you," said the boy as he and his teammates began to run.

Ninety minutes later, the boys flopped in their cots, exhausted from the laps and rigorous postgame practice.

"Cesar, I never question you as a coach, but don't you think you're pushing them just a bit too hard?" asked Lucky.

"They need to work harder. It'll make them stronger," said Cesar.

"Even steel can break."

"Baseball is baseball. On every level it should be played the right way or not—"

"Who are you trying to convince?" interrupted Cesar's friend.

⌀⌀⌀⌀

As dusk settled over the Ohio River Valley, the boys were frightened to hear crescendo-pitched screams from outside their windows. At first imagining them to be wounded people or wild animals, it was little comfort when Cesar told them that it came from *cicadas*, *crickets* and *katydids* who were just chirping their unique love songs. Armed with a vision of giant bugs capable of projecting such loud shrill noises, the boys posted lookouts at each window.

This wasn't the only punishment that this new environment visited upon these Mexican children. The densely rich grass fields and forests of oaks, maples and spruce trees were a spawning ground for pollens and molds for which the boys' constitutions had no defense. Several of them found their noses running, eyes swelling and a couple had sneezing attacks that were as cruelly painful as they were hysterically entertaining to their peers.

The Biloxi coach had offered several cigars to Cesar as congratulations for Monterrey Industrial's victory. He, Lucky and Jose sat outside in the humid night air and lit three of them.

"I hate these pests," said Cesar as he swatted a mosquito that had landed on the back of his sweating neck.

"Not half as bad as the swarms we had in the Philipines," laughed Lucky, blowing a long puff of smoke at one that flew by his face.

"After they stung you, they went after your relatives," Cesar mused.

"You know they weren't going to come out of the dugout if that minister hadn't come. I thought for sure we'd be disqualified today," Jose said.

"Would've served you right, Cesar," Lucky added. "For their sake I'm sure glad it didn't happen that way."

"You taking their side?"

"He's right, Cesar," agreed Jose.

"Admit it. Those kids are just like you," said Lucky. "As hard-headed as nails when they want something. Only difference is, you don't know what you want."

"I didn't see your satchel, doctor." Cesar shook his head.

"Don't need a doctor—an illiterate man can read you, Cesar."

"Oh, and your life is so together?"

"Are you kidding?" stated Lucky. "Mine's in pieces. That's why it's easy to spot in you."

The three men laughed, and as if on cue, they all flicked the long glowing ashes at the end of their cigars onto the ground.

21

Elite Giants

arly the next morning, Clarence brought the Monterrey Industrial team to his home.

"Buelah, honey, I invited a couple of new friends over," said Clarence as he stood on his front porch.

His wife just stared at this caravan of stragglers and glared at Clarence. "I's supposin' you's fixin' to feed them," she said suspiciously.

"Well, as long as you's cookin'," he said sheepishly.

Buelah was a soul-food connoisseur. For her, cooking was a labor of love, though she'd never miss an opportunity to complain about it. She prepared a feast of pickled cow tongue, fried chitlins, cracklin's and Rocky Mountain oysters. The latter weren't really oysters, that was just a euphemism for a part of the bull best left unmentioned. Except for the pickled tongue, everything else was deep fried in what Southerners liked to call vitamin G. The G stood for grease.

After breakfast, Buelah entered the living room where the boys were getting a blackboard session from Cesar.

"*Mmm, mmm.* Coach, these boys ain't fit to roll in a barn," she said. Their practice in the damp animal stalls had done little to improve the already over-worn uniforms. "Have 'em give me them clothes," she demanded. Buelah left no doubt that her husband may have been a big man at the pulpit when he preached the ten commandments, but in her home, she was the one who enforced them.

"Boys, give your clothes to Señora Bell," Cesar told them. All but Ricardo and Norberto complied.

"What's the matter with them two?" asked Buelah. The rest of the team was giggling. Buelah continued to stare until a red-faced Ricardo whispered into Cesar's ear.

"They forgot to put on their underwear this morning," Cesar translated.

"Shucks, I had seven brothers and raised five boys of my own. They ain't got nothing I ain't seen. Tell 'em they gots till three to give me them clothes or I's gonna remove 'em myself." Buelah turned her back and began counting to three. Laughter rose from their teammates as Ricardo and Norberto sheepishly handed the last two pairs of pants to her.

❧⦿❧

In Louisville, it's said that if the bourbon is blended just right, a man can see the aurora borealis without leaving his front porch. Whiskey-induced visions aside, residents had to rub their eyes at the sight of a Little League baseball team jogging and doing calisthenics in its underwear. Passing motorists waved and honked; some were encouraging, others mocking.

Cesar had stepped up this form of persuasion anytime any player made a mental error, even if it was answering a question incorrectly during one of their blackboard lessons. The rule was if one boy incurred the dreaded laps, they all ran with him. Cesar was determined that they should always rise and fall as a team.

Though every game along the way was important—as a single loss spelled elimination—there was something extra special about today's contest against Owensboro, Kentucky. Every one knew that the winner would receive a berth in the final round of the Little League World Series in Williamsport, Pennsylvania.

At St. Matthews Park, the reporter from the *Louisville Courier-Journal* was taking a picture of Baltazar, Fidel, Enrique, Norberto and Pepe. Its caption would read, "Mexican *Murderers' Row* Eyes Crown."

Across the way, Frankie was interviewing Coach Quinn, the

Owensboro skipper.

"Yesterday, you didn't give Monterrey a chance. How do feel now after watching them blanket Biloxi thirteen to nothing?"

"Ask me again in six innings," he said apprehensively.

During the inaugural ceremony, Cesar's boys were astonished when "The Star Spangled Banner" was followed by the raising of the Texas flag. Lucky had brought the one presented to them in Fort Worth, and he had convinced the groundskeeper to hoist it beneath the flag of Kentucky. He even got the band to strike up "The Eyes of Texas," which was that state's official anthem.

In the first inning, Sherman Chappell, Owensboro's pitcher, leaned too far over the plate and a pitched ball struck him on his head. Angel rushed off the mound and was the first to reach the fallen Owensboro player.

Angel desperately tried to find the right words, and all he could repeat was, "*Lo siento, perdóname* [Forgive me, I'm sorry]."

Chappell was a bit shaken, but fortunately all right. However, the rules stated that any player hit in the head had to be taken out of the game, even if he appeared okay.

Blake Chappell, Sherman's father and one of the team's assistant coaches, wasn't happy at all with the ruling. He demanded that Cesar take Angel out of the game—a baseball "eye-for-an-eye" so to speak. Coach Quinn came out and asked Sherman's father to return to the dugout to cool off. Cesar asked Coach Quinn if he wanted him to pull Angel.

"It was an accident, wouldn't be right to hurt two boys with one pitch," the Owensboro skipper answered.

Fortunately, the team had another ace on its roster. Bobby Woodward was averaging a phenomenal fourteen strikeouts a game—that was more than two an inning. Bobby was confident when Coach Quinn handed him the ball.

As the game progressed, whenever the Mexican boys yelled and cheered, "Come on, guys" or "Give it to them, Angel!" the umpire would warn Cesar to make his kids stop.

"Why? The other team's yelling just as loud," Cesar said.

"Taunting the other team from the dugout is prohibited," said the umpire.

"They're not saying anything bad. They're just cheering for their own players."

"We can't be sure, so tell them to keep silent," repeated the umpire.

"Where does it say that?" Cesar asked, producing the rules from his back pocket.

The umpire, knowing there was no such rule, got right in Cesar's face and demanded, "I said, keep 'em quiet. If you don't like it, go back to Mexico."

Lucky and Jose realized that Cesar wasn't going to win this confrontation so they went out and pulled their hot-tempered coach back to the dugout.

"Come on, Cesar, cool it!" José pressed Cesar to calm down.

"But he's wrong. He's—"

"He's an officer, and he outranks us," stated Lucky.

Cesar didn't say another word, but he handed out towels to each player so that when something exciting happened they could scream into their towel-covered mouths.

❦

On land once inhabited by the Ohlone Indians, the Presidio in San Francisco had been a military base since 1776. This 1,400 acre promontory overlooking the Golden Gate Bridge was home to the Western Regional Finals.

The day before, La Mesa's Lewis Riley pitched a masterpiece in beating Tucumcari, New Mexico. Today, Joe McKirahan was ahead by eighteen runs against the Euphrata, Washington team. Their tally of runs had come so early in the game that the Western Regional final held little in the way of a contest. La Mesa knew it was going to Williamsport, and the celebrating had begun by the third inning.

❦

Against Owensboro, Norberto had struck out in the Monterrey half of the first inning. As he walked dejectedly back to the dugout, he passed right in front of Rose who motioned him to come closer. She made a gesture to show him he should choke up on the bat, but his reaction showed that he didn't give much credence to batting advice from an elderly woman.

Two innings later, Norberto stepped into the batter's box with the game still scoreless. There were two runners on base, and Cesar prepped him. "Just make contact. Fidel might be able to score from second."

The three words least comforting to a player in a slump are "Just make contact." To add to Norberto's pressure, he knew that Paulina was watching him and there were only so many times he could strike out before she lost enthusiasm for him. He stared straight ahead, refusing to allow himself even one glimpse of her in the crowd, and then proceeded to miss the first two pitches.

Rose was grumbling to herself, "I's seen more games than Jackie Robinson. Choke up on the bat or choke at the plate."

Norberto stepped out of the box and looked at Rose. She was putting her hand to her throat in a choking motion. The young batter slid his hands up the barrel, stepped back in the box and slapped the next pitch up the middle for a base hit and an RBI. As Norberto settled on the first base bag, he peeked at Paulina who was flushed with pride.

Baltazar was the next up. When he went to select his bat, he, too, looked at Rose, touching each one until she nodded her approval.

"What are you doing?" Cesar asked him.

"She's a friend of the priest and he knows God," answered Baltazar as he strode past Cesar to take his at-bat.

Whether the bat made a difference, or it was merely the confidence she instilled in Baltazar, he hit a single into left. Rafael Estrello followed with a solid double.

At the end of the inning, Angel took the mound with a three run lead. He and his teammates knew that their defense was in a position to win the game. One by one, Owensboro batters came to the plate and one by one they found themselves retiring back to the dugout as Angel's pitches grew stronger and stingier. Despite being ahead three to nothing, every *Regiomontano* tensed with each pitch, knowing the potential of their powerful opponents. With every out, the Owensboro hitters were well aware of their diminishing chances, and each faced Angel with a growing sense of urgency and determination to strike a decisive blow.

The *Regiomontanos* were so focused on holding on to their thin lead that no one had time to contemplate the significance of the game until a long fly ball to center field settled into the webbing of Enrique's glove and the final out was recorded. Monterrey Industrial achieved the inconceivable. They had earned a berth in the 1957 Little League World Series.

The first words Angel Macias said to Cesar were, "Señor Faz, are we really going to Williamsport?"

Both Angel and his rival, Bobby Woodward, had performed heroically—each striking out eleven batters in a pitching duel on this humid afternoon. But in shutting out the heavily favored team from Owensboro, Angel, the ambidextrous pitcher from Colonia Cantu, had come unimaginably close to achieving a pitcher's crowning achievement. Just two errant pitches—one a base hit and one that struck Sherman Chapell for a free base—stood between him and a perfect game.

"Yes, Angel, I believe we are," an equally stunned Cesar finally answered.

✺

Monterrey Industrial was mobbed by fans and reporters. They were excited but tired, and winning meant packing up and venturing even farther north to another mysterious American city.

"LITTLE LEAGUERS' SIESTA PAYS OFF WITH FIESTA" would be the next morning's headline in the *Louisville Courier-Journal*.

Hundreds were seeking autographs, and though Cesar and Angel savored the moment, there was someone with whom Angel wanted to speak. The two made their way through the crowd to find Sherman, the pitcher who was taken out of the game when he was hit by Angel's pitch in the first inning. Though ineligible to play, he had remained with his father to watch the whole game.

"Angel wanted me to tell you and your son how sorry he is about what happened," Cesar told Sherman's father.

"No apology needed, it's part of the game," said Blake politely. "My son told me it was his fault. It was a curveball that he didn't think was gonna break into him so much, so he leaned in a bit too far."

"Well, Angel still felt horrible."

"I ain't never seen someone my age throw like him," said Sherman.

Boh father and son wished Monterrey Industrial luck in the tournament and then walked away, wondering with what might have been had one curveball not curved so much.

Reporters wanted to know more about this eighty-pound ambidextrous phenom. Perhaps it was a blessing that Angel didn't speak English or else he would have been constantly mobbed by questions.

"Coach Faz, can Angel Macias really pitch with both hands?" asked one such reporter.

"Well, you saw him playing the infield yesterday with his left arm," he answered.

"But there's a difference between throwing and pitching," said the reporter.

"Would you be willing to give an exhibition for us?" asked another.

"Yeah, let's see the kid," chimed in several reporters from the press corps.

"Well, I don't know. . ."

"Come on, coach, We read the stories. Was that just some Texas boasting?" cajoled the one who had presented the challenge.

Cesar drew Angel aside. "The press has treated us well, and our families in Monterrey deserve the positive news," Cesar told his ace pitcher.

There were many spectators who still hadn't left the bleachers, and when they heard what was about to happen, several yelled to their friends: "Their pitcher's gonna give an exhibition!" Many who were exiting returned.

After pitching the most important game thus far in his life, Angel began to throw pitch after pitch of curveballs and change-ups with his left and right arms for the press corps and other amazed onlookers. Angel was used to throwing for hours under Monterrey's blistering sun, and had Cesar not stopped him after ten minutes, he could have thrown the equivalent of another complete game.

". . .throwing baseballs that darted and hopped like Mexican jumping beans," wrote a Louisville reporter who prepared his article for the morning edition. He nicknamed Angel a "diamond devil."

It was soon time to board their bus back to Nichols U.S. Army General Hospital. Paulina's father, who had been talking to some of his neighbors, was also ready to get his daughter and leave. Norberto had a great many firsts to discover with girls and a good-bye was one of them. Before she ran to her father, she turned to give Norberto a quick parting kiss. With eyes closed, they were lucky that their lips even made contact. It was fleeting, but it was a fraction of a second that Norberto would never forget.

"*¿Qué hora es* [What time is it]?" Baltazar asked Norberto as he hurried up the steps of the bus.

"*¿Porqué* [Why]?" asked Norberto.

"*¡Es que necesito decrile a el medico el momento exacto en que mi amigo se volvío loco* [I want to tell the doctor exactly what time my friend went crazy]*!*"

❧♾❧

Even before the early news editions hit the street, word had spread about the winners of all the regional tournaments. Monterrey Industrial represented South, a region that reached beyond the U.S. border. Bridgeport, Connecticut, had captured the East; the Jaycees from Escanaba, Michigan, had won the North; and the overwhelming favorites from La Mesa, California, were the champions of the West.

Neither the players and coaches of Monterrey Industrial, nor their fans or detractors, could imagine that the *Regiomontanos* would soon participate in the most emotional and dramatic Little League World Series ever played.

But first, the team would have to get there.

❧♾❧

"We're taking up a collection for the team," Señor Claudio Villarreal told several workers at Fundidora. Each man reached into his pocket and tossed a few coins into the upside-down hard hat.

As Claudio approached Umberto Macias, he said, "You should be proud."

"Why? His chores haven't been getting done since he left. And baseball isn't going to get him a better job in Monterrey."

"Maybe Angel has his own dream," suggested Claudio.

"Dreams don't build cities, men and iron do," Umberto grumbled.

"After the iron has rusted and the men have returned to dust, what is left but the dream?" his friend said.

ഝൟ

On Sunday, Clarence invited the team to the Forest Missionary Baptist Church. To boys who were accustomed to the formality of a Catholic Mass, the service didn't sound like anything they'd ever experienced in a church.

Clarence belted out his high-energy sermon from the pulpit, and his flock responded with even more effusive outcries of their own.

"Brothers and sisters, say hallelujah for the boys from Monterrey," he sang out.

"Hallelujah," they sang.

"Now they gots to get to Pennsylvania and they ain't even got enough money for food, let alone the bus fare."

"Say it ain't so, Brother Clarence," came the chorus from the pews.

"It is so, brothers and sisters. And you all know what we gots to do."

"Amen, Brother Clarence."

In the back pews, Norberto and Enrique whispered between themselves. "Are these people crazy? Why are they all talking back to the priest?" asked Norberto.

"Maybe they're in trouble," surmised Enrique. "That's why he's yelling at them."

Outside, after the service, Clarence and two other elderly Black gentlemen approached Cesar, Lucky and José, and handed Cesar the collection box that had been passed around the congregation.

"We can't repay this," Cesar said.

"Yes, you can," said Clarence.

"How?"

"By not letting any of your boys throw up in our bus," he said as he pointed to the parking lot and an old yellow school bus that had the church's name painted above the row of windows.

"Why are you doing this for us?" asked Cesar.

"Cannonball and Smokey here played for the Giants."

"The New York Giants?" Lucky asked with incredulity, making the three Black gentlemen laugh heartily.

"The Baltimore Elite Giants," Clarence said, pronouncing the second word like *eee-light*. "Cannonball here coached Roy Campanella before he went up to the Dodgers. Campy said Cannonball could outhit, outthrow and outrun anyone he ever played with in the majors."

"Problem was he also out-tanned 'em," laughingly added Smokey.

"So you see, we's both Giants. We was Black and they's little," Cannonball said.

"What Cannonball's sayin' is we know a thing or two 'bout underdogs and folks who try to kill other peoples' dreams," Smokey clarified.

Cesar felt a little choked-up, but he managed to utter, "I don't know if I can drive that."

"We said you could ride in it, we didn't say nothin' 'bout you drivin' it," said Cannonball.

"Clarence is the only one who drives that bus," said Smokey.

⌒⌒⌒

El Hospital Universitario in Monterrey saw hundreds of patients a day, most of them unable to pay, which was why they came here from all over the city. Overworked and underpaid doctors and nurses scurried amidst the infirm, trying to do the best they could under minimal circumstances.

The blood donation area had been particularly busy the past few weeks. The state paid a nominal amount for each pint of blood to replace the constantly undersupplied reserves.

Maria del Refugio Gonzalez worked in the transfusion area and was speaking to the on-duty head nurse about a particular man who had come in to donate blood. Maria didn't recognize the man, nor did she realize that he was Angel Macias' father.

"He can't give," said the chief nurse.

"He's very determined," responded Maria.

"He's a drunk," the nurse said and turned to help other patients.

Maria returned to address Umberto. "I'm sorry, señor. The rules are very strict. There can be no alcohol in the blood."

"Wait a minute. . . you're a friend of my son's coach."

"You're mistaking me for someone else," said Maria, her emotions suddenly flustered.

"You've got to take my blood, I need the money. I need to help my son's team."

"Perhaps it is not him that you must help first," she said.

22

The Other Side
of the Glass

rankie stood in a phone booth outside the Nichols Hospital facility in Louisville. In the background she could see Cesar and his team slowly boarding the Forest Missionary Baptist Church's bus.

She and her editor had just finished arguing on the telephone; Charlie "Mac" Thompkin was the kind of boss that routinely hired, fired and rehired a person before lunch. More pressing was the fact that her car's engine wouldn't turn over and the rental company couldn't get a replacement to her for two days.

Fortunately, she knew a whole team going that way.

⟡

It was a long walk from El Hospital Universitario back to his street in Colonia Cantu, and by the time Umberto entered his house he felt about as low as a man can sink. He instinctively went for the cupboard where he knew he would find an unfinished bottle of tequila. Grasping its familiar-shaped glass neck in his right hand, he crossed the room, shoving aside a chair that wasn't even in his way. He was about to raise the tequila to his lips in his nightly ritual of self-medication when he suddenly became angry—so angry that he turned and hurled the bottle against the hearth's cinder block masonry, shattering the glass and splattering the clear alcohol. Umberto fell to his knees on the kitchen floor and wept for all the years he had suffered and made those he loved suffer more.

Sometimes, when a man leaves a bad deed unresolved, time lures him into the belief that it is too late to right the wrong. Many times before this night, a voice pleaded with Umberto, always to be beaten down by the demons of his private hell. He rose and went to the small shrine for Pedro. Grasping his son's medallion, he held its cold metal in his hands until it had warmed up. Umberto knew it was time to honor the living more than the dead. He also knew the priest was planning to send a package to the boys in Williamsport, Pennsylvania. It would be carried by one of the members of a Mexican delegation that was preparing to fly north. Umberto didn't have much time.

⋘◉◈◉⋙

As they drove northeast through the Kentucky countryside, Clarence had the radio on, and he and the boys sang combinations of Gospel and Mexican folk songs.

Several team members went up to Cesar and asked a question. The coach then tapped Clarence on the shoulder and said, "Seems my boys need a pit stop."

"We could use some gas too," Clarence answered.

In less than ten minutes, Clarence pulled the bus into a rural filling station.

"Where's your bathroom?" Lucky asked the attendant.

"'Round back," said the attendant, eyeing the group suspiciously.

Shortly, Lucky came out, but as the boys lined up to use the latrine the attendant stepped in front of it and said, "It's out of order."

"He was just in there," Cesar said, pointing to Lucky.

"It's out of order for you too," repeated the attendant.

⋘◉◈◉⋙

"Why couldn't we go?" Enrique asked Cesar after the entire group had re-boarded the bus and left the station.

"It's a 'Whites Only' toilet."

"How does the toilet know?" asked Norberto.

Cesar tried to explain, but the more he tried, the more agitated he got. Lucky, on the other hand, remained silent. He was ashamed of people like the filling-station attendant, but at that moment he felt as white as a bleached sheet.   Suddenly, Clarence started laughing.

"What's so funny?" asked Lucky.

"I've always noticed that when a white man's a coward, you call him *yellow*. When he's sad, you call him *blue*. When he's envious, you say he's *green*. When he's embarrassed, his face turns *red*. And yet I'm called *colored*."

Fifteen minutes later, the bus came to a stop along the shoulder of the road; it had run out of gas. The boys chose a grove of shrubs that wasn't "out of order."

Clarence found an empty gas can, and Lucky gazed down the road as the sun set over the Blue Ridge Mountains. Fireflies intermittently illuminated the densely wooded forest that enveloped the church's bus.

Lucky wasn't looking forward to a mile walk down the highway, but it wasn't a good idea for a Latino or African American man to walk alone on this desolate stretch of Kentucky back road.

"Can you believe that attendant?" Cesar said to Frankie.

"He just said you couldn't use the bathroom, he never said he wouldn't sell us gas," Frankie replied.

"He'd sell you or Lucky gas."

"Yeah, and your friend wouldn't be walking down the road with an empty gas can in his hand."

"Oh, it's so tragic when a white man suffers because of racism. It looks different from this side of the glass, doesn't it? Besides, I couldn't give that jerk our money," Cesar answered indignantly.

"Us stranded out here in the middle of nowhere doesn't make that jerk any less of one. Matter of fact, it kinda makes you one too," she said.

"So now I'm the jerk?"

"If the cleat fits, wear it," she answered.

"What can you possibly understand? At least you're the right color," came Cesar's retort.

"My dad never forgave me for being a daughter. Did your father wish you weren't Mexican?"

"My daddy was lynched," said Clarence with the casualness of someone who might have just said his father was from Kentucky or liked jazz.

There was an awkward silence.

"Well, we're a fine team," Clarence continued. "A displaced Chicano and a woman with a chip on her shoulder being driven by an orphaned Negro through Ku Klux Klan country."

"We just need a Jew and we'll have all the bases covered," said Frankie.

"We've got one. Hey, Koufax!" Cesar called back to his lead pitcher.

಄಄಄

"Have you had any alcohol for forty-eight hours?" the nurse asked Umberto.

"No," he answered truthfully.

To the average person, such abstinence doesn't sound difficult, let alone heroic. But the devil in the mezcal had taken its grip upon Umberto's soul, and the first two days of his denial had taken him through cold sweats, convulsive tremors, and the alternating feeling that ice and molten steel flowed through his veins until he wanted to leap out of his skin.

"And you haven't given blood in that time?"

"No," he replied.

Maria, working at the next table, looked over as she heard his familiar voice. He began rolling up his left sleeve. It was extremely hot, and she imagined him to be terribly uncomfortable dressed in such a heavy long-sleeved shirt. His choice of attire was no accident. He was hiding his right forearm, which clearly showed the telltale bluish marks of a syringe.

Umberto's eyes looked across the room and caught Maria's for an instant. He knew that Maria had seen him here yesterday donating blood, and one word from her would confirm the other nurse's suspicion and no doubt cause him to be asked to leave.

"You sure you weren't here yesterday?" asked the nurse.

"You must be mistaking me for someone else," he said. He breathed a sigh of relief when Maria said nothing and silently turned her attention back to her patient.

ᴥᴐᴑᴑᴥ

Heading north on Pennsylvania Rural Route 15, the church's bus approached the northern fork of the Susquehanna River.

The vegetation changed from the desert's shallow-rooted tumbleweeds to the forest's giant timbers of toughened bark, and so did the personalities of the boys. Though they had been gone for less than a month, this trip had accelerated their life experiences at a time when they stood on the precipice of manhood. So much maturity had been expected of them on the field and on such an arduous journey that it was easy to forget that they were just children.

Norberto lamented over having left Pauline.

"Don't worry, Beto, I'll introduce you to many girls at my school," consoled Angel. "Remember, there are plenty of fish in the barn," he added in a rather unusual paraphrase of Cesar's advice.

Mario noticed that this conversation made Enrique morose. "What's wrong, *el Cubano?*"

"My girlfriend fell for that Mexico City All-Star."

"And where is he now? Don't forget, you have home field advantage. Gloria lives in Monterrey."

The bus crossed the Susquehanna and entered Williamsport. The boys pressed against the windows and gazed at the perfectly manicured streets lined with colorful Victorian houses and red-brick commercial façades.

Williamsport officially became a city in 1866. A year before cityhood, the world's first organized baseball game was played on a grassy field near Academy Street on the north bank of the Susquehanna. The city has carried on a special love affair with the game ever since.

As the bus continued through its streets, it seemed that the city was completely dedicated to the Little League World Series. Posters, flags, banners and flyers of all shapes, sizes and colors hung from every building, light post and telephone pole, all proclaiming the grand final championship of the tournament.

In all, more than one hundred thousand kids from twenty-two countries had participated in more than seven thousand games, leaving just four teams remaining. And they now converged on

Williamsport along with tens of thousands of fans from all over the world.

The team got off the bus in front of Lycoming College. They would be staying at the dorms provided by the college, which was in summer recess. In the plaza across from the impressive administrative building was a large fountain, which spilled into a basin about ten feet in diameter.

A young couple stood next to the fountain's edge, holding hands. The man held up a coin to the woman's lips and then tossed it into the water.

"Did you see that?" Angel asked.

Enrique nodded.

"A man just threw away his money."

"Are Americans that rich?" asked a perplexed Norberto.

"It's a wishing well," Cesar told them. "You throw a coin and make a wish. It's a silly custom."

"What are they wishing for?" Baltazar asked.

"Don't know. Could be for health, for children. . ."

"Love?" asked Mario.

"Perhaps," Cesar said.

Ricardo lit up as if with a great idea. "Señor Faz, maybe you could make a wish for Maria."

"You don't get things just because you wish for them." Cesar slung the bag of bats over his shoulder and walked away.

∗∗∗

Cesar's first order of business was to visit the baseball field. He wanted to know its dimensions, its characteristics, the winds, the affects of the sun, especially how the afternoon shadows crossed the field.

Already, the talk of the town centered on Monterrey and La Mesa, even though the two might not play each other. About Monterrey, it was "Oh my, they're so small," and about La Mesa, it was "What giants!"

The day before the opening round, all four teams posed for advertisements dedicated to the sale of sporting goods. Cesar spent that time in a particularly pissy mood.

"What gives, coach?" asked Lucky, who rarely minced words with Cesar and who had come to know the moods of his friend very well by now.

"I want their minds focused on playing baseball, not fashion shows."

"No kid on your team has any hope of forgetting baseball. You drill it into them day and night."

"It got them here, didn't it?"

"What's really eating you?" Lucky asked.

"Don't you think it ironic that they're being used to sell products that none of them can afford?"

The games were scheduled to take place over three days: Wednesday, August 21, through Friday, August 23. The first scheduled matchup was Escanaba, Michigan against La Mesa, California. Monterrey Industrial would compete against Bridgeport, Connecticut the next day, and the winners of each semi-final game would meet on Friday in the Little League World Series championship game. But the next morning, the skies over Williamsport erupted in a constant downpour. Administrative duties continued on schedule, and the teams were called into the college's auditorium for obligatory physicals and press conferences.

Dr. Yasui, the Little League physician, had the task of examining the players to make sure everyone was healthy enough to play. Any child running a fever, having a sprained limb, or showing signs of any disease like chicken pox or measles was automatically disqualified. Cesar, as was customary, translated between the boys and the doctor, who carefully rechecked every part of his examination.

When Yasui finished examining the last Monterrey player, he stood up, looked at the gathered reporters and said, "It's remarkable!"

"What?" came the inquisitive response.

"They have no cavities," he exclaimed. "Not a single one in fourteen mouths."

"How do you explain that?" asked Ted Kosciusko from the *Chicago Mirror*.

"They surely can't afford dentists," observed Nick Hollander from the *Philadelphia Daily Herald.*

"Or candy," answered Yasui.

The reporters murmured as they often do when hearing something worthy of writing down.

"Do they pass?" another asked.

"Well, they're about thirty-five pounds lighter and six inches shorter than average. But healthy enough to play? As far as I can tell, yes."

The press turned its attention to Cesar.

"How did these boys first learn baseball?" asked Ted Kosciusko.

"From the radio."

"They didn't see it played?"

"They felt it," Cesar said proudly.

More murmuring as pencils scratched across notepads.

A few minutes later, the press conference was interrupted by a Little League official who came up to the podium and tapped on the microphone to get everyone's attention.

"Excuse me, I have an announcement," he said. "Today's game will be postponed, but our local meteorologist has assured us that this low pressure front is moving past and they expect it to clear up by nightfall. However, these circumstances have necessitated that we play both semi-final games tomorrow in a doubleheader."

When he said this, an assistant handed out programs. Cesar leafed through it and frowned.

"Sir," Cesar raised his hand and spoke to the official, "is it possible to switch the games? My team can't play at two thirty."

"Why not?" the official asked.

"It's their siesta time."

Despite the laughter from the assembled press, coaches and other teams, the official was not swayed by the problem.

"I'm sorry, the programs have already been printed and the schedule's set." He stepped down from the podium.

"What are you gonna do?" Lucky asked Cesar.

"If I can't change the league's schedule, I'll change ours," he answered. "We'll wake 'em at dawn, feed 'em breakfast at six, practice at eight, a quick lunch and then in bed for a nap by eleven. They don't have watches and they sure can't ask anybody what time it is."

∾⦙⦙⦙∾

That evening, the teams and invited guests all sat down for dinner in the Lycoming College cafeteria. Frankie sat with her colleagues of the press corps.

"So you've been covering them since the beginning?" Ted Koskiusko asked.

"That's right," Frankie said.

"Well, if you wanted an underdog, you sure got one."

"Bridgeport doesn't look that weak," she said.

"I meant Monterrey!"

"You think the Mexicans are the underdogs?" Everyone at her table stared at her in disbelief.

"You're kidding, right?"

"You're letting emotions overrule reason," said Arnie Pasternak from Newark, New Jersey's *Daily Record*.

"It comes with the uniform," laughed Nick Hollander from Philadelphia's *Daily Herald*.

"Easy does it, fellas," warned Frankie.

"Look, I've been following La Mesa since the beginning of the season. It's a different level of baseball," said Arnie. "I got nuthin' against the Mexicans, but next to the American kids, they look like a bunch of mutts at a beauty pageant. La Mesa's clearly the best team."

"Monterrey doesn't have to worry about La Mesa," said Ted.

"Oh really? Why not?" asked Arnie.

"'Cause they're not gonna get past Bridgeport," he replied.

A few seats down, the *Regiomontanos* were passing around a tin of *habañero* peppers and planning their midnight mission.

"Hey, look. His mom must've sent him a can of food from home!" teased one American kid when he noticed the tin in Enrique's hand.

"What's that, Chico?" another American boy asked.

"*Mmm, muy bueno!*" Enrique replied. He held up a pepper and ate it in one bite. He then held one up for the Bridgeport player, who seemed hesitant, but after a couple of dares from his own teammates, he took it between his thumb and forefinger and brought it to his lips.

Taking the smallest of bites, he turned to his buddies and said, "Don't taste like nothing," he boasted.

One couldn't have counted to ten before the boy hit the ground in tears, his teammates laughing hysterically.

Frankie turned to her fellow reporters and said, "In Fort Worth, they had to call a doctor for some poor kid."

"That's the only way they're gonna bring Bridgeport to their knees," said Nick.

"Aren't you a bit out of your league, missy?" taunted Ted.

"First of all, you don't want to call me 'missy,'" Frankie said. "And second, if you're so sure, how 'bout a friendly wager?"

"We're journalists," Ted said. "We don't bet on sports."

"Yeah, yeah, and Eisenhower's really a closet Commie. Perhaps a wager's a bit out of your league?"

"Okay, what's your bet?"

"Well, let's see. Any of you guys know where to buy a sombrero in this town?"

⋙◈⋘

"You know they wouldn't change the schedule 'cause we're Mexican," Cesar griped to Clarence. "Everyone knows Mexicans need to siesta after lunch."

"You can't run away from it, Cesar. But you also can't pick a fight every time someone calls you a name. You just gotta keep in the game."

"Until when? Until you get called out just when you think you have a chance?"

"What made you so bitter, Cesar?"

Cesar bit his lower lip and his face twisted slightly.

"I met a guy in the Philippines. He was a truck driver from Texas. Lent me a pair of dry socks once. One minute he's on a routine patrol and the next he's killed by a Japanese sniper. I'd never asked his name and I probably wouldn't have ever remembered the guy if he hadn't died. The funeral parlor in his hometown wouldn't let his body lie in the chapel or be buried next to whites. That was his thanks for dying for his country."

"Life can't be perfect cause we ain't, but it gives us glimpses."

"Like where?"

"In the little miracles, like out there on a baseball field."

"It would take more than a little miracle to really change things, and I'm not waiting for *Him* to intervene."

"Not all miracles are created by God," said Clarence.

"Yeah, some are made by powerful white folks."

"Jackie wasn't white, and he made us believe. I never forgot the day Pee Wee Reese defied the crowds and even his own teammates when he put his arm around Jackie. You and your boys are making a difference, even to white folks."

"Sure," Cesar said.

"Goodnight, fellas," Frankie said as she walked by.

"So early, Miss Frankie?" asked Clarence.

"Long day." She began to walk away and then turned and said, "Oh, I'm writing an article on Jim Crow—gonna use a sports angle. Desegregation ain't enough, the whole system's gotta change. Gonna ruffle a few feathers."

"Bet your editor will have something to say about that," Cesar told her.

"He already did, so I told him he prints the story or he finds another reporter."

"Careful, he paid your way here."

"No, he didn't. He told me to return after Louisville. Seems he'd arranged a syndicated deal. I'm here on my own dime. Besides, Charlie pays me so little, I'm effectively irreplaceable," she said and continued on her way out.

After she left, Clarence turned to Cesar and grinned.

"Were you ever so right, it almost hurt?"

"Don't even say it!" barked Cesar.

❧⊙❦

Soon after Frankie left, Clarence excused himself for the evening. The timing was good; no sooner had the minister left when two men approached Cesar and introduced themselves as members of a special Mexican delegation.

"We flew in last night and drove this morning from New Jersey," said Señor Ramirez.

"The boys will be very honored," Cesar answered.

"Yes, I'm sure," said the other man, Señor Espuela. "We were thinking that you should start Angel tomorrow. He's the stronger pitcher."

"But it's Enrique's turn."

"No foreign team has ever made it to the finals. If Monterrey Industrial wins, regardless of what happens on Friday, they'll make history."

"You'll be guaranteed a trophy," Señor Ramirez added.

"I don't know. We've been doing fine with this rotation. But I'll consider it," Cesar said.

The two men went to join the rest of their party, and Cesar thought about his options.

"They're right, you know," came a familiar voice from behind Cesar. He swiveled around to see his former boss from the St. Louis Browns, Mark Tanner. "You should pitch Angel tomorrow."

"You!" exclaimed a startled Cesar. Tanner had migrated with the team when the Browns moved to Baltimore and became the Orioles.

"Always go with your best."

"What are you doing here?"

"It's baseball. . . a World Series. Only in America," said Tanner, smiling.

"I would say it's good to see you, but it isn't."

"Come on, Cesar. It's water under the bridge by now."

"Some things don't change."

"You took things too personally. Baseball is business."

"Really? So what business brings you here?" Cesar asked.

"You."

Cesar got up to leave.

"No, really. I'm here scouting you," replied Tanner. Cesar stopped and slowly turned. "You're causing quite a stir. News made it all the way to the front office. Some of the brass upstairs figured anyone who could take these kids this far might deserve a second look."

"And?"

"We'll see if you can win a big game."

⊷⊷

Cesar did his usual rounds, but saved Angel and Enrique's room for last. None of the boys were asleep, and while Cesar could enforce lights out, he couldn't overrule the nervous excitement that kept his players awake.

"I'm thinking of starting Angel tomorrow," he said, cutting right to the heart of the matter.

"Why, Señor Faz? Did I do something wrong?" asked a confused Enrique.

"No foreign team's ever made it to the finals. I just want to give it our—"

"Best?" added a hurt Enrique.

"Look, it's my team and you'll do what I tell you to do!" Cesar barked.

"But it's Enrique's turn," Angel said as Enrique ran from the room.

"What's the matter with him? If we win tomorrow, we're guaranteed to leave Williamsport with a trophy!"

"And how will Enrique feel when he looks at it?"

"It's not about feelings," Cesar said sternly.

"It's all about feelings," answered a defiant Angel as he ran after his friend.

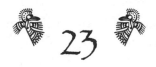

23

It's All About Feelings

esar tried to ease his own nerves by taking a walk through Lycoming College's gardens. The rains had left the smell of fresh earth, and a humid breeze passed silently and tranquilly through the grove of tall pines that surrounded the campus. The sun set late in August, and on the other side of the garden he noticed a woman talking to her dog as she walked by the flower beds.

If he pitched Enrique and they lost tomorrow, Angel would never get a chance to pitch here, a right he'd clearly earned. The fans wanted to see him; the press had already made him a hero in Mexico—it wasn't about Enrique's feelings. Sometimes coaches had to make tough decisions and the right ones weren't always the fair ones.

There was little more Cesar could do in this last evening before the start of the World Series. That night, La Mesa, Escanaba, Bridgeport and Monterrey, though thousand of miles apart, were inexorably united by the same feelings of tension, hope and anguish provoked by the anticipation of the Little League championship tournament: The American cities because they already understood the notion of dedicating themselves to kids' athletic competition, and the industrial capital of Mexico because for the first time its people were experiencing a sensation of pride in fourteen of its sons who were living and writing an incredible legend.

Cesar slept restlessly in his cot. Recurring images of disillusionment and betrayal played across his dreamscape as old wounds opened anew. His dream took him back to the Browns' locker room in St. Louis.

⋘⟨⦿⟩⋙

"So it was you spreading those comments about me," Cesar accused his boss, Mark Tanner. "I've worked for this shot for years, and I'm better than that guy and you know it."

On the wall behind the manager were photos of famous baseballers, and corkboards with papers tacked on it. There were no pennants, the kind one might find in almost any other club's offices. The Browns were perennial bottom-dwellers of the American League.

"Look, amigo, Hornsby hired you, I didn't. It's my team now, and you'll do as you're told."

"What about all those 'Wait 'til next year, Cesar' lines you gave me?"

"You don't like picking up towels, maybe you'd be more comfortable picking lettuce in the fields."

"What did you say?" asked Cesar, rushing Tanner. Suddenly, he dreamt himself to be on the crest of a huge wave breaking on the shore. He was swinging and punching and falling, until he was no longer in the confines of an office but at the edge of a slope onto which he could not grasp and which dropped away the more he struggled. . .

⋘⟨⦿⟩⋙

Cesar awoke in a cold sweat.

He had a lot to do before their 2:30 PM game time, but his train of thought was interrupted by a Little League official who presented Cesar with two large cartons.

"What's in those?"

"Uniforms," the official said. Cesar pulled one out; it was crisp white and had the word *South* sewn on the front.

"The four final teams wear the uniforms of the region they're representing," the official said.

"Thanks, but we're fine with ours," Cesar replied.

"Little League rules. Your players have to wear them, there are no exceptions," the official told him.

Cesar asked the boys to put them on. In a few minutes, Lucky and

José came in and were greeted by a team that looked more like a group of comics instead of baseball players. Chuy was wearing a shirt that dangled all the way to his feet, and Gerardo wore a pair of pants that almost reached up to his neck.

Cesar immediately called the Little League office and spoke to the man who'd brought them over, explaining that the new uniforms, made for the size of the American children, didn't fit the *Regiomontanos*. It wasn't a matter of styles or how they might look, they were simply unable to lift their arms or move their legs in these uniforms. The official wasn't swayed.

Cesar hung up and then turned to Lucky, "Quick, go find the commissioner. Tell him we've got a little problem."

While waiting for Lucky to return with Commissioner Lindemuth, Cesar asked Enrique and Pepe to fit themselves into the largest pair of pants and to stand back-to-back. "And no funny business," he teased the two blushing boys.

On the way over, Mr. Lindemuth told Lucky that the thing that kept Little League tradition so strong was that its rules were clear and unbending. "If not, it's no longer a tradition." Upon walking in the room, however, the commissioner took one look at the sorry picture of the boys enveloped in their tentlike uniforms, turned to Cesar and said, "You can use your own."

The boys were happy to put their uniforms back on. Though torn and dirty, they were a piece of the valley of Monterrey. They also would become a piece of Little League folklore as Monterrey Industrial would be the only team ever allowed to wear their own uniforms in the Little League World Series.

❦

Little League officials had notified all of the teams' managers that there would be no batting practice allowed before the games in order to protect the fields. The groundskeepers had been instructed to forbid access to any team who showed up early.

Cesar had the team's driver pick them up two hours early and asked him if there was anywhere else they could practice.

"There ain't no other fields nearby."

Cesar had the driver cruise around until he spotted what he was looking for. "There! That'll do," said Cesar.

"This ain't a field, it's a dump site," said the driver. His eyes widened as the boys ran off the bus and removed their cleats, ecstatic to feel the dirt and rocks beneath their feet.

"It'll be perfect. Thanks," said Cesar, laughing.

While the other three teams rested, the boys from Monterrey Industrial practiced the batting they would need if they were to have a chance of winning.

⊱∙⊰

Monterrey Industrial was almost late arriving at Original Little League Field. Cesar had left plenty of time, but the boys had thrown their cleats into one big pile at the practice and it wasn't easy sorting out which ones belonged to whom.

At the field, a photographer snapped a shot of Joe Caldarola, Bridgeport's pitcher, standing next to Gerardo Gonzales. Joe extended his arm perpendicularly to his side and Gerardo's entire body fit beneath Joe's outstretched arm.

"Coach, aren't your boys worried about the size of the American kids?" a reporter asked Cesar.

"Let's ask them," said Cesar who turned to Gerardo and translated the journalist's question.

"*Si no los vamos a cargar, solo les vamos a jugar,*" answered Gerardo without hesitation.

The press waited with pens, poised for Cesar to translate.

"He said, 'We're not going to carry them, we're only going to play them.'"

⊱∙⊰

In Monterrey, the newspapers interviewed the families of the players. Señora Suarez told *El Norte*, "I pray for Enrique every day. Americans are so hard to beat. I'm not used to being separated from him for so long. He is the youngest. I hope they don't take any longer."

She, like so many other mothers, had suffered the most, even through the triumph. It was they who looked each night at empty beds where their sons should have been sleeping safely at home under their protective eyes.

El Norte's article captured the community's feelings:

> The entire city, no matter what class or creed, will have its thoughts on the same thing: one more victory for los chamacos maravilla (the marvelous boys) as they face Bridgeport in the Little League World Series in Williamsport, Pennsylvania. All of the thoughts of the elderly, the young mothers and the little ones who proudly saw their brothers in the newspapers now fall on the foreign place where they are.

◈◈◈

Williamsport's Original Little League Field was built with extensive wooden galleries. Behind the diamond was a building that served to accommodate important visitors, sports reporters, announcers, and the officials and directors of the Little League organization.

The roof of the tribune on the left served as another level on which there were other visiting personalities. Bridgeport took the dugout on the third base line, Monterrey on the opposite one near first.

Every dimension of a baseball field is carefully prescribed. Whether it be the distance between bases or from the mound to home plate, limits and parameters are well-defined. The same is true of bats and gloves. Only the catcher can use a glove of any design, size or weight; all other positions' mitts are restricted to a maximum length of fourteen inches.

As had become customary of Monterrey's opponents, Bridgeport protested the size of Ricardo Treviño's glove, but when the umpire measured it, he ruled it to be of legal size. The reality was that Ricardo was so small that his glove looked oversized, hanging from the end of his thin arm.

"Five minutes, coach, I'll need your lineup card," Umpire-in-Chief Gair told Cesar.

Cesar looked over at Angel and Enrique. They had both pitched brilliantly in getting the team to Williamsport, and it would be a shame if they didn't both get a chance here. He recalled how easily Monterrey could have lost the opener against Mexico City and none of this epic would have unfolded. It was Enrique who bore the pressure of that first game and he hadn't let down the team. And it was, after all, his turn.

Calling his team in, he reeled off the starting roster. "Baltazar, second base. Ricardo, first base. Pepe, left field. Angel. . . Angel, shortstop."

Cesar looked over at Enrique, tossed him the game ball and said, "Well, what are you staring at? Start warming up."

"¡Sì, Señor Faz, sì!" replied his young pitcher who bounded out of the dugout to begin his practice pitches.

As Cesar went to hand the lineup card to Umpire Gair, he paused at the press table to borrow a pencil. He had almost forgotten to swap Angel's and Enrique's positions.

⤷◈⤶

"What's with the switch?" Señor Espuelas asked Cesar.

"You're putting your second best pitcher in and hurting your chances to make it to the finals," said Señor Ramirez.

"I heard what you said, but I made my decision. Enrique pitches," Cesar said to the two Mexican delegates who had rushed onto the field upon seeing Enrique warming up with Chuy.

"Maybe you didn't understand. We weren't suggesting, we were telling you," said Señor Espuelas.

"Where was your concern when these kids were digging rocks out of the ground to make their own field?"

Señor Espuelas paused, uncertain of what to say. He looked at Señor Ramirez and shook his head in frustration. Turning his attention back to Cesar he said, "It would be best to follow our orders if you know what's good for you."

"What can you do? Fire me?" a defiant Cesar replied.

"There are worse things," said Señor Espuelas.

"We know all about you and St. Louis. Imagine what they'll think of you when they find out the truth," threatened Señor Ramirez.

"So go tell the umpire you've decided to make a switch," Espuelas added.

"I see," Cesar said, letting out a sigh.

Cesar walked over to Umpire Gair and pointed at Señor Ramirez and Señor Espuelas. "Excuse me, umpire, but what are those fans doing on the field?"

Gair cupped his hands to his mouth and announced, "Anyone not in uniform will please clear the field immediately."

Noticing that neither Ramirez nor Espuelas moved, the umpire walked over and politely asked them, "The game's about to start, please clear the field."

"You don't understand, we're part of the Mexican delegation," answered Señor Ramirez.

"I don't care if you're with Elvis Presley, clear my field!" demanded Gair.

Cesar couldn't distinguish exactly what Señor Ramirez was saying as Señor Espuelas tugged his colleague back toward the stands, but Cesar knew it wasn't pretty. He also knew that a job vacancy had just been created at Vitro.

"Boys, come closer," Cesar spoke solemnly as the team returned to the dugout after their ten minutes of final practice. "I have a confession to make." Swallowing hard, he began, "In St. Louis, well, I. . . I wasn't exactly the coach—or even an assistant coach. I should've been, but. . . but, well, I was really. . ."

The boys listened intently as Cesar bared his soul.

"So that's the truth. Your coach was nothing but a glorified towel boy," he finished.

"We knew," Ricardo said with an air of flippancy.

"You knew?"

"Yeah," said Baltazar.

Cesar's back stiffened. "If you knew, why did you let me tell the whole story?"

"We thought it might make you feel better," Norberto answered.

"Can we play baseball now?" asked Pepe.

24

The Long Walk to First

Cesar observed Enrique's practice pitches and felt confident. The ball flew like a white dove between his glove and Chuy's, who was warming him up. He embodied the calm emotion and serenity that many players never attain at any age.

"Try to control your fast pitches and keep them low near their ankles, so it'll be harder for them to elevate their arms," Cesar advised. He couldn't help but catch Mark Tanner's eyes.

Monterrey Industrial, as the visiting team, would be up first, and Baltazar had the honor of being the first batter in the 1957 Little League World Series. When he stepped into the batter's box, he made the sign of the cross. Inside the dugout, his teammates repeated the same act.

Twelve pitches later, the top of the first inning was over. The first three batters returned to the dugout without making the slightest contact with Jimmy Caldarola's pitches.

Bridgeport didn't score in their first at bat either, but they gave the *Regiomontanos* a scare. Caldarola hit a ball that careened off the top of the center field fence. Certain it was going to be a home run, Caldarola didn't run at full speed and an alert play by Gerardo held him to a single. It was a running error that would prove costly.

In the second inning, Fidel was struck in the chest by one of Caldarola's fastballs. Fidel lay motionless for a few moments, then got up, dusted himself off and walked to first base. No one was going to allow himself to be taken out of this game unless he was on a stretcher.

Nearly halfway through the game, it was still scoreless and Cesar was growing increasingly concerned. Bridgeport had great hitters; anyone could break open the game with one swing. He didn't want his team to have to come from behind against such a strong pitcher.

Fidel came to bat again in the fourth inning. It is human nature to be apprehensive about stepping back into the batter's box after being hit with a baseball, but Fidel merely tightened his grip on the bat and hit Caldarola's first pitch into left field for a base hit.

Norberto came up with one out.

While pitchers usually receive more recognition than their teammates, it is often said that a good catcher is the brain of a team. Right now, Beto would prove his mettle at the plate, not behind it.

What happened next occurred so quickly that many in the stands missed it. Norberto sent a hit into center field. Daniel Cedrone fielded the ball and saw that he had no chance of catching the speedy Fidel, who was already running to third base. Instead, Cedrone threw to Patrick Rosati who tried, unsuccessfully, to tag out Norberto as he came sliding into second. For some reason, though the play was still live, Rosati took his eyes off of Fidel at third and walked the ball toward his pitcher. At that moment, like a fleet-footed Jackie Robinson, Fidel was off to "steal" home.

Hearing the crowd suddenly roar, Rosati looked up and saw that Fidel wasn't on third. Freezing for a moment, he readjusted and fired the ball to James Lyddy and Fidel slid under the catcher's tag and scored the first run of the 1957 Little League World Series.

"What in the world were you thinking?" Cesar asked Fidel when the young player passed him on his way to the dugout. "Who told you to run home like that?"

"You did, Señor Faz."

"I never—"

"You told me to be ready for the unexpected play at the unexpected time."

Cesar laughed at Fidel's words, but it only served to make his throat sting. It was already raw from all the yelling he'd been doing.

There was a hush over the crowd as Monterrey's 0 became a 1 on the scoreboard. The reaction was one of muted disbelief as if this wasn't the way anyone, including the *Regiomontanos*, expected the game to play out.

Perhaps no one was more stunned than Bridgeport's pitcher. Jimmy Caldarola promptly gave up a hit and a walk, which loaded the bases. After throwing three erratic pitches to Baltazar, his coach decided to relieve him at the mound. Caldarola moved to first and the catcher, Lyddy, went to pitch. Behind in the count, he walked Baltazar, which scored Norberto from third. Lyddy got the next two batters out to retire the side, but Monterrey led two to nothing.

The elation of scoring two runs in the top of the inning was quickly subdued.

Caldarola led off the bottom of the fourth with a monster smash to center field. Gerardo had no chance but to watch it sail out of the park for a clean home run, making the score two to one. Monterrey still led, but everyone knew that Bridgeport was within one swing of a tie game. Fortunately for Monterrey, the home team could not take advantage of the spark created by Caldarola's lead-off blast and stranded several base runners.

Taking the field in the bottom of the fifth, Monterrey needed only six more outs.

The inning started simply enough: Bill Basile and Joe Vitrella hit long fly balls that Pepe Maiz caught on the run. Lyddy walked and the next hitter dribbled an easy one to shortstop. Angel, usually sure-handed at that position, bobbled the ball and couldn't manage to get either runner out. With a runner on first base and the tying run on second, Caldarola, Bridgeport's best hitter, came to bat for the third time. He already had a home run, and in his first at bat, had missed another by only a few inches. Caldarola had a chance to redeem himself from his poor running play in the first inning and possibly win the game.

It's said that the hardest part of a coach's job takes place long before the game, during the hours of practice and teaching players the strategies to win. During the actual game, he must only make one or two important decisions. This was one of those moments for Cesar, and it was a move that could so easily prove disastrous.

Cesar joined Enrique and Norberto at the mound.

"He homered his last at bat, Señor Faz," said Enrique, shifting from side to side.

"I know. That's why games are won here," Cesar said, pointing to his head, "not there," then to the field. "Here's the plan. . ."

Cesar finished his sentence and then jogged off the field, leaving the pitcher alone with his catcher.

Norberto went back behind the plate, and to the astonishment of all present he made the sign for an intentional walk.

Mark Tanner turned to the man next to him and said, "Walking to load the bases? Is he insane? I knew Faz would choke under pressure."

"You know they'll second-guess you from here to Peru if Enrique walks the next batter and you end up losing," Clarence said to Cesar in the dugout.

"I know, Clarence. I know."

Any hit, walk, wild pitch or slip of defense would end Monterrey's lead. Cesar had thrown the book of conventional wisdom out the window; it was all up to Enrique now.

The entire crowd had risen to its feet when Caldarola walked to first base and the other base runners advanced. Two outs, bases loaded and a game separated by one thin run.

The tension was unbearable. Earlier, when Fidel stole home, the crowd was uncontrollably wild, but this intentional base-on-balls caused a strange opaque silence.

Cesar was suffering as all coaches do. If the boys were outplayed and lost, that would be one thing. But if his decision dashed their hopes in a single at bat, he'd never live it down.

Enrique couldn't find the strike zone for his first two pitches to Paul Miller. Norberto came out to the mound. Cesar made a move to join them but stopped when he saw Norberto wave him away. It was terribly precocious of his player, but for some reason Cesar retreated and allowed the two to huddle alone.

"If I walk this guy, then—"

"You're thinking too much, *amigo*. Imagine Señor Faz is bending over home plate," said Norberto.

From the sideline, Cesar thought it incomprehensible that his pitcher and catcher found anything to laugh about at this critical juncture of the game, but they were.

With everyone back in position, *el Cubano* wiped his brow, took the sign and fired a perfect one down the middle of the plate.

"Strike one!" yelled the umpire.

The next pitch was also dead-on, and Miller was ready. Swinging his bat perfectly level, he drove a low line drive toward the gap between shortstop and second base. Enrique was closest to the ball, but it was by him before he could react. The crowd roared, assuming it was going to be a multiple-run scoring hit.

Just then, Angel dove to his left and made an awesome stab of the ball as it ricocheted off the infield grass. Rising to his feet, he fired the ball to first base for the force-out. Miller, who was running confidently toward first, couldn't believe when he saw Ricardo Treviño stretching to receive the throw. Miller's heroics would have to wait for another game, another day, another fairy tale.

Before a stunned crowd, Enrique bounded off the mound toward the dugout. He had brilliantly pitched himself out of a jam and killed Bridgeport's rally before it had begun.

"Talk about being in the right place at the right time!" yelled Clarence.

"Planned it that way," said Cesar after his heart resumed beating. His unorthodox gamble had paid off. . . for now.

In the top of the last inning, Lyddy quickly dominated Norberto, Gerardo and Ricardo. It was time for the bottom of the sixth.

"The first strike is the most important, Enrique. Don't be like lead. Give it all you got," Cesar told him.

Enrique cleaned his forehead with a towel, fixed his hat and jogged up the dugout's steps toward the center of the diamond to finish his magnificent task.

Robert Evick made the first out for Bridgeport, but John O'Leary looped a double into center field. Enrique struck out Louis Colangelo for the second out. The lineup card called for Tommy Brannick to bat next with the tying run on second base and the winning run at the plate. Tommy was the son of one of Bridgeport's coaches.

"Hold on," Tommy's father said to him. Then to another boy who'd been sitting on the bench the whole game, "Billy, get a bat."

"Dad?" asked Tommy.

"You've struck out twice," said Coach Brannick.

"I can do it. Please!"

"Sorry, Tommy."

Billy Benzberg went to the plate to pinch-hit.

The crowd stood for the rest of the game as Enrique pitched one. . . two. . . three strikes. Bridgeport's last batter was eliminated; it was over. Enrique's valor put Monterrey Industrial in the finals of the 1957 Little League World Series. The MONTERREY insignia on the boys' uniforms, even after absorbing sweat, dirt and hostility, never appeared brighter.

Cesar Faz, Lucky Haskins and José Gonzales Torres congratulated one another. Lucky said, "Cesar, I don't know what would have happened if you didn't order that intentional walk. What made you do that?"

Cesar's voice was barely audible from screaming, so he softly whispered, "One day we'll talk about it." He knew that his coaching could only take the boys so far. In the end, it was they who were creating the miracles necessary to win.

The New York Times carried the following headline in their morning edition:

Mexicans Take an Early Siesta,
Catch Bridgeport Nine Napping

Monterrey Little League Team Wins 2-1,
as Ruiz Steals Home While Infielder is
Asleep on Play

The boys mobbed Enrique at the mound, but Cesar was thinking of only two things: the other semifinal game and a thin boy from Colonia Cantu named Angel Macias.

❧☙

Players from both Monterrey and Bridgeport had now become spectators of the later game between Escanaba and La Mesa. It was a Williamsport tradition that teams watch the games in which they weren't participating. It encouraged good sportsmanship and honored the tradition of the Little League World Series.

Joe McKirahan cracked a monster home run, his second of the game. The Monterrey boys turned their eyes on Angel, who would be facing that hitter tomorrow.

Enrique was the only one whose gaze was elsewhere. He was looking toward the parking lot. There, Tommy Brannick had left his father and teammates behind and sat dejectedly in the shadow of his dad's Buick.

Enrique made his way down from the crowded bleachers, to the parking area with a ball and glove in hand.

"*Agarra tu bat de béisbol,*" he said to Tommy.

"What?"

"*Tu palo de béisbol,*" repeated Enrique, pointing to Tommy's bat.

The Bridgeport player grabbed his bat, and Enrique gestured for him to follow. The two snaked their way between the parked cars toward the small practice field next to the one where the semi-final game was being played.

Being a good reporter, Frankie sensed something was up and followed Enrique. She found a vantage spot where neither she nor her camera could be seen by either boy.

"*¡Quedate!*" said Enrique as he motioned for Tommy to stand at home plate. Tommy watched, unsure of what to do. Enrique walked to the pitcher's mound and stared at home plate as if he could see a catcher squatting behind it. "*Soy Don Drysdale, usted es Mickey Mantle. Solo juegue béisbol.*" Enrique pretended to wave off his catcher's sign. Tommy nodded and stepped into the batter's box.

The first pitch whizzed by as Tommy took a cut and missed the ball cleanly. With no catcher, the ball bounced and hit the wooden backstop with a thud. Tommy retrieved it and threw it back to Enrique, and then dug back in the box.

The next pitch sailed high. The third pitch was a dead strike, though Tommy's bat remained frozen on his shoulder. Enrique was throwing his hardest. If Tommy was going to hit one, he'd have to earn it.

Tommy looked anxious; his hands fidgeted nervously on the end of his bat. Enrique's arm delivered the fouth pitch just as Frankie snapped her shot. Though her eye missed the moment of impact, her ears didn't. The crack of horsehide on Pennsylvania ash is unmistakable. The heads of both boys turned to the outfield as Tommy's hit arched into left field.

No words were spoken. If it had been in the real game, maybe it would have been caught, maybe it would have been the winning hit. It no longer mattered. Enrique put his arm around Tommy's shoulder, and the two walked off the field together.

Frankie took another snapshot. She knew it was the kind of candid photo that made magazine covers and won awards. She sat and thought for a few minutes as the boys made their way back to the stands. The last thing Frankie did before returning to the La Mesa game was to pull the film out of her camera, immediately overexposing it. She knew she had witnessed something meant for no one else but the two boys. She'd have to savor the moment only in her memory.

25

Catching Turtles

The journey was almost over, and which final turn it would take now rested on the thin arm of Angel Macias. He was less than twenty-four hours from his rendezvous with the most powerful battery of hitters ever seen in Williamsport.

"If you thought Bridgeport looked physically superior, you should see La Mesa," Cesar said to Lucky as the team headed back for the Lycoming College dormitories.

"They scored seven against Escanaba."

"We scored two runs against a great team," interjected José.

"A fielding error and a walk," said Cesar. "I can't count on La Mesa making mistakes like that."

Joe McKirahan, La Mesa's star southpaw, had pitched another gem. He struck out fifteen in a one-hitter against their rivals from Michigan. Ironically, McKirahan's two impressive home runs created a situation for the Escanaba coach that was all too similar to Cesar's dilemma in the earlier game when Joe Caldarola came to bat with two base runners aboard late in the Monterrey-Bridgeport game. McKirahan was intentionally walked to load the bases, but this strategy, which had paid off so well for Monterrey, backfired against Escanaba. Francis Vogel stepped in and launched a grand slam high over the center field scoreboard.

"It's on his shoulders now," Lucky said, noticing that Angel sat alone in his row on the bus.

"You think he's nervous?" asked José.

Cesar shrugged. "Wouldn't you be?"

What few realized about Angel was the greater his fear, the greater his fury when a game was on the line.

∾⦦⦧∾

Cesar stood near the fountain in front of Lycoming College. He'd arranged to meet Mark Tanner here in about half an hour. In the background, on the great lawn that stretched out from the college's main administrative building, the boys were playing pepper, and whenever a ball would get past a player, laps would ensue.

Frankie, ever on the job, took the chance to take a photo or two before coming over to join Cesar. She sat on the edge of the fountain and jotted down a few notes in her steno pad.

"Okay, boys, that's enough for tonight. I want everyone in bed with the lights out by nine o'clock," he called out to his players who slowly disbursed.

"Don't you ever give them a break from baseball?"

"Every time I do, they grill me about my love life."

"Sounds exciting."

"Yeah, as exciting as a coroner's inquest."

"What's her name?" asked Frankie.

"Who?"

"The girl back home."

"Off the record?"

"Yeah, off the record," Frankie answered, smiling, and placed her pencil behind her ear.

"Maria."

"Wife? Fiancé?"

"What's the term for a woman who'll never speak to you again?"

"I heard the game isn't over until the final out," said Frankie.

"You've been watching too many movies. Besides, I don't think I'm staying in Monterrey. Thinking of coaching up north, in the majors."

"And the boys? What about them?"

"They got along fine without me before."

"You can put your boots in the oven, but it don't make 'em biscuits."

"What's that supposed to mean?" asked Cesar.

"Means you can say what you want about somethin', but it don't change what it is. Monterrey and these boys are in you, Cesar."

"I struck out with a woman I really cared about. I got no job in Monterrey, I'm blacklisted. My folks are long gone. . . ah, what can you know?" he said with an air of indignation.

"What can I know? You ever wonder why I have a boy's name?"

"Well, it did occur to me."

"My father was a long-haul trucker out of Missouri, and Frankie Fritsche was his favorite Cardinal. I was born the week they won the 1934 World Series and I guess having a daughter didn't dissuade his desire to make me into a baseball player. Anytime he was home from the road, he'd take me to the ballpark or try to teach me the game in our backyard. At first I loved the attention, but then I grew to hate baseball. . . and then him."

"Why?"

"He left me and my mom before I was ten. You ask me what can I know? Do you know what it's like growing up with a father who wants you to be someone else—someone you can never be?"

"But at least you got better at baseball," Cesar tried to joke.

"Sometimes, you can be a real jerk," she said. She began to cry and left him alone at the fountain.

Cesar sure didn't understand women at all. He sat alone for what seemed like an hour, though only half that time had elapsed. Tanner showed up at the appointed time. The two men discussed various things, but both were careful to avoid any reference to Cesar's unhappy times with the St. Louis Browns. It was water under the bridge, and though there was no love lost between them, Cesar listened eagerly to what Tanner had to say about his future.

"I never would have pitched Enrique today. And intentionally walking Caldarola to load the bases? That took guts, Cesar, but hey, it paid off."

"Yep," the coach responded.

"Give me a call next week," his said as he handed Cesar his business card.

Cesar paused for a few moments to admire Mr. Tanner's card. On it was the raised logo of the Baltimore Orioles.

"Good luck tomorrow," said Tanner as got up and he walked away.

"Señor Faz!" came a voice from behind Cesar. The coach turned to see Angel holding two gloves.

"Angel. . . I was just, uh—" Cesar stammered as he jammed the business card into his back pocket. "What are you doing here?"

"A pitcher needs a catcher," he said and tossed his spare glove to Cesar. "Who was that man you were just talking to?"

"An executive from Baltimore."

"Executive of what?"

"The Orioles."

Angel fired the baseball real hard. *Crack!* "You're leaving us, aren't you?"

"They've offered me a job as an assistant coach. A real coaching job."

"You already have a team."

"It's the Baltimore Orioles, Angel. The major leagues!"

Angel's throws continued to increase in velocity until the sting in Cesar's glove could be heard like the short burst at the end of a whip. *Crack!*

"It's something I wanted for a long time," Cesar added.

"What? A job?"

Crack!

"No. . . respect," answered Cesar.

"We gave you that before your team was winning." Angel tossed a soft one back to Cesar. "What about Maria?"

"She's already forgotten me," Cesar said and gave Angel back the extra glove and left.

Angel stared at the water in the fountain. Shimmering beneath the surface were hundreds of silver and copper coins, each one containing the wish of a hopeful soul.

⋅⊙⊙⋅

Cesar was hurt that Angel couldn't understand how long he had pursued this goal and now he was finally being recognized as a man who could manage a real baseball team. Feeling a mix of loneliness and anxiety, Cesar took a long walk.

It is said that rivers flow toward the ocean and men flow to rivers. Soon, he found himself on a bridge that crossed over the Susquehanna River. Cesar leaned over the railing and stared at the steel gray waters that ebbed eastward. In its soft reflections, the river appeared to be a long and undulating dark mirror. He wondered where he was being led and where the destinies of these fourteen boys were flowing.

Life is so short that few men can remember the bad they have done and only a little of the good. The river took Cesar back to another time, another place and another river. He thought about catching turtles with his brother, Jorge, in the Rio San Antonio. In the summer dry spells, they would bury themselves in the muddy banks. Cesar and Jorge would look for breathing holes and then prod the ground with sticks until they felt something hard. It would take their combined efforts to grab the turtles' tails and they always ended up covered in mud. A local Chinese restaurant paid a nickel for each turtle. Times were so hard that grown men would try to steal them from the brothers. They learned how to fight pretty good defending their catch.

❧❦❧

The creak of Lucky's door could be heard down the long hollow corridor. As if on cue, a fully dressed Enrique and Angel threw back their covers. Enrique tiptoed toward the door and knocked into a lamp, which fell off the nightstand. But for Angel's quick grab, it would have shattered on the floor.

Breathing again, the boys silently slipped out of the room.

The others were already outside waiting for them.

In ten minutes, they stood in the dimly lit night before the fountain. Without shoes and with their pants rolled above their knees, the boys stepped into the slightly brackish water of the wishing well. Fishing around with their hands, they gathered coins.

"Are you sure this is right?" Mario asked Norberto as the former dropped a handful of pennies and nickels into a sock that Norberto held open.

"God is fair. He won't take away these people's wishes just because we took the coins," said the catcher.

"I was more worried about what He would do to us," said Mario.

Ten minutes later, Frankie opened her door to see the boys, still wet from their escapade in the fountain. Pepe tried his best to speak with her, but his words came so rapidly, she had to constantly ask him to slow down.

She finally heard one word repeated over and over: *telegram*. Pepe gave Frankie a handwritten note.

"Telegrams cost money. *Con qué dinero?*" she asked.

With that, Norberto and Ricardo stepped forward and each handed her a sock full of change.

"Where'd you get this. . . and why are these socks wet?"

Pepe moved close to the window and gestured toward the fountain.

"I see," said Frankie.

❧❦❧

There were only three businesses open this late in Williamsport. The first was an Esso gas station along Route 15, the second was Pomerantz's Tavern and the third was the train depot inside of which was located a Western Union satellite branch.

Frankie took care of the boys' request and then headed back to the dormitories. She was exhausted, but she had one last important stop. Sliding off her cowboy boots, she stepped into the fountain and taking a stuffed sock in each hand, released the coins back into the water.

The last one to hit the water was a silver dollar that she had been carrying around for good luck. She made sure to make her wish before sending it aloft into the wishing well.

❧❦❧

It was now past 10:00 PM. Most of the *Regiomontanos* were fast asleep, but a constant thud was keeping Enrique awake. He slid to the edge of his bunk and looked down at Angel who was having a catch with himself. The ball kept hitting the bottom of Enrique's bed.

"Quit doing that! You're keeping me up!" he told Angel.

"I can't sleep."

"Well, if it makes you feel any better, I heard that they expect more than fifteen thousand people tomorrow."

"Thanks, Enrique."

"And they're going to film the game!"

"You're not helping."

"And the radio is going to broadcast it for our families back home. If you lose, you will never have a girlfriend."

"Enrique, shut up! You're going to make me throw up." Angel stopped his ball tossing, and the two tried once again to find sleep.

After a long silence, Enrique said, "Hey, Angel?"

"Yeah."

"That was a great catch tonight. You saved my *trasero*."

"You'd have done the same for me."

After another long silence, Enrique spoke again. "I wouldn't want anybody else in the world pitching for us tomorrow than you." But Angel was already asleep.

❧

A knock broke the silence of the night in front of Señor Alvarado's house.

"Señor Alvarado, please," Fecundino Suarez said to the servant who opened the door to find both Suarez and Umberto Macias waiting on the threshold. Señor Alvarado met the two men in his marble-floored foyer. He was in his pajamas and had hastily put on a silk dressing robe that was tied about his waist.

"Señor Alvarado, we want. . .we need to make work conditions better," said Fecundino.

"Here is a list of our demands," said Umberto, handing Señor Alvarado a piece of paper.

"Demands in the middle of the night from two employees?" asked Señor Alvarado with an air of incredulity.

"Not from two employees, no," Umberto answered and stepped back to hold open the door. Outside, lining the street of Señor Alvarado's villa were hundreds of workers holding candles aloft in a gesture of solidarity. The patriarch was clearly taken aback.

"I see. But I'm sure this can wait until Monday morning—"

"No, it can't. Not the first item, at least," said Umberto.

Señor Alvarado took a moment to look down the list that he held in his clenched fist.

"You want the factories to close at one o'clock tomorrow?"

"That will give us time to be with our families before the game starts," said Fecundino Suarez.

Señor Alvardo chuckled and then said with sternness, "My family has lived here for generations and helped build these factories. They have never closed on a Friday, ever!"

"They will tomorrow, sir," said Umberto.

26

A Perfect Day

hat a great day to play baseball," Lucky told Cesar when the two awoke the next morning to cloudless and deep blue skies.

"Yes, it would be a sin to not play baseball on a day like today," Cesar replied and slid on the jersey that said Monterrey.

It was Friday, August 23, 1957, and it was indeed a perfect day.

"*Buenas días*," Cesar said, entering the room of his two pitchers. Enrique still languished in his top bunk. Angel was fully dressed and staring out the window. "You pitching righty or lefty today?" Cesar asked Angel.

"Not sure yet," Angel didn't take his eyes from the window.

"What are you looking at?" Cesar asked.

"The little bird," answered Angel.

Enrique dropped down from his top bunk and angled his neck to see out the same window. A single hummingbird was darting in and out of flowers that grew from vines clinging to the red brick.

"Boys, don't be disappointed. Padre Esteban didn't mean you could really see its wings."

"He didn't?" asked Enrique.

"No," answered Cesar. "Now hurry downstairs, you two. I want you both to eat a good breakfast."

Left alone in the room, Cesar craned his head to look out the window and gaze upon the object of the boys' attention. The furrows on his forehead deepened as he squinted in disbelief.

ᕫᖍᱟᖌᱻᔌ

Monterrey's citizens also had awakened that morning to a glorious sunrise over the Cerro de la Silla and to headlines in *El Norte* that were dedicated to the championship baseball game:

WILLIAMSPORT, PENNSYLVANIA – August 23, 1957. La Mesa, California, and Monterrey, Mexico, battle for the Little League World Championship today as the maximum honors will be presented at Original Little League Field. The official occupancy of ten thousand fans will not be sufficient for the grand encounter of the little titans of the baseball world. Everyone's thoughts, hearts, hopes and pride from these players' homes pray to God that they win.

Never had the city of Monterrey cared so much for the achievements of its athletes. Not even the bull fighter, Lorenzo Garza, or the great boxer, Panchito Billa, provoked the kind of overt joy in Monterrey like these children did.

People who weren't even interested in sports found themselves riveted to any news about the team making its way across the United States. From the most luxurious homes to the most humble shacks, everyone prayed for one more victory for the boys. Large churches and small chapels alike were being swarmed by hundreds of thousands of parishioners who lit candles to the Virgin de Guadalupe before beginning their daily labors.

Monterrey had transformed into a town that wanted to believe in miracles. Factories, offices, construction sites, bars and classrooms were invaded with thousands of radios by employees, so they could hear the games in Williamsport, and for those who didn't have access to radios, public address speakers were being hastily installed all over the city. Many of the poorest families from the barrios Cantu, Reforma and Obrerista went to the team's original field where they watched an empty diamond, imagining what was happening as the loudspeakers delivered the play-by-play. This was the drama that unfolded across an entire city transfixed by the exploits of fourteen boys, who a month ago were just lost faces in the indiscriminate sea of Monterrey's poor and forlorn.

It was nearing 1:00 PM in Monterrey, which was situated in a time zone one hour behind Williamsport's. When the minute hand struck the hour, something happened that had never occurred before on a Friday afternoon in the history of Monterrey: Whistles blew signifying the closing of the factories and workers streamed out, hurrying to get to the nearest radio or loudspeaker.

With factories, schools and the government offices left empty, Monterrey held its collective breath over a Little League baseball game that was about to begin a few thousand miles away.

❧

On the bus ride to the field, Cesar admonished his players, "You're going to see and hear applause, shouts, boos, whistles, autograph seekers, music, pictures, microphones and people—lots of them. Accept it all respectfully, but don't forget that we are here to win a baseball game and that the only way we can do it is to dedicate ourselves completely to carrying out all the opportunities possible during the game. I don't think that I am asking too much from you. When we met just months ago, you barely knew which way to run around the field. Today, you are a group of baseball players who wants to be and can be world champions."

They arrived at the field to a crowd that exceeded the official seating capacity. Some estimated it was more than sixteen thousand people, many of whom sat on a long berm behind the outfield.

Frankie took her place in the area reserved for the press; present were reporters from every major news publication. Many of her colleagues were worried it wouldn't be a contest, and a few seemed genuinely concerned that a La Mesa blowout could get embarrassing.

Cesar, Lucky and José stood on the field; all three were in awe of how many fans who had seen them play in other cities were here for the Little League World Series. They even saw Betty and Benny Little, the owners of Busy Corner in McAllen, Texas, and some of the other Good Neighbors of the Texas Valley who had traveled all this way to cheer on the team they had adopted as their own.

"Uh-oh," said Cesar when he noticed another member of the Mexican delegation approaching him.

"What's wrong?" Lucky asked.

"His buddies fired me yesterday for pitching Enrique."

"Then what are you worried about? Tell 'em you have but one job to lose for your country."

"Were you this funny during the war?"

"Yes, as a matter of fact I was. Anyway, we'll see you in a few. We don't want to spoil a tender moment between you two." Lucky and José went to greet several of the folks they recognized from Texas.

The Mexican gentleman joined Cesar. "Señor Faz, we haven't met. I'm Eloy Cantu," the man began.

"Look, you already fired me, and you can't blackmail me with St. Louis 'cause I already told the boys."

"What are you talking about? I just arrived this morning. What's this about you being fired?"

"I'm sorry, I thought you were with the Mexican delegation."

"I am. The governor of Nuevo León personally asked me to be here in his stead. I just wanted to wish you and the team good luck before the game."

"Thank you, sir."

"And I know this may be too little too late, but I have a package for you from back home. Don't lose it. I think there's money in it for the boys." As Señor Cantu handed Cesar an envelope, a man who appeared to be his assistant came running toward them.

"What is it, Rodolfo?" asked Señor Cantu.

"We have a problem. Señor Caballero won't be able to broadcast today."

"Why not?"

"He lost his voice while screaming during yesterday's game."

"I have a little experience on the radio. Tell him I'll do it," said Señor Cantu.

An open party line had been established among callers in New York City, Atlanta, San Antonio and finally to the termination point in XET's broadcast booth in Monterrey. In small rooms in each of these relay points, men held two telephones to their heads: one to hear and the other to pass on the baseball game's action. The last man in the chain broadcast the commentary through the radio.

The Brooklyn Dodgers had loaned their special emissary, Emmett Kelly the Clown, to entertain the crowd. A rousing cheer went up as the local Air National Guard unit sent four jets in a flyover of Original Little League Field.

When Cesar returned to Monterrey Industrial's dugout, Clarence was preparing to give his blessing. Turning to Cesar, he asked, "I understand the prayer to the Virgin of Guadalupe, but why do they always want the 108th Psalm?"

"One hundred and eight," Cesar held up a baseball, "is the number of stitches on the ball."

In plain sight, across the field in the La Mesa dugout, was a team of great baseball players, born and raised in the California sun, playing the game since they could barely walk. Their nine starters eagerly awaited their chance to show the world what they could do on a baseball diamond.

After the blessing, Clarence looked at the boys, who still stood on the edge of the dugout. "I think they're waiting for a last pep talk," he said.

"I'm not much for sermons—" Cesar began to tell them.

"That's Padre Esteban's job," interjected Norberto.

"That's right. And, fortunately, I have his words here with me." Cesar reached into his back pocket and pulled out a folded postcard from Hillerich & Bradsby Company, the Louisville Sluggers factory. "He wrote this before he left and told me to read it to you if you reached the finals."

Cesar began to read aloud from the small card: "Padre Esteban here, boys. When you take the field today, think of the courage of Juan Diego. Remember, after the bishop threatened him, he ran away, lost his woman and hid in a bottle. He even tried to avoid our Lady. . ."

The boys gave one another some perplexing looks. This was a version they had never heard.

". . .It was the bottom of the ninth with two outs, and even though Juan Diego tried to blame the ump and stall the big game, he crossed that hill, scored the winning run and became a hero. And like him, if you keep your faith, the Dark Virgin will help you show La Mesa what you're made of," Cesar finished reading.

"Señor Faz, how did Padre Esteban know we would play La Mesa?" asked Ricardo.

"He's a man of God, that's how," Cesar said.

With faith in the perfect answer, the boys put their hands together in the middle, let out a cheer and bound up the steps to the field.

Cesar folded up the postcard and went to stuff it in his back pocket. However, the thick envelope given to him by Señor Cantu caused the postcard to fall to the ground. Cesar was too preoccupied with watching Angel warm up to notice.

Angel began his practice pitches slowly so that his arm would gradually take form. He was all business now and only talked to Cesar to answer questions with a short *yes* or *no*. The only sign of life in him was the burning concentration in his eyes, which didn't leave the catcher's glove. By the end of the warm-up, Angel's pitches found the center of Chuy's targets with uncanny accuracy.

The field was cleared and the official announcer began, "Ladies and gentlemen, the line up for the game today. For Monterrey, Mexico: Macias, pitcher; Villarreal, catcher; Treviño, first base. . ."

The crowd stood while the Naval School Band from Washington, DC played "The Star Spangled Banner." And then for the first time in all the games that they had played in the tournament, the *Regiomontanos* watched their country's flag being raised. It was accompanied by music, but because the naval band didn't know the tune, the tinny sounds originated from a Philips portable electric gramophone that had been hastily set up in the scorekeeper's booth. Someone from the Little League organization had procured a vinyl recording of "Mexicanos, al grito de Guerra," the Mexican national anthem.

Cesar watched his boys proudly admire their flag: red and green with the eagle of Tinochtitlan on a field of white. A few, like Fidel who was the most accustomed to the Mexican flag's protocol, sang along with the music: *"Tus seines de oliva/De la Paz el arcángel divino/Que en el cielo tu eterno destino/Por el dedo de Dios se escribió* [Your forehead shall be girded with olive garlands/by the divine archangel of peace/For in heaven your eternal destiny/has been written by the hand of God]."

About halfway through the anthem, the stylus began to skip, repeating the same line. Not knowing what to do, the boys merely sang the same line over and over again until the scorekeeper mercifully moved the phonograph's needle.

Monterrey would take the field first. As the boys jogged to their positions, each one found himself momentarily alone in his thoughts.

Fidel Ruiz, taking third base, recalled the cold winter winds and the hot suffocating summers as he got on and off a van that was filled with bottled drinks which he delivered to help make money for his family.

Enrique Suarez walked to center field and thought about bringing food to his older brothers who worked at Vidriera, the glass bottling factory.

Baltazar Charles' eternal smile didn't reflect his humble home or give a hint of his sadness for his sick younger sister, Patricia.

Pepe Maiz thought of his mother who, though affluent, visited churches in the poorer barrios and ladled milk for mothers unable to provide it for their own children.

In right field stood Rafael Estrello, punching his fist into the glove that his mother had helped sew from a hybrid of materials she had scavenged in their neighborhood.

"I'm going to need both coaches in two minutes," Umpire Gair said, standing briefly at the top of the dugout steps.

"What's this?" Clarence asked, stooping to the ground to pick up the postcard that had dislodged from Cesar's pocket. After a moment of inspection, "Oh, it's Padre Esteban's postcard," he said.

"I'll take that," Cesar said hastily, but it was too late. Clarence's eyes had already noticed something quite unusual about the priest's inspiring letter. "The padre sure had a way with words," Cesar said, sliding it back into his pocket.

"Yes, yes he did," Clarence said with a knowing smile.

Only the two of them would ever know that the postcard was blank.

⁂

In all the times his boys prayed, Cesar had beseeched them never to ask for victory. It hardly seemed a fair thing to do, especially if the other team was calling upon the same Almighty for a victory of their own. But today, Cesar kneeled for a moment in the dugout and prayed for his team to win.

"Coming down!" yelled Norberto, letting Gerardo know that all was ready.

Norberto caught Angel's pitch and threw it to second base, where Gerardo was ready. Sweeping the ground as if tagging out a phantom runner, he tossed the ball to Baltazar, who pivoted and threw it to Fidel, who then threw it across the diamond to first base. Ricardo, the youngest player on the team, caught the ball, walked toward Angel and handed it to him.

"It's all up to you now, Angel," said his gutsy first baseman.

Angel said nothing. He chewed a piece of gum that Cesar had given him before he took the field, and his eyes never left Beto's glove.

The only thing needed to begin the Little League World Series was a shout from Umpire Gair. He examined his watch and looked toward the official announcer who was seated in his box. He checked his watch again and with a dramatic shout of "Play Ball!" the 1957 Little League World Series began.

Lewis Riley took a last practice swing before stepping into the batter's box. Angel stepped onto the rubber. Everything was ready. Everything was as it should be.

It was indeed a perfect day to play baseball.

34 & 35. Enrique Suarez takes the Waco pitcher "downtown."

36. No rest for the weary. Even between games, Cesar's coaching was relentless.

37. The boys circle around Cesar and begin warming up for the next opponent.

38. A *Regiomontano* slides home for another run.

39. The boys have conquered Texas and taken their flag.

Louisville

Angel 'Devil' To Opponents

40. & 41. The Louisville newspapers are abuzz with talk of an amazing Mexican pitcher (Angel Macias) who can pitch both left and right-handed.

42. Ambidextrous at the plate as well as the mound, Angel clobbers one lefty.

43. Gerardo Gonzalez slides into home during Monterrey's 13-0 rout of Biloxi, Mississippi.

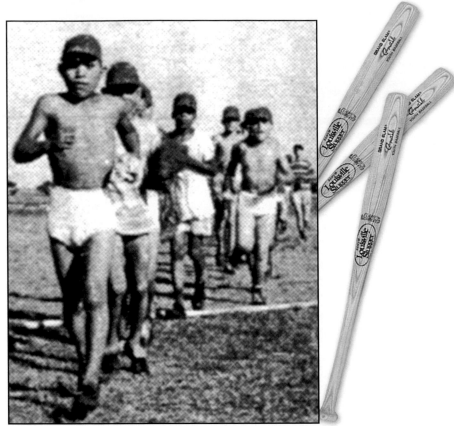

44. No uniforms, no problem. The team does roadwork
in their underwear as their uniforms are being washed.

45. Rounding third on the way to another run against
Owensboro, Kentucky.

46. Rafael Estrello heads for home during a Monterrey rally.

47. The local press labels the Monterrey batters: "Murderers Row."

48. Led by solid hitting and the great pitching of Enrique Suarez and Angel Macias (shown here being hoisted on the shoulders of his teammates), Monterrey defeated Biloxi (13-0) and Owensboro (3-0) to earn a berth in the 1957 Little League World Series. Next stop: Williamsport, PA!

LITTLE LEAGU

WORLD SERIE

1957

WILLIAMSPORT
PENNSYLVANIA
AUGUST 21-23

49. & 50. The official program for the World Series (pictured above) is being sold in the grandstands before the game.

LITTLE LEAGUE BASEBALL
WORLD SERIES
1957
WILLIAMSPORT, PA.
Not Transferable

Section A
Game 4

51. Admission ticket for the 1957 Little League World Series.

52. Wide lens shot of Original Little League Field in Williamsport as seen from centerfield. Behind home plate stands a two-story loggia for reporters and dignitaries.

53a. An incredible relay from Enrique Suarez stops a Bridgeport runner from scoring.

53b. Angel making a put out at second base during the Bridgeport semi-final game.

The New York Times

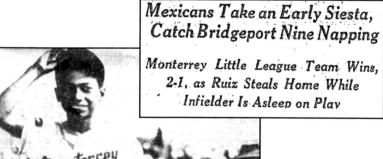

Mexicans Take an Early Siesta, Catch Bridgeport Nine Napping

Monterrey Little League Team Wins, 2-1, as Ruiz Steals Home While Infielder Is Asleep on Play

54. Enrique Suarez pitches a gem, beating Bridgeport 2-1. *The New York Times* headline mentioned the pivotal base running of Fidel Ruiz.

55. Monterrey represented the Southern Region.

56. Commemorative pin.

57. La Mesa, California was the best of the Western Region.

58. Before the game, the team receives a blessing from a local Catholic priest. The image would appear in Life Magazine.

59. An announcement of the championship game, which would be broadcast on XET, Mexico's largest radio station.

GLADIOLA

LA MANTECA VEGETAL PERFECTA PARA
COCINAR Y . .

K—O

EL MAS FAMOSO DE LOS ACEITES COMESTIBLES .

PRESENTAN HOY A LAS 13:00 HORAS, DESDE
WILLIAMSPORT, PENN.

El Campeonato de Beisbol

Pequeña Liga

ENTRE LOS DOS EQUIPOS FINALISTAS:

MONTERREY y LA MESA, Calif.

..CLARO que a través
de XET!

60. One of the dorm rooms at Lycoming College shared by the boys.

LA MESA
California

61. In the La Mesa dugout, pitcher Lewis Riley calmly awaits his chance to duel Angel Macias.

62. The opposing captains (Fidel Ruiz of Monterrey and Francis Vogel of La Mesa) shake hands at home plate while Umpire Howard Gair looks on.

88-Pounder Hope of Monterrey In Little League Series Today

Angel Macias, Ambidextrous, Is Team's No. 1 Pitcher, Batter and Fielder

By MICHAEL STRAUSS
Special to The New York Times.

WILLIAMSPORT, Pa., Aug. 21 — A baseball player, who virtually out-Merriwells Frank Merriwell, will play with the Monterrey nine of Mexico tomorrow when the Little League World Series gets under way.

The Eastern debut of this pint-sized athlete was deferred today because of rain. A deluge just before game time washed away the Mexican team's semi-final round contest with Bridgeport (Conn.).

But when the lads from south of the border open the series, leading them will be Angel Macias. He is an ambidextrous youngster, who hits from both sides of the plate, and who can play all nine positions.

Because of the postponement, tomorrow's program will be made up of a double-header. Paired in the second contest are Escanaba (Mich.) and La Mesa (Calif.).

Angel, a five-foot eighty-eight-pounder, not only is his team's best batter but he also is Monterrey's top fielder and twirler. Back home, in practice games, he has been known to register strike-outs on three or four pitches while tossing with alternate hands.

Although the Mexican team is the lightest, youngest and shortest in the present four-way club tourney, it is conceded a fine chance of taking it all.

To gain the semi-final berth, the Mexican boys had to defeat

Associated Press
Angel Macias

field, he keeps changing around, depending on how he feels.

If Macias is pitching, the opposing line-up is scanned to determine which hand he'll use. A preponderance of left-handed batters means southpaw hurling.

Surprisingly enough, the youngster doesn't care to grow up to be a pitcher. He wants to be a center-fielder. His favorite player is Mickey Mantle.

"Mantle is a turn-over hitter like me," the lad explained to

63. Earlier that morning, *The New York Times* headline placed Monterrey's hopes on the arm of the thin Angel Macias.

64. Angel Macias takes the lonely walk to the mound to commence the biggest game of his life.

65, 66 & 67. Angel sets, winds up, and delivers... The World Series has begun!

27

Simply Perfect

"Angel Macias prepares to throw the first pitch of the 1957 Little League World Series. First up for La Mesa is the pitcher, Lewis Riley," began announcers in two languages.

"Here's the windup and the pitch. It's a hard line drive to right field. . . Wait! What a catch by Ricardo Treviño at first!"

Riley hit the ball so hard, a surprised Ricardo barely had time to reach up and get his glove on the ball. Judging from its trajectory, it looked like it would have surely kept going until it hit the right field wall.

It was only one play, but it was significant. A double or a triple would have most likely resulted in at least one La Mesa run and a great psychological edge. Instead, La Mesa had nothing to show for Riley's solid contact.

With one down, the infield passed the ball around the horn and then back to Angel, who still chewed his gum and said nothing.

Norberto called for a curveball for the next batter, Leonard Tobey. He hit one off the end of his bat that was easily fielded by Angel, who tossed the ball to Ricardo for the second out. John Hardesty was third, and with two strikes in the count, a wicked changeup left him staring at the plate as the umpire called his third strike.

Monterrey passed its first defensive test.

Riley now took his place on the mound. He had a dominating fastball, and at five feet nine and a half inches he was the tallest pitcher the boys had ever faced. The height of the mound only accentuated his stature as the *Regiomontanos* stared up at his incoming pitches. But just as Don Quixote had his mythical battle against the one-eyed giants, Angel and his eight fellow Sancho Panzas were ready for the challenge.

Baltazar grounded out to Byron Haggard at second base, and Pepe followed with a similar consequence for the next out. Angel, batting third, took a base on balls. Enrique was batting cleanup, but Riley's fastballs overwhelmed him and the first inning was over.

Joe McKirahan, the slugger who had creamed two homers the day before, was La Mesa's fourth hitter. Francis Vogel, who also had homered against Escanaba, took his practice swings in the on-deck circle.

Without the slightest recognition of whom he faced, Angel pitched a fast ball for strike one. McKirahan dug in, but Angel, cold in concentration on his next two pitches, sent curveballs toward the corners of the plate. McKirahan's intense swings missed both pitches and provoked a wave of surprise among the thousands of fans. Few Little League pitchers had the courage, astuteness and ability to manage those types of pitches.

The fans strained forward as Vogel hit a sharp grounder to Baltazar, who in turn threw it perfectly to Ricardo for the second out. An offensive threat had been handled, but just as quickly another one stood at the plate in the form of Jerry Wilson. Again, Angel worked on pitching to the corners of the strike zone with low, fast curveballs, and he struck out Wilson to end La Mesa's second inning.

Angel still hadn't uttered a single word and continued to chew the gum that had long since lost its flavor.

Fidel went down on strikes to lead off the bottom of the second. Rafael adjusted his glasses with both hands as he held the bat between his legs. He entered the batter's box and looked at Riley. After a strike and a ball, Rafael hit a pitch up the middle. Haggard dove, but the ball went by him into center field for a clean base hit. Rafael, the boy from the small town of Guadalupe, who had never spent a single night away from home, was the first player to get a hit in the Little League World Series final.

For the next batter, Riley lost control of a ball and hit Norberto. The impact was hard, but Beto shrugged it off and made his way to first base. It was a good opportunity, but Riley was able to retire Gerardo and Ricardo to end Monterrey's threat.

Angel took the mound again in the top of the third. La Mesa's center fielder, Dennis Hanggi, took two fast curveballs for strikes. He then received one fastball at chest height that he couldn't resist. He was out before the ball even touched Norberto's glove.

Angel and Norberto's strategy for the shortstop, Robert Brown, was different. Angel sent two quick balls and then a changeup. Brown seemed to swing before the ball reached him. After Brown's strikeout, Haggard, the second baseman, ended La Mesa's third at bat with an infield pop-up.

Riley opened the bottom of the third by striking out Baltazar, but Pepe was able to connect with one of Riley's pitches, sending the ball flying into left field for a clean double.

Pepe looked to his coach for a strategy, but the only thing Cesar yelled to him was "Try to make any play! Don't hold back!"

Riley however, after walking Angel, worked through Enrique and Fidel, and Monterrey was again unable to capitalize on having a base runner in scoring position.

The game was still scoreless, and the crowd became strangely quiet. Everyone expected La Mesa would already be ahead by several runs, but so far Monterrey Industrial had been the only team to get runners on base.

Angel Macias went out to the center of the diamond for the fourth inning. Riley, now at bat, failed at the hand of Angel's low pitches. The left fielder, Tobey, hit a ball toward Gerardo, who fielded it and threw him out at first, and Hardesty hit a grounder to Ricardo, who tossed it to Angel to end the top of the fourth.

Rafael, Norberto and Gerardo all went down in the bottom of the fourth. It was during this Monterrey at bat that someone handed Cesar a message. He was so focused that he crumpled the paper, not noticing that atop the stationery was the Great Seal of the United States of America.

This time, as he tried to stuff it in his pocket, he removed the envelope that Señor Cantu hand-delivered from Monterrey. It was torn, and worried that the pesos within might fall from his pocket, he went to hand the envelope to Clarence. As he did, he spied a chain dangling from a small tear. Opening the envelope, he pulled out the chain and found a medallion of Our Lady of Guadalupe wrapped in a handwritten note.

⋴⊚⋵

McKirahan had come back for revenge. His power was incredible for a twelve-year-old. Angel wiped his forehead, fixed his cap and looked for Norberto's signal. Hitting more than a dozen home runs during the tournament, McKirahan's shots didn't just score runs, they made statements. Angel began his movement against McKirahan. Strike, ball, ball, strike. Angel watched as McKirahan, anxious to win the game in one at bat, swung wildly at the air for strike three.

Vogel entered the batter's box; Angel chewed on the same piece of gum. Vogel gripped his bat and missed three fastballs. By the time he realized he was out, the boys of Monterrey were already passing the ball to one another around the horn.

Up to this point in the game, the crowd had clearly favored the American team. With two outs in the top of the fifth, the sentiment of the crowd was about to dramatically hinge on one wild play.

Wilson hit an infield dribbler that Angel, Fidel and Ricardo all went for. Wilson, noticing that first base was uncovered, slowed down, confident that he had a base hit. Fidel fielded the ball and threw to first anyway. A fraction of a second before Wilson's foot touched the base, Norberto caught the throw and tagged the shocked base runner out.

The crowd exploded enthusiastically.

In the hundreds of thousands of games that these spectators had seen in their collective lives, few had ever seen a catcher—even in the pros—with the baseball acumen and presence of mind to shadow the runner down the first base line.

"That was incredible, Beto!" exclaimed Cesar.

"I just didn't want to run anymore laps," Norberto answered.

The inning was over. Perfection was preserved.

⋴⊚⋵

José shouted out the names of the first three Monterrey hitters due up in the bottom of the fifth inning: "Treviño, Charles and Maiz!"

Ricardo got his bat and walked to the on-deck circle with a slight limp, the cumulative effect of having taken dozens of kicks and cleats to his right leg in the previous twelve games.

Cesar stopped him. Feeling a shift in the momentum and even in the crowd's sympathies, he knew if Monterrey had a window through which to strike, it had just been opened a crack.

"Ricardo, do you want to win the championship?"

"Sì, Señor Faz."

"Then do anything you can to get on a base, even if it means getting hit by a pitch. Get as close to the plate as you can. If you get hit, don't worry. We'll get someone to run for you. Get on base, *Zurdo*, and we'll win."

A faithful and obedient Ricardo did just as Cesar asked of him. At the risk of being injured, he got as close to the plate as he could. Riley couldn't find the strike zone and ended up throwing four straight balls.

As the announcer called out Baltazar's number, Cesar sent in Mario Ontiveros to run for Ricardo, who limped off the field. He had done his duty, and no one could have expected more of him.

As he had done with Ricardo, Cesar spoke to Baltazar before he went to bat.

"Balta, you want to win the championship? You have to bunt the ball perfectly so that Mario can get to second. McKirahan and Hardesty are going to try for it, so you have to hit it toward Riley. He'll be off balance after pitching but that'll give Mario the best chance. Balta, you have to touch it perfectly. You lay down a perfect bunt for me and we'll win."

Cesar then went to first base and told his pinch runner, "Mario, as soon as you see Balta square to bunt, run to second as fast as you can, as fast as you have ever run."

Everyone on La Mesa's defense knew a bunt was coming, so their infielders crept closer. Baltazar squared and laid down an exquisite bunt. Time seemed to exhale slowly as the ball made its way to a spot perfectly equidistant from the pitcher, catcher and third baseman, all of whom could do nothing but hope it rolled foul. By the time it gently came to rest on the chalk line, Mario had made it to second base and Baltazar stood safely on first.

Mario, who had slid into second, got up and dusted off his pants, looking to Cesar for the next sign.

Pepe was up next. He was one of Monterrey's best power hitters, but a selfless Pepe knew that this was a classic scenario to lay down another bunt, sacrificing himself to move Mario to third base and all that much closer to scoring. In a game where both pitchers were performing well, one run scored by either team could become the margin of victory. But Cesar had long ago thrown away the book of practical plays.

He called Pepe, Angel and Enrique—his next three hitters— together.

"Look, there isn't going to be any more bunting," whispered the coach. "That's what La Mesa is expecting. We are going to hit hard now. One of you guys has to do this so that we can win." Cesar then ran down the sideline to tell José the plan. He appeared like a general rallying his troops in the height of battle.

"Hey, Pepe," Enrique called his teammate, "I think our underwear got switched in McAllen."

Pepe smiled.

The stadium's occupants rose to their feet as Pepe stepped up to the plate and Riley readied the first pitch. The tension could be felt throughout the entire field and in Mexico, where hundreds of thousands were listening to the radio and praying.

When the defense for La Mesa saw that Pepe wasn't preparing to bunt, their infielders backed up a few steps and got ready for a possible double play. Riley pitched and Pepe's bat connected, sending the ball flying between shortstop and second for a base hit. Mario, who had already been running on the pitcher's release of the baseball, rounded third base without even looking back, his leather helmet flying off as he slid into home for the game's first run. Monterrey Industrial had scored against one of the best defenses in all of Little League baseball. The crowd's reaction showed their amazement as a hush fell upon them.

Angel flied out, but Enrique followed with a double, which scored the hard-running Baltazar and Pepe. Fidel walked and Rafael struck out. An infield hit by Norberto loaded the bases for Gerardo.

At four feet seven inches and weighing sixty-five pounds, Gerardo was fourteen inches shorter and one hundred pounds lighter than La Mesa's center fielder Dennis Hanggi. He made contact for another infield hit and another run as Enrique touched home plate.

Francisco Aguilar pinch hit for Mario Ontiveros, who as a pinch runner had replaced Ricardo. Riley was able to get Francisco out to end the fifth inning, but the damage had been done. It happened so fast that La Mesa barely had time to react. To the astonishment of all who watched or listened, Monterrey Industrial led La Mesa four to nothing going into the top of the sixth—and last—inning.

⎯⎯⎯⎯⎯⎯

Before the Monterrey rally ended, Angel had been sitting all alone at one end of the bench.

"Señor Faz," said Ricardo, "no batters have gotten on base. Angel's pitching a perfect—"

Cesar quickly cupped a hand over Ricardo's mouth and pulled him to the opposite end of the dugout. "No one, I mean no one, says one word to him about this or anything else!"

Angel, still working the same piece of chewing gum, was as cool as Cesar had ever seen an athlete. When Francisco's out was recorded, Angel carefully placed the chewing gum on the bench, as if saving it for later.

"We are just going to get outs for you," Cesar told Angel. "Don't think about anything else but your pitching. Don't change anything, don't let up. Even if we trade runs for outs, we will still win. Throw strikes and give it all you've got, so we can end this once and for all."

This inning would be Angel's farewell performance, never again would he defend Mexico in a Little League uniform. Thousands of fans knew it, and the young pitcher knew it too.

Angel made the sign of the cross and gave Cesar a last look before he went to the mound. The crowd was completely under Angel's spell as he began his first practice pitches. It was as if they were witnessing more than a miraculous baseball phenomenon; they were watching a boy mature into a young man before their very eyes.

Awaiting him were Hanggi, Brown and Haggard, each hoping to

be the spoiler and ignite a rally by La Mesa. Fidel replaced Ricardo at first base and Francisco came in at third. There was not a single spectator who was unaware of what possibility was unfolding. The scoreboard said it all. Through every inning, La Mesa's tally showed nothing but zeros. None of them had reached first base "by hook or crook, on hit, walk, or error".

Everything was ready as Norberto put on his catcher's mask. The bottom of the last inning of the Little League World Series was about to begin.

۞

La Mesa would need four runs to tie, a formidable number, but the team was not the sort that got this far by quitting. They had shown countless times that they could explode for many runs in a single inning. For that, they would need to get runners on base, and the first one who could achieve this would break the spell of near-perfection that Angel was weaving this magical afternoon.

The prize was just sixty feet away. One runner to first base by any means: a hit, a base on balls, a fielding error, a wild pitch, a batter hit by a pitch. Any mistake by Angel or his teammates and one runner could quickly become two, three or more.

Dennis Hanggi led off.

Angel brought Hanggi to an even count of two balls and two strikes. Defending the plate, Hanggi popped the next pitch straight up in the air in foul territory along the third base line for what looked to be an easy play for the first out. Angel and Norberto converged on it, but at the last second Norberto waived off his pitcher. "I got it!" Beto cried out, but the ball hit his glove and popped out. It was a missed opportunity and a second life for the La Mesa batter to change the course of the game.

Norberto was clearly upset. Everyone on Monterrey Industrial knew the stakes. They wanted to win, but they also wanted this particular glory for Angel.

"Sorry, *Flaco*," Norberto said with heartache in his voice.

"Let's strike him out instead!" Angel said to relieve his catcher's mind. These were the first words that Angel had spoken the whole game.

The quieter the audience got, the more cold and calculated Angel became. He so resembled a hunter after his prey that even his teammates didn't recognize him. Hanggi swung his hardest and best at Angel's next pitch, but Angel's determination proved to be the margin of victory in this duel.

"One out!" Señor Cantu cried into the telephone through which he had been relaying the action.

Fred Schweer was sent in to pinch-hit for Robert Brown. He hit a sharp ball off Angel's left leg and the ball careened toward Baltazar who was moving in the opposite direction. The crowd collectively gasped as Schweer hustled to first base and the end of perfection. Baltazar barehanded the ball and from his knees threw the runner out at first. Fidel, who had stretched for his throw, ran off the bag to congratulate Baltazar.

"Two outs now!" continued Señor Cantu. "Angel Macias is one out away from pitching the only perfect game in the finals of the Little League World Series."

The crowd in Williamsport began to chant. "An-gel. . . An-gel. . . An-gel. . ." rose a cry that could be heard all the way to Monterrey. But the only world that existed for Angel was contained in the forty-five feet between his right hand and Norberto's glove. In his mind, the rhythmic chant of the crowd became a monosyllabic *thud*, *thud*, *thud*, like a ball hitting a cinder block wall on an abandoned dirt field near Vitro.

La Mesa's final hopes rested on Byron Haggard's bat. He dug in and waited for Angel's delivery. Pepe, like his fellow outfielders, had only one thought on his mind. If a ball were hit into the outfield, he'd dive face first if need be to prevent it from falling to earth and ruining Angel's bid for baseball immortality.

But as is often the case on a hero's journey, Angel had created his own challenge. Only twice in the game did he let the count run to three balls: in the second inning and now in the last inning with two outs. Something in the stands had distracted him. Standing in between a break in the third base bleachers was a father who had hoisted his young son on his shoulders.

"Time!" Cesar yelled and hustled out to calm down his pitcher.

"Are you going to take me out?" asked Angel.

"No chance. You woke me up once from a perfectly good siesta, now you're going to finish what you started."

Angel felt the hardened gum between his teeth.

"What does it matter? They just beat you down eventually."

"I was wrong. Everyone's counting on you."

"Not everyone," said Angel, his eye drawn again to the father and son. Cesar looked in Angel's direction and saw the object of his distraction. "My father is ashamed of me," Angel said, fighting back tears.

"I meant to give this to you last inning, but Beto's play made me forget." Cesar reached in his back pocket, withdrew the medallion and handed it to Angel, who immediately recognized it.

"How did you—?"

"Your father sent it. He's very proud. . . of you."

Angel reached behind his neck to clasp the medallion.

Umpire Gair took a few steps toward the mound and summoned Cesar. "I don't mean to disturb your chat, but there are 16,001 of us who thinks there's a baseball game going on here," he stated.

"You can do this, Koufax."

With the game on the line, the young pitcher looked at Cesar with steely eyes. With neither pity nor anger, he stated, "I'm not Sandy Koufax. I am Angel Macias."

Cesar nervously walked back to the dugout. On the mound, Angel felt the ball in his fingertips. Finding the seam with two of his fingers, he wound up and fired.

Strike one.

The crowd roared.

The windup, the pitch, strike two!

Angel received the ball back from Norberto, who gave him his sign. Angel nodded. Looking up, he noticed the moon could already be seen on the horizon, though it was still daylight. Cesar's words before his first game in McAllen, Texas, played through his mind: "The birds in the sky, the waters of the river, even the sun will wait until you're ready." He held up the ball until it eclipsed the moon perfectly. The world held its breath until Angel was ready.

Hundreds of flashbulbs fired as Angel's curveball began to break about five feet from the plate. Haggard swung and missed the ball.

Its forty-five foot journey ended snugly in the leather folds of Norberto's glove.

It was simply, utterly, humbly, audaciously, undeniably *perfecto*.

ⓔⓞⓞⓓ

The stadium erupted in an uncontrollable ovation. Photographers snapped pictures and journalists frantically wrote shorthanded summaries of what they had just witnessed. Exuberant fans pushed past the policemen who tried to restrain them from storming the field.

Fidel was the first player to reach Angel and then came Baltazar, who hugged his pitcher. Norberto didn't even have time to take off his equipment as he ran to the mound with the winning ball in his hand, followed by the rest of the team.

Cesar made his way to Angel, and when his young pitcher saw him, he leaped into Cesar's arms as photographers captured the moment for posterity.

28

CAMPEONES
del MUNDO

elayed by one minute and forty-seven seconds after the final out—XET broadcast the words, "*¡Campeones del mundo—son campeones del mundo* [Champions of the world]*!*"

The excitement of the moment was so great that Señor Cantu, who wasn't formally trained in radio protocol, said a few words that could not be spoken in polite society.

If the jubilation at Original Little League Field could be felt in downtown Williamsport, the outburst of joy in Monterrey could be felt rippling across all of Latin America. In a simultaneous explosion, people screamed, danced in the streets, beat their chests and many fainted from exhilaration. Cars stopped and honked their horns, factory and train whistles blew, and police and fire trucks rode around the city with sirens wailing.

❧☙

An hour later, thousands of fans still lingered, celebrating as if the young Mexicans were the hometown team. The field was filled with reporters, photographers and people of all ages. Many of the Monterrey players had sat down to continue autographing and the fans chatted to them in English, to which the boys could only smile in return.

After being labeled by many as *foreign* baseball players and by some as *invaders*, they were now the pride and joy of two nations, and especially of fourteen families who anxiously awaited their return home.

The time to board the bus and return to their dorms had come, and the fans surrounded them to say good-bye. Some girls tried everything to hug and kiss them through the windows. Lucky asked one young girl why she was crying and she told him it was because the boys were leaving. He told her that with some luck, Monterrey Industrial might return to Williamsport the following year.

"Yeah, but it'll be different. These boys won't come back."

The team had become emissaries. Unapologetically Mexican, they were proof that there were no obstacles between people when kindness and faith were immense.

Back at Lycoming College, Cesar turned on all the showers and a fully dressed Angel was the first one to dive in. In the middle of laughter and fun, each player went into the showers until there was not one dry Mexican uniform.

Cesar recalled weeks earlier when he had said to the boys that they had to choose between five things: "The movies, candy, sodas, swimming or being champions." Tonight, he let them have all five.

⌘

The next morning, telegrams and newspaper articles were being delivered to Cesar, Lucky and José in such volume that they didn't have time to read them all. They came from the four corners of the world, from dignitaries to simple fans. Cesar did, however, take the time to read one article. It was written by Herman Masin, the legendary sports chronicler.

Viva Monterrey

US baseball fanatics recently fell in love. The object of their affection was a young Little League team from Monterrey, Mexico. Imagine a baseball club where everyone is on average about four feet, nine inches tall and weighs less than eighty pounds. They traveled more than two thousand miles in a month and played in thirteen games in a foreign country. Arriving in the arid and dusty land of McAllen, Texas, this

past July, nobody there or back in Monterrey
considered the little team as anything more than
a speck in the canyon.

It was time to bid farewell to the Pennsylvania community that
had all but been seduced by the boys' noble humility. As the team
waited in the parking lot, their stuff packed in small bundles and old
paper bags, Cesar was in his room, gathering the equipment that he
had lugged over his shoulder for almost a month.

"Knock, knock," said Frankie, standing at the threshold of Cesar's
door.

"Frankie! I'm glad you came," he said.

She entered and sat on the other bed, which had been used by
Lucky. "Great game, huh?" she said, smiling.

"Yes, it was. Thanks for the good coverage," Cesar replied. "I
thought you were still mad."

"I was wrong, Cesar," she said.

"About me being a jerk?"

"No, you still are," she teased, "but I'm glad Mac gave me the
assignment. It let me meet you and the boys. I thought about our
conversation the other evening. I'm going to St. Louis for a bit to
visit my father."

Frankie ran her fingers along a satin banner that had been given
to Monterrey for their victory. She suddenly felt sad, as if something
given to her was being taken away, even though she had resisted
accepting that thing in the first place.

"Won't he be shocked by the assignment you got stuck with. A
baseball story of all things. I can see now why you hated the game."

"You and the boys made it okay. No, you made it more than okay.
You made me miss those lazy Sunday catches with my dad."

"Hey, are you still looking for that angle in the story?" asked
Cesar.

"Always," Frankie answered.

"You can write about how the Monterrey coach gave his kids bad
baseball advice."

"You're kidding."

"Nope. I told them the game wasn't won on the field but in here," he said, tapping his head. "I was wrong. It's won in here." Cesar placed his hand over his heart.

"There may be hope for you yet, Cesar Faz. You take care now," Frankie said, and stood up, kissed him on the cheek and left.

Cesar soon joined the boys in the parking lot. The team, still resembling a band of wanderers, boarded the bus that would take them to their next destination: New York City. But this time, they would be arriving as conquering heroes.

29

¡EL PRESIDENTE!

The bus passed slowly down West Fourth Street, allowing the boys one last look at Original Little League Field and a town that had embraced them and offered them admiration.

A few hours later, the smallest baseball team found themselves in the biggest city in America. After having begun their journey in a motel in McAllen, Texas, the boys were now staying in a luxurious hotel in Times Square. The banquets they partook of in grand dinning rooms contrasted sharply from the cold meals they had eaten on so many occasions, and the same team that had to hitchhike to the game were now being transported in limousines.

They were celebrities in a city teeming with the wealthy, powerful and famous. A subway operator saw the boys and exclaimed, "You're the ones I saw on TV this morning!"

Even a policeman who was patrolling Fifth Avenue stopped and asked them, "You guys are the ones that won the world championship, right?"

They visited many tourist attractions—the Empire State Building, St. Patrick's Cathedral, the Bronx Zoo, Radio City Music Hall—and had even circumnavigated Manhattan on the Circle Line Ferry. As part of a promotion, Macy's gave each boy forty dollars and an hour to run around the department store, buying whatever they wanted. Without exception, every single one thought only of what to get for his parents or siblings.

As exciting as these attractions were, there was one place the boys wanted to go that meant more to them than any other in New York City.

Located at 55 Sullivan Place in the Flatbush section of Brooklyn was one of the oldest major league ballparks in the United States. Built on top of the Pigtown garbage dumps, it opened on April 9, 1913, and was named Ebbets Field. It had been home to the Brooklyn Dodgers for forty-four years and would be so for only one more month. Today, the Dodgers would play the St. Louis Cardinals.

Ebbets' right field fence was a work of art that only "bums" from Brooklyn could have designed. It had 289 different angles caused by numerous protrusions from its unique construction. Rising above it, since World War II, was an immense Schaefer Beer sign. The official scorekeeper would light up Schaefer's *H* for a hit and one of its *E's* to signify an error.

The boys, still in their uniforms, filed into the stadium and stared in awe at the massive bleachers and roof, all held up by huge steel girders.

Sal Maglie tossed a ball with Gerardo and Baltazar, and joked with reporters that "Maybe these kids could teach me a few things." Before the game, Roy Campanella went to his locker and gave Norberto his spare catcher's glove.

The crowd gave Monterrey Industrial a rousing ovation and the boys settled into their seats to watch the game. Don Drysdale started for the Dodgers, but he had to be relieved, and eventually it was Maglie who struck out the final Cardinal batter with the bases loaded in the ninth inning to hold on to a six to five victory.

The fact that the Dodgers, last year's pennant winners, were struggling to hold on to third place didn't matter at all. The boys loved every minute of their first major league game.

A local sportswriter noted that the boys had become so beloved that if they stayed in New York City, "the Yankees would have to move their franchise to San Francisco."

After the game, Angel asked if he could enter the visiting team's locker room. Sandy Amoros, the legendary Dodger outfielder from Cuba, volunteered to take him in. Though Amoros warned him that the Cardinal players might not be in a good mood given their loss, Angel insisted that it was important, so in the two went. Angel made his way toward Stan "the Man" Musial, one of the most heralded players of all time. He wanted Musial's autograph.

"It's for his coach," Amoros translated as Angel handed Musial the old worn baseball with which he and Cesar had first played.

"What's this?" asked the famous Cardinal when he recognized his own smudged and nearly obliterated signature. "Did I sign this already?"

"Apparently you did, but his playing catch rubbed it off," Amoros told Musial.

"Some people think his writing is pretty valuable," Amoros said to Angel.

"Tell Señor Musial that if he had signed a photo we never would have played with it," Angel replied with the innocence that only a twelve-year-old can have.

Musial broke out into a hearty laugh and turned to his teammates. "I guess it's good not to think too highly of yourself. This kid and his coach are batting around one of my autographed balls."

⌘

Dwight D. Eisenhower awoke the morning of August 27, 1957, with a full schedule, typical for the President of the United States. Being the president and commander-in-chief was a logical progression for the hardworking Kansan who, as a five-star general during World War II, had led the allies to victory in Europe.

The Cold War was on and today's edition of *TASS*, the Soviet Union's sanctioned newspaper, announced, "Successful tests of an intercontinental ballistic rocket and explosions of nuclear and thermonuclear weapons have been carried out in conformity with the plan of scientific research work in the USSR."

Outside the Oval Office were dozens of people waiting to see President Eisenhower: Senators, congressmen, members of the Cabinet, leaders of foreign governments, unions, lobbyists, military commanders—most of whom fit into rigidly defined fifteen-minute segments of the White House schedule. But right now the president was excited to meet the fourteen boys of Monterrey Industrial. Eisenhower's chief of staff had sent Cesar a hand-delivered message in the fourth inning of the Little League World Series, which Cesar had unwittingly crumpled into his back pocket. Luckily, he had found it before he and the boys had jumped, fully clothed, into the Lycoming College locker room showers.

The president's personal secretary, James Haggerty, welcomed the team and escorted Cesar alone into the Oval Office. There, standing in front of his desk in a gray suit, was the President of the United States.

"Good morning, Mr. Faz. It's a pleasure to meet you."

"Good morning, Mr. President. It is an honor," answered Cesar.

"Mr. Faz, I want to congratulate you. You're a great baseball coach."

"Thank you, Mr. President. I'm not that good. What happened is that I have a great team."

"You have a great team because you are a great coach. Accept it. You have done something big for your country." Cesar didn't feel it was the time or place to inform the elder statesman that they were both Americans.

After a few minutes of conversing privately, the president then asked the boys to come in. Cesar and Lucky had spent hours teaching them how to greet President Eisenhower in English. Each was to shake his hand and say, "Good morning, Mr. President," and then give his own name.

Cesar warned them that the president was a very busy man and would not likely spend much time with them or engage them in any conversation. Of course, children can often derail the best laid protocol.

Ricardo extended his hand and said, "Good morning, Mr. President, I am Ricardo Treviño."

"What position do you play, son?"

"¿Qué posición juegas?" Cesar translated.

"Why are you asking me that, Señor Faz? You already know that I play first base."

"First base," Cesar said to the president.

"Mr. Faz, he said a lot more than that," responded President Eisenhower.

"He was telling me that I already knew what position he played."

"Oh good, please tell him that I thought that first basemen were usually tall so that they could catch high and low balls."

"Ricardo, the president thinks you're too short to play first base," Cesar continued translating.

"Tell him that I'm short, but I'm really good!"

When the president heard Cesar's translation of Ricardo's answer, he stretched out his hand again and said, "Well, then, I have to greet Ricardo again because he's really good."

The boys gave President Eisenhower a rousing cheer: "¡Rah, rah, rah, el Presidente!" They posed for photographs, and the images would be seen around the world—even studied in the Kremlin.

President Eisenhower went to his desk and handed each boy a pen. Engraved on it were the words, "Stolen from Dwight D. Eisenhower." When Cesar translated the words Angel immediately dropped it saying, "Ah, they're going to throw me in jail." The president's smile confirmed it was a joke, and Angel reached to pick up the fallen pen. The president offered him another instead, and Angel took the one from his hand and the one from the floor, saying, "Me llevo las dos [I'll take both]."

If only Sergeant Harbush, the border guard who didn't think the mojaditos worthy of speaking of the President of the United States, could have seen the boys taking turns sitting and spinning in the same chair from which President Eisenhower led the free world.

30

Small Changes

The Mexicana de Aviacion Douglas DC-6 arched from the sky and made its final descent into Benito Juarez Aeroporto in the heart of Mexico. José led the boys in a chorus of an old song, "Mexico is my capital! Here I bring this song. Inspired by a shawl, also green, white and red—the same as my country. Mexico is my capital!"

A motorcade escorted the team to the Presidential Palace. As they rode through the streets of the capital, police motorcycles roared ahead and all around them flowed a sea of excited faces watching from sidewalks, cars, buses and every available window. They were bombarded with flowers, kisses, cheers and people screaming, "¡Viva Mexico! Viva Monterrey!"

The team was greeted at the palace by many dignitaries, hundreds of members of the press corps, as well as the *Diablo Rojos*, the professional Mexican baseball team. They had won the Mexican AAA League Championship the year before, but their fame didn't keep these grown men from openly weeping when they met the boys.

At 11:15 AM, the boys were received by Adolfo Ruiz Cortines, the president of Mexico. The boys delivered a personal message from President Eisenhower to him.

After the formal greetings, President Cortines asked Angel, "*¿Que pensaste durante el último out de tu juego perfecto* [What were you thinking during the perfect game]?*"

"My coach helped me a lot. I didn't realize that I was pitching a perfect game until the end of the fifth inning. In the last inning, I got nervous, but Señor Faz came out to me and gave me encouragement."

"What did he tell you?" asked *el presidente*.

Angel looked at Cesar for a moment. Perhaps he wanted to tell the president of how he'd interrupted Cesar's siestas, but then he decided these were memories best left on a dirt field in Monterrey between a pitcher and his catcher.

"Señor Faz told me to give it all I had, and that was exactly what I did. Thanks to my great teammates and to God, I was able to make good pitches and overcome the obstacles—and for that I am very grateful," said Angel like a true champion.

It was clear that the president had learned of the dirt field that the boys played on in Monterrey, because after giving them each a beautiful trophy, he told them, "The Government of the Republic will fund the construction of a baseball park in Monterrey with the most modern commodities to perpetuate your triumphs."

⚭⊙⊙⚭

From the day their dirt field was blessed by Padre Esteban through the first game in the small town of McAllen, Texas, and all the way to Williamsport, the boys had never missed visiting a Catholic church or receiving a blessing before their games. And always, uppermost on their minds, was the Dark Virgin of Guadalupe.

In Louisville, they made Cesar pledge that if they played, he would visit Her basilica. It was with no small irony that their triumph was the reason that Cesar found himself in Mexico City. They left him no chance to delay keeping his promise.

When the boys entered the basilica, lights in the nave came on and the organ gently played the notes of the "Guadalupe Hymn." The team was greeted by *Canonigo* Salvador Escalante. They followed him up to the *comulgatorio* where they knelt and gazed upward to Juan Diego's cloak; emblazoned inside its flaps was the sacred image of the Virgin Mary.

Canonigo Escalante said, "Young athletes, you are where you should be right now, before our Mother, Virgin Guadalupe. You left our country to find triumph by strength, intelligence and spirit.

You come here to pay homage with your innocent and powerful hearts..."

After they had received the canon's benediction, they quietly prayed, "We thank you, Dark Virgin, and offer to you our thirteen victories."

That was when something happened, which had never been witnessed in the four centuries that the church stood on Tepeyac Hill, a place reserved for solemn acts of prayer and penitence. When the boys started to leave, the thousands present, who had been kneeling in quiet meditation and prayer, rose in a spontaneous outbreak of applause. At first, the boys looked apprehensively at this outpouring of love and wondered if it was sacrilegious, until they noticed the canon himself joining wholeheartedly in the ovation.

It was finally time for the boys to go home.

❧

"It's been quite a ride," Lucky said to Cesar and José as the airplane headed north from Mexico City to Monterrey.

"You think? Four weeks ago they crossed the Rio Grande with their underwear in paper bags and a few days ago they're at the White House, shaking hands with the most powerful man in the world," stated José.

The three men laughed.

In the rest of the cabin, the boys recounted their favorite moments.

"I can't believe how big Ebbets Field was," Norberto said to Ricardo.

"I can't believe you said that to Roy Campanella!" Ricardo scolded him in return.

"But he *doesn't* look Italian!" answered Norberto. In truth, though Campanella is considered to be the first black catcher in the major leagues, his father was Italian.

In the row across from them, Angel was demonstrating something on a baseball to Enrique. "This is how Sandy Koufax holds the splitter." Enrique took the ball and tried to mimic Angel's grip on the seams.

"Come on, Angel, spill it. What did Stan Musial tell you?" asked Enrique.

"Sorry, trade secret."

"What are you daydreaming about?" Baltazar asked Mario, who lay back with a wide grin.

"All those beautiful girls in Macy's."

Cesar moved farther back in the cabin to join his players.

"Ricardo and I are eleven years old, Señor Faz," Roberto exclaimed. "We can play on next year's team!"

"Yeah, next year," responded Cesar with a lackluster tone. The boys took it as a sign of his exhaustion and understood that he was not yet ready to begin strategizing about next season.

"They've got no chance against Monterrey Industrial. We've got the best coach in the world!" Ricardo proudly proclaimed.

Angel looked at Cesar. He knew the truth. Cesar planned to tell the boys of his plans, but not now. Not at the moment of their greatest glory. The plane's sudden lurch made Cesar queasy, and he excused himself to the lavatory. Lucky stuck a finger down his throat and pretended to gag, which made the boys laugh. They only stopped when Cesar almost opened the rear door of the plane, thinking it lead to the restroom. Fortunately, an alert stewardess quickly corrected Cesar's mistake.

Later, Angel sat in the copilot's chair, pretending to work the controls. All of the team members had been named honorary pilots of the Mexican Air Force, and as such, each had been given wings and was allowed to take a turn at the controls during the flight.

Gazing down upon the earth from the cockpit, Angel had never dreamed of what things could look like from here. He saw what appeared to be a great white ocean in which the spine of some giant reptile broke its cottony surface. The spine was the long jagged range of the Sierra Madres, and the ocean was a vast sea of clouds that filled every crevice of its valleys. Like liquid vapor, one such cloud poured up and over the top of one ridgeline, spilling down the other side. Angel didn't appear concerned that this cloud seemed to defy gravity, his mind had become a *tabla rasa* upon which a world he had lived in but never truly noticed was slowly revealing its wonders to him.

Soon, he rejoined the team as the pilots prepared the plane for its final approach. Back in the main cabin, the boys were all glued to the windows as the plane flew over the heart of Monterrey. If the drone of the engines hadn't been so loud, the boys would have heard the screaming from a mile below. No one in the history of Monterrey had ever witnessed the sight the boys now beheld while descending from five thousand feet.

"*¡Es increible!*" Fidel said, not being able to blink for fear the image would disappear like a dream upon waking.

Beneath them, more than a half-million souls, almost the entire population of Monterrey, had been lining up for hours, waiting for their little heroes. Even from this altitude, the boys could see that the entire twenty-mile route from the Northern Airport to the city's center was lined on both sides with teems of men, women and children.

"For us?" asked Rafael.

"You guys are their heroes," Cesar answered.

"They don't even know us," said Fidel.

"They know what you've done."

This was more than they had ever expected from the town that only a few months before saw them as the dispossessed. This was the first moment they really grasped the gravity of what they had accomplished.

∽⟩⟨∽

The governor of Nuevo León published the following message in all of the city's newspapers:

TO THE BOYS OF THE MONTERREY TEAM, WORLD CHAMPIONS OF LITTLE LEAGUE BASEBALL

I cannot wait till you arrive. In this short message, I would like to welcome you back to Monterrey and cordially recognize you for your sports victory. You have brought our city triumph against other foreign nations.

You have motivated all of Mexico to succeed. We admire and appreciate the kindness you have displayed through your faith and love of country. That is what directed you toward triumph.

When you arrive home, you will find love from your parents, friends, schoolmates and teachers. You will find the respect of all citizens. Grasp all of this as your most intimate rewards for all of your hard work in sports and for humankind. You have increased our patriotism with your tenacity, discipline and modesty. We are very proud of your performance, and we would like to make a celebration in honor of you, who have displayed such effort and bravery.

All of the homes of Nuevo León feel sentiments of admiration and kindness.

Sincerely,

Sr. Raul Rangel Frias

Governor of Nuevo León

For almost a week, the city of Monterrey had been busy planning the biggest celebration in its history. Small changes, some so small as to be noticed by the boys, were adding up to become part of a huge miracle, united by baseball and faith.

The official tribute would take place that evening, August 30, at seven o'clock, on the western balcony of the Governor's Palace. The official program was organized by the students of Angel's school. Many of the children who had given Angel a hard time because of his humble background were now honoring him, working all night making *piñatas* for the homecoming party. By order of Gen. Domingo G. Martinez, the Seventh Military Regiment and the Eighteenth National Service Infantry were to provide an honor guard for the team.

꧁◌◌꧂

Touching down, the aircraft came to a stop on the tarmac and the pilot cut its engines. Even before the blades had stopped spinning, a gigantic and crazed crowd approached the plane. The owner of the urban bus company had offered his whole fleet to bring thousands of people to the airport for free.

The fans surrounded the aircraft so tightly that soldiers had to create an opening through which the boys could deplane. Wearing their same uniforms and walking, as always, from smallest to tallest, they stepped out into the enveloping ocean of a crying and cheering populace. They were emotionally and physically drained, and in many ways what their admirers demanded of them was way beyond the limits of children.

Twenty convertibles waited to drive them the nearly twenty-five kilometers into the city's center, and the closer they got the denser and more frenzied the crowds became. Less than a mile from the Governor's Palace, the motorcade came to a sudden halt. Two long cargo trains were crossing *Avenida Alfonso Reyes*. The army commander in charge of the procession radioed the conductors who immediately began to brake the massive locomotives. After a sustained screeching with sparks flying from iron rails, the trains rolled to a stop and then each—with a loud whistle and blast of steam from its undercarriage, reversed directions and opened a breach so that the honored baseball players could pass.

During the delay, thousands of screaming fans broke through a chain-link fence and had to be controlled with powerful fire hoses. Dozens of others managed to climb onto several of the convertibles. As the motorcade restarted, the car carrying Enrique and Rafael overheated from the weight of so many occupants. Instead of moving them to other cars, the crowd pushed their vehicle off the road and hoisted the boys on their shoulders and began to carry them the rest of the way. Cesar was worried, but he had no way to reach his two players. He could only pray that the citizens, in their loving hysteria, would protect the boys.

Behind them, the screams of Diesel Machines 6518 and 6206 could be heard as their whistles joined the multitudes of proud *Regiomontanos*.

After two hours of forging through the crowds, the motorcade finally reached its destination in Benito Suarez Plaza. People leaned over rooftops, sat on window ledges, hung from posts, and appeared from every available nook and cranny.

Night had overcome the day when the boys entered the Governor's Palace. Crafted from huge blocks of rose quarry stone by artisans in the last century, its classical architecture was in keeping with the colonial era of the vice-regency. One exterior wall adjacent to the portico was unveiled to reveal an inscription of the boys' names and victories carved into the stone for posterity. An artillery company began a twenty-one gun salute, which lit up the sky like lightning.

The boys carried bouquets of flowers for their mothers, and as each player was reunited with his own, shrieks of joy could be heard above the crowd.

Baltazar's sister, Patricia, held him so tightly, he thought he'd suffocate. But he was so happy to see her that he didn't care.

Angel, the boy with iron nerves, cried as he hugged his mother. Releasing her, Angel then stood before his father.

"Sorry, Papa, I didn't mean to leave my chores undone for so long."

"The chores can wait."

Angel took off his medallion and handed it to Umberto.

"For Pedro's shrine."

"No," his father said, gently grasping Angel's hand, which still clutched the medallion.

"It's for you, my son."

Umberto picked Angel up and held him tightly in his strong arms and at that moment, Angel knew he was finally home.

☙⊙☙

The City Council declared the boys Distinguished Citizens for which they received special certificates. They were also admitted into the Nuevo León Sports Hall of Fame, and to cap off their accolades, the headmasters of Nuevo León University and *Tec de Monterrey* presented each player with a full scholarship for the remainder of his education. For most boys, it would mean the difference of whether they would finish high school and even consider attending college.

Norberto turned to Enrique and shouted over the crowd, "Maybe you'll become an engineer after all!"

"I bet he'll even get a date with Gloria Jimenez," added Ricardo.

"To the heroes of Monterrey!" announced the governor with his arms raised high, sharing for a moment the feeling of unadulterated triumph.

Cesar finally found Padre Esteban and handed him a souvenir from Ebbets Field—a Brooklyn Dodgers' jacket. "They were lucky their priest loved baseball," Cesar said as he helped Padre Esteban slide his arms into its satin sleeves.

"Baseball is okay," said Padre Esteban, shrugging.

"What do you mean? You never missed a game."

"For their sake."

"But I assumed you loved—"

Padre Esteban motioned for Cesar to come closer as if he were about to impart a terrible secret. "One day, by accident, I tuned in to a Dodgers game. After Mass the next Sunday, I played it for the boys and they loved it. Do you know how hard it is to keep a dozen boys in church for two hours?"

Both men suddenly noticed Enrique being hugged by Gloria.

"Looks like you're going to be in for some new competition," said Cesar, laughing.

The roar of the crowd continued, and Cesar spotted the one person he desired most yet was most afraid to desire. He swallowed hard and approached Maria through the jostling fans. It was time for him to face the music.

"Cesar."

"Maria, I can explain. I—"

Before he could finish mumbling another apology, Maria threw her arms around his neck. "I feel the same way!"

"You do?"

"At first I was angry, but then I got your telegram."

Telegram? Cesar thought. *I never sent her a telegram. Wait a minute...* Cesar looked over Maria's shoulder and saw his players watching and grinning mischievously.

Cesar swore he could see them mouthing the words, "The unexpected play at the unexpected time. . ."

cᴏⓈⓋᴏ

As the official ceremony ended, the team passed one last time onto the palace's main balcony to wave good-bye to the hundreds of thousands of people who had gathered. Police vehicles waited to take the boys and their families to their homes. Cesar said good-bye to his players as a father might with his children. . . with a kind look and a prayer.

Cesar and Maria sat for a while. Few words were spoken, though Cesar knew he had something very important to tell her. He just couldn't bring himself to spoil the moment.

Something Maria finally said brought Cesar back to the fork in the road.

"I'm not sure whether my father will see you this time. But I can try," she said hopefully.

That was when Cesar told her of his being fired and the fortunate timing of his job offer from the Baltimore Orioles. He hadn't even said that he was going to take the job when Maria stood up sharply and said, "I can't believe I waited for you all this time and now you're telling me you're leaving?"

The joy of their reunion had all but evaporated. Cesar didn't understand a lot about women. He even wondered if knew as much as his boys, but he did know how to count and this was unequivocally strike three.

Cesar offered to take Maria home, but she told him she thought it best that he didn't; her father would probably beat him senseless when he saw that his daughter had been crying and that Cesar was the cause. Some of her friends were just leaving the square at that moment, so she bid him farewell.

Cesar decided to walk home. After hours of cheers and screams, the lonely silence of the street contrasted starkly to his ears. It was here that Cesar and the boys' paths diverged. Everything had come to an end.

In a few days, Cesar would pack his few belongings and leave behind the Cerro de la Silla mountains, perhaps forever. Baltimore, with its bustling harbor and urban grit, awaited him.

Despite it already being the next day, he had told Lucky that he'd

		VISITING CLUB	
BATTING ORDER			
No.	Name	Age	Psn.
15	Riley, Lou	12	6
4	Tobey, Leonard	12	7
14	Hardesty, John	12	5
5	McKirahan, Joe	12	1
13	Vogel, Francis	12	2
5	Haggard, Barney	12	4
16	Hougaie, Dennis	12	3
4	Haggard, Barney	12	4
15	Blackwood, Tom	12	8
Reserves			
13	Musgraves, Dave	12	
15	Baker, Richard	12	
11	Schweer, Fred	11	
14	Brown, Robert	12	
12	Gowins, Richard	12	
Mgr. Bob McMullan			
Coach - Ralph McKirahan			

68 & 69. At 5'9" Lew Riley was the tallest pitcher the boys had ever seen. He also had a wicked fastball. Fidel Ruiz (on the ground being attended by medical personnel below left)

learned firsthand just how fast. Fidel would shrug off the pain and finish the game. Nothing to sway a Monterrey player from his rendezvous with destiny this afternoon.

70. John Hardesty tries to tag out a Monterrey runner at second base. Lew Riley, like Angel, had pitched brilliantly for four innings. Things were about to "head south" for La Mesa in the bottom of the fifth.

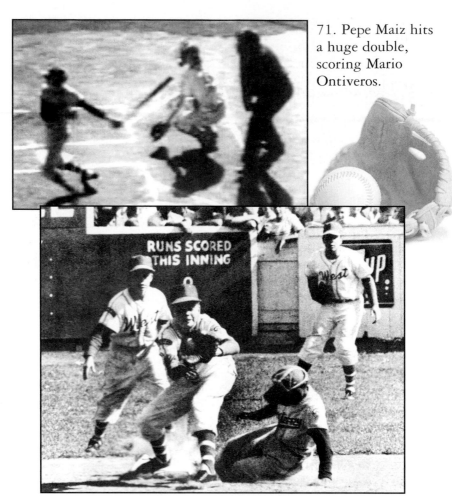

71. Pepe Maiz hits a huge double, scoring Mario Ontiveros.

72. One play earlier, Mario Ontiveros was safe at second after Baltazar Charles' perfect bunt.

73. Enrique scores the last run of a four-run fifth on Gerardo's infield hit. Notice the ball arriving just as he crosses the plate.

74. The perfect game is preserved by a step.

75. Behind every great pitcher is a loyal catcher. Norberto pats his friend on the shoulder as Angel prepares for the final inning and baseball immortality.

76. The greater the pressure, the more fierce was Angel's resolve. Here, he delivers the last of his lethal strikes as. . .

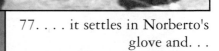

77. . . . it settles in Norberto's glove and. . .

78. . . . Angel leaps for joy as . . .

79. . . . he is mobbed by his teammates: the 1957 World Champions!

80. Angel and Norberto hold up the "zeroes," showing that no runs or hits were earned by La Mesa.

81. Moments after victory, Angel leaps into his coach's arms.

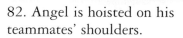

82. Angel is hoisted on his teammates' shoulders.

83. Back at Lycoming College, the celebrating boys jump, fully uniformed, into the showers.

84. & 85. A baseball championship wasn't the only thing the Monterrey boys captured while in America. Enrique Suarez may have taught a few Americans about baseball, but this adoring fan has something special to teach him.

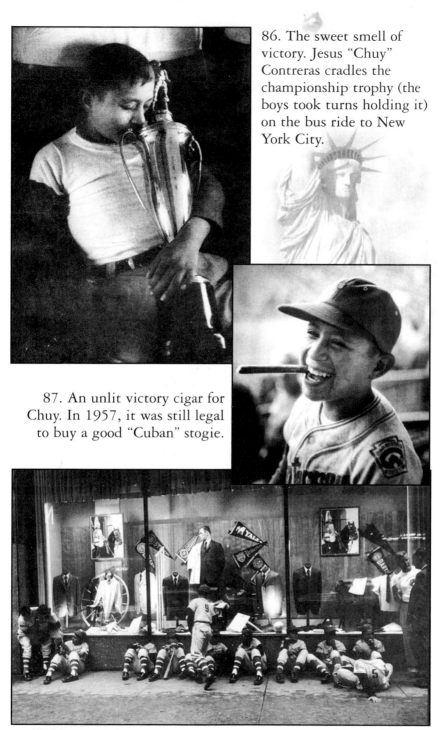

86. The sweet smell of victory. Jesus "Chuy" Contreras cradles the championship trophy (the boys took turns holding it) on the bus ride to New York City.

87. An unlit victory cigar for Chuy. In 1957, it was still legal to buy a good "Cuban" stogie.

88. The team sits in front of a New York City department store window.

89. Angel deposits a subway token in the slot. The boys will ride the Rapid Transit No. 7 train to Flatbush—home of Ebbets Field and the Brooklyn Dodgers.

90. The team enters the field that a month ago, they had only heard about on the radio. On August 25, 1957, they were guests of the Brooklyn Dodgers who played the Cardinals that day.

91. Angel poses in Ebbets Field with Dodger pitchers Carl Erskine and Sal Maglie. They each hold one of his equally dominating pitching arms.

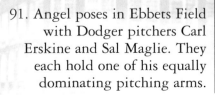

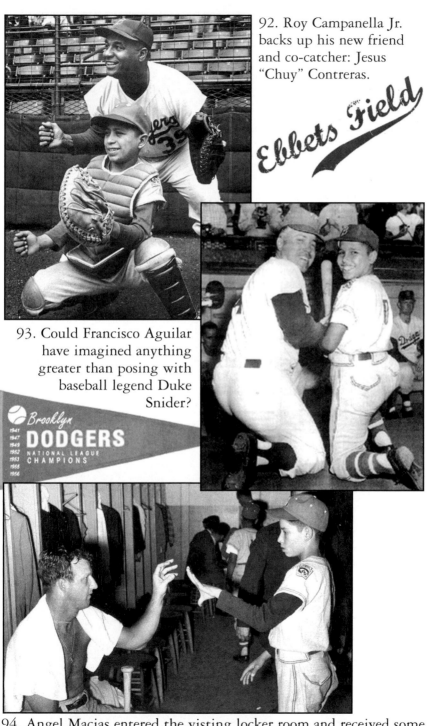

92. Roy Campanella Jr. backs up his new friend and co-catcher: Jesus "Chuy" Contreras.

Ebbets Field

93. Could Francisco Aguilar have imagined anything greater than posing with baseball legend Duke Snider?

94. Angel Macias entered the visting locker room and received some personal tips from St. Louis Cardinal great: Stan "The Man" Musial.

95. & 96. The team proudly shows President Eisenhower their trophy.

97. With a borrowed camera, Norberto *"el Verdugo"* Villarreal tells a photojournalist from the Associated Press that he's blocking the shot.

98. A Supreme Allied Commander and a World Series victor. Angel Macias walks one-on-one with President Dwight D. Eisenhower along the White House portico.

99. Richard M. Nixon smiles as Angel places his cap on Senator Lyndon B. Johnson's head. Both men would become future Presidents of the United States.

100. An awe-inspiring sight: the boys pause at the Lincoln
Memorial and pay respects to America's sixteenth President.

101. Not to be outdone, Mexican President Cortines presents
Angel and his teammates with a special trophy—even bigger than
the one they were given in Williamsport.

102. While in Mexico City, the team makes the most important
stop of all. They visit the Basilica de Guadalupe where they
dedicate their victories to the Virgin Mary. The boys receive a
standing ovation in the church from an enthusiastic congregation.

EL MEJOR PREMIO

103. "The Best Moment: Coming Home to Mama!"

¡OTRA VEZ CON MAMA!

104. Each player had a wreath of flowers which he presented to his parents as the team arrived at Monterrey's Northern Airport. With over 500,000 fans waiting for hours to see them, the boys had no idea how much Monterrey had fallen in love with them during their odyssey.

105. A heroes' welcome continues as the boys are passed from shoulder to shoulder.

106. & 107. The fans go beserk as the team's motorcade winds its way to the Governor's Palace.

108. Fans jammed the town squares to catch a glimpse of the team.

109. Mario Ontiveros was right, love is a lot like baseball and Cesar Faz didn't strike out after all. Here, Cesar and Maria are pictured after a different Monterrey Industrial team won the 1958 Little League World Championship. In 2008, Cesar and Maria celebrated their 50th wedding anniversary.

see him tomorrow, though he really meant later that evening. They planned to celebrate Cesar's last evening in Monterrey the way they'd baptized many a bar on the waterfront of Luzon, Philippines, and in the Barrio Antigua.

Soon, Cesar was on Matamoros Oriente in the barrio called Nejayote, standing before a house where the street dead-ended into the Rio Santa Catarina. Three faded stars were still visible in its window. He didn't need to search for his door key; he hadn't locked it before he had left. No one would break in. If they had, there would have been little to steal.

c∕ᴓᏀᴕ

"To Cesar Faz!" said Lucky, and he raised his beer. The sun had long set on the day after the celebration, but Cesar, Lucky, José and their cronies continued the revelry deep into the night.

"Good luck in Baltimore," José said.

"Watch out, Yankees," said another. "With Faz coaching, the rest of the American League hasn't got a chance!"

Last rounds were downed, and Cesar embraced his friends and watched them scatter down the cobblestoned streets to their separate lives. Returning home, he retired to his bedroom. It previously had been used by his father as a printing room. He tried to sleep but couldn't find its peaceful release. His fatigue was not just the physical one brought on by the long trip, it also was the exhaustion of feeling alone again.

He arose and went to the kitchen. He wasn't sure why. There was no food or beverage there, but it was a different room.

That's when he saw it. Someone had obviously entered his home when he was away.

On his table was a very worn baseball. Over a bluish smudge was the fresh ink of Stan Musial's new signature. Surrounding it were the hand-scribbled names of the boys of Monterrey Industrial's very first Little League team.

Cesar had what is known in many parlances as a moment of clarity. He took a long shower, got dressed and waited impatiently for the sun to rise. When dawn finally came, he found a pen and some paper and wrote an important letter, which he would mail on his way to his destination. It was addressed to the management of the Baltimore Orioles. They wouldn't understand his decision, but frankly it didn't matter. He had far more important things on his mind.

He would speak with Vitro's management and ask for his job back. He would be respectful and firm, and worst case, he would find employment elsewhere.

But first, he had another stop to make. Though it was still cool, he began to sweat with excitement. It was the kind of nervous anticipation he felt before the Little League World Series. Making his way down to Platon Sanchez Street, he knocked on the door. It was not yet seven thirty, and he knew his face might not be a welcome one this early or at any other time of the day. But he was determined to do the impossible: He was going to convince the umpire to give him a fourth strike.

A barrel-chested man opened the door and squinted as he looked straight into Cesar's eyes.

"Good morning, Señor del Refugio. I'm Cesar Faz, and I've come to ask your permission for your daughter's hand. . ."

Epilogue

Roses in Winter

The Valley Transit bus pulled out of the station in McAllen, Texas. The one night's layover here had given Cesar a chance to rest, so he could arrive that afternoon in Monterrey, refreshed for the event. It also afforded him the opportunity to revisit the city he had first traveled to almost fifty years ago in 1957.

He had been visiting his niece's family in San Antonio. It's a long way by bus from there to Monterrey—over twelve hours—and it's a lot faster to take a flight, but Cesar never liked airplanes when he was younger, and now, in his eighties, he avoided them altogether.

McAllen had changed a lot. Home Depots and strip malls with Starbucks coffeehouses now lined old Business 83, the road on which the Grand Courts Motel and its small swimming pool had once been. The Busy Corner diner was now a clothing outlet and the fields of Baldwin Park housed a mobile home community.

Even the bus was a lot more comfortable than the one he and his team had ridden in 1957: air conditioning, reclining seats, even a toilet. No, it was nothing like what he remembered. Then again, he was sure McAllen thought the same thing when it looked at him.

In less than twenty minutes, the bus crossed the McAllen-Hidalgo-Reynosa International Bridge. It made Cesar think of another bridge and another time—this one was a few miles upriver; and the last time he traversed it, he was on foot trailing a group of twelve-year-old baseball players.

Cesar would have been happy to stay longer in San Antonio, but later today he had to join the surviving members of that team—nine of the original fourteen—for a dedication of a new Little League field. It wouldn't have mattered if he had been in China, he would have rowed home to be here for these "kids."

He thought about the word *kids* for a moment. He still saw them that way, even though they were all in their early sixties. He laughed softly to himself—he remembered when he thought of being in one's sixties as incredibly old, but now what he wouldn't give to be that young. Except, of course, he wouldn't trade one moment of the last forty-nine years he had spent with his wife, Maria Faz del Refugio Gonzales.

She was asleep in the seat next to him. He had thought about awakening her as the bus went through McAllen, but he decided to mercifully spare her the tour down memory lane, a trip she had graciously listened to for nearly five decades.

⤳⊙⊙⊙⤳

"*Última Parada, Monterrey*," came the bus driver's announcement when they reached their final destination. Maria Faz del Refugio Gonzales slowly opened her eyes and smiled at Cesar. He loved rising before her each morning just so he could be awake when she greeted the day.

The Fazes made their way to Estadio de Béisbol Monterrey, Monterrey's professional baseball stadium and home to the AAA Sultanes. With a seating capacity of 33,000, it was built by the construction company owned by Pepe. Standing on field level, Cesar looked with pride at the red, white and green shawl of the Mexican flag that flapped defiantly on the pole in center field. As he approached the dugout, he could see the "kids."

"Glad you made it for the game, Señor Faz," said Enrique.

"I had nothing better to do today," Cesar replied.

"You have nothing better to do *any* day," said Ricardo.

Cesar didn't respond; he was already studying the competition. The old-timers of Monterrey Industrial were going to play a few exhibition innings against the Sultanes.

"They look tough," Cesar said. "Okay, remember—"

"We know," interrupted Angel. "Be ready for the unexpected play. . ."

". . . at the unexpected time," chimed in the rest.

"Speaking of unexpected, remember this?" Cesar asked and quickly tossed a ball at Angel. The pitcher's reflexes were still keen as he caught it in his left hand.

"It's traveled quite far for a baseball," said Angel, rotating it slowly in his hand while he gazed upon the autographs that covered its surface.

The Sultanes were warming up along the first base line. Besides building the stadium, Pepe also owned the team, but today he wasn't here as an executive. He had just come out of the locker room wearing a jersey made especially for today's ceremony. Across its flannel apron was displayed MONTERREY. Except for its larger size to accommodate both age and portliness of better living, it was a replica of the shirt he had worn in 1957.

Also present on the other sideline were the twelve-year-old boys of the new Monterrey Industrial team. Their shirts also said MONTERREY, but they were made from modern materials—like those worn by the pros of today. The young team looked with respect upon the first *Regiomontanos* to ever wear Little League uniforms.

An old man tended to the oasis that surrounded a small sanctuary to Our Lady of Guadalupe. The old man, an honorary groundskeeper of sorts, lifted a faded copper can and let a stream of water drizzle onto the beds of the most inexplicably red roses. Stopping his task, he paused to gaze at the field, admiring the efforts of the elderly players. Most of them were struggling to throw the baseball around the diamond—alive was the desire, but long gone was the fluidity. A few, like Enrique and Angel, could still play pretty well, but on the other end of the spectrum, Alfonso Cortez was slowly losing his eyesight from diabetes.

Sadly, heart failure had taken Lucky nearly twenty years earlier, and though Padre Esteban had also passed away, he had left behind an indelible legacy and an old radio that he had donated to the Tec de Monterrey.

Ricardo, the "baby" of the team at only sixty-one, bent over to scoop a low throw from Gerardo. Ricardo's groan was quite audible, and it appeared for a moment that he might have split his pants.

Soon, the stands were filled with people of all ages. Some waved banners and flags, some ate *tortas* and *churros*, but all gazed in wonder at the three generations of ballplayers who now lined up on the first and third base lines.

The mayor of Monterrey said a few words and then introduced Eloy Cantu Jr. who stood at home plate, his features partially obscured behind several microphones.

"Ladies and gentlemen, please welcome the Sultanes, Monterrey's team of today," Eloy said, and the crowd applauded. He took a deep breath and then continued. "In 1957, my father flew to Williamsport, Pennsylvania, and had the honor of broadcasting the final game of the Little League World Series. Nearly a half-century has passed and, unfortunately, so have many of our citizens who witnessed that event, including my dear father. But I am consoled and deeply honored to stand before you today to introduce the surviving members of that team who made history for our city and our country."

A huge standing ovation ensued. Eloy wiped a tear from his eye as he surveyed the ecstatic crowd who cheered for the 1957 Little League World Champions. In some part, he felt they paid tribute to his father, whose contribution of August 23, 1957, had linked his memory with this miraculous event. Eloy regained his composure, and his words forced their way through the lump in his throat.

"Also here today are the members of the new Monterrey Industrial team. In 1988, Hurricane Gilberto wreaked havoc upon this city. Hundreds lost their lives. The original field these boys played on was destroyed and Monterrey Industrial ceased to be. Many of you are too young to recall that tragedy, but today I have the pleasure of announcing the site of their new ball park and the rebirth of that team," he proudly proclaimed. He turned to the young players and said, "You are our future."

❦

"Full count!" yelled the umpire.

Angel took the catcher's sign and readied himself to pitch.

Norberto was gone, and a younger player from the Sultanes was filling in. That position is too grueling for an old man, but Angel would have given anything to see his beloved catcher squatting behind the plate.

Pausing to look at the crowd, Angel savored the moment, knowing that even "the birds in the sky would wait for him." He wound up and released his pitch.

"Strike three!"

An inning later, the announcer's voice came over the PA system: "One out now, Monterrey Industrial still holding onto a one to zero lead. But Angel seems to be tiring. Señor Faz has called time-out and is going out to calm down his pitcher."

"You seem distracted," Cesar said to Angel as the two men met on the mound. "You tired?"

"They're driving me nuts." Angel motioned toward center field.

In the outfield, Pepe and Enrique were having an argument. Cesar hadn't quite made it all the way there when he could hear them squabbling, and he knew right away what it was about.

"I'm Duke Snider," said Pepe.

"No, I am," answered an equally stubborn Enrique.

"I called him first!"

Cesar shouted over their argument: "Okay, that does it! None of you are Duke Snider. Now play ball!"

"Now look what you did!" Pepe accused Enrique.

"Kids!" Cesar said and rolled his eyes skyward making his way back to the dugout.

❧

The old groundskeeper put down the watering can and walked over to the dugout. Years of factory work had left his fingers gnarled from arthritis, and his face had the weathering of a man who had spent the better part of his life at sea, though he had never been closer than a hundred miles to either ocean that surrounded Mexico.

"Missed you at Mass on Sunday," said Umberto. "First time since I can remember."

"I was visiting some family in Texas," Cesar replied.

"Never been there."

Cesar looked over Umberto's shoulders at the new Monterrey skyline that silhouetted the Royal Mountains beyond.

"It's okay, but not as beautiful as Monterrey."

"Strike three, you're out!" came the cry of the umpire. Umberto and Cesar looked at the mound for an instant.

"Your son still has quite an arm," said Cesar.

"And the voice of an angel," said Umberto, smiling

"That was an amazing summer, wasn't it?" Cesar asked.

"They owe it all to you," Umberto said with a soft look in his eyes.

Cesar shrugged his shoulders. "I just taught them a little baseball. They taught me I could see the wings of a hummingbird."

It was finally time to leave. Cesar rejoined his wife and reached out his hand for hers. He loved holding her hand, whether in front of thirty thousand spectators or when the two of them walked alone in the small park near their home.

Just as Cesar was about to lead Maria into the darkened corridor of the Stadium's exit, he paused a few steps beyond the first base line. Looking back one last time at his "boys" who a half-century earlier had molded a rock-strewn pile of dirt into a baseball diamond, he realized that men do what they need to do before God and other men, but on occasion children do things that transcend fairy tales.

In Their Own Words

Cesar Faz (born/November 6, 1918)

Though I worked for several years at Cristaleria and Vidriera Monterrey, I spent the majority of my career (thirty-six years) at the famous Fabricacion de Maquinas (FAMA). I retired after having risen to general manager of industrial relations.

I remember every detail from that 1957 season, but what amazed me the most was the total lack of experience and knowledge of the children at the beginning of the trip. I still remember how Jesus "Chuy" Contreras had never been in a car, and four weeks later he was in the White House with the president of the United States. This was a great journey for all of us.

After the miraculous event, I returned to work for FAMA and got married in 1958 to the love of my life, Maria del Refugio Gonzales. We live in San Nicolas, where we raised five children: Cesar, Maria Eugenia, Virginia Guadalupe, José Javier and Claudia de Jesus, who got her name because she was born on Christmas. I kept in touch with the Little League, and I am now a voting member of the Mexican Professional Baseball League. From 1985 to 1991, I was the Nuevo León State Sports Director. I am proud to be in the Mexican Baseball Hall of Fame, but even more surprising to me is they named a street for me in Colonia Industrias del Vidrio. But no trophies or streets or even if they named a whole plaza for me could equal in magnitude the honor of leading these fourteen boys to their triumph.

Angel Macias (born/September 2, 1944)

I remember my Williamsport, Pennsylvania, experience as one of extreme joy and innocence. I was most impressed with the support that the American people gave us. When we got there, we were so out of place, so different and so small that we caught their attention. The American kids were more used to this and they were more serene, less emotional, but we were smiling and jumping and screaming.

When I came back, I studied all the way to high school at the Instituto Regiomontano. Finally, I decided to play professional baseball and signed with the California Angels' organization. I played for them and other teams up to 1974, when I retired from baseball and went back to Monterrey. I immediately resumed my university studies, obtained a bachelor's degree in business and administration, and began working for Grupo Alpha.

In 2001, I returned to baseball as the director of an academy where I can give young talented players the opportunity to improve and become the best they can be. Each year, graduates from the school go to American Major League Baseball teams, and each of them leaves Mexico with a piece of me and the dream of Monterrey Industrial. I married a beautiful angel named Josefina Martinez, and we have three daughters: Josefina, Martha Patricia and Diana Laura.

Enrique Suarez (born/August 11, 1944)

I live very near the field where we first began our baseball. On Monterrey Industrial, we never had any illusion about how far we could get in the tournament, but we made it all the way. The thing that stands out the most in my memory is we were young and fearless, and we could not be intimidated by any of our opponents because we had nothing to lose. Even though we were all great companions, I remember Norberto Villarreal as a very good friend and I miss him very much. He was the first to pass away.

After Williamsport, Pennsylvania, we all got scholarships to continue studying in private institutions. It was a big break because my parents never could have afforded any education for me. I was sent to the Instituto Regiomontano, a well-known school for the privileged classes. I always felt a big contrast between my background and that of my classmates. Despite the scholarship, I had to quit after ninth grade. We had so little money that I had to get a job to help my family make ends meet.

I lost touch with my teammates for several years and found myself reunited with such good old comrades through the efforts of Señor William Winokur. Every time he comes to Monterrey, he treats the whole team to lunch at Los Gatos, a restaurant famous for its roasted goat. Sometimes I feel as if no time has passed, even though there are a lot of old men at the table now. The 1957 championship changed all of our lives, we went through something that can never be taken from us. I know we will always have one another until the very last one of us is alive.

José "Pepe" Maiz (born/August 14, 1944)

I was very impressed during the first couple of nights that I experienced with my teammates in McAllen, Texas, because some of them would wake up on the floor. At first I thought they had fallen, but soon I discovered the shocking truth: They had never slept on real beds. This contact with people of less resources than I was accustomed to opened my eyes and made me re-evaluate everything I had. They really taught me a humility that I believe became a fundamental part of my personality.

After returning from Williamsport, Pennsylvania, I continued playing baseball in other leagues, having a chance to play in additional international championships. In 1961, I had a very difficult decision to make when I was invited by a scout to play for the San Francisco Giants. I was excited by the prospects, but my father was adamant about me finishing my studies at the Monterrey Institute of Technology where I ultimately earned a bachelor's degree in civil engineering and a master's degree in business administration and finance. I spent one of those years as an exchange student in Wisconsin, where I learned English and discovered new sports like American football.

After marrying Maria Lourdes Domene, I worked several years for the city of Puebla but then returned to take over my father's company, Maiz Mier Construction, a responsibility I hold to this day. In 1982, when I became the president of Monterrey's professional AAA baseball team, the Sultanes, I promised two things: to make them champions again (they had not done so for twenty years) and to build them a new stadium. The latter took eight years, and Sultanes Stadium is one of the biggest baseball arenas in Latin America. One year later, our team captured the championship and did so twice again that decade.

I have been fortunate enough to receive many honors and recognition during my life, but I hold four inductions to be the most important: the Latin American Hall of Fame in Laredo, Texas; the Tec de Monterrey Hall of Fame; the Mexican Baseball League Hall of Fame, and finally the Williamsport Hall of Excellence, where I am the first Mexican to be so honored. I am also proud of having a family and being able to pass on my values to our four children: José, Mauricio, Maria Lourdes and Eugenio.

Norberto "Beto" Villarreal (born/September 23, 1944) as told by his widow, Maria.

Norberto's experience in Williamsport, Pennsylvania, was one that changed his life and status forever. Every one of them was amazed by the reaction that the whole city of Monterrey had when they returned home in glory. Norberto, as well as all of the other kids, got a scholarship to continue studying and did so until he was hired by Trailers Peña to work as a jornalero at their plant and to play baseball for their team. He was a hero and moral leader of his neighborhood. Whenever there was a problem or a fight in the barrio, they would wake up Norberto and call for his assistance. He was known to be a great pacifier and inspiration for so many youths.

When he was eighteen, he married me, Maria de Jesús Celestino. We formed a family with four children: Claudia, Jesus Antonio, Adriana Guadalupe and Judith. After working and playing baseball for Trailers Peña, Norberto began an intense search for stability, changing jobs and professions often. He built car parts in a factory, a few years later he became a *tránsito*, a street-patrolling police officer who rode a motorcycle. Soon after this, he decided to look for a new life in the United States, where he worked in construction and learned all the skills needed to build a house. He returned to Monterrey and became an *alguacil* (a sheriff) for a few more years. The stability he sought proved elusive again as he left that job to be a barman in a nightclub. Norberto's last profession was managing several cantinas with his older brother. Cirrhosis ended his life in 1996.

Beto was a good and well-liked man who never asked anybody for any breaks. His life was challenging, but he found happiness in his family and in his memory of victory with his teammates of Monterrey Industrial.

Baltazar Charles (born/January 28, 1945) as told by his widow, Bertha.

Norberto Villarreal introduced Baltazar to Señor Faz, who was completing a team to go to the United States. There was something about this group of kids he started playing baseball with that was different, and finally there was hope for his life.

But Baltazar almost didn't go with Monterrey Industrial because he didn't want to leave his sister, Patricia, behind. It was she who eased his conscience, convincing him that it would hurt her more if he missed this amazing opportunity. Seeing her in pain always deeply troubled Baltazar, and he worried about her every day he was away. He kept going with the inner desire to win for her.

The most heartfelt and earnest experience he had from his voyage across the United States to Williamsport, Pennsylvania, was the opportunity to meet his heroes. Walking into Ebbets Field to see a Brooklyn Dodgers' game was something that he would remember forever. He would tell everyone this story whenever he had a chance.

Even though Baltazar had a scholarship, he didn't finish his high school studies. Patricia's condition continued to get worse, and she died by her twelfth birthday. When she became most seriously ill, Baltazar dropped out of school to stay by her bedside. She told him not to worry for her. She said the best moment of her life was that summer when her brother was traveling on his incredible journey to Williamsport. She would wait anxiously each day for their father to bring home *El Norte* to see if there was news about Monterrey Industrial and if Balta was mentioned. And when he was, she said those were the moments she could not remember her pain. She was so very proud of him.

Without the benefit of an education, Baltazar's choices for work would have been limited to manual labor in the factories. But the skills he had developed with Monterrey Industrial allowed him to pursue the thing he loved the most—after family, of course—and he became a professional baseball player. He played for the Diablos Rojos, the Mexico City team that had received them in tears when they entered the nation's capitol.

Norberto played baseball with teams from Houston, Texas and Monterrey. When he was thirty-six years old, a terrible slide got him a very badly broken foot and ended his baseball career. He began working in Fibras Quimicas, where he stayed for seventeen years, and finally he entered PEMEX, the Mexican oil company, where he worked the last eight years of his life. He died of a heart attack when he was fifty-nine years old. Even after his injury and when his job made great demands on his time, he always found the time to train and play with the children of our neighborhood, emulating Señor Faz's ideals.

The experience of 1957 and losing his sister were the two biggest turning points in Baltazar's life, though they existed at opposite ends of happiness and sadness. My husband always said, "If I was born again, I would trade all my baseball games and all my trophies to make Patricia well." But God had a different fate for each of them, and Baltazar made the best of what God gave him. He was a good and decent man, and he had a tough life that he never complained about. I could not have found a better husband, and we were very happy together. I know, though, that those years he played on baseball teams and even the hours coaching neighborhood children right up until he died were the happiest times of his life.

Ricardo Treviño (born/September 11, 1945)
I am the son of Eusebio Treviño and Oralia Cantu. I remember coming home from the Diego De Montemayor Elementary School where some employees of Estrtucturas de Acero used to play baseball across the street from my family's house in Colonia Reforma. I was probably nine or ten years old. But a big shock for me was at that time my father decided to try his luck and moved to the United States, but he went alone.

He used to visit for a couple of weeks each year, but he would always leave again. I always missed my father. When Monterrey Industrial went to Williamsport, Pennsylvania, he was living in Milwaukee. When I saw him a year later, he told me that he had heard all about our championship from the news and that he was very happy. Even when my father finally became a U.S. resident, he never wanted to take me there, so I stayed in Monterrey where I continued playing baseball.

After playing in the Pony and Colt leagues where I participated in international tournaments, I became a professional baseball player when I was only seventeen years old, leaving my high school and joining the Sultanes, Monterrey's home team. At twenty-three, I retired from baseball, knowing that I wanted to do something else with my life. I married Irma Rivera and had four children: Ricardo, Rolando, Marcela and Adriana. After leaving the Sultanes, I entered the jewelry industry, and I have my own company named Pedregal Joyerías that I share with my sons. I also have a large cattle ranch north of Monterrey, and my teammates think of me as somewhat of a cowboy.

I think life is about committing mistakes and moving forward—that is the only way to progress. Being the sole player who went to Williamsport twice (Monterrey Industrial won the Little League World Series in 1957 and 1958. Ricardo was on both teams and is also the only player to be on two winning championship teams), I have a hard time distinguishing my vague childhood memories from what happened each year. But I will forever remember the brotherhood and camaraderie that still remains for the players until this day.

Rafael Estrello (born/March 18, 1945)
I remember a lot about our adventures in Williamsport, Pennsylvania, but one vision that stands out more clearly was when we first boarded an airplane. I was struck with fear and amazement of flying. In the middle of the flight, Cesar stood up and walked to the back, looking for the bathroom. Suddenly, a flight attendant ran screaming toward him, scaring all of us. But she saw him about to open the back door of the plane. This was a terrifying moment. Imagine what could have happened!

I studied through high school at Prepa #1 and began working for Cajas de Carton Monterrey, where I also played baseball for a few years. I held a few different jobs, with companies such as Aceros Planos and Cervecería Cuauthemoc Moctezuma. Recently, I have been working as a traveling salesman, where I get the opportunity to visit many parts of Mexico. I have five children: Alma Dolores, Maria Elena, Rafael Mario, Norma Helia and Carlos Alberto. I will always remember my thirteen brothers, my teammates on Monterrey Industrial.

Fidel Ruíz España (born/April 24, 1945) as told by his widow, Maria.

Fidel told me many stories about the 1957 Little League World Series Championship. Like the time when he got lost and everyone looked for him. He scarcely made it to the game on time, and everyone was angry at him. After a few innings, they had forgiven him for his mistakes. He never forgot about sitting on President Eisenhower's chair. He was one of a few members of the team who got *two* presidential pens. He didn't steal it, as the president joked about Angel, since Fidel had learned his lesson about stealing back in the military camp.

The promise of a scholarship made it possible for Fidel to study at the Escuela de Contadores, where he graduated as an accountant and went to work in the office of Maiz Mier Construction with his friend Pepe Maiz. Fidel was married two times: First, when he was eighteen years old, (he had four children) and the second time at thirty-five, to me, Maria Angelica Cepeda. We had two children, Fidel Jr. and Angelica. I will always remember him helping them out with their homework and asking them to always give their best. Knowing what he had accomplished for all of Mexico made our children listen very closely to his advice.

Unfortunately, Fidel had many health problems, and at fifty-nine years old he succumbed to a heart attack and joined his mother and father in heaven.

Gerardo Gonzales (born/February 14, 1945)

I was the third child of nine whom Felipe de Jesus Gonzales Cantu and Maria de Jesis Elizondo Lopez would have in their marriage. I remember playing baseball at the dirt field behind Fabricación de Máquinas, where I would walk all the way home and feel safe in Monterrey. We were dreamful and innocent children; we had no sense of evil or wickedness. I was nicknamed *La Pinny*, a common nickname for short people. Because of my height, I was given a uniform with the number three since the team was numbered by height. Only Jesus "Chuy" Contreras, who was number two, was shorter than I was. Señor Faz, of course, was number one, though he never wore his numbered shirt during our games.

I am not sure what bravery came into me when I said "We are only going to play them, not carry them." I didn't mean it to sound brash; I just didn't really understand what the reporter expected us to do about how big the American boys were. And they did seem like giants to me then.

I studied at the Instituto Franco Mexicano all the way through high school and then moved on to the Universidad Autonoma de Nuevo León, the state university where I obtained a PhD in mechanical and administrative engineering, a master's degree in business administration and a master's in industrial engineering.

When we got back from Williamsport, I played for a few more years in other leagues, but I knew that baseball would not be for long. I began working for the Commission Federal de Electricidad in 1968 and stayed there for thirty years. At twenty-nine years old, I married Blanca Rita Guevara, and we had Blanca Rita, Ana Beatriz, Gerardo and Gabriel.

"*La union hace la fuerza*" (teamwork makes everything easier). This lesson from Williamsport has helped me on the baseball field and everywhere else in life. What do I recall the most? I remember that my nickname changed thanks to Williamsport. At the electrical company, instead of *La Pinny*, my coworkers called me "the Champ."

Jesus "Chuy" Contreras (born/February 23, 1945)

I remember knowing Baltazar Charles and Alfonso Cortez a little bit before our Little League World Series Championship. I loved how we all got along, and I still remember that we never imagined we would win more than one game. Now, as a Little League coach for the Cuauhtemoc League, I am well-known and respected. I have followed the steps of Señor Faz, and try to discipline my team as well as we were in 1957.

When my father passed away after thirty-five years at the brewery, I had my mother, Maria Zenaida Leija, move in with me, and I have cared for her ever since. It is an obligation that I happily accept, but as a result I never have felt the opportunity to marry and have children. In many ways, Little League baseball has been my legacy and its participants "my children." I encourage them to study hard and to play the sport they love the best that they can.

Mario Ontiveros (born/December 6, 1944)

I remember 1957 and our team with great pride. Being so young and at that age so naive, compared to twelve-year-olds today, made us experience our adventure as an amazing journey. Even though Señor Faz managed us with very harsh discipline, I had lots of fun and surprises. Once, we had to ask a man with a truck to take us to a game in McAllen, Texas, as we didn't have a bus. So we all got into the back, and as it drove off three of us fell out onto the street. Now we laugh about it, but imagine how scared Señor Faz was.

I must give Señor Faz a lot of credit for what happened and for the success that we had. For example, we had never played at night in Monterrey, so this was something new that we had to deal with in McAllen. Señor Faz, who had a lot of baseball experience, told us not to look at the lights and taught us how to find the ball in the unusual shadows cast by them. I think that discipline is one of the greatest values I learned from this experience, and I have used this lesson all my life. It was put to its greatest test not long after that baseball season.

It took only a few months after I got back to Monterrey as a hero for fate to take away my father. I was thirteen years old, and after school each day I had to work with my mother to help feed and clothe my four younger brothers and sisters. I loved baseball, but I could not manage to study all day, work late into the evenings and weekends, and still find time for the game that I had fallen in love with and that had loved me back so dearly.

My mother bought a tortilla machine and a bicycle for me, which that I used to deliver the tortillas to clients and companies. Thanks to a lot of hard work and teamwork, she and I watched our family grow and prosper. Without the maturity I learned on the road with Monterrey Industrial, I never would have had the strength to become a man so quickly. I miss my father every day, but I thank God he lived to see us become champions. I know he would be proud of me if he could have seen how I helped my mother raise their other children.

At eighteen, right after finishing high school, I went to work at Vitro´s Fabricación de Maquinas. I was offered a scholarship (the government would pay for my education no matter where or for how long), but the financial needs of my family made it necessary for me to forego that dream. I never felt badly about it, I knew that God had granted me the greatest dream of all, so it was just my turn to help make my bothers' and sisters' dreams possible.

I worked at Vitro for thirty-five years, starting from the bottom and moving up the engineering department supervisor. The salary I earned allowed my siblings to keep studying all the way to college.

I married Consuelo Rosales Garza when I was twenty-six, and we have three children: Victor Alberto, Jessica Rocío and Susana. My wife and I live happily at our house in Colonia Industrias del Vidrio.

Roberto Mendiola (born/November 24, 1945)

I studied at the Alvaro Obregon High School, but I used to skip class and go play with my friends. I never liked school, but when I say something now to children, I tell them to study hard and to pick a sport. I really believe that sports will keep them safe from vices and addictions.

When I was eighteen, I began working for the national telephone company managing lines. I married Maria Ines Rodriguez Lozano when I was twenty-five, and we have three children: Roberto Manuel, Mirna and Eduardo Alejandro. After working thirty-one years and moving upward until I held the highest union-based job in the company, I retired.

I am so grateful for my Little League World Series experience. I remember the feeling of being the champions and how as we won each game we didn't realize the magnitude of what was going on. Not until we came home did it sink in. I also remember being in those military bases, sitting with my teammates in a room and simply fooling around. Señor Faz kept us under control, but that didn't mean we couldn't have fun and joke around. We were kids!

Alfonso Cortez (born/September 22, 1944) Nearly blind from diabetes, the following was dictated by Alfonso to Virginia Faz, one of Cesar's daughters. Sadly, Alfonso passed away several days later on Sunday, July 22, 2007.

I have been married to Alma Elena Bernal for thirty-two years. We have five children: Alfonso, Adriana, Alejandro, Nelson and Patricia.

My father died when I was thirteen, very soon after that baseball season of 1957. When that happened, I had to start working to support my family. I sold lubricants and then real estate. I remember Angel, Pepe and Enrique ("el Cubano") the best. I also remember that Cesar was very strict and kept us on a short leash, but we all respected his discipline.

When we crossed the Potomac River into Washington, DC, we stopped in to say hello to President Eisenhower. He said hello without standing up when we first came in. When I approached him, his guards immediately stood between us and through Cesar I learned that they said I shouldn't come near the president. I told him, "That's not my president. My president is Ruiz Cortinez." President Eisenhower was very gracious and laughed a lot. He even let us sit in his chair.

In Mexico, we got to meet President Cortinez. When we told him that President Eisenhower let us sit in his chair, he did the same for us. He told us that the only people to ever sit in it were presidents, Pancho Villa. . . and now the Little Giants of Monterrey Industrial.

I have very few mementos of that season. My uniform and any photographs or trophies that I had were all lost when my house burned down. One of my vivid memories, though, was piloting the plane that brought us to Monterrey. Each of us took a turn, and I happened to be in the cockpit when the Cerro de la Silla mountains came into view. I cried. I can never describe the pride I felt at that moment in myself, my teammates and in my country.

Francisco Aguilar (born/January 12, 1944) as told by his widow, Gloria.

Francisco's biggest memory and impression of their journey was Kentucky Fried Chicken. As simple as it might sound, he was charmed by the crispy flavor of it and would speak of it his whole life. He always thought of these places the way one might think of an eternal friend and frequently visited some of them.

After returning home, Francisco kept playing baseball and studying, because of the government's scholarship, until the second year of accounting school. He then became a professional baseball player and coach. He gave baseball clinics after he retired from the game.

After we married, I confessed to Francisco that I didn't know about him and the team. I was probably the only one in all of Nuevo León to be ignorant of such a huge event in our history. But he was always very humble and shy about his participation, even though people stopped him and patted him on the back almost every day of our marriage.

After our wedding, he began working at the Government and State High School No. 16 until he retired eighteen years later. Sadly, my husband passed away several years ago after suffering from diabetes. Our children, Gloria, Francisco and Nancy, remember him with the greatest pride and affection. I sometimes wake up in the middle of the night, still hoping that he has just gone to the kitchen for a snack. And I often hear his voice when I am lonely and think that I cannot face another hardship. That is when I hear him tell me his favorite expression, "Never give up," as the *niños campeones* never gave up.

José Gonzales Torres (born/August 26, 1926)

After World War II, I worked for the American Metals Company in Monterrey. Their headquarters were in New York City, and they sent many Americans who brought a love and desire to play baseball to work in Mexico—the game reminded them of home. In 1947, I helped organize an adult Catholic league that was comprised of the first baseball teams in Monterrey.

Long before the 1957 Little League World Series, I was well aware of the needs and poverty of the children of Monterrey and felt that they deserved a space for recreation and development outside of their schools. Williamsport, Pennsylvania, made all this possible.

I became good friends with Cesar Faz and Lucky Haskins during our adventure in 1957. Since I had some previous experience as a journalist and photographer, I became the team's press manager and took most of the pictures that appeared in the Mexican newspapers and magazines. I also participated as a reporter in the 1968 Olympics, which took place in Mexico City. I continued coaching several baseball teams until I was named director of Mexico's Little League.

I worked for CEMEX in the engineering department and then the archive department for twenty-two years until I retired at age sixty. All the while, I contributed articles and photographs to UPI and the Associated Press. I was married but my wife and I never had any children.

Harold "Lucky" Haskins (born/ circa 1905) as told by his daughter, Barbara.

I don't know a lot about my father's life before World War II or the reasons that motivated him to leave us with my mother in Wisconsin. But she would have none of that, and my three siblings and I were dropped off at the border with an offer he couldn't refuse. The war had a great impact on my father; he was always a stickler for structure, discipline and rules, which is probably one reason he loved sports so much.

He ran a program in Monterrey that sent legal aliens to the United States to work until that program was shut down by anti-Mexican policies of the mid-1950s. Before he began his own bottling company, he worked as a sports instructor and teacher at the American School of Monterrey. He also taught the local university students how to play American football.

During the trip to Williamsport, Pennsylvania, he had to abandon his bottling company and finally lost it. His love for sports and especially for the Monterrey Industrial team was greater. When he and the team returned, my father worked for other schools and opened a souvenir shop called Paco, which was located right beside the Ancira Gran Hotel.

He remarried and had three more children. Our names are Patrick, Michael, Robert, Barbara, Richard, Jimmy and Rafael. In 1968, my father decided to return to the United States. He relocated to McAllen, Texas, the very first place that he and the boys went to play. He soon began working in sports again, this time forming a program for mentally and physically challenged people. He would always proudly remember the 1957 Little League World Series Championship and everything that they had to go through to be able to play. In December 1980, my father died. The McAllen veterans gave him a military burial because he had been a US Navy officer.

Without his efforts, it is unlikely that the boys of Monterrey Industrial ever would have had the opportunity they did to make history and change all of our lives.

ﻌﻌﻌﻌﻌ

Amazingly, after two and a half years of tracking down the participants of the 1957 Little League World Series, the only player whose whereabouts remained a complete mystery was that of the pitcher for La Mesa, Lewis Riley. Not one of his teammates had seen him since high school, and Internet searches for him proved fruitless. A private investigator searched birth, marriage, tax and death records all to no avail.

Miraculously, Lewis Riley surfaced recently. This was the brave young man who, fifty years ago faced off against Angel Macias in a historic duel for the championship. This chapter was originally intended for just the Monterrey Industrial team, but here is a special treat from this gracious La Mesa star.

Lewis Riley

On August 23, 1957, I pitched in the final game of the Little League World Series. I didn't realize it then, but my team, La Mesa, was playing the first foreign team, Monterrey Industrial, to appear in a championship game. From all appearances, the game seemed even more of a mismatch than David and Goliath.

For one thing, we fourteen Californians were mostly enormous twelve-year-old boys playing a team of mostly tiny, rail-thin boys from Mexico. I was five feet, eight inches, and my team's average height was five feet, four inches. The Mexican ball players, on the other hand, averaged four feet, eleven inches and more than a few seemed to suffer from malnutrition.

At our living quarters in Williamsport, Pennsylvania, where the four teams in the Little League finals ate their meals together, Monterrey Industrial always stuck around for seconds and thirds, while we and the other two American teams headed for the recreation room to play Ping-Pong and watch television.

We Californians were a cocky bunch. Not only had we beaten the best teams in America, where baseball was king, but we were facing a team that appeared to tire so easily they had to take a nap every afternoon. (At the time, I didn't realize the benefits of a siesta.)

I was not only one of La Mesa's starting pitchers, but I was also the team's lead-off batter. I prided myself in being able to give our team a jump start in most games by getting a hit or at least drawing a walk—but not that day on August 23, 1957. And the two batters who followed me also were retired quickly.

Not to worry, we thought to ourselves as we took the field. Even a blind squirrel finds an acorn every now and then. I took the pitcher's mound and easily retired the side in the bottom of the first. We "Goliaths" felt confident that we would jump ahead and not look back, which had always been our modus operandi. The game remained scoreless after three of the six innings. We not only had not scored any runs, we also failed to reach first base safely. Nine boys up, nine boys sent muttering back to our bench.

I'll never forget the pitcher; his name was Angel Macias and he was ambidextrous. So far though, he seemed to need only his right arm, and he was getting stronger with each inning. Angel was throwing pitches I'd never seen before. It was like trying to hit flubber, but I was determined to right the ship when I lead off the fourth inning.

So much for determination. Angel struck me out as if I were swinging blindfolded at a piñata. It was the first time in the Little League tournaments that I became discouraged, and for the first time I could see doubt creep in the eyes of my teammates. The two batters behind me were also easy outs, which meant that Angel had a perfect game for four innings.

I strode to the mound in the bottom of the fifth inning, bloody but unbowed. Though my team wasn't hitting, I still was pitching well. Monterrey had yet to score a run.

Then the wheels fell off. I hit the first batter in his side, which was hard to do since he was stick-thin. The next batter bunted, and suddenly flustered, I threw away the ball. I was not used to making such mistakes, and my tender psyche began to fall apart. Before I knew it, Monterrey had scored four runs. We were in need of a major comeback, but first we needed a hit.

As fate would have it, we got neither, Angel Macias pitched the first and—to this day—only perfect game in Little League World Series Championship history.

At game's end, my teammates joined me in a tear fest. By dinnertime, though, we had recovered enough to clean our plates and to enjoy ourselves playing Ping-Pong with our conquerors. The Mexican ballplayers spoke no English, but we still had a good time mingling with them, including their tiny catcher who was, amazingly, pointing out our hitting weaknesses. When it came to me, he raised his hand next to my chest, indicating I had trouble with high pitches. I could only laugh because he was right.

When I hugged Angel, who had a magnetic smile when not on the mound, I said, "One more at bat and I would have hit a homer." He just smiled.

An Author Reflects

esides having a wife and three children whom I adore, the best thing about life is when I wake up, I might discover something amazing. Once in a rare while, the discovery is so profound that it actually sets my life on a new course.

September 12, 2004, was just such a day.

The weather in Malibu, California was typically perfect, and I was having breakfast at Marmalade's Café with a friend, Anson Williams. For those who don't recognize his name, he played Potsie on the show called *Happy Days*. He had read a rough manuscript of my first novel, Marathon, and liked the way I wove a story.

"Can I tell you a true story I heard about when I was a kid?" Anson asked me. "Perhaps it'll be your next book."

I have heard many stories, so I assumed the odds that he was in possession of the topic of my next book were about as likely as snow in Malibu. Anson then proceeded to tell me that there was once a group of boys from Monterrey, Mexico who overcame adversity to win the 1957 Little League World Series.

I decided then and there that it would be my next book project, but it quickly evolved into something far deeper for me. I did as much homework as I could in the vacuum of my office until it was time to see who on the team was still alive and if I could find them.

First, I spoke to the Little League organization in Williamsport, Pennsylvania, who was very cooperative but had no phone numbers or addresses. They suggested I call Betty Pujols in the Puerto Rico office, which administrated all Little League activities in Latin

America. She gave me a phone number for José Gonzales Torres who had been the assistant coach on Monterrey Industrial's historic journey. Through him, I was able to reach Cesar Faz.

I was so happy to learn that he was still alive. My first words to him were "Señor Faz, sir, I am calling you with the most heartfelt respect and admiration. I apologize that I have been unable to find someone to introduce me to you, but I would like to visit with you for a few minutes to speak about the 1957 team."

Cesar could not have been a more gentle and gracious man, and when he agreed, I felt as if I had uncovered a pearl in an oyster.

Planning my first trip to Monterrey, I took another bold step. Internet searches of the Monterrey Industrial champions revealed many stories concerning José "Pepe" Maiz, the team's left fielder. Though recruited by the San Francisco Giants, his father had insisted he pursue an education instead. Pepe studied engineering at Tec de Monterrey and helped grow the family construction business into a world-class operation. Besides having built many of Monterrey's bridges and office towers, he was responsible for the construction of the city's professional baseball stadium, one of the most impressive baseball parks outside the United States.

Pepe had gotten Monterrey on Major League Baseball's short list of possible cities for relocating the Montreal Expos. It didn't get awarded the franchise, but Pepe is not the kind of man to give up easily on bringing a Major League Baseball team to Mexico. If anyone can do it, it will be him.

When I called him, I wasn't sure how I would get through to the chief executive of a major construction company, but to my shock his secretary said, "Hold one moment," and he personally picked up the line.

I was fortunate in my first "hits," as José, Cesar and Pepe were the only members of the team who spoke English fluently (as had Lucky Haskins). Angel claims he can understand it pretty well, and I'm sure there is nothing that he could not do well. Angel lived in the United States for several years, playing in the majors for, as poetic justice would have it, the California Angels.

Cesar was the first one I met. His son drove him to the Hotel Quinta Real where I was staying. I immediately recognized him as I walked into the lobby. His eyes were dark and penetrating, though the years had softened his countenance. We talked down the sun.

The next morning, I met Pepe at the headquarters of Maiz-Mier Construction. The walls of his small and cluttered office brimmed with photos of him posing with dignitaries and business magnates, but at the center were the pictures of him as a twelve-year-old playing in the season of a lifetime.

Packed away in boxes were several scrapbooks with hundreds more photos and newspaper clippings from the summer of 1957. I asked him if I could bring them back to my office in Los Angeles where I could scan them into my computer. It was an insane request. He didn't even know me, and I was asking to take his precious mementos back to California with a promise to send them back when I was done. He gave them to me without even asking for my ID or contact information.

Angel Macias happened to come by Pepe's office while I was there. He runs the well-regarded Baseball Academy where young Mexican hopefuls are taught the rudiments of the game to propel them to the highest levels of competition. He invited me to his home where I interviewed him with the help of a translator who accompanied me during my stay.

The same thing happened that had occurred at Pepe's office. There were irreplaceable pictures on Angel's wall and he let me take them, frames and all, back to my hotel, without the slightest worry that I wouldn't return them. They knew the Dark Virgin of Guadalupe still watched over them, and though I had no intention of misappropriating or misplacing the mementos, I knew I would guard their property with my life.

Through Cesar, Pepe and Angel, I met the rest of the surviving members of the team. Sadly, Lucky Haskins had died of a heart attack in the early 1980s. Norberto Villarreal, Baltazar Charles, Francisco Aguilar, Alfonso Cortez and Fidel Ruiz, the speedster who had stolen home to "Catch Bridgeport Nine Napping," had also passed away, before they turned sixty. Fortunately, nine of the fourteen boys were alive and all still lived in their beloved Monterrey.

Though many of the factories still exist, Monterrey has become a truly modern metropolis with diverse businesses and attractions. It's clean, safe, and the people are undeniably friendly and proud of their hometown.

After a few days, it was time for the formality of permission to use their names and likenesses. Previous suitors had focused exclusively on Cesar and Angel. It was logical: the coach and the pitcher who threw the perfect game. But I made an important decision. Since every member of the team had sacrificed equally to get to Williamsport, any deal would involve all of them or none of them. I knew I would have to make my pitch to the entire team, surviving family members included.

While Angel rounded up the roster, he and Pepe warned me that Enrique Suarez held some bitterness about the event and had fallen out of touch with his teammates. The reason was understandable. Enrique had pitched and won the same number of games as Angel. In addition, Angel's productivity at the plate had been minimal, but Enrique hit six home runs to lead the team's offense. Despite these feats, any discussion of the 1957 season always focused on Angel and his perfect game. Every reporter wanted to interview Angel. *Angel* talked one-on-one with Eisenhower. *Angel's* picture made the *New York Times*. If it hadn't been for Enrique's clutch performance against Bridgeport the day before, there would have been no game the championship game in which *Angel* could be perfect.

Angel understood this, and always accorded Enrique respect, but it was still a tough pill to swallow for a twelve-year-old boy or a sixty-three-year-old man still living in the shadow of his famous teammate.

"I'm not sure he'll speak with you," warned Pepe, but I had to try.

It took a few attempts to reach Enrique at home, but when my interpreter was able to get him on the phone, I told him, "I know who the real hero of the Monterrey Industrial team was. His name was Enrique." I wasn't being patronizing; I was paying tribute to a boy who—as much, if not more than anyone else—had led them to victory.

Enrique invited me to his home. It's the same one he grew up in, in Colonia Cantu. He was in great physical condition, trim and very tan. I could see why they called him *el Cubano*. During the interview he sat on his living room couch, holding hands with his wife of more than forty years. The pride in his voice was as resonant as if he were describing an event that happened just last week. At one point, he excused himself to retrieve something. When he returned, he showed me his old glove and baseball bat. But the best treat was his perfectly preserved uniform, draped neatly on a hangar. It was so small; it looked like it was more suited for an eight-year-old than a boy of twelve. It was fashioned from of soft flannel that uniforms used to be made of. He let me hold it up, and it still showed the stains made from grass and dirt.

I reached out and ran my fingers along the stains, knowing they came from fields in Monterrey, Texas, Kentucky and Pennsylvania. Touching them linked me to that time and place.

ᥱᨆᨖᨆᥲ

The next afternoon, I found myself at the Cuatemoc Brewery next door to the Salon de la Fama del Beisbol, the Mexican Baseball Hall of Fame. I sat in the middle of a large U-shaped table surrounded by every living participant and the widows and children of those who had died. It was not a warm and fuzzy gathering. They grilled me.

Besides a novel, I made it clear that I wanted to develop a screenplay and produce a film about their story. I laid out my ideas, telling them that it was not my intention to make a documentary. I saw their accomplishment as the incarnation of that part of the human spirit which stands for something noble, that willpower in the face of adversity. And the more I learned about their religious devotion, the more I knew the story was not about baseball but about faith.

When Ricardo Treviño asked to speak for the first time, I knew we were at the moment of truth, that point in the interview when my involvement—or lack of it would be decided. Ricardo was a gruff and portly man who was a cattle rancher and drove a Ford F250 pickup with custom rawhide seats. At eleven years of age, he never backed down from a fight or cried when being spiked at first base. Time hadn't eroded his toughness.

"Have you ever published a book?" he asked.

"Not yet, but I'm close," I answered.

"Have you ever made a movie?"

"No," I replied.

"Have you at least written a screenplay before?"

"No."

"Well, then what gives you the right to think you can do it?"

I turned to my interpreter and said the only thing that came to my mind. "Ask Señor Treviño what gave him the right to win the Little League World Series?"

My translator hadn't even finished my sentence when I saw tears streaming down Ricardo's face. One could have heard a pin drop; no one said a word while he regained his composure. After a minute or so, he looked straight at me, and my translator shared his response.

"Many have come to us over the years. You're the first one whom I believe has the right heart. I don't know if you will succeed or not, but I'm putting my faith in you."

⁂

After Monterrey, I made a special trip to Mexico City to see the Basilica of the Virgin of Guadalupe. I had the same curiosity that a tourist or historian might have when visiting Buckingham Palace, Stonehenge or the Colosseum in Rome. I assumed I would view it with detached respect. As we pulled up, my guide informed me that the original basilica was sinking and that a new church had been constructed on a site next to it. That new church, which rises in front of the old one, has the 1970s architectural style akin to Space Mountain in Disneyland.

M.I.T., my alma mater, and Wall Street, my first career, were good training grounds for cynicism in both the divine nature of the universe and the spiritual virtues of humankind. The basilica was going to begin my education anew. Entering the church, I saw a moving sidewalk, the kind you might find at an airport, though this one was fairly short and zig zagged back and forth in a small rotunda. Stepping onto it, I looked skyward and suddenly felt my breath suspended in midflow. There, in a gold glass-encased frame, was an open garment—the very *tilma* worn by Juan Diego. Emblazoned on its aging fabric was the resplendent figure of Mary, her head bowed slightly.

Apparently, the best scientists in the world can't explain how the image got there. I have learned that there are just some things that science cannot and perhaps will never be able to explain.

Afterward, I made my way to the original basilica. It's more than four hundred years old and, unfortunately, as much of Mexico City was built on land-filled swamps, the church is noticeably sinking into the fragile earth beneath it. A preservation project is under way to shore up its foundations, but for now one is still allowed entry onto its unevenly sloped stone floors. Inside the cathedral, steel ropes crisscross the dimly lit space, each one supporting a massive concrete pillar. I was not born Catholic but I lit a candle and prayed. And there on the sacred ground on which Juan Diego once knelt, I felt the power and purpose of something far greater than myself.

めⓄⓄ

As part of my research, I visited every place the team stayed or played, though some of the fields and accommodations have long since vanished. Of all the happenings on their journey, one stuck out most in my mind. It was not Norberto's game-tying home run against Houston or Enrique's brilliance against Bridgeport, nor was it Angel's perfect game. It was their walk from Reynosa to McAllen; the sacrifice to play one game. It was really, really far. I was in an air-conditioned automobile, and it still seemed like a long drive. I was exhausted just imagining being with them on their trek through the thirsty desert.

I also tracked down as many of the team members of La Mesa as I could find. It interested me that only one La Mesa player still resided in his hometown, yet every Monterrey player remained in his.

I found the grown boys of La Mesa to be helpful in providing me an insight into life back then and, of course, their interwoven fate with Monterrey Industrial. At first, I was concerned about how much they would want to discuss an event in which their fame was based on losing.

My concerns evaporated when their catcher, Francis Vogel, selflessly told me, "In many ways, I'm glad they won. Whatever winning could have meant to me, I know it meant so much more to them. I always felt it was their destiny and everything happened the way it should have."

⸎

Back in the early 1970s, I played Little League baseball in my hometown of Tenafly, New Jersey. I was pretty good, even though I never rose to the level of competition that the boys of Monterrey Industrial and La Mesa did. Still, it was a turning point in my life. It transformed me from an introverted boy who lacked self-confidence to a proud young man who believed there was something I could do well.

Today, Little League is played by more than three million boys and girls in over eighty-two countries. Though unheard of before Monterrey Industrial's improbable victory, non-US teams now win many championships. And why not? Baseball has become an international pastime, and what better diplomacy than games played by children?

The poet Robert Frost once said, "Nothing flatters me more than to have it assumed that I could write prose, unless it be to have it assumed that I once pitched a baseball with distinction."

It's too late for me to be a great pitcher, so I can only hope my prose will improve. In baseball terms, one for two isn't bad. But I have learned it isn't too late for me to grow as a person, and my association with these boys-turned-men has allowed me to do just that.

Invaluable to me have been the hours spent interviewing the players, some of their widows and Cesar Faz. This book would not have been possible without their remembrances, as well as Cesar's writings and memoirs. I have taken dramatic liberties as a writer, but the baseball details are accurate. More importantly, I have remained steadfastly faithful to the soul of the story and what these kids accomplished from their lime-dust field in Monterrey's barrio to the manicured green diamond in Williamsport. They made this world-weary and too often cynical adult believe that anything is possible, even seeing the wings of the littlest bird.

The Roster

1957 Monterrey Industrial Little League Team		
Name	**Uniform Number**	**Position(s)**
Cesar Faz	1	Head Coach
Angel Macias	8	Pitcher, Shortstop
Enrique Suarez	14	Pitcher, Center field
José "Pepe" Maiz	15	Left field
Norberto Villarreal	13	Catcher
Baltazar Charles	9	Second base
Ricardo Treviño	7	First base
Rafael Estrello	12	Right field
Fidel Ruiz	11	Third base
Gerardo Gonzales	3	Shortstop, Center field
Jesus "Chuy" Contreras	2	Catcher, Utility
Mario Ontiveros	5	Utility
Roberto Mendiola	6	Utility
Alfonso Cortez	4	Utility
Francisco Aguilar	10	Utility
José Gonzales Torres		Assistant Coach
Harold Haskins		Manager

The Box Score
1957 Little League World Series

La Mesa Northern Little League • La Mesa, California				
Lineup	At Bats	Runs	Hits	Putouts
Riley, p	2	0	0	1
Tobey, lf	2	0	0	0
Hardesty, 3b	2	0	0	1
McKirahan, 1b	2	0	0	5
Vogel, c	2	0	0	6
Wilson, rf	2	0	0	2
Hanggi, cf	2	0	0	0
Brown, ss	1	0	0	0
Haggard, 2b	2	0	0	0
Schweer[1], ph	1	0	0	0

[1]*Pinch hit for Brown in the 6th.*

Monterrey Industrial Little League • Monterrey, Mexico				
Lineup	At Bats	Runs	Hits	Putouts
Charles, 2b	3	1	1	0
Maiz, lf	3	1	1	0
Macias, p	3	0	0	0
Suárez, cf	3	1	1	0
Ruiz, 3b	3	0	0	0
Estrello, rf	3	0	0	0
Villarreal, c	3	0	1	12
Gonzáles, ss	3	0	0	0
Treviño, 1b	1	0	0	6
Ontiveros[1], pr	0	1	0	0
Aguilar[2], ph	1	0	0	0

[1]*Pinch ran for Treviño in the 5th.*
[2]*Batted for Ontiveros in the 5th.*

	1	2	3	4	5	6	R	H	E
La Mesa, CA	0	0	0	0	0	0 -	0	0	1
Monterrey, MX	0	0	0	0	4	x -	4	4	0

The Schedule

	Opponent	Score	Pitcher
McAllen, Texas			
Monday, July 29	Cuidad de Mexico	9–2	Suarez
Tuesday, July 30	McAllen	7–1	Macias
Wednesday, July 31	Mission	14–1	Maiz
Thursday, August 1	Weslaco	13–1	Suarez
Friday, August 2	Brownsville	6–1	Macias
Corpus Christi, Texas			
Monday, August 5	Laredo	5–0	Suarez
Tuesday, August 6	West Columbia	6–0	Macias
Fort Worth, Texas (Texas State Championship)			
Friday, August 9	Houston	6–4	Suarez
		(Maiz, extra inning)	
Saturday, August 10	Waco	11–2	Macias
Louisville, Kentucky (Southern Regional Championship)			
Thursday, August 15	Biloxi, Mississippi	13–0	Suarez
Friday, August 16	Owensboro, Kentucky	3–0	Macias
Williamsport, Pennsylvania (Little League World Series)			
Thursday, August 22	Bridgeport, Connecticut	2–1	Suarez
Friday, August 23	La Mesa, California	4–0	Macias

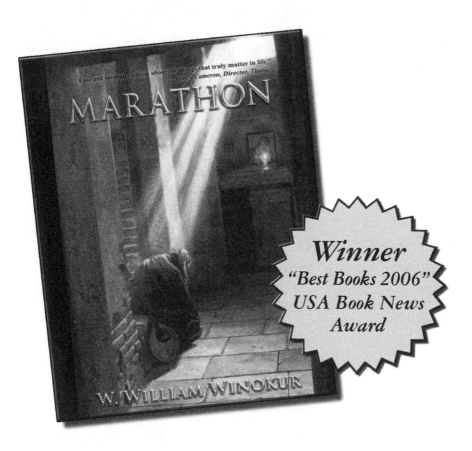

Critics Praise **MARATHON**

"Epic and intimate, a book about the things that truly matter in life."
—*James Cameron, director*

"This is a book to be read, re-read and treasured."
—*David Compton, Roundtable Reviews*

"You'll fall in love with the goodness, gentleness and humanity of Ion Theodore as well as his beloved country—I was truly sad to see the novel end."
—*Joanne Benham, Readers View*

"The story is layered by a master craftsman. A myriad of emotions will cause these pages to quiver, capturing readers' hearts and drawing them deeper into this novel."
—*In The Library Reviews*

"W. William Winokur weaves fact, fiction, poetry, biography, history and mythology into a beautiful story that sensitively explores eternal questions about life's meanings."
—*Evelyn Sears, BookPleasures.com*

"Marathon is the best novel I've read in the last ten years! Really a literate jewel!"
—*Maria Stasinopoulos, National Society of Greek Writers*

"Greece's tumultuous history comes alive in this moving saga. Marathon is a dramatic first novel by a promising writer."
—*Arianna Huffington, syndicated columnist*

"This is truly a deeply involving first novel by an extremely talented contemporary American author. I encourage anyone who can read to read Marathon."
—*Martin Landau, Academy Award®-winning actor*

MARATHON'S PROLOGUE - RESURRECTION:

One day, I became suddenly and frighteningly aware of having lived without knowing the first thing about myself. I hadn't been in a coma, nor was I suffering from disease—it was a veil of a more obscure nature. Now, my eyes are open and I see the world as a blank slate upon which I can press the sharp edge of my soul.

I am called Marianna, but I was born Maria Anastasia. Maria is in remembrance of the Blessed Virgin; Anastasia is Greek for *one who will be resurrected.*

As Marianna, I never thought of myself as being susceptible to flights of mysticism or prone to believing in things hoped for. I was brought up in a secular world whose pendulum had swung away from spirituality. And until now, *destiny* sounded like an ideal embraced only by young poets and tortured romantics.

For years, I wandered through cultural clichés—the free love of the 60's and the decadence of the 70's. Then I grew tired of the banal and traded it in for the corner office and the comforts of a Long Island suburb. *Brotherly love* and *making a difference* were beautifully selfless mantras but they didn't pay my mortgage, let alone a summer rental in the Hamptons. Everything had become an economic equation: how could I accumulate the greatest amount of anything with as little sacrifice as possible. Even the concept of my fellow man had become another cliché. I found myself amid a heap of souls too preoccupied with themselves to achieve anything for humanity—and I had neither the courage nor the imagination to dig myself out of the ruins of beautiful ideas gone awry.

I tried to maintain a separation between what I did for a living and what I did for a life. I had even lost the ability to feel for those closest to me, failing one of the most important of those people when he needed me the most.

In one's lifetime, the chance to choose the right path rarely visits more than once. But I have been granted, a second opportunity to rise, and in doing so I learned an invaluable lesson: to *find* the truth you must first *seek* it—*if* you seek it you must be *willing* to find it.

There are moments in each person's life that mark turning points, choices by which we alter our fate to degrees great and small. What we see of the world, with whom we bond, how we speak to another human being—all these decisions determine who we are, both in our eyes and to those around us. Do we realize the significance as they happen, or is it only in hindsight that their import becomes recognizable? I do not know the answer, but I do know that such an event has irrevocably changed my life. But what intrigues me more is how I perceived life the instant before the event. An entire potential existence was eradicated as a new life course was suddenly plotted and I have abandoned my regret of roads not taken.

I am Maria Anastasia.

I want to set down the story before my memories fade into chaos. It is a journey of salvation and redemption that began thousands of years ago in the sun-drenched mountains of Greece—the birthplace of the Gods.

Photo Credits

The publisher gratefully acknowledges the following entities for granting permission to reprint the photographs contained in this book:

Photo no. 96 © Corbis Images

Photo no. 31 © Corpus Christi Caller-Times

Photo no. 29 © El Norte

Photo nos. 58, 67, 69, 53a, 86, 87, 88, 92, 97, 98, 99 and 100 © Getty Images

Photo nos. 55, 57, 62, 64, 68, 71, 73, 74, 77, 78, 79 and 84 © ITN Source

Photo nos. 17, 49, 51 and 56 © Little League Baseball, Inc.

Photo nos. 40, 41, 47 and 48 © Louisville Courier-Journal

Photo nos. 5, 7, 8, 9, 10, 11, 12, 16, 18, 20, 21, 22, 23, 33, 36, 37, 42, 50, 104, 105 and 106 © Televisa, S.A. de C.V.

Photo nos. 34, 35, 38, 39 and 43 © United Press International

Photo nos. 30, 32, 46, 54, 95, 101 and 102 © Wide World Photos, Inc.